Dale Mayer

Tuesday's Child

Book 1

Psychic Visions

i

TUESDAY'S CHILD
Dale Mayer
Valley Publishing
Copyright © 2011

ISBN: 0987741101
ISBN-13: 978-0987741103

DEDICATION

This book is dedicated to my four children who always
believed in me and my storytelling abilities.

Thanks to you all.

ACKNOWLEDGMENTS

Tuesday's Child wouldn't have been possible without the support of my friends and family. Many hands helped with proofreading, editing, and beta reading to make this book come together. Special thanks to my editor, Pat Thomas. I had a vision, but it took many people to make that vision real.
I thank you all.

CHAPTER ONE

2:35 am, March 15th

Samantha Blair struggled against phantom restraints. *No, not again.*

This wasn't her room or her bed, and it sure as hell wasn't her body. Tears welled and trickled slowly from eyes not her own. Then the pain started. Still, she couldn't move. She could only endure. Terror clawed at her soul while dying nerves screamed.

The attack became a frenzy of stabs and slices, snatching all thought away. Her body jerked and arched in a macabre dance. Black spots blurred her vision, and still the slaughter continued.

Sam screamed. The terror was hers, but the cracked, broken voice was not.

Confusion reigned as her mind grappled with reality. What was going on?

Understanding crashed in on her. With it came despair and horror.

She'd become a visitor in someone else's nightmare. Locked inside a horrifying energy warp, she'd linked to this poor woman whose life dripped away from multiple gashes.

Another psychic vision.

The knife slashed down, impaling the woman's abdomen, splitting her wide from ribcage to pelvis. Her agonized scream echoed on forever in Sam's mind. She cringed.

The other woman slipped into unconsciousness. Sam wasn't offered the same gift. Now, the pain was Sam's alone. The stab wounds and broken bones became Sam's to experience even though they weren't hers.

The woman's head cocked to one side, her cheek resting on the blood-soaked bedding. From the new vantage point, Sam's horrified gaze locked on a bloody knife held high by a man dressed in black from the top of his head down. Only his eyes showed, glowing with feverish delight. She shuddered. Please, dear God, let it end soon.

The attacker's fury died suddenly. A fine tremor shook his arm as fatigue set in. "Shit." He removed his glove and scratched beneath the fabric.

In the waning moonlight, from the corner of her eye, Sam caught the metallic glint of a ring on his hand. It mattered. She knew it did. She struggled to imprint the image before the opportunity was lost. Her eyes drifted closed. In the darkness of her mind, the wait was endless.

Sam's soul wept. Oh, God, she hated this. Why? Why was she here? She couldn't help the woman. She couldn't even help herself.

She welcomed the next blow – so light only a minor flinch undulated through the dreadfully damaged woman. Her tortured spirit stirred deep within the rolling waves of blackness, struggling for freedom from this nightmare. With one last surge of energy, the woman opened her eyes, and locked onto the white rings of the mask staring back. In ever-slowing heartbeats, her circle of vision narrowed until the two soulless orbs blended into one small band before it blinked out altogether. The silence, when it came, was absolute.

Gratefully, Sam relaxed into death.

Twenty minutes later, she bolted upright in her own bed. Survival instincts screamed at her to run. White agony dropped her in place.

"Ohh," she cried out. Fearing more pain, she slid her hands over her belly. Her fingers slipped along the raw edges of a deep slash. Searing pain made her gasp and twist away. Hot tears poured. Warm, sticky liquid coated her fingers. "Oh. God. Oh God, oh God," she chanted.

Staring in confusion around her, fear, panic, and finally, recognition seeped into her dazed mind. Early morning rays highlighted the water stains shining through the slap-dash coat of whitewash on the ceiling and the banged up suitcases, open on the floor. An empty room – an empty life. A remnant of a foster-care childhood.

She was home.

Memories swamped her, flooding her senses with yet more hurt. Sam broke down. Like an animal, she tried to curl into a tiny ball only to scream again as pain jackknifed through her. Torn edges of muscle tissue and flesh rubbed against each other, and broken ribs creaked with her slightest movement. Blood slipped over her torn breasts to soak the sheets below.

The smell. Wet wool fought with the unique and unforgettable smell of fresh blood.

Sam caught her breath and froze, her face hot, tight with agony. "Shit, shit, and shit!" She swore under her breath like a mantra.

Tremors wracked her tiny frame, keeping the pain alive as she morphed through realities. Transition time. What a joke. That always brought images of new age mumbo jumbo to mind. Nothing light and airy could describe this. Each blow leveled at the victim had manifested in her own body. This was hard-core healing – time when bones knitted, sliced ligaments and muscle tissue grew back together, and time for skin to stitch itself closed.

Sam understood her injuries had something to do with her imperfect control, paired with her inability to accept her gifts. Apparently, if she could surmount the latter the first would diminish. She didn't quite understand how or why. Or what to do about it. Her body somehow always healed, the physical and mental scars always remained. She was a mess.

The physical process usually took anywhere from ten to twenty minutes – depending on the injuries. The mental confusion, disconnectedness, sense of isolation took longer to disappear. She paid a high price for moving too soon. Shuddering, Sam reached for the frayed edges of her control. It wouldn't be much longer. She hoped.

Nothing could stop the hot tears leaking from her closed eyelids.

This session had been bad. Apart from the broken ribs, there were so many stab wounds. She'd never experienced one so physically damaging. Nervously, she wondered at the extent of her blood loss. If she didn't learn how to disconnect, these visions could be the end of her – literally.

Just like that poor woman.

Sam hated that these episodes were changing, growing, developing. So powerful and so ugly, they made her sick to her soul.

Several minutes later, Sam raised her head to survey the bed. The pain was manageable, although she wouldn't be able to move her limbs yet. Blood had soaked the top of the many Thrift Store blankets piled high on the bed. Her hollowed belly had become a vessel for the cooling puddle of blood. Shit. The stuff was everywhere.

The metallic taste clung to her lips and teeth. She rolled the disgusting spit around the inside of her mouth, waiting. She wanted to run away – from the memories, the visions, her life. But knowing that pain simmered beneath the surface, waiting to rip her apart, stopped her. Weary, ageless patience added to the bleakness in her heart.

Ten more minutes passed. Now, she should be good to go. Lifting her head, she spat the bloody gob onto the waiting wad of tissue and noted the time.

Transition had taken fifteen minutes this morning.

She was improving.

Oh God. Sam broke into sobs again. When would this end? Other psychics found things or heard things. Many of them saw events before they happened. She saw violence – not only saw, but experienced it too.

Occasional shudders wracked her frame from the coldness that seemed destined to live in her veins. The odd straggling sniffle escaped. She couldn't remember when she'd last been warm. Dropping the top blood-soaked blanket to the floor, Sam tugged the motley collection of covers tighter around her skinny frame. Warmth was a comfort that belonged to others.

She wasn't so lucky. She walked with one foot on the dark side – whether she liked it or not. And that was the problem. She'd been running for a long time. Then she'd landed at this cabin and had been hiding ever since. That was no answer either.

Her resolve firmed. Enough was enough. It was time to gain control. Time to do something. This monster had to be stopped. Now.

Christ, she was tired of waking up dead.

CHAPTER TWO

10:23 am, 16th May

The police station, a huge stonework building, towered above Sam, blending into the gray skies above. Or maybe she just felt small. Insignificant. She couldn't imagine choosing to spend time in this depressing place. It only needed gargoyles hanging from the dormers to complete the picture of doom.

The entire idea of what these people did defeated her. She understood the necessity, yet given her insider knowledge, this whole human viciousness thing was too much. She wouldn't be here now except another woman had been murdered.

Given her past interactions with the police, even that wouldn't have been enough to make her sign up for more. The last cop she'd dealt with had been one bad-assed bastard.

No. The ring had brought her here.

This morning's killer had worn a similar ring to the one Sam had seen several months ago in another vision. She'd caught only a brief glimpse of it then, with the memory surviving transition to burn an indelible mark on her heart. Even the mask and gloves had looked similar. The biggest nail in this guy's coffin had been the energy. Like DNA, energy was unique, a personalized signature so to speak. Both killers had the same energy, the same variations in wavelengths and ripples. Even the same type of vibration. But that was hardly police evidence.

Knowing that some asshole had killed again, filled her heart with sorrow and slowed her steps. Several fat raindrops splattered her face – the joys of living along coastal Oregon.

The weather didn't bother her; the crowds and noise did. And the smell. Exhaust, sweat, and perfumes mixed to become something only a city dweller could love. No, the outlying community of Parksville suited her perfectly. The trip into Portland was only twenty minutes on a good day.

Strangers with umbrellas shouldered past her. Would any of them believe her if she told them about the murders she'd witnessed, experienced? She'd faced distrust and skepticism with every foster family. As a precocious six-year-old, she'd told her foster mother's coworker to look after her son better. She'd been punished at the time. But when the boy had drowned in his backyard pool, Sam had really suffered. She'd been dumped back into the system and the label 'odd' had been added to her file. Her *gift* scared people.

Today, she had no choice. She had to come here. She couldn't stand by and let this guy kill again. Still, it was a long shot to ask the police to believe her when she couldn't supply a time frame, a name, or even the location of victim or killer. She just didn't know.

She squared her shoulders. Hitched up her faded jeans. No more. Disbelief or not, she had to do this. She ran up the last few steps.

The interior of the station felt no less imposing. Twenty-foot ceilings lined with dark wood created a doomsday atmosphere. Great. She lined up and waited. When her turn arrived, she stepped to the counter.

The officer glanced at her. "Can I help you, miss?"

Wiping her damp palms on the front of her jeans, she took a deep breath and muttered, "Yes." She paused, eyeing him carefully. How could she tell the good cops from the bad ones?

The older-looking officer, his expression encouraging and steadfast, helped calm her nerves. Except her ability to judge people had never been good. Sam hesitated a moment longer before the words blurted out on their own accord. "I need to talk to someone about a murder."

He raised his eyebrows.

"Two murders." Even she recognized the apology in her voice.

His eyes widened.

Okay, she sounded like she had one screw loose. Still there wasn't any delicate way to approach this. She dropped her gaze to her tattered sneakers, almost hidden beneath her overly long pants.

"What murders, miss?" His voice, so kind and gentle, contrasted with the sharpness of his gaze.

Shifting, she glanced around. She didn't want to talk about this out in the open. The line of people started several feet behind her. Still... She leaned closer. "Please, I need to speak with someone in private."

She twisted the ribbing of her forest green sweater around her fingers – a response to the intensity of his gaze. Catching herself, she stilled, as if locked in space and time. Not so her stomach, which roiled in defiance. This had to happen now, or she'd never be able to force herself back again.

When he nodded, she breathed a deep sigh of relief. "Thank you," she whispered.

"Go take a seat. I'll contact someone."

Sam spun away and stumbled into the next person in the line behind her. Flushing with embarrassment, she apologized and retreated to a chair against the far wall. She closed her eyes and rubbed her face as she tried to calm her breathing. She'd made it this far. The rest...well...she could only hope it would be just as easy.

It wasn't.

"Okay. Let's go over this one more time." The no-nonsense officer sat across from her in the small office. His crew cut had just enough silver at the tips to make him distinguished-looking, accenting what she suspected would be a black and white attitude.

He scratched on the paper pad for a moment and frowned. He tossed his pen and opened a drawer to search for another one. "*Two* women have been murdered? You just don't know *who?*" He glanced from his notes to her, in inquiry.

She shook her head. "No, I don't."

"Right," he continued, staring at her. "You don't know by *whom?* You say one man killed both women, but you don't know that for *sure?* And you don't know *where* these women could be. Is that correct?"

Sam nodded again. Her fingers clenched together on her lap.

"Therefore these women, *if* they existed and *if* they were murdered, could have lived *anywhere* in the world – *right?*" He quirked an eyebrow at her.

"Right, but..."

"Just answer the question. Could these women and their supposed killer be, for example, in England?"

Her shoulders sagged. Why couldn't anything be easy? "Theoretically, yes. But I'm not—"

"I have enough dead women right here in Portland to go after. Why would I waste time working on a 'possible two more' that could have happened anywhere? Not only that...you're saying that one woman was strangled and then stabbed and the other one was just stabbed. That's not normal. Killers tend to stick to the same method for all their kills." His annoyance pinned her in place. "Prove that a crime has happened."

The detective tilted his head back, his arms gestured widely. "Show me a body, either here or somewhere else, and I'll be happy to contact law enforcement for that area. Until then...if you don't have anything else, why don't we call it a day?" He waved in the direction of the door.

Sam stared at the irate officer, her initial optimism long gone. The problem was, everything he'd said was true. She didn't have anything concrete to tell him. She'd hoped the description of the ring would help validate her story. Frustration fueled her irritation. Both boiled over.

"It's because of my abilities that I know these murders occurred close-by." Sam poked her finger toward the floor. "I'm not strong enough to pick up images from so far away. These *are* your cases — you just need to identify them."

"How?" he snarled. "You've given me no physical descriptions, no names, and no location markers. How can I identify them?"

All the fight slipped down her back and drained out her toes. She studied him for a long moment. How could she get through to him? "The first woman will be in your case files and for this morning's victim...chances are it hasn't been called in yet. I'd hoped that knowing there was more than one victim would make you take notice." She paused. "Can't you use the ring to track the killer down?" She leaned closer. "He *will* kill again, you know. You *will* remember this conversation later."

He shrugged, his eyes darting to the open doorway. He was obviously wishing she'd disappear, preferably forever.

Sam assessed his face and found only disbelief. Her shoulders sagged. It wasn't his fault. He'd reacted as she'd expected. Skeptical and derisive. Sam flipped her braid over her back and rose. She'd tried. There'd be no help here.

"Fine. I don't have any proof, and I didn't think you'd believe me, but...well, I had to try."

She straightened her back, thanked the glowering officer, and escaped into the hallway. Ahead, the front glass wall glinted with bouncing sunlight. Freedom beckoned. Her pace quickened. By the time she'd rounded the corner and caught sight of the front entrance, she'd broken into a half run.

***

11:10 am

Detective Brandt Sutherland smiled at the young rookie. "Thanks, Jennie, I appreciate this."

Pink bloomed across her features, accenting her age, as did the ponytail high on the back of her head. Did they still wear those in school? As a new recruit, her arrival last week had caused quite a stir, her fresh innocence a joy to the department full of jaded detectives.

"Sure, any time." She gave him a shy tilt of her lips at first, which then turned into a real grin before she hurried back to her desk. Still in the hallway, Brandt opened the file and glanced at the photos. His stomach dropped. His mood plummeted further as he checked out the other pictures in the stack. Another one. Damn it.

A commotion down the hall caught his attention. Glancing up, he frowned. What was that? A small bundle of moving clothing and flying hair bolted toward him. Brandt jumped out of the way. His open file smashed against his chest, only to end up in her path anyway as the tiny woman dodged sideways in a last-ditch attempt to miss him.

"Easy does it. Watch where you're going." He reached out to steady her as she stumbled. His hand never quite connected as she slipped away like thin air.

Huge chocolate eyes, framed by long velvet lashes, flashed. "Excuse me," muttered the waif before she continued her sprint to the front door, her long braid streaming behind her.

"Wait," he shouted, but she'd gone, leaving Brandt with an impression of soft doe eyes – evocatively large, yet filled with unfathomable pain. Brandt felt like he'd just been kicked in the stomach – or lower. Mixed impressions from those eyes, flooded his mind. Frustration. Defeat. Pleading for help, but no longer expecting to receive any. Yet, he could have sworn he sensed steel running through her spine. Somewhere along the line, life had knocked her down, but not out. Never out.

He took several steps after her, only to watch her bolt out the front door.

Who the hell was she? He shook his head in bemusement. Two seconds and he'd felt enough for a psychological profile. Yeah, right. Still, how could anyone have that much torment going on and still function? Staring after her, he wished she hadn't escaped quite so fast. He didn't know what she needed or why, but surely he could have helped somehow.

His curiosity aroused, he walked into the office at the end of the hall, and studied the lone occupant. "Kevin, were you just talking to that young lady?"

"What young lady?" Detective Kevin Bresson looked up from his keyboard, his gray eyes confused and disoriented. Reaching up, he jerked on the knot of his tie.

"The tiny one that's all eyes."

Kevin's brows beetled together and then comprehension hit. "Oh, the skinny one." He shook his head and grimaced. "Jesus, I'd stay away from her, if I were you."

Brandt stared toward the front entrance, unable to forget her haunting image. Or his inclination to follow her. A compulsion he had trouble explaining even to himself. "Why?"

"The moon must be full or close to it – the wackos are coming out of the woodwork."

"She's nuts?" Brandt pulled back slightly, jarred by Kevin's comment. "No way."

"Yup, crazy as a bedbug." Kevin checked his desk calendar, pointed on today's date. "Look at that. I'm right. It is a full moon tonight."

Brandt readily admitted he didn't know much about the cosmos, still he'd have bet his last dollar there'd been sanity in those eyes. There'd also been a hint of desperation, as if she'd hit the end of her rope maybe, but at least she'd known it.

"So what did she want?" Brandt worked to keep the interest out of his voice.

Kevin tossed his pen down on the desk and leaned back. "She tried to tell me this crazy-ass story about waking up inside another woman while she was being murdered." Kevin snorted. "I've heard a lot of stories over the years, but that one topped my list."

Brandt straightened, stepped closer. "She's a psychic?" He didn't quite know how he felt about that.

Kevin shot him a disgusted frown. "If she is, she's not a very good one."

Brandt frowned. "Why? What did she have to say?"

"Something about a killer murdering *two* women. *Both* times, she says she witnessed the murders as they happened, from *inside* the dead women's bodies." Kevin shrugged as if to say *People, what can you do?* "Even odder, she says this killer used a different MO each time."

That was unusual, yet not unheard of. He only had to think of the animal he was hunting. If he was right about him, this guy constantly changed his methods.

"Did she offer any proof? Some way to identify the killer? Did she know who the women were?" At Kevin's shaking head, Brandt felt pity for the woman. He hadn't been here at this station for long and he didn't hold a position that invited confidences – only, detectives were the same across the country. Some were good cops with limited imagination, some had too much imagination and had a hard time playing by the rules. Kevin appeared to be squarely on the side of the disbelievers and rule makers.

Brandt, well, he'd admittedly done more rule breaking than was probably good for him. Old-fashioned detective work did the job most times, but not always. And he didn't give a damn where the help came from, as long as it came. He couldn't resist asking, "Anything concrete?"

"Nope," Kevin answered with a superior half-smile. "I told you – lots of nothing."

Brandt stared out the hallway teeming with people. It had to be lunchtime. "Damn." Just before walking through the doorway, he turned back one last time. "Nothing useful?"

"Nope, nada."

Disgusted, Brandt walked away. At least that partly explained the panic in her eyes.

"Except the ring," Kevin called out, snickering.

Brandt spun around. "Ring? What ring?" He walked over and put his palms on the desk. "You didn't mention a ring."

Kevin leaned back in surprise, his hand stalled in midair. "Hey, easy. I didn't think anything she said mattered."

"Fair enough." Grappling for patience, Brandt threw himself down in the chair. "What *did* she say?"

"Fine." Kevin shifted to the side and reached for his notebook. He flipped through the pages until he found what he wanted. "She didn't say much," he said, frowning at his notes. "She woke up twice 'inside' different women while they were being murdered. She sees what the women see and when they die, she snaps back into her own body."

Brandt frowned, puzzled. "Odd ability to have. Where does the ring fit in?"

"She said that when staring out of the women's eyes..." Kevin rolled his eyes at that. "She couldn't see much of the attacker because he wore a full ski mask, like a balaclava. You know the ones with only eye holes and a mouth hole. She remembers his eyes being black and dead looking. And..." he paused for effect.

Brandt glared at him in annoyance. "Come on...come on. Stop the melodrama."

"Jeez, you're a pain in the ass today. What gives?"

Brandt rolled his eyes. Camaraderie was slowly developing with Kevin. Brandt had joined the East Precinct four weeks ago, but on a temporary basis. His boss had arranged for Brandt to have an office and access to all files, current and cold, as he searched for information on a potential serial killer, before heading up a task force if his findings warranted one.

He'd come into contact with this killer years ago and had run him to ground in Portland a year ago. Then nothing. A year. He couldn't believe they still didn't have a lead. This killer had become his nemesis. His Waterloo.

Most of the guys here had accepted him. It would take time to develop more than that. Time he didn't have.

"Fine then." Quirking one eyebrow, Kevin continued to read. "She mentioned seeing a ring during the one murder, and then she thought she recognized it again during the second one," he said in an exaggerated voice.

"Did she describe it?"

Kevin nodded and glanced down at his notes. "Some sort of four-leaf-clover pattern with a diamond in each of the leaves. A snake, or something similar, coils between them. According to her, one of the stones was missing."

Brandt sharpened his gaze. "Color? Size? Gold? Silver?"

Kevin searched again through his notes and shook his head. Casting an eye at Brandt, he said, "She didn't say and...honestly, I didn't ask. I thought she was off her rocker." He scrunched his shoulder. "Jesus, her cases aren't even related, yet she says it 'feels' like the same killer. Something about having the same energy signature. Whatever the hell that means." He dropped his gaze, a frown furrowing his brow as he doodled on the corner of his notepad. "I gather you're not dismissing her story?"

Brandt considered that. He'd used psychics before. In fact, he'd been friends with Stefan Kronos for a long time. The reclusive psychic was a difficult person to get close to. And even more difficult to be close with. The man was painfully honest. Brandt knew what valuable information they could give, but also knew using them could be a crapshoot.

"I don't know what to think. The changing MO thing is unusual, but it happens. That's why I'm here, after all. Still, if she had concrete information, it would have been easy enough to check out against our cases. But she didn't though, did she?"

Kevin shook his head. "Not really. The last murder happened this morning, which could mean that we haven't found the victim yet, or it happened in a different country and we'll never hear anything about her. Oh yeah, this morning's victim had a tiled ceiling with deep crown moldings and frilly pink bedding. That is, if any of this can be counted on." He waited a heartbeat. "Here. Go for it. I'll log it in, but you can have this." He ripped off several pages from his notebook. "Personally, I think it's all bullshit."

Brandt half nodded and walked back to his office. Bullshit or not, he'd still check it out.

An hour later, Brandt slumped back in his computer chair, stumped. Killers were normally predictable in their methods. They stayed with what worked and few killers changed that. Those that did had been in business for a long time. They'd evolved. This made them incredibly difficult to hunt – as he well knew.

He checked Kevin's notes again. With only a comment or two on the women's hair and the way they'd died – it would be hard to identify the victims. He had too many possibles to sort through. In a busy metropolis like Portland, murder was an everyday affair.

Speaking into empty air, he said, "This is ridiculous. I need details, damn it."

He needed a time frame or details of the victims themselves. How could Kevin not have asked for more? Not that he could blame Kevin. The city was overrun with nutcases. Who could tell them from the *normal* people these days?

He scratched down a couple more questions before returning to his screen. This particular nut had a name – Samantha Blair. He tried to fit the name to the image of the skinny, panicked woman from the hallway.

Back at his screen, he brought up all the information the database had to offer, which was scant at best. She was twenty-eight years old with no priors, no outstanding warrants, and no tickets or parking violations.

The phone rang, interrupting his search.

"Hello."

"Hi, sweetie. How are you today?"

Brandt leaned back with a grimace. "Mom, I'm fine. I told you yesterday, the headache was gone when I got home. Nothing to worry about."

"Yes, dear. I just wanted to call and make sure you're feeling better."

"I am. How are you? Are you ready to leave that place yet?" Brandt pivoted in his chair to stare out the window. The sun had managed to streak through a few of the gray rain clouds, lighting the sky with colored swaths.

His mom should be sitting out on her little deck in the assisted living center a few miles out of town. She'd been happy there – too happy. This was supposed to be a temporary situation. Somehow, every time he mentioned her leaving, her lung condition or diabetes acted up or she came up with some other excuse to stay a little longer. The center didn't mind. They were in the process of adding a new wing to accommodate more seniors. His mom had money and paid her way. It was to be closer to her that he'd requested the switch in location to this particular station.

"I'm not that good. My hip has mostly healed, but it still feels weak." She sniffled slightly.

Brandt grinned. What her hip had to do with a fake cold was anyone's guess, still she pulled out a sniffle every time.

Her voice almost back to normal, she asked, "Do you have time for lunch today?"

"No. Today's not good."

"Oh dear. Well, how about tomorrow then?"

"Mom, I'd love to if it's just the two of us. No more prospective girlfriends, okay?"

"Now honey, I wouldn't do that. You explained how you felt about my 'interfering,' as you called it. But, still," the raspy voice dropped to a sad whisper, "I do want to see you settled before I die."

"Oh, hell," Brandt muttered. The sweet long-suffering tones somehow managed to convey lost hopes and dire endings soon to come. "Mom, you aren't dying. And I am in the hands of a good woman. Many good women in fact." Her shocked gasp made him grin.

"Don't say that. You need a wife, not those...those," she spluttered.

He couldn't help but chuckle at her outrage. She deserved it for her constant interfering in his private life. Her persistence came closer to smothering than loving.

Brandt groaned under his breath. He straightened, stretching his back. "Enough about my girlfriends. Mom is there anything else you need, because I've got work to do."

"No, I'll save it for lunch tomorrow at the Rock Cafe. Be there at one o'clock like you promised."

Brandt's chair snapped forward, his feet hitting the floor hard. "What? What's this?" She'd hung up on him. "Damn it."

Irritated, he stared at the phone in his hand. His mother's machinations were legendary, and though he hated being outmaneuvered, it was his fault. He'd been letting her get away with this for thirty-four years, so there'd be no changing the status quo now.

Good humor restored, he turned back to his computer screen. According to Kevin, Samantha lived in the nearby community of Parksville where she worked at a local vet's office part-time. The sparse facts didn't begin to explain the haunted weariness that had so touched him. He'd seen a similar look in the families of victims and those at the bottom of their world.

He forced his attention back to Kevin's notes. It appeared Samantha had said something about both women having long hair. The one from several months ago had been a blonde who'd been strangled. So, how many unsolved cases could he find with long-haired murdered victims?

His fingers flew across the keyboard. Three cases listed for the last year. One of them flagged as possible prey of the Bastard, the serial killer he'd followed to Portland. A killer that had been active for decades, possibly all over the States, with no one connecting the dots – until Brandt.

This killer's victims were always young, beautiful women that were either happily married or in strong, committed relationships. All had been raped. And that's where the similarities ended. Some women were strangled in their beds, some stabbed in their living rooms, others tortured for hours. Portland was the geographical center of the most recent attacks.

The police had an old DNA sample that had degraded over the years and a couple of hairs from very early cases – and no one to check them against. This asshole had started his career before the labs became so sophisticated. He'd adapted and learned well. To date, they had no fingerprints and no hits on any databases.

That's why Brandt had trouble convincing his boss that they had a serial killer. Hence his job, pulling together everything he could find to get the backing for the task force to hunt down this asshole.

A knock sounded on the door. "Move it, Brandt. We've got another one."

CHAPTER THREE

11:27 am

Sam sat in her dilapidated Nissan truck at the stop light. Who was that man she'd mowed down in the hallway? It might have been a fleeting contact, but he'd left a hell of an impression. Strong, determined, surprised and even concerned. Sam wrapped her arms around her chest. Not likely.

A honk from behind catapulted her forward. She drove down Main Street before pulling into the almost empty parking lot at the vet's office, her insides finally unfurling and relaxing after the tough morning. The animals always helped. It's not that she didn't like people, because she did. But the foster home mill hadn't given her much opportunity to understand close relationships.

Whenever she'd tried to get close to another child, either they or she'd ended up shipped out within a few months. Sam had grown up watching the various dynamics around her in bewilderment. From loving kindness, to sibling fighting, to lovers breaking up and making up, everyone appeared to understand some secret rules to making relationships work.

Everyone but her.

She'd tried several relationships, even had several short-lived affairs. In the last few years, they'd been nonexistent.

Sam locked her car and walked through the rear door of the vet hospital – her kind of place. She had a kinship with animals. They'd become her saving grace in an increasingly dismal and lonely world. She stashed her purse in the furthest back cupboard, peeled off her sweater, and tossed it on top. Then she tucked in her t-shirt and got to work.

Moving through the cages, Sam grinned at Casper, a tabby cat who'd lost his leg in a car accident. "Hey buddy, how're you doing?" She opened the door and reached inside. Instantly, the cat's heavy guttural engine kicked in. She pulled the big softy out of the cage, careful for his new stump. The bandage had stayed dry at least. That had to be a good sign. She gave him a quick cuddle. "Okay, Casper, back you go. I'll get you fresh water. And how about a clean blanket?"

Sam bustled about taking comfort in the mundane and in the service of others – animal others. She hummed along until she came to the last cage. Inside, a heavily bandaged German shepherd glared at her. She halted at the hideous warning growl.

She stretched out a hand to snag the chart hanging from the front of the cage.

The growls increased in volume.

Sam stepped back to give the injured animal more space. She'd intruded in his comfort zone, something she could respect. Bending to his level, she spoke in a soft voice. Without his trust, taking care of him wouldn't be pleasant for either of them. And this guy looked like he'd seen the worst humanity had to offer.

The growl deepened, but stayed low key – a warning without heat.

Sam could respect that, too. She sat cross-legged at the edge of his space and continued to talk to him until he calmed down.

"Hey, Sam. I didn't hear you come in." Lucy, the gregarious vet assistant's voice boomed throughout the furthest corners of the room, giving Sam no opportunity to ignore it. She hunched her shoulders at the intrusion, keeping her eyes locked on the dog.

"I came in the back," she called out in a low voice.

The dog stared at her.

Sam shifted slightly and narrowed her gaze. The shepherd's gaze followed every movement. She grimaced. Strange, but she could almost sense his interest.

"There you are. What are you doing sitting on the bare floor like that? You're going to catch a cold." Lucy's voice sounded behind Sam's shoulder.

Sam jerked then twisted around to greet the large older woman, and for a startling moment saw another Lucy instead – Sam's murdered best friend Lucy, from a decade ago. The long familiar brown hair appeared braided off to one side, with her sweet smile spread across her face. The image was old and faded and yet still heart wrenchingly clear.

Pangs of guilt wiggled in Sam's belly. The dog's low growl tore through the image. Sam shook herself, concentrating on the office manager and not her old friend. "Hi, Lucy."

The older woman fisted her hands on ample hips. "Come on out front and have a warm cup of tea."

Sam glanced at the dog. His black gaze locked on the two women.

Lucy reached down a beefy hand to help Sam get to her feet. Sam winced. This morning's vision had left her stiff and sore. Her police disaster had left her aching.

With slow careful movements, Sam brushed off her clothes and hung the chart back on the dog's crate.

"Jesus girl, you're freezing. Lord, this child can't even take care of herself, let alone no animals."

Sam shook her head at Lucy's habit of directing comments to the almighty above. Still, she had a point. Cold, Sam's constant companion, had settled deeper in her bones. She found herself propelled to the front offices and the small cozy lunchroom. There, a hearty nudge pushed her to the closest chair. Within minutes, a hot cup of strong tea with a gentle serving of cream arrived before her.

Lucy, with a second cup of tea, took the chair opposite Sam.

Unable – and unwilling – to stop them, Sam confronted memories of the other Lucy. That Lucy had loved her tea too. The two of them had shared many cups. During one such moment, Sam had broken her own rule and had trusted her enough to tell her about her 'gift.' Poor Lucy. She'd thought it had been so cool. Then one night after drinking too many B52s, she'd told everyone, once again making Sam an oddity – an outsider. And reminding Sam of a sad truth – even friends couldn't be trusted. A lesson she hadn't forgotten since. Her friend had died an ugly death. And Sam hadn't been able to help her. More guilt.

Sam sighed.

"Heavy thoughts," said Lucy gently. "Care to share?"

Sam's mouth kicked up at the corners. "Nothing worth sharing," she murmured.

Lucy leaned back with an unsurprised nod. "Just so you know I'm always here if you ever want to talk." After a moment, she continued in a bright cheerful voice. "Here, try one." A plate of cookies appeared beside the hot mug.

"Thanks." And Sam meant it. Choosing a peanut butter cookie, she bit into it. She closed her eyes, a tiny moan escaping. In the darkness, the rich, buttery peanut taste filled her mouth. Delicate yet robust and sooo good.

"Not bad, huh?"

Sam nodded, wasting no time in popping the rest of the morsel into her mouth. Lucy nudged the plate closer. Sam grinned, and snatched up a second cookie. Lucy gave her a fat smile of pleasure.

Her mouth full, Sam considered the woman beside her. This Lucy gave from the heart, freely offering acceptance and reserving judgment. Sam understood the value of the gift. At the same time, all that emotion made her nervous

"Thanks for the tea and cookies." She took her cup to the sink.

"What do you think of our new patient?"

"The German shepherd." Sam spun around. "What happened to him?"

Lucy rose and brought her cup to the sink. "Sarah found him." Lucy turned around, "You remember my daughter, Sarah? She works at the seniors' facility..." Without waiting for a response, she continued talking. "She called in to say a resident had found the dog injured in the parking lot. Dr. Walcott drove over and picked him up."

Sam watched as Lucy turned on the hot water and dribbled a little dish soap over the cup in her hand. Sarah, she vaguely remembered was activity coordinator at a home between here and Portland.

Lucy gazed at Sam. "He was in tough shape. And since he woke up after surgery, well..." She placed the clean cup upside down on the drying rack. "He won't let any of us near him unless he's sedated."

Sam chewed on her bottom lip. "Is he eating? Drinking?"

"Through his IV," Lucy said with a small grim smile. "We'll see what he's like when it comes time to check his wounds. Don't get too attached. His prognosis isn't good."

Already halfway through the doorway leading to the back of the hospital, Sam stilled and glanced back, seeing only concern in the other woman's eyes. Resolutely, Sam headed back her charges.

The shepherd's low growl warned her halfway.

"It's okay, boy. It's just me. I'll be taking care of you. Give you food, fresh water, and friendship. The things that help us get along in life." Although she kept her voice quiet, warm, and even toned, the growl remained the same.

She couldn't blame him.

He might be able to get along without friendships, but she wanted them. Except for her friendship with Lucy, she'd never had that elusive relationship that others took for granted.

Sam approached the dog's cage with care. According to his chart, he'd had surgery to repair internal bleeding and to set a shattered leg. On top of that, he'd suffered several broken ribs, a dislocated collarbone and was missing a huge patch of skin on both hindquarters. Written in red and circled were the words: aggressive and dangerous. The growling stopped.

Sam squatted down to stare into his eyes. The dog should have a name. He didn't give a damn. But a name gave the dog a presence, an existence...an identity.

"How about..." she thought for a long moment. "I know, how about we call you Major?"

The dog exploded into snarls and hideous barking, his ears flattened, and absolute hate filled his eyes.

"Jesus!" Sam skittered to the far corner of the room – her hand to her chest – sure her heart would break free of its rib cage.

"Is everything okay back here?"

Sam turned in surprise to see one of the vets standing behind her, frowning. "Sorry," she yelled over the din of the other animals that had picked up the shepherd's fear. She waited for the animals to calm down before continuing. "I'd thought of a brilliant name for the shepherd, but from his reaction, I think he hates it."

The vet walked over and bent down to assess his patient. "It could have been your tone of voice or the inflection in the way you said the name. He'd been abused, even before this accident." After a thoughtful pause, he added, "I'm not sure, but it might have been kinder to have put him down."

"No." Sam stared at him in horror. "Don't say that. He'll come around." At his doubtful look, she continued, "I know he will. Give him a chance."

That she seemed to be asking the vet to give her a chance hung heavy in the room, yet she didn't think he understood that.

He stared at her, shrewdness, and wisdom in his eyes.

Then again, maybe she'd misjudged him. She shifted, uneasy under the intense gaze.

"We'll see. We'll have lots of opportunity to assess his progress as he recuperates."

Sam had to be satisfied with that. She knew the dog was worth saving and so, damn it, was she. Her salvation and that of the dog's were tied together in some unfathomable way. She could sense it. She'd fight tooth and nail to keep him safe.

In so doing, maybe she could save herself.

***

11:45 am

The Bastard had been busy.

Brandt grimly surveyed the room. The woman lay sprawled across the bed, killed by multiple stab wounds if the massive blood loss was anything to go by. Any number of perps could have done this, but Brandt knew the scene would be clean. Squeaky clean, just like every other one he blamed on this asshole.

And the woman would have drugs in her bloodstream, just enough so she wouldn't have been able to struggle – at least not much. A signature obvious from the more recent cases. Brandt frowned. This case would move to the head of Brandt's list. Ammunition for a task force to put this asshole behind bars.

His fists clenched and unclenched. Christ, he wanted to kill the Bastard himself.

Blood spattered the walls, carpet, the trashed bedding…a few drops even going so far as to hit the ceiling. A large pool of black blood had congealed on the floor beside the night table. This woman hadn't been murdered – she'd been butchered. She had to have been in a drugged sleep at the time of the attack. The only signs of struggle were on the bed, and not many of them, at that.

She also had long brown hair with a hint of a curl in it at the ends. Or would have had if the stands weren't flattened by the weight of the dried blood. The bedding was some kind of ruffled rose paisley thing. Two points to Samantha Blair. Deep crown moldings on the ceiling gave her a third.

"Brandt, the young man who called this in is waiting out back."

Adam was the youngest member of the team, with only six months' experience behind him. Always pale, today his red hair and freckles stood out more than ever, giving his face a clownish appearance. He tried to look anywhere but at the body on the bed. "Kevin said you can take the lead. He'll be here soon."

Another test. Fine with him.

"Then, let's go have a talk with the guy out back." Brandt headed outside of the brick house to question the waiting man. Tall, slim, and overwrought, the mid-twenties man sat on the brick step, his hair was brush-cut and his head cradled by his folded arms. His blue shirt was soaked with tears and his shoulders heaved and shuddered even as Brandt watched.

Brandt waited to give the young man a moment. "Jason Dean?"

The younger man snapped to his feet, nodding in between the tears. "Yes, that's me. Is...is she being taken away now?" He wiped his eyes with his sleeve, like a young child.

Brandt glanced back inside the small dwelling swollen with law enforcement and CSI. "Soon. The coroner isn't quite done yet."

The man's face paled even further, and his bottom lip trembled. He took several deep, bracing breaths and nodded.

With gentle coaxing, Brandt managed to get the whole story out of him.

They both worked for the same company and had been going out for close to a year now. They'd gone out for dinner and drinks last night before returning to her place. He'd stayed for several hours, leaving around one-thirty in the morning. When she hadn't shown up at work, he'd called numerous times and then had slipped over to check on her.

After finishing with Jason, Brandt walked back inside to wait. Within minutes, Kevin arrived with the other two homicide detectives on the team, Daniel and Seth. Brandt paced back and forth in the hallway, chewing on the information in his mind while he filled them in on what he knew.

"It's him, isn't it? The one you're always talking about?" Daniel, the second youngest member on the team asked, a frown wrapped around his forehead. He tucked his thumb into his pant pockets. Daniel's paunch matched his wife's five-months-pregnant belly – a fact the team teased him about mercilessly.

Each team member in the East Precinct pulled long hours. Brandt respected that. He wasn't here to rock the boat. But any cases that could be the Bastard's, he wanted in on. Simple. And so far, nothing. Except more bodies.

Grimly, Brandt watched as the gurney was wheeled into the bedroom.

"Chances are good it's him. Toxicology should confirm it." Brandt leaned against the bedroom wall and tried to assess the scene – a difficult task with his emotions still unsettled. He'd have to wait for the tests to come back to know for sure.

She'd been deliberately arranged with her legs splayed wide apart, her arms above her head. Open display, mocking and degrading her for maximum humiliation. Another similarity between the killer's victims, posed…yet not always in the same way.

Irrational rage from a rational mind.

"Okay, we're ready to move the body." One of the CSI team spoke to them.

Brandt nodded. "Thanks. How's the scene? Are you going to be able to get much?"

The investigator shook his head. "Not much. The scene is clean. We might find something when we run our tests, but I'm not counting on it."

"Her name was Mandy Saxon," said Brandt abruptly. Her purse sat on the kitchen table, unopened and undisturbed, along with a briefcase of work she'd brought home. She'd been an accountant, a thirty-year-old junior member of a successful firm here in Portland, with her whole life ahead of her.

Now it was all behind her.

Stone-faced, the detectives watched two men bag and load the body onto the gurney before wheeling it out the door. Brandt would catch up with her at the morgue tomorrow.

Turning back, he caught sight of the coroner leaving.

"James, have you got a time of death?"

The grizzled coroner answered, "The best I can do at the moment, is between two and five." James shook his head. "I'll have more after the autopsy." The coroner walked out after smacking Adam's shoulder.

Turning back to the crime scene, Brandt watched as one of the CSI officers picked a tiny object off the carpet with tweezers. He waited until the item had been bagged and tagged.

"Stanley, what did you find?"

The man stood, holding the bag aloft for Brandt to see. "It appears to be a diamond or a zirconium. Have to wait until I get it back to the lab to know for sure."

Brandt stared at the tiny twinkling object. "Earring?" It could be the right size. He turned toward the open doorway. The stretcher had long gone. He'd have to wait to check what jewelry the victim wore.

He walked over to the open jewelry box on the dresser to rummage through the few quality items inside. All the settings appeared intact. None matched the stone.

Stanley, who'd worked alongside Kevin and his team for over a decade, joined him. "I'll run it through some tests. It's pretty small, probably part of a design."

Like a four leaf-clover design? Brandt couldn't remember the exact details of Ms. Blair's statement. Had the ring always been missing one jewel or only the last time she'd seen it? Had she even mentioned that detail? He'd have to wait until he got back to the office to be sure – but it felt right.

That waif's story sounded beyond wild, but that look in her eye had been real. Whatever demon drove her, she believed in it.

Staring down at the tiny jewel, Brandt realized he couldn't discount it either.

"Okay, keep me posted."

Stanley nodded and headed back to his kit with the evidence bag.

It took another hour before the room emptied, leaving only the brutal evidence of death behind. Bloodstains perpetuated the smell of death. Vestiges of violence remained behind. Brandt swore he could almost see and hear the play-by-play of her death from the scene laid out before him.

He didn't have psychic abilities in the normal sense, still, like many of his coworkers, he had a strong intuition. Whether it had developed through his years of police work or through his long friendship with Stefan, didn't matter. He'd learned a long time ago to listen to it.

And right now, it was screaming at him.

***

2:20 pm

Kevin Bresson pulled into the station parking lot. Lunch was over and the place was packed as usual. Around the back of the building, he found a spot and parked. "Home sweet home," he said to Adam, who was sitting in the passenger seat beside him.

"If you say so."

Kevin glanced over at him. "Can't be cynical at your age. Come on, you haven't been on the force long enough for that. Give it a decade or two like me – then you've earned the right to be sour."

Adam got out and closed the door of the black SUV. He waited while Kevin grabbed his bag before walking to the rear entrance.

"I'm not being cynical, exactly. But it's a little hard to stay positive when you come from scenes like that one."

Kevin's normally stern face darkened. "I know what you mean."

Adam held the door open for him. "Do you think Brandt is right? That there's a serial killer working here?"

Kevin's pace never slowed as he headed for the elevator that would take them to their third floor offices. "I don't know. I've only seen some of the evidence. It would take more to convince me fully. Still, he has got a couple of valid arguments. Too many to discount his theory."

"He thinks this is another one."

"And that's possible. We'll work on it the same as every other case, and either he'll pull it for his list or he won't. We have enough work to do without keeping tabs on what he's up to."

"Right."

Kevin entered the waiting elevator with Adam on his heels. He was tired and fed up. The last thing he wanted was for Brandt to be correct and that a serial killer had been operating under their noses for decades. Just as the door was about to shut, a yell went up.

Kevin stopped the doors from closing long enough for Dillon Hathaway to get on.

"Thanks Kevin."

Dillon grinned that affable smile that always pissed Kevin right off.

"I hear you caught another bad one this morning. Let me know if you need any of my expertise to close this for you."

Kevin stiffened. Just because the 'kid' had a couple of college degrees didn't make him better than the veterans on the force. Now if Dillon had some experience to go with that piece of paper then people might be more inclined to listen. As it was, Dillon, in his late twenties, had only about six months of experience. Kevin wondered why he hadn't gone into business.

He had that wheeling dealing kind of attitude and dressed the part too. He'd have done well.

Covertly, he studied Dillon's designer suit and lavender shirt. No wonder the guys in the department laughed at him. Although, it was his insufferable know-it-all attitude that made everyone want to kick his ass.

Adam wouldn't stay quiet. Kevin shot him a warning look, but it was too late.

"I think we can handle it. Other people, beside you, know how to do their jobs, you know."

Grinning, Dillon put his hands out in front of him in exaggerated supplication. "Hey, no problem, Adam. Just wanted to let you know that you can call on me any time. But I understand pride. So just trundle along in your usual way."

Kevin clenched his jaw and rolled his eyes. He did take pride in the number of cases he'd closed over the years. But no matter how many he solved or how many assholes he put behind bars, there were always a dozen more ready to take their place. If Brandt was right, they were in trouble. A serial killer with the skills to stay undetected for decades was just bad news – for everyone.

But working with Brandt was a different story than asking this young upstart for help. Brandt might be new to the department, but Kevin respected the man – unlike Dillon. Brandt was a straight up kind of guy who you could count on in a tight spot. What made working with him hard was his special assignment status. Not that he played the maverick card, but he worked with his own agenda.

Kevin wasn't sure what Brandt did all day exactly, only that he showed up for their meetings and any crime scenes that fit the parameters he was searching for. Cushy job if you could get it. As long as he stayed out of Kevin's way then he could work on all the task force preparations he wanted to – no harm done.

The elevator opened. Kevin, already focused on his job at hand, pushed all worries of Detective Brandt Sutherland from his mind.

CHAPTER FOUR

3:45 pm

Sam hit the next rut hard, bouncing across it before she had a chance to maneuver her truck to the left. Her driveway had more potholes and grooves than drivable surface – a free bonus with the cheap rent. Her little pickup shook hard with the next hit and never had a chance to stop trembling before it bounced again.

Sam grimaced. She'd soon be black and blue just from the trip home. Great, more bruises. As if she needed more pain. Turning the last corner, she leaned forward to see her favorite view.

The tree line opened to the full valley and lake. Glittering water glistened for miles. She lived for this moment. The hills and mountains in the horizon bled into wonderful shades of blue and the trees...the greens and yellows, an oil canvas of joy. She smiled. This vista sustained her soul as food never could.

Parking the truck, Sam hopped out. Off to the left she could see her small cabin nestled just far enough back from the shore to give a front yard. She realized once again how blessed she was to have been given a chance to live there. A perfect place to stop running.

When she'd found it, the owners – an older couple – hadn't wanted to rent it out. She'd been in dire straits and once they'd sensed that, their attitude had changed.

Sam appreciated their change of heart. Life had dished out a couple of bad months. She winced. Who could talk in terms of months? Her life had been a cesspool for years.

The sun twinkled overhead. She smiled at the sky. Opening the driver's door, she started to hop back in when pain lashed through her. Black tentacles reached inside her skull and clutched her brain, dropping her to her knees.

She cried out, her hands cradling her temple. She doubled over, rocking back and forth, as darkness filled her mind. Her chest constricted. She struggled to breathe. Then she started to panic.

Just before she lost control, the curtain of blackness ripped aside. Sam breathed hard, struggling with the new images. They weren't of her truck or of the woods around her.

She stood outside a coffee shop in an area she didn't recognize. The only familiar thing came from behind her. A feeling, a gaze, an energy. Comprehension hit her slowly. "No," she cried, her hands covering her eyes. Pain seared her heart as her mind finally understood. Nothing could stop the tears from welling up and tumbling down her cheeks.

The killer had just found another victim.

***

3:55 pm

Brandt preferred to gain information in a less formal way, yet his badge did loosen tongues. Or it had until Parksville. The rotund postal clerk hadn't recognized Sam's name until Brandt gave her a description. She'd clammed up immediately, to stare at him suspiciously. When he brought out his badge, she became even more belligerent – if possible.

"You can ask your questions over at the vet hospital as she works there part-time." She turned away to speak with another customer.

Dismissed, Brandt left – his curiosity aroused. He walked across the street to the Parksville Veterinarian Hospital and asked his questions there.

"Sorry, we don't give out personal information on our staff." The older woman was striking in her own way, except for the waves of protectiveness rolling off her. Odd, she too saw him as the enemy. Not an unusual reaction from the drug runners and hookers on the streets, but from someone who looked more at home dishing out apple pie and lemonade – very strange.

Brandt turned his badge her way.

She raised one eyebrow, yet didn't relax. Instead, she held out her hand. Brandt passed over his badge and watched as she wrote down the information before passing it back.

"Now, can you provide me with her address, please?" he said in his most official voice.

She appeared to consider his words. What required consideration he couldn't begin to understand. "Excuse me," he snapped. "Does she work here or not?"

"Yes, that's true. She does." The dragon smiled as if happy to be able to answer him.

"Good. I *need* her address and her phone number." Using his well-honed eagle eye, he stared her down.

To no effect.

"I don't think she has a phone." She assessed him again, with that same calculating look of his grandmother. "Why the interest?"

"It's personal, ma'am." Brandt had been thinking to save Samantha unnecessary questions about the police looking for her. Then he saw her knowing glance and groaned. Heat flooded his face.

The older woman smiled.

Brandt shuffled his feet as if still in high school himself.

Her smile widened.

Shit. Brandt couldn't believe it. He shook his head to clear his thoughts and tried to regain control of the wayward conversation.

"Police business," he clarified, hoping to get this conversation back on the right direction.

After another long look, the dragon, as if realizing he couldn't be put off, walked toward the desk, wrote something on a small scratch pad, and held it out to him. "Here you go – her address. Now, if you'll excuse us, we have to take care of our customers." She motioned to several people waiting behind him. "Hello Mrs. Caruthers. What's the problem with Prissy?"

Brandt snatched up the paper and strode through the front glass doors. Once outside, he glanced down at the address.

"Shit." She'd given him the same PO Box address he already had. Technically, she'd done what he'd asked, while avoiding giving him what he needed.

"Is there a problem, sir?" A competent-looking older man approached him. "I'm Dr. Wascott. This is my office. Maybe I can help you?"

Brandt smiled, happy to find someone normal in the town. "I'm Detective Sutherland." Brandt once again reached into his pocket and pulled out his badge. "I'm looking for directions to Samantha Blair's place."

"Oh." The older man smiled, his bushy brows giving him a Rip Van Winkle look. "That's easy. She's at the old Coulson homestead." He turned and pointed out the direction. "Head up the highway to the large gingerbread-looking house. Turn right onto the dirt road past the house and follow it all the way down to the lake. She's pretty isolated down there, but seems to enjoy it." He opened the front door of his office. "There's no problem, I hope?" He paused and looked back at Brandt, one eyebrow raised.

Brandt shook his head, tucking the slip of paper into his shirt pocket. "Not at all, I'm just checking on some information she gave us."

"Didn't think so. She's not the type." Smiling, the vet walked inside, the glass door shutting behind him.

Brant stared up the road. A gingerbread house – that should be easy.

***

4:09 pm

Sam dragged her sorry ass out of the truck and up the wooden stairs. The vision had left her feeling as if she'd gained a hundred pounds. Every shuffling step had become an effort. That insight into a killer's mind had been downright unpleasant. Knowing he'd found another woman, hurt her. That she'd had the vision at all terrified her. It was yet another sign her 'talent' was changing. And she didn't like it one bit. Her head throbbed from the remnants of sensory overload.

Moses barked excitedly, his madcap tail waving in the wind. He shoved his wet nose into her hand.

"Hey boy. Sorry to be so long today." She scratched the big dog's head. The golden haired Heinz 57 mix easily came to her mid-thigh. She smiled at the oversized black paws. Moses had been the main man in her life for a long time.

Shifting her library books, picked up over her lunch break, she strode up the front steps. On psychic phenomena, these books might hold the answers to her perpetual problem. At one time, she'd asked experts for help. Unfortunately, she'd chosen the wrong kind of expert.

Images of padded walls and needles slammed into her mind. Ruthless, and with more experience than she'd like to admit, she slammed them right back out again.

Moses slumped to the deck in his usual jumble of muscle and sinew, thumped his tail once, and fell back asleep.

"Good companion you are, Moses."

His tail thumped again, but he couldn't be bothered raising his head. Sam bent down to stroke his back. Her fingers slipped in and out of the thick golden pelt, enjoying the silky contact. A great sigh erupted from him, and he relaxed even further.

Sam laughed at his total exit from the world. He had the right idea. She needed sleep, too.

Exhaustion from her vision had caught up to her. Even running a hand over her forehead brought a tremor to her spine. After putting on the teakettle, she walked into the bathroom, dampened a washcloth, and wiped her face. The cool wetness helped refresh her.

Catching sight of her face, she winced. Her porcelain skin – always translucent – now seemed paper thin, transparent even. She looked friggin' awful. She closed her eyes, shocked at how far her health had sunk. If she didn't find answers soon, her 'gifts' would kill her.

She was halfway there now.

While she walked through the tiny cabin, loneliness crept in. She stared at the plain walls, her hip propped against the counter and a hot cup of tea warming her hands. The support walls were old logs and the floorboards had been cut from hewn wood. They'd worn down in places and would have some incredible stories to tell if they could talk. Unfortunately, in her case, they could. Depending on the day and the strength of her energy as to what signals she picked up, the stories went from unsettling to downright nervy.

Moses raised his bushy head and growled. Sam glanced around, puzzled. "What's the matter, Moses?"

He growled again, staring at the place where the driveway drove out of the evergreens at the top of the ridge.

Sam gazed out the living room window, but couldn't see anything. Living out here, wildlife often shared her space. She loved watching the deer make their way to the river for a drink. Thus far she'd also seen raccoons, coyotes, and once, in the evening, a bear. If the animals left her in peace then she'd be happy to return the courtesy.

A faint rumbling told her what she needed to know. A vehicle. She retreated into the house, a leery eye on the driveway. It didn't take long before a black pickup bounced into view and rolled to a stop at the porch stairs.

A tall, rugged man got out, removed his sunglasses, and tossed them on the dash. He appeared vaguely familiar, yet she couldn't place him. Using the one gift that she'd come to accept, Sam assessed the waves of determination pouring from his shoulders. This man was nobody's fool. And he wanted something from her.

Moses growled again.

That face. The lock of brown hair falling down on one side, piercing eyes and a 'take no prisoner' attitude, dressed in denim. He was a cop. Recognition flickered. He was the man she'd almost run into at the police station. Curiosity and fear mingled. What could he want? Her stomach acid bubbled as tension knotted her spine. She chewed her fingernail as his six-foot frame climbed the stairs.

The heavy pounding on the other side of her head startled her. She cursed silently, but with full force, letting it bounce around inside her mind. She wiped her moist palms on her jeans, and opened the door.

"Yes?"

His brow furrowed. "Samantha Blair?

She frowned. "Maybe. Who's asking?"

An odd light shone deep in his Lake Tahoe blue eyes. "Detective Brandt Sutherland, at your service, ma'am."

"Your badge, please," she said.

His eyebrow quirked, still he didn't say anything. He reached into a back pocket and withdrew it for her.

Sam plucked it from his fingers. She read the number on it several times, committing it to memory.

He reached for the badge. "Satisfied?"

Sam handed it back to him. "Maybe. What can I do for you?"

Tucking his badge away, he stared at her, an odd glint in his eye. "You spoke with Detective Kevin Bresson at the station this morning, correct?"

Nerves knotted her stomach tighter, pulling down the corner of her mouth. Sam frowned at him. What was he up to?

"Yes. You saw me there." Her stomach heaved. "What's this about?"

He shifted his weight. Why? He didn't seem the type to feel discomfort about much in life.

"May I come in?"

She considered his request for a long moment before opening the door wide.

Moses followed, staying close to her side, and nudged her leg. She dropped her hand to his head, reassured by his warm presence. "Good boy, Moses."

Big brown eyes laughed up at her, his tongue lolling to one side.

"Moses, is that his name?"

Sam nodded slowly, studying this lean muscular male, hands fisted on his hips, as he watched her. Raw sex appeal oozed naturally from his very presence. She frowned. He was too damn appealing. She didn't like that. Cops were not her favorite people. Sexy ones definitely didn't make her list.

Glancing around the small living space, she realized she didn't know what to do. She'd never had any company here before. Did a police visit count as company? Did she sit down with him? Offer him a cup of tea or what? Awkward – and hating the uncertainty – she repeated abruptly, "What do you want?"

He surveyed the simple living room, walked over to an old sofa, and stopped. "May I sit down?"

With a new perspective, Sam saw the threadbare furniture for what it was – shabby signs of dire poverty. It wouldn't have mattered any other time – after all, she lived it. She didn't understand why it mattered now. "Sure."

She sat on the couch opposite, trying to understand why he intrigued her. He glowed – with life, with health. He had so much vitality that everything around him paled by comparison. His energy was a beacon she couldn't help but find attractive – the lure of warmth and strength, something she'd experienced little in life. He dwarfed everything in the small open room. Sam felt tiny, insignificant against his more dynamic presence.

He reached across and placed his huge hand over hers.

Sam froze. His touch burned into her icy hands. Heat flared. So did confusion. Attraction. Hatred. Pain. Heat. Everything rolled together. Her gaze flew up to meet his.

He squeezed her fingers. Only then did she notice she'd been twisting her fingers around and around in a nervous pattern. A habit she'd tried to break for years. She yanked both hands back and tucked them under her thighs, leaning back. Heat still pulsed inside her veins. Heat she wanted to nestle closer to, yet couldn't explain why. Or didn't dare try. Nervous energy bubbled up. She clamped down hard and forced her errant muscles into stillness. Sam waited for him to speak.

"Are you okay?"

She jerked her head up and down.

"Good. Then let's go over the statement you gave Detective Bresson."

"Why? He didn't believe me."

"But maybe I will," he countered. "So, please, from the beginning."

The beginning. She cast a careful eye over him.

He prompted. "You said you woke up inside a woman's body as she was being murdered?"

Oh, that beginning. Relief blossomed, and she settled back into the couch. Slowly, succinctly, she explained her story again.

"Any idea if his ring had real diamonds in it?"

She glanced at him in surprise. "No. I wouldn't know the difference."

"Could you see the woman's hair?"

"This one had long brown hair. I think it had a slight curl to it."

He raised an eyebrow at her and pursed his lips. "Curly?"

Sam swallowed hard several times, overwhelmed with the memory. Soft and feathery, the dead woman's beautiful curls had stroked against her neck with every twist and turn of her head as she fought for her life.

Locking down her grief and stiffening her spine, Sam explained. "I could feel it curling around my neck."

The look on his face eased.

Sam had no idea if he believed her or not.

"Can you tell me anything about his height, the clothes he wore, the type of mask he had on...anything?"

His mask. Shivers raced down her spine. The madness in those eyes – those glowing orbs still made her nightmares hell. Green neon had shone with joy at the pain he had inflicted.

Sam could hardly speak. Her voice hoarse from unshed tears, she explained what little she'd seen, and the impression the killer had left on her. She hunched her shoulders against the lingering horror, hating the power the memories held over her.

He asked a few more questions. She slid into monosyllabic answers, wishing he'd finish and leave.

Finally, he snapped his notebook closed and tucked it into his shirt pocket. "Thanks." He stood and walked to the door, and turned back to face her, pulling out a business card.

"I don't know if I believe you or if what you've given us even helps, but I appreciate you having come in to share your information. If you think of anything else, please let me know." He nodded politely and walked out.

Now that he appeared ready to leave, Sam's emotions scattered. She didn't know what to make of him. His presence confused her. Interested her. Intrigued her. Memories dictated that she should be angry, scared even. But she was none of those.

Sam trailed him onto the porch. The detective hopped into his truck and drove off. He never looked back.

Sam stayed, bemused, until his truck bounced and shuddered out of sight. For the first time in years, a faint hope came into being. Maybe something could be done after all.

"And just what the hell was that all about, Moses?"

His heavy tail brushed over the wooden planks. Not much of an answer, still it was the only one she was going to get. She headed back inside, Moses at her heels. A chill settled into the room — or maybe it was into her soul.

She wandered around the now seemingly overlarge, empty space...lonely space. The ancient floors creaked under every step in a rhythm that was almost comforting.

The detective probably considered her a suspect by now and if not he would soon. That's how they worked. The police were suspicious of anyone odd. She knew that. She'd come under their scrutiny more than once. But especially from one detective.

Her thoughts blackened at the reminder. That man had been out to get her, and she'd only been trying to help. Damn him.

Even if this detective did put her on his suspect list, she had no one to blame but herself. She'd known it was likely to happen. Still, she'd had to do something. Those women had no one else.

A shiver of apprehension raised goose bumps on her arms. The last thing Sam wanted was to have her life examined under a microscope. She avoided people because she couldn't stand their questions. And sooner or later, everyone asked questions.

***

5:19 pm

Brandt grinned at his mother's antics. He'd stopped in at her self-contained unit in the seniors' complex, for coffee and to apologize for canceling out on lunch tomorrow. It didn't take more than a few minutes to realize that some things never change.

A beautiful young woman, Lisa, knocked on the door not five minutes after he arrived. Maisy wasted no time inviting her in to meet Brandt.

An obvious setup, yet no different from what his mother put him through on a regular basis in her quest to see him married. Not that old age had crept into her bones, nor had her health deteriorated. Still, she sought grandkids in the worst way. And she had no compunction about using underhanded methods in achieving these goals.

Studying Lisa more closely, he could see the classical beauty his mother would think appropriate. Baby blue eyes with a guileless innocence, long straight blond hair and a slim, but curvy shape. And none of it mattered to him.

All he could see were Sam's haunting eyes. He had no idea if Sam's body curved or bumped. He knew she had a slight build and that she didn't eat enough. With her oversized sweater on, not much else showed. He didn't quite know how he felt about this interest, but was willing to see where it went.

He understood that his 'type' was fluid and fluctuated on impulse. He considered that normal. That didn't mean he chose to go out with all of the women who appeared on his radar.

"Brandt. *Brandt?*"

Brandt focused on his mother and smiled sheepishly. Her knowing smirk immediately put him on his guard. With a sinking feeling, he realized he'd been staring at Lisa too long. He groaned softly. Maisy's smirk widened.

"Now Brandt, I know she's adorable. Do try to concentrate, dear."

He rolled his eyes and stood up. "I'm sorry, ladies. You'll have to excuse me. It's time for me to head out."

"Oh, no," Maisy cried out. "You never stay for a real visit. Won't you stay for dinner at least?"

Trust her to ignore the fact that he'd been here for dinner just a couple days ago. Today, he'd come straight from Samantha's hideaway, needing a touch of normalcy after seeing her. Only to realize that he preferred Sam to the Lisas of the world. How contrary could he be?

He excused himself from dinner and said his good-byes. The sky had clouded over giving an unusual darkness to the horizon. Once in his truck, his mind immediately returned to the tiny woman with a huge impact. Sam and that overgrown mutt, Moses, had chosen a singular existence out in the middle of nowhere. The dog had been protective when Brandt first arrived. After a once-over he'd gone and lain down. A guard dog would never have done that.

Pulling off to the side of the road, he called into the office for updates. Then he tried calling Stefan, his difficult, contrary, and incredibly gifted psychic friend. And left another message.

Given the lateness of the hour, he decided to go home and mull over the contrariness of human attraction.

CHAPTER FIVE

11:05 pm

Lying in bed that night, Sam couldn't sleep. Her overwrought mind refused to let up. The tantalizing possibility that she was meant to do something with this gift worried at the frayed edges of her mind. Depressed and unsettled, she fell into a fitful sleep, her dreams dark and disjointed pieces of past visions.

Screams jarred her from a deep sleep. Confusion turned to fear when Sam realized the horrific sounds were coming from her own mouth. Even worse, she had no idea where she was.

Terror overwhelmed her. Her fingers spasmed in a death grip around a strange steering wheel as the car she drove careened further out of control. Still trying to toss off the remnants of sleep, Sam yanked hard on the wheel in a futile attempt to turn it. The mid-sized car plowed through a steel barricade to hang suspended in midair before plummeting to the rocks below. Screams ripped from her throat and she reefed again on the useless steering wheel, helpless to stop the deadly impact. Her foot pounded on worthless brakes. The front grill of the car crumpled and metal buckled upward. The car slammed into the first of the rocks below, snapping her forward into the windshield.

Agonizing pain radiated off her shattered spine. Grinding metal, exploding glass, and continuous crunching sounds filled the air as first the bumper flew off, then the rear window shattered outward. The car tumbled, smashed on a huge rock, careened to the left and flipped end over end before coming to a hard landing on its wheels, right side up at the bottom of the cliff.

Then utter silence.

Sam trembled. Shock and pain pulsed through her veins even as her blood dripped out one beat at a time onto the shredded seat beside her. God, she didn't want to die.

She wanted to live. Please, dear God.

Someone help!

Blood streamed over her face, her spine...where a shearing heat set off continuous stabbing pain. The steering wheel jammed into her ribs. The front dash had crumpled into a mess of twisted steel and plastic. The famous Mercedes emblem now hung drunk in midair over the remains of the once beautiful cream leather seats.

Sam couldn't feel her right arm. And wished she couldn't feel her left. She closed her eyes, willing away the image of bone shards that had sliced through her sweater, a few loose strands of wool clinging to the ends. Heart wrenching sobs poured from her throat, tears coated her cheeks. She was alone. And dying.

A brilliant flash of light engulfed the car as the fuel from the pierced gas line flashed into flames. Heat seared her lungs and scorched her hair, the strands melting against the inside of her car window. Panicked, she screamed as flames licked at her feet, burning, and cooking the flesh right off her bones.

Agony. Pain. Terror.

A voice whispered through the blackness of her mind, so odd, so different it caught her attention. She strained to hear the words.

"Let go. It's time to let go."

Sam stared through the flames, stunned. *Let go of what?* She couldn't hear over the roaring fire and could barely see, but knowing that someone was there stirred her survival instinct and she started fighting against the seatbelt jammed at her side. She was saved. Just another minute and they'd open the door to pull her free. She'd be fine.

"Please hurry," she cried out.

"Let go. You don't need to be in there. Let it all go, and come with me."

She peered through the golden orange windshield to see a strange male face peering at her through the flames.

He smiled.

"Come with me."

"I want to, damn it. Can't you see I'm trapped?" she screamed, her vocals crisping in the heat.

"Release yourself. Come with me. Say yes."

The pain hit a crescendo. She twisted against it, hearing her spine splinter. The car seat melted into her skin. So much pain, she couldn't breathe. Blackness crowded into her mind, blessed quiet, soothing darkness. She reached for it.

"Let go. You don't need to go through this. Hurry."

She started. Why wasn't he opening the door or getting others to help? He should be trying to save her. Shouldn't he? Sam, so confused and so tired she could barely feel the pain overtaking her body. Where had he gone? She tried to concentrate. His face was now only a vague outline that rippled with the heat waves. A soft smile played at the corner of his mouth. The flames burned around him, weird as they centered him in the warm glow. She wanted to be with him. To live.

"Here, take my hand."

Dazed and on the brink of death, Sam focused on the hand reaching for her. She struggled to raise the charred piece of flesh that had been her arm and reached out to grasp his.

She was free.

Overwhelmed, cries of relief escaped. She turned to hug her savior, her head just reaching his shoulder. He stood beside her, the same radiant beaming look on his face. His blond hair glowed, and he had the brightest teeth.

She sighed. This beautiful man pointed to her right arm. Confused, Sam glanced down at her burned arm, realizing she could feel none of her injuries. Just like her other one, her broken arm had miraculously healed – whole, smooth, and soft. Her skin hadn't looked this good in ten years.

Realization hit.

She spun around to find a massive fireball below. What the hell? She had to be dead. But instead of the horror or shock, she expected to feel, she felt good. In fact, she felt great. She turned to the ever-smiling stranger.

"Let's go, sweetheart."

Sam didn't know why he'd called her that, but she bloomed under his loving gaze. Honestly, she was so damned grateful to be out of the car, she let him get away with it.

Holding hands, they floated higher into the cloudless blue sky. Then when the crash site below had become a tiny speck, Sam felt a hard flick on her arm and the words, "Thanks. I can take it from here."

And she woke up.

***

6:05 am, June 16th

Stunned and disoriented, Sam lay rigid in bed. The sense of loss overwhelmed her. *He* was gone. She needed his gentle warmth. He made her feel loved and cared for. Bereft, hot tears welled at the corners of her eyes. She didn't want to be back here in her own body. She wanted to be that other woman. That lucky woman.

Sam stopped in shock. That woman was dead! How lucky could that woman be? She'd be fine now, happy and at peace...with that man at her side. Lucky to be so loved.

And who the hell was he?

Sam couldn't believe her vision. Even now, instead of being overwhelmed with shock and pain, she felt uplifted.

Mystified, she questioned the difference this time. Not the death itself, that part unfortunately, had been normal, right down to the excruciating pain. But afterwards...? She didn't know who the man had been or what he might have been to the victim, but he'd cared about her. She wished she'd had her wits about her to talk to him at the time. Now it was too late.

There'd been one other major difference in this vision.

Always before, Sam had been forced to endure the horror of what one human being could inflict on another. This had been her first accident. Or was it?

What's the chance someone killed the woman to make it appear like an accident?

Sam narrowed her eyes, thinking. Given her relationship to violence – and there's no doubt the woman had died a violent death, had foul play been involved? Sam replayed the video locked into her psyche. The brakes hadn't responded, neither had her steering wheel – then they weren't built for flying. Suspicion remained. Intuitively, she felt more was involved. But could she prove it? No. She did know the woman had not been sleeping at the wheel or drunk. Living her last moments had given Sam clarity into the woman's mental state. There hadn't been any drugged or hallucination type of sensation.

Her car had to have been sabotaged. Sam snorted and threw back the blankets. So what? Just because she 'thought' foul play had been involved didn't mean it had been. Or that she could convince the police of it.

Grabbing up her journal, she wrote down as many details from this vision as she could. A process she went through every time. The impressions about the man were so clear, so poignant she had to write them down. Finally, she was done. Closing the book, she put it beside her bed, ready for the next time. She stared at it for a long moment. If anyone found her journals...she glanced over at the box beside her suitcase...they'd be used as evidence against her.

She had to question what her role was this time. She hadn't been able to help the poor woman. If she had a 'gift' then she wanted – no *needed* – to use it to make a difference. And had yet to do so. The idea, the concept...to help the victim find justice tantalized her. And then again, attempting to help these women meant working with the police. Bile immediately bubbled up in her stomach.

Sam leaned over, reaching for clean jeans and a t-shirt – dressing while deep in thought. Making a quick decision, she reached for the card and punched the number on her cell phone before she had a chance to change her mind.

"Hello?"

Fear caught her sideways. Words refused to come out.

"Hello. Who is this?"

The sharp demanding tone made her wince. She glanced at the clock on the stove and grimaced. He'd been asleep.

"God damn it, answer me." Anger reached through the phone to squeeze her vocal cords.

Samantha rushed into speech. "It's me. Huh, hmmm, Samantha Blair."

"Samantha," he said, enunciating the words slow and clear as if trying to place her.

"You came out to my place at the lake to ask me some questions yesterday," Sam started to explain.

"Oh. That Samantha." The anger shifted down to a growl.

She could almost see him shift into gear.

"What can I do for you?"

"Umm." Now that she had him on the phone, she didn't quite know what to say. "I know that some of the stuff that I told you might have been a little difficult to believe." She paused, not quite knowing where to go from here.

"Maybe," he answered, huskiness clouding his voice as if he was still groggy from sleep. It did funny things to her stomach.

She focused on his answer, his wariness. Determinedly, she forged ahead. "I saw an accident happen this morning. I thought if you could verify these details, you might have more faith in the other information I gave you."

Dead silence.

Oh God, why had she called him? She chewed on her bottom lip. What madness possessed her to call? She glanced out the window. It was just starting to get light outside.

"What kind of car accident?" His voice sounded brisker, more alert.

"A woman drove over the cliff and crashed onto the rocks below." She hesitated for a moment then rushed into speech. "The thing is...this time I recognized the spot. She drove off at Emerson Point."

"Emerson Point?" Now she had his attention. He was all business.

Feeling reassured, she continued. "Yes. She went through the guardrail. The car landed on its wheels before exploding."

"Hmmm. Time frame?" He cleared his throat.

That husky sound made her stomach do a slow tumble. Sam struggled to consider his question. But images of him leaning against the head of his bed, running a hand through his ruffled hair, the blankets resting low on his hips made her swallow and close her eyes. What had he asked? Oh yeah, it had been something about time frame. Had the accident been in real time? She cleared her throat. "About thirty, maybe forty minutes ago.."

"You think?"

She hated the apologetic tone in her voice. "I woke as it happened. All I can say is that I think it played out in real time."

More digestive silence.

"Right. Make of car, color, and license plate? Anything specific that you can tell me."

"I experienced her death the same as always. So, I couldn't see the license plate because I was, in effect, driving the car. She drove a dark colored Mercedes. I don't know the model."

"How did you know the type of car then?"

"Because I could see the logo inside the car."

Sam could hear the scratching of pen on paper. She waited.

"Right. Anything else?"

"Her name was Louise." Sam's voice hitched and stopped, surprised. Where had that come from? The name danced through her head. It felt right.

She took a deep breath, knowing this could be the point where he suspended belief. "And I think she was murdered."

***

6:30 am

Brandt rubbed the sleep from his eyes. Jesus, what a way to wake up. Every time he spoke with this woman, he couldn't get a grip on her. Was she for real?

He threw back his duvet and headed for a shower. At least this time, she'd given him something concrete. If it checked out.

Two hours later, at the station, he stood frowning down at an accident report in his hands. Incomplete as yet, just chicken scratch as the cop on the scene hadn't had a chance to finish the paperwork.

"Jackson, any sign of foul play?" Brandt glanced up from the paper, his piercing gaze nailing the young traffic cop.

"No, sir," Jackson said shifting his large weight from one foot to the other. "Not that I could see."

The younger man rubbed his face, fatigue pulling on his skin, giving him a much older appearance. The job did that to everyone after a while. "There isn't much left. The fire burned everything to ash."

"There weren't any secondary vehicle marks on the highway indicating she might have been forced off the road?"

"No, nothing like that. Her car headed straight for the guard rail, went through and over."

Brandt shot him a hard look. "Suicide?"

Jackson shrugged. "No idea."

He looked like he didn't give a damn. It must have been a long night. Brandt nodded and handed back the report. "We'd better find out." He turned away, heading down the hallway.

"Uh, Brandt, sir?"

Brandt stopped before slowly turning around. "What?"

"Do you know something about this woman? Something that pertains to the case? Because this seems straightforward. Open and shut type of thing."

You mean, 'you don't want to be bothered' type of a thing, Brandt thought, his cynicism rising to the surface. Too often, it was more a case of working in the areas where progress could be made and leaving the time-wasting for others. Still, his placement here put him in an awkward position.

"Maybe," Brandt answered. "Then again, maybe not." He turned and walked away. He needed to talk to Samantha again.

The hot July sun shimmered between the leaves to bounce off the hood of his truck as he drove past the gingerbread house. The place was a remarkable landmark. Further down, fir growth grew thick on the left and several poplar groves dotted the fields on the right. Signs of improvement done over the years blended into the natural habitats. Drainage ditches ran along the side of the well-maintained road. Generations had put their heart and soul into developing this place.

Brandt could only wish he had something as nice to pass on to his kids.

Kids. He grimaced. He didn't dare go there. It led to his mother and all her machinations. The truth was, at thirty-five he'd given it a whole lot more thought than he wanted to admit. Especially to his mother. He saw the worst that people could do to each other, and at other times, events were so poignant they made his heart hurt. It was at those times, he gave serious thought to his future. Thankfully, these lapses were short-lived. The divorce rate in his profession was out of this world. He'd be willing to try, but honestly, he'd never met anyone he couldn't live without.

Besides, it would take a unique woman to accept his work.

He rounded the last corner. The old homestead sprawled off to one side, lazy and serene. Except for the dog barking on the porch, the cabin appeared deserted.

Braking, Brandt brought the truck to a gentle stop beside her red one. Was that rust or paint that gave the vehicle its color? He studied it closer as he opened his door and hopped out. It didn't look road safe. He frowned. She needed a better set of wheels.

The screen door banged shut.

Brandt turned quickly. Sam stood, arms akimbo, apparently surprised to see him.

"Louise Enderby drove her Mercedes off the highway between 5:45 and 6:15 this morning," he said as way of greeting. Alarmed, he watched the color drain from her face. Brandt reached out to steady her, except she pulled back before he had a chance to make contact. His left hand still in midair, Brandt blinked at the speed she'd moved to avoid him.

In general, women liked him. He couldn't remember a time when one had avoided his touch. He didn't know if he should be amused or insulted. Instead, he felt oddly hurt.

"Why did you come?" she asked.

He glanced at her in surprise. "I thought you'd like to know."

She frowned. "You could have called me."

"But then I wouldn't be able to see you in person. By the way, was this morning's call an emergency?" He raised his eyebrows.

Samantha frowned. "I couldn't leave her alone in the car."

Interesting wording. Alone. He had to know. "Why?"

Her solemn gaze studied him for a long moment. She sidestepped the answer. "The bastard needs to be caught."

Brandt's heart stalled before starting again – double time. "The bastard?" Did she know about the serial killer he'd been chasing this last year? How could she know anything? Unless she was for real? God, could she help? Hope flared deep within.

"The killer."

Oh, that bastard. Damn. His heart rate returned to normal. "I'd like to ask you a few more questions. May I come in?"

She took a step back, paused, then stepped off to the side giving him room to pass.

Brandt walked inside. It seemed as bleak as he remembered. The threadbare furniture, plank floors – everything clean yet old. Bare kitchen counters...only one mug stood by the sink full of water.

He stopped in the middle of the room and turned to stare at her.

She hadn't moved.

What was wrong? He opened his mouth to ask, when she walked to the stove and put on a teakettle. As usual, she had on a sweater several sizes too big that hung almost to her knees, only this one was a brown cable type of thing. Threadbare jeans and white cotton socks completed the picture. And the perpetual braid down her back. He eyed her outfit. She barely made five feet and her clothes accented her thin frame, but there were hints of curves in all the right places.

"Do you want a cup of tea?"

He'd rather have a coffee, yet with no coffeemaker in sight, there didn't appear to be much choice. And her offer could be deemed a definite step forward in the social game. Even for a prickly female like her.

"Thank you. I'd appreciate that."

He watched as she pulled out a teapot and teabags from the cupboard. She never made idle chitchat or unnecessary movements. Economical all the way. She fascinated him. He couldn't think of another person like her. He walked over and sat on the same sofa as last time. "This is a nice place."

"I like it."

"Have you been here long?"

She shot him a suspicious look. "You mean you don't know already?"

His lips quirked. "I'd like you to tell me."

Samantha shrugged. "I've been here close to six months now."

"And before that."

She rolled her eyes. "Before that, I was somewhere else."

"Of course you were," he murmured. Her full history had been on his desk half an hour after he'd learned the details of the car accident she'd 'seen.' It hadn't taken long as there'd been little to add to what he already knew. Today's accident had opened doors for him. He wanted to learn the extent she was willing to fill in the missing details.

"Did you sabotage her car?"

She froze in the act of pouring water into the teapot. Her back went rigid. Fury visibly radiated through her bunched shoulders, rage-like waves he could almost touch. Ever so slowly, she finished filling the pot and replaced the kettle on the stove. Just as slowly, she turned around.

Brandt prepared to be blasted and found himself stunned at the pain evident in her eyes. Anger, yes, but he'd also hurt her. He grimaced. Damn, he'd judged that badly. He couldn't figure her out and had automatically tried to shock her out of her silence. Instead, it appeared he'd locked her deeper inside.

"I'm sorry. I had to ask."

She stared down at the kitchen floor, the muscles in her jaw twitching. She walked to the small fridge and pulled out a carton of milk. After a long moment, she shuddered once before answering, "When I have these visions, I'm not on the outside looking in. I'm inside these people staring out." She shot him a look. "Believe me, it would be much easier if it were the other way around."

That was understandable. If what she said were true, she must experience what they experience. He didn't think that included the pain – no one could stand that. Still, being inside must forge a personal connection. And how hard would that be given the eventual outcome?

He waited until she'd brought his tea. "Can you do this at will?"

"No."

Did that make it better or worse? Brandt stayed silent. She didn't offer any more information. "What about controlling it?"

"I wish."

"So, what can you do?"

"Endure." She bit her lip afterward, but it was too late. The word had slipped out.

God. Brandt paused, cup midway to the table. So softly spoken, the word said so much. He stared at her. She didn't like her gift. She hadn't learned to live with it yet. Or to control it. It controlled her. A rush of sympathy washed through him. Gifts like these, if real, were very unforgiving.

Few people had strong psychic abilities. Of those, some went insane. Some survived – barely, and a select few learned to control them and lived quite well. From what he'd seen, she could be one of the stronger ones. Except without the control, she was dangerous. Very dangerous.

Stefan had often extolled the dangers of psychic power without training. Brandt narrowed his eyes. Maybe Stefan could help her. If she'd accept any help. He stared at her in consideration.

Uncontrollable power was a disaster waiting to happen.

He should get the hell out and not come back. Even as he thought it, he knew he wouldn't. He couldn't. He needed to learn more about her. To understand her. After confirming the details of this morning's accident, he was willing to buy into her story as a psychic. But his personal interest bothered him. Especially when his better judgment told him to leave her alone.

She sipped her tea, apparently comfortable under the intensity of his gaze. She didn't fidget, move around, or make artificial conversation.

"Well," she asked. "Did you make up your mind?"

He lowered his cup. "About what?"

"Whether to believe me or not."

"I'm willing to believe up to this point. Your information checked out on the car accident and until I find out otherwise, I'll give you the benefit of the doubt."

"Gee, thanks." She peered over the rim of her teacup, derision in her voice .

Exasperated, he said, "You can't expect me to jump for joy over all of this. I'm a cop. I like things to be cut, dried, and clear. I also know that it rarely happens. So if there is information that can help, then I will listen and say thank you."

She stared at him, a frown between her brows.

He had no idea what she was thinking. Samantha had the odd distinction of being the only person to throw him off balance every time he saw her.

She shrugged. "What questions did you come to ask me?"

Damned if he could remember.

He took another drink of tea while he racked his brain. Oh yeah. "I'm hunting a particular killer. I wondered..." He leaned forward. "Can you find people?"

She cocked her head to one side and narrowed her gaze. "I don't know. I've never tried." Almost apologetically, she added, "I don't have any formal training in this."

He nodded. Stefan would have a heyday with her. He thought about it for a half second, then grabbed his notebook from his pocket and wrote down Stefan's phone number. He continued to ask several general questions about her abilities and the things she'd seen.

Ripping the note off, he placed it on the coffee table between them. She could contact Stefan on her own if she wanted to. He asked one last question. "Is there any particular trigger for the visions?"

That caught her off guard. She stared at him, her eyes flat, haunted. "Yes."

"And that is?" he asked.

"Violence."

DALE MAYER

CHAPTER SIX

10:19 am

"You can't put him to sleep. He's been doing great. I don't understand." Samantha blocked the cage containing Soldier, the name she'd settled on for the injured German shepherd. The rest of the staff faced her as one group.

"Samantha, we warned you about his lack of progress. He isn't adapting to people. No one will be able to handle him. The shelter won't take him now."

"Then why did you save his life?" Damn, she hated to beg, but someone needed to stick up for the dog. "If he was worth saving then, he's worth saving now."

Lucy stepped forward, placing a comforting arm around Sam's shoulder. "Honey, we tried to warn you. We hoped he'd get better, but he hasn't."

"He just needs a little more time." Samantha didn't know what tactic to try next. Her hand clenched again, fingernails sliding into half-moon impressions already there. She knew she had to keep trying. She hated the compassionate looks from her co-workers, hated their detachment. No one had taken the time to get close to Soldier like she had. It wasn't fair.

Just this once, she'd broken her own cardinal rule and gotten close. Too close. Her heart ached. She couldn't stand the thought of something happening to him.

That made it an easy decision.

"I'll take him," she said abruptly.

The room exploded.

"No Samantha, you can't do that. He could be dangerous."

"Sam, that's a bad idea."

"I wouldn't recommend that."

Sam refused to listen. They didn't understand. She *had* to give Soldier a chance.

"I have to try. He's not comfortable here. If I take him home, he'll have an easier time of it. He needs to learn to trust again. He can't do that here."

"And then what?" Casey, the only female veterinarian on staff, spoke the collective voice of reason. "What if he attacks you?"

"He won't." Sam answered with more confidence than she felt. Stubbornly, she repeated, "I have to try."

Dr. Wascott walked over and squatted down before the German shepherd's cage. Dangerous growls filled the room.

"Sam, I can't let you do that." He sighed. "He's dangerous. I can't have that on my conscience."

"Well, I don't think he is. But, if you give us a chance and it turns out he doesn't improve or gets worse then...then you can put him down."

Standing up, the vet snorted, his hands on his hips, staring at her in concern. "At that point, no one will be able to get close enough and we'll have to shoot him."

Some truth existed in his words, but Sam wouldn't be swayed. Not now that she'd sensed a sign of weakening. "I'll need to borrow a cage to transport him." She double-checked the size of the dog. "And a hand to load him."

"The only way I'll agree is if you keep him in his cage for at least another week." He reached out, placing a hand on her shoulder. "I'll come and see him then and re-evaluate. He's too dangerous to be free right now. He could hurt himself and anyone in the vicinity."

Sam interrupted him. "Which is why my place works. There's no one around for miles." Tossing him a smile of thanks, Sam headed out to her pickup to make room in the box.

Moving Soldier went well, with everyone's help. Once Sam made it on the road, she kept checking the rearview mirror to make sure the cage hadn't shifted.

Driving gave her time to think. Like about the name and phone number Detective Sutherland had left behind, with a casual comment. "He's a strong psychic whom I've worked with in the past. Call him if you need someone to talk to."

Then he'd left, seemingly not realizing what a bombshell he'd left behind. Sam had snatched up the paper, read the name *Stefan*, then tucked the information away in her purse. She'd wanted to grab the cell phone and call right away, but hadn't a clue what to say. Now, excitement bubbled in the back of her mind. Terrifying her with the possibilities. She hadn't been able to call yet. In truth, she'd rather have Brandt with her when she made contact. Less awkward that way.

Sad to say, but this had gone a long way to improving her opinion of this particular detective. She wrinkled up her face at another truth. To have the handsome detective believe her would be great. To earn his respect, now that would be a bonus. There was just something about that look in his eyes. As if he cared. As if he cared about *her*.

How sexy was that? To actually know that someone was listening, paying attention. Just his focus on her with such intensity made shivers go up her spine. His dynamic features, so alive and always shifting, intrigued her. But then so did his lean muscles cording his neck and forearms.

Goose bumps raised on her arms, even though she drove in the heat of the melting sun. For the first time that she could remember, she'd found a man that intrigued her. She grimaced. That a cop had been the one to bring her dormant sexuality back to life was beyond ironic. Women had been attracted to men in uniform since time began. Just not her. Too many bad memories.

The trip had to be hurting the dog in the back, yet she hadn't heard him complain once. The cabin came into view, surprising her at the speed of today's trip. Once home, she backed the truck up to the porch.

Moses waited, wagging his golden plume of a tail. She hopped out, gave him a swift hug, and went to open the tailgate. It stuck, as usual. She pounded it a couple times before it finally dropped. Moses bounded into the truck box, eager to check out the new arrival.

He loved other dogs. Most of the time, they loved him. Soldier curled a lip, but other than that showed no reaction. Sam watched their interaction carefully. Except for a low warning, Soldier ignored the other dog.

Sam, hands on her hips, spoke to the dogs. "Now would be a good time for the detective to show up. We could use his help – or rather his muscles." The cage rested on an old blanket. She'd had plenty of help loading him, now she'd have to tug on the blanket to drag him off.

Despite working alone, the blanket system worked well. Although, by the time Soldier had been safely moved to the porch and under the overhanging roof, Sam's limbs were shaking from the effort. Soldier never made a sound.

Even now, he lay there and regarded her with his huge eyes blackened with pain. They locked on her as if he understood. Her heart melted a little more.

Sam collapsed beside his cage, her breathing ragged. "There you go, boy. Life will be much nicer here." Using the bottom of her t-shirt, she wiped the rivers of moisture from her forehead.

Moses and Soldier sniffed each other through the steel mesh as Sam rested and watched. The patient needed fresh water, clean blankets, medicine, and food. Lord, she needed food. And a shower.

With full bowls of food and water, Sam returned to see Moses stretched out against the side of the cage, staring at her reproachfully.

"Don't look at me like that. I can't let him free. He might take off." Placing the bowl down, she unclipped the front door.

"Hi, Soldier." Soldier's dark pain-filled gaze locked on hers. He slumped lower.

"Shit. Are you hurt? Damn it. I knew we shouldn't have moved you. I'm so sorry, Soldier. I had to. They were determined to put you down."

He closed his eyes, his mouth growing slack.

Fear clutched her heart. She struggled to open the tight clasp on the cage door. The closure snapped open and she stretched a hand toward him.

He didn't growl and only opened one eye. Pain clouded his gaze, but a much less heated warning remained.

"What's the matter, no more fight left inside? Or are you prepared to give me the benefit of the doubt after rescuing you from there?" She stroked the thick, lush fur. Dried blood decorated his dark coat. As her fingers worked deeper and deeper, she found sand and grime worked in to skin level. "Poor guy. It's been a long time since anyone cared about you, hasn't it?"

Sam's knees and back ached from the cramped position. She scrubbed his back and neck for another moment. While she worked, she told him about his new life, using a quiet calm voice. She didn't know if it helped or not, yet knew it was what she'd like done if she were in the similar situation.

Stupid. It's not as if she'd ever be huddling in a cage. She stopped, her fingers deep in his thick fur, stunned by the correlation. She might not have been in a cage, yet she'd been living as if she were an injured animal anyway. Wary, hiding from the next blow that life would deal her.

She laughed. "Enough for both of us, huh?"

The cage door clipped her as she backed out, making her curse. Moses whined. Soldier even lifted his head. With both dogs' gazes on her, Sam managed to extricate herself from the wire. She stayed on her knees for a long moment, considering the door. If she disliked it, imagine how the dog liked it?

But if she left it open, would he run away? Or worse, get hurt? The cage offered safety for him. But what kind of life did he have without freedom? As he'd still be in the cage, she wouldn't be going against her word to her boss. Not that he'd see it that way.

Moses stuck his nose on her neck, reminding her she'd been motionless for too long.

Wrapping her arms around his neck, she gave him a warm hug, burying her face in the thick ruff. "Oh, Moses. Tell me this is going to work out for the best."

She reached down to shut the cage door, and stopped. Both dogs stared at her, ears up. Soldier couldn't go anywhere right now. His injuries would stop him from running away. But what about her agreement with the vet? She made a gut decision.

"Fine. We'll try it your way."

Sam walked into the cabin, the cage door wide open behind her.

***

7:22 pm

Whistling cheerfully, the tall, heavily built man tugged on the lead he awkwardly held in his left hand along with one of the two dog crates. He should have made two trips, but he'd had enough for today. It was time to head home. Past time.

He'd held his temper all he could this day. He was quite proud of himself. It took inner strength to remain calm when inside he despised being here, despised the people, and particularly despised the women.

He should get an Oscar for that alone.

No one appreciated how hard it was for him here. No one. He was capable of so much more. Still, it was their loss and his gain. He knew he could do more. In fact, he *was* doing more – they just didn't know about it. A malicious joy seeped through him.

"Hey, Bill."

Jack, one of the organizers, had chased after him and almost reached him. He sighed, took the last few steps to his van, and put down the crates. Damn, these dogs were getting heavier every time he had to take them anywhere.

"Good class today. Thanks, buddy. Did Dolly Seymour ask you about fitting in a new session next week? This would be another private session."

Bill opened the back door to the van. "She mentioned something about it. I haven't confirmed availability yet. I'll have to call her in the morning."

"No problem. This is the same group from last week. They want to work on individual training, so maybe you can see your way into accepting this one."

Bill had a grin plastered on his face. On the inside, though, he was tired of smiling. He was tired of being nice all day, and he was fucking tired of the whole mess. Surely, his luck would change soon and he could split. "No problem. If I can, I will."

"Good enough. We'll see you later then."

Jack headed back into the clubhouse. As he opened the door, a slinky brunette in tight-ass capri pants and a shorty midriff top walked toward him, a tiny white Lhasa Apso sporting a big pink bow, in her arms.

Bill grinned at the beautiful woman walking toward him and stopped loading his stuff into the back of the van to talk with her. "Hi, Caroline."

A bright smile broke across her face. "Thanks for today's class, Bill. I'm just sorry Jared couldn't be here today. He'd have really enjoyed it."

Bill smiled as expected. In truth, if he heard one more thing about her husband, Jared, he was liable to scream. If there was one thing he couldn't stand – it was gushing females, particularly when they were gushing about their males.

Still, he managed to keep an eye on her nicely rounded ass as she walked past to her black Porsche several vehicles down.

He just might have to do something about that...and her.

***

2:30 am, June 17th

Screams echoed in the darkness. Sam twisted and pulled, struggling to get away from whatever held her fast. She couldn't get free. In a blind panic, she realized her body no longer answered to her commands. Her eyes opened. She shuddered. Shearing pain melded with terror as she took in the blood dripping to the floor. It ran down the folds of the floral bedspread to soak into the cream carpet waiting below.

"Please don't...no more." A voice not her own spoke the words in her head. A blow shattered her breastbone. Her screams poured into the small room. Sam barely flinched. Her attacker laughed.

"Like I'm going to listen to you, bitch. You like this. You must. You let that useless husband of yours beat you all the time." His hideous laughter added to her horror. God, how could he laugh at her? He was an animal. She died a little more at his unexpected pleasure. Monster.

Maybe it had something to do with his unseemly pleasure, or maybe it came from her absolute fury at yet another murder, but somewhere deep inside, Sam's consciousness attempted to reassert itself. In a weird way, she became aware of both worlds at once. Her awareness built, a small step at a time, allowing her to put a slight distance between her and the dying woman's. Fog grew between the two realities, buffering her from the poor woman's pain and fear.

Groggy and disoriented, Sam tried to snap out of the psychic episode fully, only to slam back inside the injured woman. Her body lurched uncontrollably. Sam tried to ward off the oncoming blow, but couldn't make the right arm move.

"Stupid woman. What good are those looks of yours now? It's far too late to run away." The fists lashed out, once, twice and then yet again. Muscles tore and internal organs bled under cracked bones. The poor woman arched her back, lifting high off the bed. Both women screamed. Cries echoed inside and outside of Sam's mind, building, and blending into a crescendo of terror.

"Why are you doing this?" Blood trickled down the corner of her mouth. Sam didn't know who spoke – her or the victim. It didn't matter, the words were the same.

"Because I can, bitch." Mocking laughter echoed through the small room.

"But...?" She gasped, fighting the vomit in the back of her throat. "Why me?"

"You're weak. You deserve killing. Staying with an asshole like that. Besides, I hate him. Maybe the cops will think he's good for this one."

"No," she gasped. "Please, don't."

"Too late."

He raised his fist and landed a blow below her eye socket. Bone shattered, making little scrunching noises. There'd be no white knight coming to the rescue. Ever. There was only Sam and she didn't know how to help.

Through the bloody haze, Sam, desperate to take something useful back with her, struggled to open her good eye. Swollen and bloody and not her own, made the job damn near impossible. Light slid painfully under her sore eyelids. She struggled to bring the scene in focus. The bastard was getting off her bed. Blood splatter covered his shirt and jeans. He wore unrelenting black with the blood standing out in dark wet spots. He wore gloves and a ski mask. Same height and same build.

Same energy pattern. Damn, him again. At least she thought it was him.

Only one eye could see. Sam couldn't even tell if this man wore a ring or not. The light in the room started to fade, as if the sun were setting at rapid speed. Except the curtains were closed and it was the middle of the night.

Her vision narrowed, locked on her killer's face. The circle grew smaller and smaller. Sam knew her time was almost over. She could only watch with painful understanding as the circle of light reduced to a pinpoint before finally, thankfully, blinking out. Forever.

It was over.

Sam woke in her own room, minutes later. For the first time, grief didn't overwhelm her. She was angry. She hurt for the victim and her family. But even more, a deep pulsing fury permeated her soul. That asshole had way too much fun doing what he was doing. He had to be stopped.

When she could, she shifted upright. Pain still coursed through her body, but the anger provided a dense barrier, letting her cut through the pain. Inner excitement grabbed hold. This time she'd had some kind of conscious awareness. She'd kept a part of herself intact while living what that poor woman had experienced.

Poor soul. Sam sniffled. Why was this guy doing this? Surely, he had a reason — more than just for entertainment.

Lying back down, she thought about the details from the vision. Once again, the killer had been fully hidden, so no face or ring showed. There'd been light-colored walls, a plain white ceiling, and a cheap floral bedspread. Again, nothing helpful.

It was six in the morning now. Surely, someone would find the woman today? Depression set in.

Tucking the blankets around her, she reached for the phone. There was no answer at Detective Brandt's number. She hung up. Then changing her mind, she redialed and this time left a message. Afterward, she sat, undecided, before dialing the station.

Five minutes later, she was sorely regretting that action.

"I'm sorry, ma'am, could you repeat that?"

"Could you please have Detective Sutherland call me? I know this sounds bizarre, but I can't give you any more information. A woman has been murdered." Samantha tried to keep her voice from showing her frustration. Just going over the details hurt. Damn it, why wouldn't anyone listen to her?

She cleared her throat from the confused emotions clogging it. "Excuse me, could you just pass the message on, please?" She shifted the phone to the other ear.

"I'll see that he gets your message," replied the cold voice on the other end of the phone.

"Thank you," she answered, and hung up. There was nothing else to do.

It took twenty-five minutes to hear from him.

"Samantha?"

"Yes," she answered, relief rushing through her. "It's me."

"And?" he asked, concern in his voice.

Sam took a deep breath, snuffling back tears. "He's killed again," she whispered.

Dead silence.

She scowled into the phone. She could almost hear the gears in his mind churning at lightning speed.

"Did you see him?"

"I saw him, not the ring. He kept his gloves on the whole time." She shivered at the memory, still fresh in her mind. "He wore all black, including the ski mask."

"Can you identity him in any way?"

Sam shook her head then realized he couldn't see her. "No. Not really. I might recognize him by size, carriage, maybe his way of moving. His gaze..." Sam closed her eyes and swallowed hard, hating the fear clinging to her skin. Some belonged to the various victims and to a certain extent – some of it was hers. The killer breathed evil. She got a grip again. "It won't stand up in court, but I would recognize his energy if I ever saw him again – at least I think so."

"What does that mean?" His sharp voice cut through the lines.

She stiffened. "When he kills he lets himself enjoy it. Energy has its own individual pattern and changes with moods, etc." She paused for a moment. "I think I might recognize it again, but I can't say for sure."

"Hmm."

Sam waited in edgy silence.

"Is there anything you can tell me about the victim?"

"Like what?" She relaxed slightly. With it, fatigue set in. She was so tired.

"Like where she lives, a house, an apartment...something to help us find her faster."

Samantha sighed. "When you're being attacked, you don't think, 'I'm so and so and live at 146 Pine Street.' Women think about being rescued, and why them, and toward the end..." Sam caught back a hiccup of a sob. "Toward the end," she continued, her voice a hint above a whisper, "they only think of those they're leaving behind – their loved ones." Sam could barely hear him through the chaos of her emotions, yet, she could sense his sympathy. She could hear him scratching down notes. "He beat her to death."

"He beat her? No knives?"

"No. He hated her husband. The husband beat her so he took her away from him. If that makes any sense."

"Nothing a killer does, makes any sense."

Sam hesitated. "Another thing. Her eyes were damaged. It was hard to see clearly." Sam stared bitterly out the large bedroom window, where raindrops started to ping against the panes of glass. She would see another sunny day, but the poor women wouldn't.

"Can you tell me anything else? Her name? You got the name of the car victim."

"That was different." Violent imagery coursed through her mind. Was there gold to be mined in there somewhere? "Just a minute." Sam closed her eyes, trying to let the images she'd been forcing back, flood her mind. Maybe, there was something useful there. Fists. Blows. Blood. Screams. Red. Pain. Grief. Sam doubled over, gasping at the emotional onslaught. She fought to stay conscious, scared all over again as the pain and images took her back into the horror. *There.* What was that?

A name. Sam fought to leash the demons in her mind, scrambling for the safety of her physical reality, desperately wanting to return to her small cabin by the lake. She shuddered and opened her eyes.

A whitewashed ceiling stared back at her.

She shivered. How could anything so bizarre happen in such a calm and normal setting?

"Sam, damn it, answer me." Brandt's voice screamed through her phone, dragging her attention back to the task at hand. "Are you there? God damn it!"

"Brandt." Sam's vocal cords sounded wrong to her own ears, hoarse and rough. She tried again. "It's okay. I'm here."

"What the hell happened? Jesus, you said just a minute. I thought you'd gone to get something."

Sam frowned. "How long was I gone?"

"At least two or three fucking minutes." His voice calmer now. "I almost hopped into my truck to drive out to your place. Jesus, don't scare me like that again."

Sam shook her head. That long? No, surely not. She stared uncertainly at the small plastic clock on the milk crate that passed for a nightstand.

"So what the hell was that all about?" Brandt blasted her, obviously pissed now that she'd returned.

"Sorry, I didn't mean to worry you. Her husband's name was Alex."

"Husband? Was he the killer?"

"No." She rushed to explain. "That's what the killer wants you to believe."

"So, the husband was a wife beater?"

"I think so."

Silence through the phone as he digested that information. When he spoke again, he was all business. "I've got to take another call. I'll need you to come to the station and give a statement. How about eleven? I'll see you then."

Sam stared down at the dead phone. "Shit. That was so *not* what I wanted to happen."

CHAPTER SEVEN

8:55 am

Approaching the same imposing building for a second time was no easier. She glanced at her cheap watch. Right on time. The station had called just over an hour ago asking her to come in for nine instead. Two hours earlier meant two hours she didn't have to wait and worry. Taking a deep breath, she straightened her shoulders and walked in.

Her reception, this time, was quite different. After letting the front desk know she was there for her appointment, she was taken to a small room and left alone. Sam shivered as she took in the square table and two chairs. No windows, no couch, nothing to indicate comfort. This appeared more like an interrogation room. Silently, she walked to the far side of the table and sat down. Sam didn't need any other cues to understand she could be in serious trouble.

She just didn't know why.

The door opened, admitting an older grizzled cop. "Miss Blair, thanks for coming in. I'm Detective Stan Robertson."

Sam grimaced. Warily, she watched as the man pulled out the other chair and sat down, dropping a file folder on the table.

"So you're a psychic, are you?"

She replied, "Somewhat."

He glanced over at her, his bristly eyebrows slightly raised. "Explain."

"Sometimes I get visions, but I can't read tarot cards or anything like that."

He opened his folder and started writing notes on his pad of paper. She tried to read his chicken scratch. It proved impossible. She waited until he'd finished writing before asking a question of her own.

"Why did you call me in?"

"You reported a murder." Calm, quiet, he gave no inkling of his reaction to her report. He could be writing out a grocery list for all the emotion he showed. Sourly, she realized he'd probably been on the force so long nothing fazed him.

"Where's Detective Sutherland?"

"He's off duty right now. He'll be in soon."

"I'd prefer to speak with him." Actually, she wanted to speak with only him, suddenly realizing she might not have the chance. What the hell was going on?

"We'll have him call you to follow up." His demeanor suddenly changed. "So where were you when this murder happened?"

"In bed, sleeping."

His disbelief should have been an early warning. It wasn't.

"The same bed as this woman?"

Blindsided, she slumped in her chair. So, that was it. She was a suspect. Wait a minute. She sat straight up. "Did you find her?" she asked.

"Why don't you tell me?" He smirked at her and returned to note-taking.

Sam didn't know what to think. Every time she stepped forward to help, she became a suspect. But stupid her, she kept coming back for more. When would she ever learn?

"So where were you at..." the officer stopped to look at his notes, "between midnight and four this morning?"

"At home," Sam answered, her shoulders slumping. "And yes, I was alone."

"So you have no alibi." He jotted something down.

"If I'd known ahead of time that I'd need one, then I'd have made an effort to be with someone. But I didn't." Sam glared at the man sitting opposite her. She didn't want to be here. She should have told Brandt that she couldn't come.

"I'd like to talk to Detective Sutherland," she repeated.

"Yeah, we'll get on that right away."

He never moved.

Sam snorted before subsiding into silence. She was past helping him.

"Let's get back to exactly what you were doing the evening leading up to the death of your friend."

"She wasn't my friend. I didn't know her. I don't even know where she lives." It took effort to keep the wobble from her voice. She didn't think she'd ever get used to the accusations or the mockery that often accompanied the disbelief. She eyed the officer writing extensive notes. What the hell could he write to fill two full pages?

Without a word or a glance her way, he got up and left the room.

Sam waited with mounting frustration, and when an hour later, she was still sitting there, the frustration morphed into an insidious fear. She couldn't stop trembling. She interlocked her fingers and sat on them. *Focus, you idiot. Don't let them get to you. You can do this. There's no reason for them to hold you here much longer.* Using a mantra that had helped her in the past, she mentally repeated: All will be well. Everything happens for a reason. All will be well.

Shit happens. That was the other mantra of her life. And it sure as hell had.

All will be well. All will be well. All will be well.

The door opened suddenly.

She forgot to breathe.

The same detective she'd seen at the very first meeting walked in.

She sighed in disgust.

"I'm Detective Bresson. I need to ask you some questions."

"Why? You didn't believe me when I walked in here the first time. What's changed?"

He ignored her.

Sam listened in disbelief as the questioning started all over.

An hour and a half later, Sam was shown the front door, the officer's words echoing in her head. *Don't leave town.*

Go where? Bitterness overwhelmed her. She had nowhere to go.

***

10:50 am

Brandt checked his watch as he pulled the pickup into the side parking lot and hopped out. With any luck, he'd have time to grab a mug of coffee before Sam arrived. He'd tried contacting the police artist last night without success. He'd left a message. Hopefully, she'd gotten it and had shown up, too.

Sam had too much valuable information locked inside her head not to take advantage of it. Their police artist had an eerie interpretation of people and events as well. Maybe together, the two of them could produce a little bit of useable magic.

He pushed open the side door and nodded at Jensen, just leaving. Walking straight to the lunchroom, he snagged a mug, filled it with coffee, added cream, and headed to his desk. So focused on his time frame, it took him a minute to notice the unusual silence in the station.

Glancing around, he frowned. People weren't smiling at him. No one said hello or good morning. What the hell?

"Hey Adam, what's up?" The younger man was hunched over his keyboard, staring at his monitor as if it held the answer to life on it. He started; red flushed over his face and neck. He mumbled and refused to face Brandt.

"What?" Brandt walked over until he stood directly in front. "Adam, talk to me."

Adam's shoulders slumped. "I think you'd better talk to the captain."

Brandt stiffened. "The captain? Okay, how about a heads-up first?"

Adam finally glanced around the office and then met his gaze. "Personally, I think she might be on the up and up, but there's some that think she's in this neck deep."

"She?" The caffeine had yet to kick in or his brain hadn't woken up yet. Either way, nothing about this was making any sense.

"Your little psychic friend."

His stomach soured. "Sam? What does she have to do with this?" Brandt checked his watch. She should be out front waiting for him by now. "Has she arrived already?"

Adam looked at him, puzzled. "She just left."

"Left?" Brandt searched the large open room, hoping to catch a sign of her. "Why? I asked her to come in at eleven. I wanted her to meet with the sketch artist."

Adam lowered his voice and leaned closer. "She arrived hours ago. They just let her go."

Black, blinding anger coiled deep inside, stirring in anticipation of freedom. "They?" Brandt's voice was cold and thick. Who the hell had gone after Sam without talking to him first? Who the hell dared? Because that asshole had a surprise coming. Sam was *his* source and no one else's.

Adam ducked and peered from side to side, checking to see if anyone was watching them. The two of them always talked. They were on the same team for Christ's sake. Brandt leaned closer. "Talk to me," he ordered the younger man. "I want it all, and I want it all now."

Adam flushed even redder. "I don't know the details. Ask Kevin."

Kevin. Brandt thought about it for half a heartbeat. Yeah that made sense. Kevin's black-and-white view of the world matched his black attitude. Kevin didn't appear to trust anyone. Damn it. It was time to have a talk with Kevin. Brandt hated feeling like he'd been targeted.

Just then, Dillon joined them. Both men half-turned away from Dillon who belonged to one of the other teams. He wasn't privy to their work.

"What secrets are we discussing now?"

Both men gave him a baleful look. Adam walked away without saying a word.

Brandt studied him. Why would he even begin to step in where he wasn't wanted? Brandt had little to do with him, thankfully. He'd always appeared a little too slick. That had nothing to do with his fancy suits. Today, he wore another pinstripe suit and what appeared to be a damask shirt. This kid was looking the part. Brandt just didn't know what that part was.

"No secrets here." Every department had a misfit or two. This station was no different. The captain here was quite tolerant — as long as everyone did their job.

Brandt didn't know Captain Johansen well. Big, beefy, and built, his physique gave rise to the nickname of B-cubed. He kept a military-style haircut that showed more white than gray and had a huge squared off jaw. Buzz Lightyear anyone? Yet, he had a reputation of being a straight shooter with his men, and fair on most issues. But on the question of psychics, well Brandt had no idea where he stood.

It was hard being an outsider. He was here to do a job, allowed to join the team in order to complete a job, yet not quite a member of the team. Obviously some of them thought differently about him. But going behind Brandt's back was never acceptable.

Dillon half-laughed and shifted his position, his hands sliding into his pants pockets. "Are you sure? It sounded juicy when I went to walk past. Couldn't help but stop and ask."

He grinned in a way that pissed Brandt off. He needed to talk with the captain now. He needed to find out what the hell was going on. Brandt spun on his heels, slopping coffee on the floor and headed for the captain's office.

***

11:00 am

The door to the captain's office was closed when he arrived. He knocked hard.

"Come in."

Brandt strode in and stopped short. Kevin was seated on the left. The captain sat behind his huge mahogany desk. There was a sense of expectation. They'd been waiting for him.

His defenses went up.

"Come in, Brandt. Take a seat."

"I'd rather stand." He struggled with it, but his voice actually sounded normal. Tight but calm.

"Fine. Whatever you're comfortable with. But you also need to be comfortable with the fact that Kevin is entitled to speak with any witnesses he sees fit. That includes this Samantha Blair." The captain's beetled brow met in the middle as he peered over his glasses at Brandt. "That is why you're here. Isn't it?"

Brandt choked back the words clogging his throat. He had to remember he was a guest here. "Correct. And it's possible that detectives at this station work differently than they would in most other stations – but that would surprise me."

Normally detectives built a rapport with their witnesses. They might ask another detective to go and talk to someone, to see what shook loose. Most detectives, as a basic courtesy, would mention to the other detective that they needed to talk to one of his connections before they interviewed someone involved in his case.

Captain Johansen cleared his throat. "Yes, we do things a little differently here."

Brandt's gaze cut to the captain. "That different?"

Once again, Captain Johansen exchanged glances with Kevin.

"We deal in good old-fashioned police work here. Not black magic." Kevin couldn't stay quiet any longer.

"That's what this is all about? Because she's a psychic?" At Kevin's nod, Brandt snorted. "Then you could have had the decency to talk to me, couldn't you? I've worked with Stefan Kronos for over a decade."

"I'm not sure that I believe his work either. However, many of my friends do, given his success record. This woman is a flake, pure and simple. I don't want her involved in my cases." Kevin's sarcasm underscored his point of view.

Interesting that Kevin had heard of Stefan. "You haven't given her a chance, have you?" Brandt turned to confront him. "I believe in her. She's given valuable information and I think she can help."

"I interviewed her. She doesn't have anything to offer." Kevin stood up. "I don't have time for this. As long as you have something reasonable to offer to my cases, feel free. But if you're going to bring in a psychic, use her for your cases, not mine. She can hang you, not us. You're only visiting here. And you won't destroy *our* reputation with your fucked up ideas."

Kevin strode out, leaving an uncomfortable silence behind.

Brandt looked back at Captain Johansen, who stared back. "Is that the official stand?"

He pursed his lips, thinking. "For the moment. I'm certainly not a fan of using psychics. But I do know Stefan's work. So I can't discount them either. Let me know if she comes up with anything we can use. Other than that, don't confuse the issue between hard work and easy answers."

***

11:20 am

Kevin walked through the commons, staring straight ahead. Most of the office knew what had just happened. The interior walls were very thin.

He didn't give a shit. Let them talk. As long as they didn't bring it to him, he could care less. He had work to do, and gossip wasn't one of his job duties.

Neither was dealing with flakes. Even harmless ones. But he'd had to check it out further. Now he'd done so, and now he could wash his hands of her. Good riddance.

If only Brandt would see things his way. He'd expected more of this 'visiting detective.' Brandt seemed to be a straightforward kind of guy. He'd always dug in and helped where needed and he sure as hell knew how to get the job done. But this psychic stuff was just plain weird. That he'd trumped Brandt's witness, wasn't something he was prepared to get into. Not on a murder case.

Besides, like religion, there was just no telling where individual beliefs lay.

That was fine with Kevin. He didn't push his beliefs down anyone's throat and expected the same courtesy – especially at work. Kevin shook his head. Christ, a psychic!

Even his wife had laughed at him.

***

12:30 pm

Brandt pulled the truck up to the cabin in a spew of dust and dirt. Moses stood on the porch barking at him. At least the dog showed some sign of guarding the place. He cut the engine and hopped out, slamming the door behind him.

"Hey Moses, how are you doing, big guy?" Brandt eyed him warily, certain that Moses posed no threat. Still, one never knew. He climbed the steps, hand outstretched toward him.

Moses walked a step closer. Just as Brandt was about to touch him, a deadly growl erupted from the far side of the porch before rising into a hideous howl. Moses backed up and took up his fierce barking again.

Brandt started. "Jesus. What the hell is that?" He could just make out the oversized cage further down the porch, half covered in old gray army blankets. He took a hesitant step closer, only to stop as the growl grew to crescendo.

"Easy, take it easy." He didn't know what Samantha had inside that damn cage, but if it were relative in size, it had to be huge.

He glanced at the closed front door, sure he was being watched. Samantha had to be hiding behind the curtains. Ignoring the cage for the moment, he rapped on the door. Samantha opened it promptly, confirming his suspicions.

"Hi."

The door shut in his face, leaving him staring at worn, peeling wood.

He closed his eyes and groaned. Shit. After what the team had put her through, he couldn't blame her. Then neither could he blame the team. He might have done the same thing under different circumstances.

"Samantha, I had nothing to do with this morning's appointment. The detectives called you in because they had questions. I'm sorry for the way it went down. Still, it's our job to ask."

Silence.

"Crap." It would take a bomb to get her out of there now.

"Would it help if I said I didn't know about this morning's meeting until after you'd left? I had nothing to do with it. Honest."

More silence.

"That was the rest of the team. They don't have much faith in psychics and wanted to check you out for themselves."

Dead silence.

Shit. He so didn't have time for this. He searched for ideas. Moses had slumped to his usual position of full-relaxed mode on the porch. The cage was quiet, but Brandt sensed the awareness emanating from the wire structure.

"Nice pet you've got there. Sounds dangerous. I may have to put him down as a danger to society."

The front door crashed open. "Don't you touch him," she snarled as she raced toward the cage.

He grinned. Like taking candy from a baby.

As she caught sight of his grin, she stopped her headlong rush and changed direction to charge him instead. He laughed even as he deflected her blows.

"You bastard. You did that on purpose." She took another swing at him, her knuckles grazing the top of his nose.

Still laughing, he snagged her wrists.

"You're right. That was low, but I had to get you out of the house."

He was loath to let go of her wrists. Not wanting to get clipped was only one reason. The ire in those velvet eyes spoke volumes about her temper. No, it had more to do with the shape and fit of her against him. He switch to holding both her wrists with one hand. The fingers of his other hand sank deep into the always-present sweater – this time a deep forest green one – before finding her warm flesh below. Her frame – surprisingly solid. The purple fire shooting from her eyes made him grin. Even as he watched, she ran her tongue over her lips.

His stomach clenched. He reached and tugged her long braid.

He stared at her hands gripped in his. Blue veins wound from her fingers up and under her sleeve. He frowned and loosened his hold.

"Sorry." He grimaced as pink rushed through to her pale fingertips. "I didn't mean to hurt you."

Samantha tugged her hands free and stepped away from him. "I'm not hurt."

He glanced from her hands to her face, frowning. Somehow, he didn't think she'd tell him if she were. She wasn't going to change on his say so.

"May I come in?"

She shuffled her feet, but refused to look at him. More evasiveness. Not a surprise, coming from her. He waited for a moment before adding, "Please."

CHAPTER EIGHT

1:15 pm

Sam didn't want to let him into her space. She didn't know how her ire had died so suddenly. But she didn't want to let it go just yet.

"Are you okay?"

She twisted around, brushing her hair from her eyes. "What the hell do you care?" The words burst out with more punch than she intended. Better to appear calm and rational than let him know how hurt and betrayed she really felt.

"We need to talk." he responded.

"What could there possibly be left to talk about?" She turned and walked into the cabin.

Brandt came in behind her.

She strode to the fridge and pulled out a jug of cold water. "Why won't you leave me alone?" she asked, without turning around.

A large muscled arm reached into the glass cupboard above her head, pulling out two tall glasses. He set them down on the counter and tugged the jug free from her fingers.

He appeared so in control, she wanted to scream at him. Her life was in turmoil. She watched as he poured two glasses.

Pissed at her reaction, she snatched one up and walked outside. Her nerves were rubbed raw. She could only take so much.

"I can't."

His answer hurt. She escaped toward Soldier. Her stocking feet whispered along the porch. Soldier still heard her. She couldn't see him, but she sensed his attention. "It's okay, boy. It's just me." The sensation of wariness coming from the cage never relaxed. She couldn't blame him, hers hadn't disappeared either.

A low growl erupted in the far corner.

"What's in there?" Brandt asked from behind her.

Sharper, higher pitched growls had the two of them backing up a few paces.

"That's some huge cage," Brandt said, his voice carefully moderated.

"He's a good-sized dog. And he obviously likes his space."

Brandt snorted and walked to the stairs and sat down. "You think?" He took a big drink, still staring at the cage. "Is he dangerous?"

"No." She amended her answer after a quick thought. "At least, I don't believe so."

He arched his eyebrow. "You mean you don't know?"

"I just got him," she muttered. She didn't think Soldier would really hurt anyone – unless they got too close.

She could feel Brandt's gaze burning her face. A hot flush washed over her cheeks. "So why are you here?" she asked.

Silence. She heard his heavy sigh on the air. From the corner of her eye, she saw his head turn, his focus on the view before them.

"I came to explain. I went to meet you for our eleven o'clock appointment. That's when I heard they'd called you for a visit earlier."

"Visit." Disbelief made her shake. "Did you say visit?" Her voice rose alarmingly high. "How could anyone call that a visit? How about calling it a Gestapo session, or maybe an interrogation?" She glared at him. "But a *visit*, it was not."

With Moses at her side, she headed down to the end of the dock. The water glistened in the late sunlight. Her knee buckled sideways as Moses leaned against her, whining.

"It's okay, boy. I'm fine." She laid a gentle hand on his bushy fur, enjoying the comfort of his touch.

"Are you?" Brandt faced the lake. "That's actually why I came — to check up on you."

She stiffened.

He hesitated. "I'm sorry I wasn't there, I might have been able to ease it slightly. But don't get me wrong, they would have brought you in regardless. They needed to check you out after you reported the third victim."

Sorry? She threw him a stunned glance. He wished he could have been there? Well, so did she. Overwhelmed and unaccountably relieved, Sam dropped to sit down on the dock, her suddenly weak legs dangling over the edge. Somehow, the day didn't seem so bad after all. Moses slumped down to the ground at her feet.

Brandt stood beside her, looking as if he wanted to say something. Sam didn't care. She had enough to deal with keeping the bubbling lightness inside from making its way outward. The last thing she wanted was for him to see her relief.

The silence grew uncomfortable. "What?" She didn't like the indecision on his face.

He shrugged.

"Come on, fess up. What?"

He sat down a little apart from her. "Do you have other skills? You know like telekinesis or telepathy — anything?"

His tone came across light and amused, yet Sam sensed a serious thread through it all.

"You mean like mind reading? She sharpened her gaze, trying to figure out what he meant. No, he was too sensible for that. Wasn't he? Searching his face, she had to ask, "You don't really think I can read your mind — do you?"

He shifted his weight and stared out across the lake.

She grinned, her first real one in a long time. As the realization swept through her, a giggle escaped. She slapped her hand over her mouth, astonished at the sound. Moses raised his head and whined. She giggled again. Then she couldn't help it; she laughed aloud. When he cocked his head to one side and stared at her, she laughed harder, threw her arms around the dog, and hugged him close.

She watched Brandt shake his head, as if he only just realized he'd crouched down beside her, his puzzled look clearing.

"What's so funny?" he asked, aggrieved.

Another giggle escaped even as she fought to control herself.

She wiped her eyes. "Sorry. God that felt good. I haven't laughed that hard in years." It took another couple of minutes before finally, she heaved a big sigh and relaxed. Peace settled upon her, ill fitting at first, but she slowly grew more comfortable with it. Another sigh escaped, and she stretched out on the dock. The sun had lost most of its heat, leaving a slightly cooler air to wash over her heated skin.

"Well?"

"Well what?" Then she remembered – mind reading. Another giggle escaped. He shot her a dirty look, and she tried hard to stifle the rest. There was no way to stop the grin that split her face. "I'm not telepathic. I can't read minds. Okay?"

He peered at her intently. She stared back, still grinning, but serious.

He nodded once and lay down on the warm dock beside her.

Sam smiled, the wooden boards warm beneath her shoulders. It was a gorgeous day.

She was dimly aware of Brandt stretching out on the other side of Moses. She could feel his gaze. She smiled slightly and closed her eyes. Content.

Her thoughts free floated in the newly created space in her mind. Stress had fled in the face of her laughter, leaving room for peace and contentment.

Images, both colored and not, danced, enjoying the freedom to roam. Faces, images, names, and places. Nothing followed a pattern as free association flowed. In an uncharacteristic move, she let them. Amazed at the clarity, Sam could only watch in awe. Where did these come from? She recognized some of them – and some she didn't.

"What are you thinking?"

"Hmm?"

"I asked what you were thinking."

"Not thinking – seeing. Pictures, images, events." She smiled lazily, never opening her eyes.

"Anything on the murderer?"

She froze. It didn't help. The moving images sped up, tumbling over each other, impatient for their moment in the light. One face flashed, followed by another and then another. Without warning, the film stopped. A camera trained on one woman. But Sam was inside that woman staring at the camera lens. The faint reflection on the camera lens showed the vague outline of a beautiful laughing brunette. The woman smiled into the camera, amused at something the photographer said. She turned her head. Sam caught glimpses of a huge green park, flowers in brilliant vibrant beds. Several other people mingled. Someone called out a name. Her head twisted around. Her name. She was called Annalea. Sam recognized her basic essence. Sam had connected to this same soul the other day.

"Annalea."

"Who?"

She knew. "That's her name." Sam opened her eyes to a slowly darkening sky.

"The murderer?" he asked. His voice sounded stunned, his tone disbelieving.

"No," she whispered, grief already clogging her heart, breaking up her voice. "He's stalking his next victim. Her name's Annalea."

***

2:10 pm

Even an hour ago, Sam would have said what she was doing was impossible.

It defied logic. But there it was.

She stood on the steps of the police station, staring up at the imposing front. What was even worse, was that somehow...somehow she'd been convinced to do this willingly.

Un-freakin-believable.

"Problems?"

Sam started. Brandt stood several steps above her, staring down at her with a questioning look on his face. She rubbed her damp palms on her faded jeans, glancing at her scuffed runners showing too much wear, then up at him. She wrapped her arms beneath her breasts, not quite knowing what to say. Her thick sweater was long and didn't seem to make a bit of difference to the chill deep in her bones. She stared around at the busy street before turning her gaze on him again.

"Yeah, this isn't exactly my favorite place to 'visit.'"

He grinned at her. "It will be different this time."

Should she believe him?

"I promise."

Sam raised her face to the sun, took a deep breath, got a grip on her whacked-out emotions, and strode the remaining few stairs. Once inside, she kept her focus on Brandt and followed his lead. Within minutes, she was sitting at a large table in a spacious lived-in room. It was much more pleasant. This looked like a meeting or a conference room. The sideboard held papers and books. One of the tables held used coffee cups and even a dirty plate.

"Do you want a cup of coffee before we get started? I'm not sure we have any tea."

Feeling as if she'd been caught snooping, Sam quickly nodded. "Thanks, coffee is fine. Black, please."

Brandt flashed a quirky grin as he left.

On her own, Sam glanced around at those passing through. There were no windows in the room. She'd have felt better if she could have seen the world outside – to have less of a caged feeling. She did much better in open air. She tilted her head. Maybe she should look at going into horticulture. That was outside, away from people. Yeah, she'd do well with plants. Too bad they didn't do well with her.

"Here you go. Careful, it's hot."

A cup of steaming coffee was placed before her. The heat drew her like a magnet. She wrapped her hands around the mug, almost moaning with joy.

At that moment, she looked up to catch Brandt's quizzical gaze. She flushed.

"I'm a little cold, that's all."

He raised one eyebrow and refrained from commenting.

Sam returned her attention to her coffee, staring at it longingly. With the steam still rising, she tried a sip. She choked, hastily putting it down again. She coughed again, trying to clear her throat. Dear God, how could they call that coffee? She snuck a glance at Brandt. He hadn't noticed.

Sam didn't know what to say. Brandt sat down across from her, sipping his own coffee. God, he actually seemed to enjoy it. He flipped through a file on the table. Every once in a while, he stopped and wrote a few notes on a pad of paper.

"You'll get used to it."

Surprised, Sam asked, "Get used to what?"

"The coffee." He flashed a grin at her. The wicked glint in his eyes caught her sideways. Her heart stopped, before suddenly thundering on.

"Like hell," she said when she finally managed to speak.

"You're right. I lied. You never get used to it."

A sudden commotion at the door caught their attention. An older woman, hauling a large case bustled into the room. "Sorry I'm late, Brandt."

"No problem, Irena. Grab a seat."

Irena banged the case down and shrugged out of her coat. "The weather has gone to hell out there."

"Has it started raining?"

"Not yet, but the sky is ready to explode at any minute." Irena opened her case.

Sam gawked. Wow, what a kit. She watched as Irena pulled out an art pad and a small case of art pencils.

"Okay, so what are we doing today?"

Brandt quietly explained. Sam listened, watching Irena's face intently. Her expression wrinkled once before settling into the same old cynical look. Whatever.

Brandt stood up. "Sam, I'm going to leave you in Irena's hands." He smiled at the two women. "I'll return in an hour or so to see how the two of you are getting along."

Sam watched him walk out.

"So." Irena pulled a large sketchpad toward her and reached for a thick art pencil. "Let's get started."

An hour later, Sam was so engrossed that when a heavy hand landed on her shoulder, she shot out of her chair and spun around to face the danger. Brandt.

"Jesus," she snapped when she could, her hand still covering her pounding heart. "Don't do that."

"Sorry." He held his hands out in supplication, yet his twinkling eyes paid lie to that statement.

Sam glared at him before slowly retaking her place.

"If you two are finished, can we get at it?" Irena glared at them both. "We're just about done."

Brandt walked around to stand behind the artist. He gave a quiet but deadly whistle. "Wow."

***

2:34 pm

Irena shot him a look. "I'm not done yet. Get lost."

Brandt glanced over at her. He reached for the picture beside her on the table. "Is this yours, too?"

Irena took a quick peek in between her strokes. "Yes. We started with that one."

Sam slid lower in her chair under Brandt's intense gaze. "Why?"

"I do that sometimes. I started with a strong visual to help her to focus on the details. Why?" Irena frowned at him.

Brandt didn't answer. He studied the diagram. Something twigged, but he couldn't place it. The detail depicted was incredibly scary. Christ, she was good. Inside, he turned cold. His team members were going to have a heyday with this. Anyone would point out the three possibilities – either she was an incredibly gifted psychic, had a deadly twisted imagination, or she'd been there. He knew which one Kevin would lobby for.

He studied Sam, slouched in the chair. She lay with her eyes closed; gray smudges underlined her eyes, accenting her translucent skin and the fatigue.

The picture disturbed him. Irena was good. In this piece of work, she'd been damn good. The eerie details made it come alive – or appear even deader. In fact, the picture was damned near perfect. Tossed bedclothes, half on and half off, portrayed the violence with uncanny accuracy. The pool of blood on the mattress and the overturned lamp on the night table added to the impression of a great wrong having been committed. She'd given a death scene a terrible sense of life.

Softy, he questioned her further. "Sam – this level of detail?" He paused shaking his head. "Did you tell Irena about the blood dripping down on the mattress or the lamp overturned?"

Stretching her arms over her head, Sam shook her head. "I knew the bedding had been tossed around and that there was massive blood loss. I thought the lamp had dumped because the light came from the floor region. The layout details are all from Irena."

"You realize this level of detail is what will bother the other detectives?"

Sam bolted upright to stare at him. "Bother them, how?"

Pulling a chair up beside her, Brandt laid the sketch down. "They're going to say this picture has been envisioned from someone in the room, not from someone in the body, because if you were to see from her eyes only, you wouldn't have these details in your viewing area."

Sam peeked at Irena, who was listening to the conversation. "I gave her some details, her years of experience in this job allowed her to fill in the rest. But make no mistake, that picture..." She stabbed the sheet once again in his hand. "Is from one of my visions." She ran her hand through her hair. "Sorry, maybe I'm just overreacting from this morning." She turned to Irena who'd kept working, her pencil swiftly forming and pulling visions off the page.

Silence ensued in the large room. Brandt knew they were the center of attention. He cleared his throat and cast a glance in Irena's direction. She was studiously working on her drawing, keeping her head down.

"I didn't mean to imply anything. But for anyone who doesn't really understand how your abilities work, this...stuff seems, well I guess it's a little freaky, and they're going to question it."

She nodded, refusing to face him.

"Brandt, Captain Johansen wants to see you."

Damn. He glanced around at Adam, who tilted his head in the captain's direction. Brandt shook his head and motioned toward Sam.

Adam grimaced. "That's why."

Great. Cops preferred to work with what they could see, hear, and touch. That's why he'd brought Sam in today. For these pictures. That, and to hopefully shake loose more details from Sam's psyche.

"Now. And you're to take the picture with you."

Brandt glanced around the room only to find everyone suddenly busy – heads down. He glanced at Sam's bent head. "Don't panic. I'll talk to him. Everything's going to be fine. I promise."

Her eyes said she didn't believe him.

Frustrated, picture in hand, he strode past the younger detective to Captain Johansen's office. It felt like walking a gauntlet as everyone openly watched. He rapped hard on the closed door.

"Come in."

Brandt pushed the door aside and entered the room. The shades were now open, showing the heavy storm clouds of Portland beyond. Tall office buildings mixed with high-rises in the skyline. A busy world operated out there and for once Brandt wished he could join it.

"Sit down."

"I'll stand, sir." He stared straight at the captain and handed over the picture.

"What do you think?"

Surprised, Brandt could only stare at him. The captain glared up at him. "I think the two of them did a hell of a job."

The two men exchanged hard glances.

"Did she add anything new?"

"Not to this one. They are working on the next picture right now."

He nodded. Taking his time, the captain examined the picture in detail. "Does the photo match the crime scene?"

"I haven't had a chance to compare it yet. Still it lines up with what I remember."

The captain nodded again. "Does Stefan Kronos know her?"

That threw Brandt off balance. "I haven't asked him."

A keen glance came his way. "Maybe you should. Kevin doesn't feel this woman is to be trusted. In fact he puts her at the top of the list of suspects."

"He would." Brandt couldn't hide his disgust. "Kevin has yet to listen to her seriously."

"What makes you think she knows anything?"

Brandt pointed toward the sketches. "That."

The captain stared at the black image again, his lips pursed. "The question is whether the picture is too exact?"

"I'd have to compare it to the crime scene photos."

The captain nodded once. "Then do that. While you're at it, get her fingerprints and if she's willing, her DNA. That will either clear her or implicate her. She's either who she says she is or she's a suspect." He handed the sketch back. "Make sure we know which."

Brandt couldn't believe what he'd heard. "You might want to remember she came in willingly. She doesn't have to be treated with suspicion."

"Then don't. Just ask her. If she's innocent she won't mind." The captain's lips twitched into a wolf smile that made the hairs stand up on Brandt's neck. He returned to the stack of papers on his desk, clearly dismissing Brandt. "Now get those fingerprints and DNA and get her out of my station before I have a mutiny on my hands."

Brandt pulled open the door and shut it quietly behind him. Fingerprints weren't out of line; the DNA was.

Somehow, he had to gain Sam's cooperation.

Thankfully, she was still focused on the pictures. He watched for her reaction as he asked, "Would you mind offering your fingerprints so we can convince the naysayers that you weren't involved?" He tapped the paper for emphasis. "Like I said, some will take this the wrong way," he added in a low voice.

Sam froze. Irena even stilled for a long moment before her pencil returned to scribbling furiously.

Once again, Sam straightened. Calmly, she studied him. Once again, Brandt felt like a lowlife. It didn't matter that this was needed to rule her out, and it was only commonsense. No. It was the right thing to do and would stop the many conjectures and innuendos that were going to fly. Still, he felt like he'd kicked a puppy. Or maybe a cornered barn cat. "It's common to take fingerprints to rule out people."

"Only when they've been at the crime scene." Her voice was low and troubled.

Brandt tried again. "I know you're telling the truth. I've just finished telling the captain that exact same thing. That doesn't change the fact that some people here aren't going to believe anything you or I have to say."

That brought a sharp glance his way.

"If you do this, it quiets the talk and shuts up those that want to put you as the prime suspect."

"No, it won't," she scoffed. "It will rule out that my fingerprints match those you have on file, but anyone who wants to disbelieve is still going to say that I could have worn gloves."

Damn. He was hoping she wouldn't figure that out so quickly.

She hopped to her feet. "I have nothing to hide. I came here to help so take my damn prints." She walked over to stare out the window, her face lean and hard, hurting.

Brandt hated feeling like a heel. It would help if he could explain it further. This wasn't the time or the place.

"I'm sorry. This really is the best way."

"Whatever. Just take the prints and let me go home."

"Fine." Brandt knew his irritation was unreasonable. She had a right to be dismayed, upset even, but this tired out acceptance upset him. Now that she'd agreed, how could he approach the idea of DNA? He hesitated, wondering how to start.

She gave him a long flat stare. "What?"

He sighed and rubbed the top of his head. "The captain would also like your DNA while we're at it."

She closed her eyes and swayed unsteadily.

"Easy. Don't faint on me. This is just a Q-tip in the mouth kind of thing. It's not major." He studied her pale face. "Did you eat?"

Her eyes opened, showing black unreadable pools. "Not much."

"Let's get this over with so you can get some lunch."

Sam checked her watch. She was so tired. She'd probably need food before making the drive back to Parksville. Right now, though, all she wanted was to be home alone.

"Make it fast. I need to return to the clinic."

Where she felt loved and supported, he had no doubt. He understood how she felt. "By the way, have you called Stefan yet?"

"No. But it might be the first thing I do when I get home."

He nodded. "That's probably a very good idea."

CHAPTER NINE

4:14 pm

For about the hundredth time, Sam wiped first one hand and then the other on her jeans. Her fingers clenched on the steering wheel. Weariness still pulled on her, although much less so. Going to work for a couple of hours had helped some. Especially considering she'd managed to sneak in, take care of the animals, and sneak out without seeing anyone. The last thing she'd wanted was company.

Moses lay in his usual place, his tail wagging. There was no sign of Soldier. Sam parked and went inside.

She scrubbed her fingers, up one side and down the other, then she washed them all over again. Using a tea towel, she dried her hands and inspected them again. That there'd been no fingerprint ink to wash off, didn't change the fact she saw it every time she looked. She shivered and tugged her worn sweater around her tighter. Even though the sun shone high overhead, her bones were chilled. It had been a hell of a day.

Sam could only guess at what Brandt and the other detectives were learning about her now. She reached for the hot water and soap again.

***

4:25 pm

Brandt refused to feel guilty. He'd done his job. That's all. That picture of hers changed everything – and had cemented the captain's opinion. At least he'd agreed to make good use of what she had to offer, with the caveat to keep him in the loop.

He pushed his chair away from his desk and reached behind his head, locking his fingers together. The captain was right. Brandt needed to ask Stefan about Sam. He'd give Sam another day to contact Stefan on her own, then he'd bring the two of them together, regardless.

He'd worked successfully with Stefan for years. He knew good psychics could offer invaluable help unavailable through traditional police work. He also knew they were unusual people. They didn't see the world the same as the rest of the population. Senses overloaded easier and they retreated to spaces that soothed their raw souls.

Sam had her home at the lake for a physical retreat, did she have anything else? Stefan had a beautiful log house, yet his real solace was his art. His stunning, but tortured paintings were known the world over.

"Brandt."

Brandt frowned. Kevin. He sighed inwardly. "Kevin. What's up?" He eyed the other detective warily. They hadn't spoken since the meeting in Captain Johansen's office. Right now, Kevin sported a huge smirk on his face.

Kevin walked to the desk, holding out a sheaf of papers. "Just some research for you. Maybe this will convince you she's not quite what you want her to be."

He dropped the papers on Brandt's desk and walked out.

The top fax was a newspaper article. Brandt checked the date, March 10, 1998. The headline read *Young Psychic Leads Police on Merry Chase.*

Shit. Brandt sat down for some heavy reading.

***

4:45 pm

Kevin couldn't help feeling satisfied. Damn that felt good. Vindication. Now maybe Brandt would get that witch off his mind and off this case. And the same went for himself. Since this morning's meeting, he'd had a hard time focusing.

Finally, he'd broken down and researched Ms. Blair's background

He'd gotten lucky. After just an hour, he'd managed to get enough information to convince anyone – even Brandt. At least it should be enough. As a precaution, he'd copied them and given one set to the captain to read as well.

Handing the papers over to Brandt felt good. Damn good.

This woman was treacherous.

He didn't want her anywhere near his cases.

***

8:25 pm

Waning light flashed on the ripples in the lake. Sam swam effortlessly through the flickering rays. The evening was silent, except for the splashes as her arms cleaved through the water. The long shadows drooped after the heat of the afternoon, dipping deep into the lake for the refreshing coolness. Even the birds were silent.

Sam continued to swim for another twenty minutes. Tired and content, she dove under the surface before rolling over to float on her back. She closed her eyes and rested. The serenity of the evening slipped under her anger and pain, gently tugging them free to disperse amongst the ripples. Deprived of all else, but the sensation of water lapping on her heated skin, Sam lost herself in the moment. Her breathing slowed and she relaxed deeper. How healing. A heavy sigh, coming from nowhere, released into the air.

A short bark cut through the tranquility. Sam rolled over to see Moses at the end of the dock, waiting for her. He barked again and jumped around, wagging his tail. Sam laughed, slowly swimming toward the dock. "I'm fine Moses. Don't worry, I'm coming in."

Moses barked once more before lying down to watch her approach. She'd almost reached him when Moses sprang to his feet and turned to face the house. He barked once.

Hugging the dock, Sam peered through the shadows. A shadow slowly separated from the tree line. Soldier. Sam watched in wonder as the big dog limped toward them.

Tears of pride melded with droplets of the lake as Sam hopped out of the water. "Hey, Soldier. Good to see you on your feet, boy."

She stayed at the end of the dock, her feet dangling in the water and watched his progress anxiously. "You can do it, Soldier. Just a little more." He seemed so weak. Head down, his spine hunched in pain as each foot touched down. Still, he kept coming. He stopped at the end of the dock and lowered his haunches. He stared down at them and whined.

Moving slowly but confidently, Sam stood up and walked the few steps over to the dogs. Soldier curled his lip, although he didn't growl. Sam bent over and patted him gently on his shoulder. His fur was stiff with dirt. She glanced at the fresh water all around them. It would be a bad idea.

Soldier glared up at her, his lip curled higher.

"Yeah, I hear you. Not quite ready for a dip in the lake are you? Maybe in a couple of days, okay?"

She picked up her towel and dried off. Wrapping it around her, she slipped into her sandals and calling to the dogs, she walked up to the cabin. Single file, they trooped behind her. At the front door, she waited for Moses to come in. Surprised, she watched as Soldier ambled in behind Moses. She felt honored. He'd obviously decided this was home.

Sam smiled, whispered, "Good night guys," and headed to her bedroom and a good night's rest.

That night, her dreams were wild and even more colorful than usual. The scenes were brighter than normal. They screamed at her overloud and overbright – overwhelming her in their sensory onslaught. A sexual haze had her twisting and moaning as her body moved to an internal heat she'd never experienced. Large capable hands stroked upwards over her belly, caressing the smooth contours. Slowly the fingers slid higher and higher.

Sam caught her breath when the hands stilled, the tension coiling tighter inside. She wiggled closer, trying to move into his hands. Warm laughter tickled her ear. She groaned, not understanding the driving need that had overtaken her body. A part of Sam struggled to clear her mind. She didn't have a lover.

His hands moved again. She sighed with relief, her breath floating out into the blackness of the night. That small part of her rational mind questioned the unusual sexual overtones and the wild colors floating through her mind.

The rest of Sam's awareness centered on the tormenting fingers and sparks igniting along her nerve pathways. Sensations burned as fire seared over her skin. She churned with an inner heat, a heat that built to the point of pain. Finally, the hands reached the swell of her breasts – and stopped. Sam couldn't help herself, she tried to shift into those magic hands, but they gripped her ribs, stopping her. A groan escaped.

"Shhh," whispered the dark voice. "We have all night."

Sam shuddered at the promise. The promise and something else. Something wrong, something off. It bothered her, except she was too caught up in the sexual tension to want to figure it out. She arched high off the bed as he cupped her full breasts and squeezed gently. They coaxed then relaxed then returned to torment her again.

Sam cried out.

Dark laughter wafted through the room.

She shivered. There it was again. That nebulous feeling of something wrong. What was it?

The hands returned to torment her again. "Please..." She tried to reach for him, needing him closer.

And found she couldn't.

Just as the sensation of wrongness returned, Sam realized her arms were caught above her head. Caught and held by one of his hands. And the clouds in mind, blurring her clarity.

He laughed again. Dark laughter became black as his other hand, the one that had so gently cradled her breast, squeezed hard and then harder again.

Sam arched up, screaming in agony.

And woke up.

Still in shock, Sam curled into a tight ball and rocked back and forth under the comforter, her hands cradling her tender breasts. She bolted upright, peering into the dark corners of her bedroom. Relief washed over her. She was alone. "Dear Lord. Thank you." It had only been a dream.

A dream. Was it possible?

She stilled. A dream or a vision. She shuddered, the shakes wracking her body once again. Dear God, is this what that animal was doing? Seducing his victims with their own sexuality then turning on them? No. Sam examined the memories. Something had been very wrong, but she couldn't put her finger on it. Everything had a surreal look, an overly loud and overly colored appearance to it. A thought burst into her consciousness.

Drugs. The woman had been drugged.

Had the other victims? Sam realized her earlier visions had started too late to be able to identify something like that. She wouldn't have noticed a needle prick amongst the other pain. Panic for her life would have dispelled the rest of the drugged dullness away from her thoughts.

Sam started crying, quiet painful sobs of possibility. She didn't want to know any more. She couldn't deal with it. Not this. After tonight, she might never let another man touch her again — ever.

Touch.

She froze. The guy in her dreams hadn't worn gloves.

Had it been him? Another asshole? Or had it truly been just a nightmare? She shuddered. It had seemed so real. A wet dream gone bad in a big way. Sliding deeper into her bed, Sam pulled the covers to her chin. Only it wasn't enough. She hopped out of bed, snatched up an old nightshirt from the box on the floor, and pulled it over her head.

For the second time that day – she felt violated.

***

9:35 am, June 18th

Brandt strode down the hallway. One of his priorities this morning was to connect Sam with Stefan. He'd finally managed to reach him early this morning. Now all he had to do was to get Sam to agree to meet him. And he needed to talk to Sam about her past workings with the police.

The research Kevin had brought him had been less than flattering. Still, Brandt knew that Stefan had some less-than-stellar moments at the beginning of his career as well. The article hadn't given her age and was years ago. She'd have been young and green. Not to mention untrained, which she still was. Hence his push to connect her to Stefan as soon as possible.

Nothing he'd read had given him any reason to disbelieve her. He suspected Sam could be instrumental on his proposed task force. Not to mention many other ongoing cases. He hoped to cultivate her skills on a regular basis. Even if that meant returning to his old station. At least there, his old captain was amiable to psychics. Ideas percolated through his brain. He'd talk it over with some of his friends – and Stefan, of course.

Brandt never had liked authority. He still didn't, but with age came understanding that those above were just doing their job to make it better and safer for everyone. Or at least it was supposed to work that way. However, just as there were good and bad guys on the streets, the same could be said of the police department. One still had to believe that most of the bad guys were outside the force.

"Hey Brandt. Ran the fingerprints you asked for. She checks out."

Brandt lifted his head. The youngest of the three technicians walked into his office. His name eluded him – something European like Pieter. Brandt smiled and held out his hand for the papers being offered. "Anything interesting?"

"No rap sheet, if that's what you are asking." The tech pointed to the second page. "This might be of interest. Yeah, she was also a suspect in a missing child case in Spokane, Washington, years ago."

Brandt's gaze sharpened on the younger man's face. "What? A suspect?"

The tech shook his head. "Apparently she had information for the police, only they didn't believe her. The end result made her a suspect for a while, until the child was found safe and sound."

Brandt digested that as he scanned the paperwork. "Thanks, I'll take it from here." Now he understood Sam's odd reaction yesterday. She'd already been through this. Once again at his office, he pored over the report. So, eight years ago she'd tried to help and failed – been mocked even, based on Kevin's material. This file showed she'd tried again five years ago. The Spokane P.D. hadn't mocked her; they'd made her a suspect.

Brandt shuffled through the file. What was missing in the report was how the child had been found. Had Sam contributed to the little girl's safe return? He might need to call the detective listed on this particular case file. Grabbing a folder, he wrote Samantha's name on the tab and stacked the growing collection of material inside. Brandt leaned back in his chair, hands locked behind his head.

Her connection to this killer bothered him. It could be the same asshole that he'd been tracking. Both of them changed the method of death, but as far as he could tell, they both favored beautiful young women between eighteen and thirty-five – and all were middle-class, working females.

His mind flitted through the elements he knew. Sam's killer wore a ski mask, which didn't make sense. Usually the guys who planned on killing their victims didn't bother with masks. After all, there wasn't going to be anyone left behind to identify them.

He had no way of knowing if the other cases in his files were the same. The victims were all dead. There were never any witnesses, and little forensic evidence left behind. Then there was the ring. If Sam had anything concrete, the ring might just be it.

She was also connecting with a lot of victims. Most serial killers took time between kills. Sam's visions occurred with only days between them. Some killers went on a killing frenzy until whatever drove them, drained out of their system. Then they went quiet. Sometimes the quiet period lasted months to years. Brandt knew his best chance of catching this killer was before he went off the radar again. Who knew how long it would be before he resurfaced again.

***

9:50 am

Dillon walked into the conference room. Not only had he missed the meeting this morning, he'd also missed breakfast. He was hoping there'd be some scones or a Danish left over. Walking to the sideboard, he smiled. One huge blueberry muffin. Perfect.

He snatched up his prize and walked toward the double doors. Several papers lay discarded on several chairs. He turned the closest one over. It was a picture of a ring. Wasn't that the one Brandt was researching? He'd heard about it, but this was the first he'd seen it.

Walking to his desk, he muttered about the dinosaurs in the office. It was hard being a forward moving kind of guy in this place. The mantra around here was always about 'good old fashioned detective work.' Christ, who needed all that legwork? Technology was meant to be used. The same for the media. They were always helpful. At least Dillon had found them so. The Internet was, of course, the best. Why didn't the station have a website where pictures like this could be posted and give the public an opportunity to email or phone in with their information?

Of course, this was an old argument, and he'd gone several rounds with Captain Johansen over it – and lost every one. Dillon had wanted to host a regular five-minute slot on both the local television station and the radio stations. That had been shot down, too. Still, accessing the public was the cheapest and fastest way to gain information. The department's man-hours, logged trying to find and interview people, were incredibly expensive.

He took a large bite of his late breakfast muffin. He could understand Brandt not wanting to take that step. Like Dillon, Brandt was new here and didn't want to rock the boat. Dillon stopped chewing as an idea formed. If he arranged everything correctly, Brandt would get the information he needed, and Dillon could prove his theory. More ammunition to take to the captain. In a way, Dillon would be doing this to help Brandt. Who knew what new information could come to light.

He grinned. He'd have to think this through. Yet...it sounded like a hell of an idea.

***

10:15 am

Brandt rubbed the back of his neck. The screen scrolled, searching for more cases linking to his killer. Just then, his phone rang, distracting him.

"Hello."

"Detective Sutherland. This is Nancy from Willow Health Clinic."

The manager from the long-term care home. He groaned silently and closed his eyes, his fingers pinching the bridge of his nose. "Hi, Nancy. How are you doing?"

"Umm, I guess I'm fine. The thing is I need your help with Maisy again."

His shoulders slumped. He knew it. His mother was up to no good again.

"What's the problem?" He winced and held his breath.

"Umm, well..." She stopped.

Brandt shook his head, he knew already. Checking his watch – did he have time to whip down there? "Is she causing trouble again?"

"It's not so much causing trouble...more like she's stirring up the other residents."

He shut down his laptop. "Would you like me to come by and talk with her again?"

"Yes, yes. That would be wonderful. She's such a fun lady to have around. I hate to even ask you. But the Board has already stretched the rules for her several times, and I'm not sure that she can skate by on this one."

Brandt ran fingers through his hair. "How bad is it this time?"

"She's setting up pools again."

Brandt grinned. "That doesn't sound so bad."

"No," the harried woman on the other end of the phone said. "It's the subject matter that's the problem. Would it be possible to have you stop in sometime today?"

"No problem," he said. "I'm heading in your direction soon, so I'll be there before lunch."

"Oh, thank you. I certainly don't want to upset her. She's interjected such life here," Nancy said warmly.

"No problem. I'll see you in about an hour." Brandt rang off. Standing, he grabbed his briefcase and coat then locked up his desk.

Dillon stuck his head around the door.

"Hey Dillon. What's up?" Brandt barely withheld his grin at Dillon's suit of the day. This was the classic pinstripe with a matching tie in reverse stripes. But it was in forest green, black, and white. Mafia anyone?

"I'm just checking that you still need information on this?" He held up the sketch of the ring. "I missed whatever you said at this morning's meeting." Dillon raised an eyebrow in question.

"I'm looking for the owner. If I can trace it to a store, sorority, or something like that, I might be able to figure out who bought it."

Dillon stared at the sheet, frowning. "It's a simple enough design. But I don't think I've seen one like it." He turned the page slightly. "Is one of the stones missing?"

"Yeah, the last time it was seen, one stone appeared to be missing. The others are clear – diamond or zirconium, maybe."

"Gold, white, brass – do we know?"

"No. Gold in color is all I have."

"Shouldn't be too hard to track down. Have you talked to the jewelry stores here?"

Brandt walked around his desk to stand at Dillon's side, giving the sketch another glance. "I talked to several so far, I've faxed it to several more. So far, the same thing. Not in stock anywhere and no one remembers one quite like this in the last decade or so." Brandt considered the pattern. "It could be a custom job. I'll have to contact the local designers and see."

Behind him, Dillon asked. "Have you checked online?"

"Yes and no. I have a couple of people working on it."

Dillon nodded. "Okay, I'll keep an ear out and let you know if I find anything." He turned and walked toward the doorway. He stopped and turned around. "Oh yeah, while I have the chance, I also wanted to ask if the rumors were true?"

"What rumors?"

The younger man grinned, a perfect toothy smile. Some serious money went into that look. "That you've brought in a psychic on this case."

Brandt refused to let irritation show. "Love rumors, don't you?"

Dillon smirked. "Yeah. The grapevine here is rampant."

Brandt frowned at him, hoping to quell his interest. "Well, you can't believe everything you hear."

"True." Dillon turned, as if to finally leave again. "Let me know if you need any help with anything."

"I'll be fine, but thanks for the offer." He motioned Dillon to precede him out of the office. "Time to head out." Brandt checked his watch. He was running late.

CHAPTER TEN

10:45 am

Sam found it hard not to worry while she worked with the animals. It's not as if she lacked for topics. After last night's vision, she was now worried about *not* telling the police. Her instinct reaction had been *no way*. Not after yesterday. Today in the light of day, she knew she needed to tell Brandt.

The worry about what information the police had dug up on her, nagged at her. What if Detective Sutherland contacted that deputy from Nikola County? There was a lot of ancient history there and none of it looked good for her. Chances of the detective believing her story over that rogue deputy's version were nonexistent. She already knew that law enforcement protected their own. What were the chances the deputy had forgotten her? Not great.

"Sam, can you give me a hand?" The voice called through the swinging double doors.

Sam quickly closed the door to the rabbit cage she'd been cleaning and headed for surgery room one.

She pushed open the door. "Jesus." She jumped forward to help. "You could have called me earlier." She reached out to support the large, sleeping Newfoundland dog that was in danger of sliding off the small table. "Time to get a larger table?"

The other two women laughed. "Careful with the front legs. He's got stitches across the ribs on that side." The three women carefully maneuvered the large animal onto a second table. Then waited to receive him and then move him into an even larger cage.

Once inside, the dog's wounds were checked, his tubes adjusted for the cage walls and the door closed. Sam stepped over to look at the injured animal. He had to be a hundred and fifty pounds. "What happened to him?"

Dr. Valerie Brown, the older of the two, smiled and said, "You don't need to whisper, he's not going to wake up."

Sam's lip twitched. "I know. He's beautiful."

The other woman, Dr. Brenda Torrance, stripped off her gloves. "Yup, he's gorgeous alright, only he needs to stop arguing with cars."

Sam sent a sharp question her way. "What, another car accident?" She glanced at the sleeping animal. "How horrible."

"We'll move him to the back room after he wakes up from his anaesthesia."

Sam narrowed her gaze. Funny lights played over the surface of the dog's thick fur coat. Weird. Shivers raised goose bumps on Sam's skin. A vision reached into her brain and took over her sight. The dog was hurt worse than the minor repair held together by the stitches. Images crowded her – the dog up in the air, tumbling before hitting his left hip on a fire hydrant.

"Did he get the cut from the car or from the landing?" She focused on the animal's body, searching for any clues as to what else could be wrong.

"The front grill of the truck ripped a strip of hide off him. Why?" Valerie asked.

Sam gazed at her vaguely. "What? Oh, his left hip doesn't look right. But I'm sure you took x-rays, so that hip must be just bruised and not broken."

Deliberately, Sam left, as if to return to the cages to finish her job. In the other room, she stopped outside the door and listened.

Behind her was a weighty silence.

"What was that all about?"

"Damned if I know. Were x-rays done?"

A rustle of papers. "No, the owners brought him in for stitches. They saw the accident. They didn't want to go through the expense of x-rays, if not required. A check-up was done before we came on for the day." More papers were shuffled. "What do you think, should we do x-rays?"

"I hate taking over cases already in progress. I was told this animal just needed stitches. Shit."

Silence except for a brush of clothing and soft muttering. Sam could only hope they were checking the dog's hip a little more closely. Nodding encouragement that they couldn't see, Sam followed their actions with one ear to the door.

"Damn. We need to x-ray his hips. Let's call the owners."

"She's right?"

"I don't know, but there's something wrong. Who did the intake on this animal?"

"I'll have to check the paperwork when we're done."

Sam grinned. She whispered to the empty room. "There you go boy. Now you'll be fine." She listened for another moment before heading to finish her work.

It wasn't until later that she realized this was her first vision around an animal. Sam had actually seen the energy over the injured part of the body. The goose bumps had been the first inkling of something wrong. Her heart positively lifted with joy. To be able to do something for animals would be wonderful. Now, if she could learn to control it so she could use it at will. More questions for Stefan.

"Sam, can you run and do a pickup for us?"

Sam spun around, her hand rushing to her chest.

"Sorry." Valerie reached out an apologetic hand. "I didn't mean to scare you."

Sam blew out a noisy breath, letting her hand drop down.. "I must have been miles away."

"It's these shoes. They should be sleuth shoes." Valerie lifted her practical working shoes to peer at the soles.

Sam waited until she had Valerie's attention. "What do you need?"

"I need you to run over to where Lucy's daughter works and pick up an injured cat. If you don't mind. It's about fifteen minutes from here." Valerie checked her notes briefly. "You were right, by the way, the dog's hip was dislocated and the ligaments and muscles are badly torn."

"Oh, how sad. I'm glad you could fix him." How could she refuse to go get the cat? Her shift wasn't over for at least an hour. Besides, they were doing right by the dog.

"Of course, we'll pay for your time and your gas."

Sam brushed her hand in the air. "It's no problem. I'm almost done here. Give me directions. I'll just wash up and get ready."

"Great. I really appreciate it. We've been so busy that I haven't taken the time to say how much I appreciate your efforts here. Thanks." With a grateful smile, Valerie headed to the office.

Sam stared, bemused, at the flapping doors. It's a good thing she'd left. Sam didn't have any response to give. She couldn't remember the last time she'd received a compliment like that.

It was kind of nice.

***

11:00 am

It had been a busy morning already. And still Bill wasn't quite done. He shuffled the contents in the bed of his truck. He'd promised to bring the dogs over to the palliative care center. Those patients loved seeing the animals. It was the least he could do for those dying folks. It was either make their last days a little sweeter or knock 'em off early.

He grinned. It would be so easy. Only, it wouldn't mean the same thing for him. It wasn't just getting his rocks off – well that

117

was a huge part of it – but he needed certain things in order to get there. It used to be easy. Now everything had to go exactly right or he couldn't enjoy himself.

Starting with the victim – just anyone wouldn't do. The right victim was everything to him. He was a selection specialist. And he'd made a mistake last time. Not on the girl, but on the method. He'd tested a new drug on her. Bad decision. She'd reacted terribly, slipping into unconsciousness before he could really enjoy her. He'd left – beyond pissed. Now, he'd need a fix again...and soon because of that.

He'd expected to hear about her on the news, but so far nothing. Stupid cops, they'd probably written her off as a suicide. He grinned. That worked for him. Fooling the cops kept things challenging. Over the years he'd even wondered what drove him, but had come to the conclusion that it didn't matter, as he was past the point of stopping. He refused to dwell on it.

He also didn't like the mask thing. The bloody wool itched. He preferred to stay anonymous. Not take any chances. When he'd first started, he hadn't taken the same care. During the first couple of rapes, he'd sweated with the droplets falling onto the women's skin. Early on, he'd tried using alcohol on one woman's skin to remove any sweat or saliva and had quickly discarded that. He'd ended up with a bloody mess. If being uncomfortable was the price then that was fine with him. The gloves also didn't thrill him because he wanted the skin-to-skin contact. Every once in a while, he still succumbed to the temptation, but was always careful to put them on immediately afterwards. Why the hell it mattered at that point, he didn't know, except he'd been doing it that way for so long logic couldn't even begin to win over superstition. What worked, worked and that was all there was to it.

A shrink would have a heyday with him. Yeah, he was paranoid. Still, he was in this for the long haul and didn't plan to screw up anytime soon.

***

11:10 am

Brandt pulled into the parking lot at the Willow Health Center. He parked at the front and walked inside. The offices were off to the right. He headed there first.

"Hi, Nancy."

The tiny older woman looked up in surprise. Then a big smile broke out. "Detective Sutherland. Thank you so much for coming."

He shook his head. "She's my problem, not yours."

Nancy grinned. "Except that while she's here, she's also our problem."

There was no arguing that logic. "I'll walk down and have a talk with her before she goes for lunch."

"Good. She might be in her room, or she could be over with the animals today. I'll be there in a couple of minutes."

"Oh, right. It's pet day, isn't it?" The center had a well-loved program where family members were allowed to bring pets in to see the various residents for an hour to two. Sometimes, special dogs and cats came in to keep the people company or put on small shows. The older people loved it. It was a highlight for them.

Brandt walked down to his mother's room.

"Mom?" He knocked gently.

"Come in."

Brandt pushed the door open to find several other people in there. A hushed silence descended when they recognized their visitor.

He heaved a sigh. "Yes, the cops have been called. Mom, what the hell are you up to now?"

Maisy ran over to him and gave him a big hug. "It's lovely to see you dear, however, there's no reason to use profanity."

What could he do? She was his mother. He rolled his eyes and wrapped his arms around her frail body in a gentle hug.

He grasped her shoulders gently and held her at arm's length. "Mom, we have to have a talk."

***

11:20 am

"Here it is." Sam slowed, pulled into the long driveway, and parked. There was a familiar truck parked to the right. She frowned. There's no reason it should be Brandt's truck. There had to be hundreds of those here in town. Her pulse jumped, and she couldn't help searching the area for him. She didn't want to see him, not really, yet couldn't hold back the pulsing excitement at the thought of it. Traitorous hormones.

She walked inside. Large and open with multiple comfy couches, the lobby had a friendly atmosphere. Sam could see people feeling welcome here. Bright yellows and moderate oranges blended with the lush palms and overgrown dieffenbachia plants filling each corner.

The front counter stood empty. Sam pursed her lips. There didn't appear to be a bell to ring for service either. Sam frowned. She checked her watch. Surely, it was early for lunch? Not knowing how a place like this worked, Sam found herself choosing between two corridors and took the left one. Various doorways along the hallway were identified by numbers. They appeared to be apartments or self-contained suites of some kind. They didn't look like the hospital rooms she'd assumed they would be.

Having never known anyone living permanently or temporarily in a place like this, she found herself wondering at the circumstances that would leave them here. Did these people not have family, or were they alone like she was?

Were they happy here? Or did they pine away, always wishing for a better life? Living alone for so long, a place like this could seem like a prison. Surely, some of these people had families to live with?

Laughter drifted toward her. Curious, Sam followed the sound. Glancing back, she saw the reception desk remained empty.

The hallway opened up into another large sitting area with many tables surrounded by people. Some played cards, others were engrossed in chess, and still others were petting several dogs. Animals. Now that was a nice touch. Sam smiled at a particularly large feline that strolled regally between several legs, her leash getting caught up – to everyone's enjoyment.

Sam looked around for someone in charge. Everyone appeared to be in the same age category – old. There was one younger man with a basset hound on a leash. The dog appeared comfortable, sprawled in place and showing no interest in being dragged across the room. Sam smiled. The dog was gorgeous. Evidently, several of the residents thought so too. Several bent to pat the dog's long ears and rotund belly.

No one appeared bothered by Sam's presence. In fact, no one even seemed to notice her. She continued past the group and headed down a quieter corridor where there were several more doors.

One opened, and a small woman with a nametag on her shirt walked out. *Finally*. Sam stopped. "Excuse me. Do you know where I can find either Sarah or Nancy?" Belatedly, Sam read the nametag.

"I'm Nancy. Sarah has gone home for the day. How can I help you?"

"I'm here from the vet hospital in Parksville to pick up an injured cat."

"Oh my goodness. You've been walking around here looking for me, haven't you? I'm so sorry."

Sam smiled at her. "No problem. How is the...?" Her voice trickled to a stop as a large man stepped out of the room behind Nancy. "Brandt?" She blushed and quickly corrected herself. "Detective Sutherland, I mean. What are you doing here?"

Nancy jumped in. "Oh, do you two know each other? That's wonderful. Why don't you stay here for a moment while I try to locate the poor cat?" With a bright smile the cheerful woman hastened down the way Sam had come.

"No, I'll come..." But Nancy was already gone.

"Too late. Nancy can move very quickly when she wants to."

"Brandt, who are you talking to?" A spry lady with bottle-blue hair came to the door. "Oh." She smiled, a little too brightly. "How nice. Brandt, invite your friend inside." She turned to Sam. "Hi, I'm Maisy and Brandt is my son."

Sam smiled weakly. "Hi." Of course, this was Brandt's mother.

"Come in, child."

Sam found herself manoeuvred into the small suite where several curious seniors instantly surrounded her. Behind her, she could hear Maisy whispering loudly to Brandt.

"Now I know why the others wouldn't do. All you had to do was tell me about her. This is wonderful." Maisy beamed.

Sam closed her eyes. Uh, oh.

"Mom, don't start with me."

"Of course not. I'm too happy to argue with you." She bustled over to regard Sam like a unique species under a microscope. "Move everyone, give the child some space." She snagged Sam's arm and led her to the couch. "My goodness there's not much to you, is there?"

"There's enough. I'm actually quite healthy." Sam tried to defend herself while allowing Maisy to shove her gently onto a flowery couch that probably had many stories to tell. For all the gentleness behind this woman's gestures, Sam sensed a steel core. She might be Brandt's mother, but Sam doubted she had let him get away with much.

A warm cup of tea was placed in her hand, followed by a small plate heaped high with cookies.

"Oh, no. The tea is just fine, thank you."

"Nonsense. You need to eat more."

A polite way of saying she was too skinny.

Another silver-blue head popped around the corner. "So your son is here, is he? Now you're going to get it, Maisy."

"Nonsense. He can solve this." This came from one of the people that had been in the small room the whole time.

Brandt interrupted. "Let's return to why I'm here. Mom, what are you up to now?"

She rose with a gentle smile on her face. "Surely, they didn't call you over this little bit of fun we're having, did they?"

Multiple voices chimed in with their take on the situation.

"Mom, this is the third time this month. What's gotten into you?"

"Why nothing. Besides, this isn't my fault. This time it's your fault."

Brandt shook his head, clearly confused.

Sam couldn't believe it. She watched in bemusement, drinking her tea, as fifteen elderly people in the room crowded around Brandt, all of them talking at once.

"Okay, one at a time. Come on everyone, calm down. Jackson, you take it easy – I don't want you having a heart attack again. Colonel, good to see you. Do you know what Maisy is up to this time?"

The colonel laughed a deep Santa laugh that charmed Sam. "Of course. She's acting as a bookie again."

"Mom?" Brandt spun around to see his mother calmly counting a column of figures. "What are you doing?"

"Nothing much. Just taking bets on Joshua's love life." She snickered. "Or lack of it."

Several giggles and guffaws filled the room.

"Joshua?"

"Yeah, the sour puss that runs this place. He has a new girlfriend, so we're betting on how long before it all goes south. Personally, I don't see it making it to the end of the month."

More laughter as several other people boasted what time they'd bet on.

Brandt groaned. As always, his mother had fired up her social circle. Brandt just stood, his mouth working, only no words came out.

Sam giggled.

Everyone spun to stare at her. Maisy hopped to her feet and walked around her son. A delighted smile lit up her face. "Oh my, child, that sounded a little rusty."

Sam's eyes widened at that comment. She knew she didn't laugh often, but surely calling it rusty was a little extreme.

"Brandt, I like her. Except she's all skin and bones." She turned to Sam. "Surely, you're not one of those hung up on all those fad diets are you?" Disapproval swept the room.

"No, ma'am. I'm not dieting." Fat chance. Sam thought of the belt she'd had to notch tighter this morning. She was losing weight quicker than she could eat.

"You're all eyes too. Life has been hard on you, hasn't it?" Maisy didn't wait for an answer, which was a relief as Sam had no idea how to answer. Maisy grabbed her arm, tugging the sweater up her arm. "Dearie, you're positively skinny." The blue veins pulsed along the top of Sam's arm. Hurriedly, Sam pulled the oversized sweater down to cover the top of her hand.

Maisy patted her hand before releasing it. "It's okay child. We're not criticizing you. We're all friends here." She smiled up at her son. "Brandt, tell me about this beautiful waif in your life."

All eyes turned to Brandt. Sam's were wide with horror.

Brandt found his voice, just not the volume control. He bellowed, "Mom, stop."

Maisy stared at him, affronted. "Now you listen to me, young man, I haven't even begun."

Grimly, Brandt glared down at her. "You can stop right now. This is a semi-official call because once again you are creating a disturbance. Do you *want* to be evicted from this place? Go somewhere else where you won't have all your friends? This has to stop."

"Harumph."

"Don't give me that. I've told you before, no more betting. Taking a simple wager between two people is one thing, Mom. Setting up a betting book on something like the administrator's love life is going too far – again." Brandt was adamant.

Sam sat bemused as chaos erupted around her. It went on for at least ten minutes before Brandt managed to calm down the outrage.

Watching him, Sam realized that several of the elderly people were staring at her openly. She probably wasn't the norm for Brandt's women.

Her lips quirked in a tentative smile at several of them.

They all smiled big fat grins back at her.

"What's your name, dear?"

Turning to look at Maisy, Sam replied, "My name is Samantha."

"That's a beautiful name." Maisy beamed at her, apparently having no trouble ignoring her son glaring down at the two of them.

Sam wasn't having the same success. Her glance darted between Brandt and Maisy.

"Mom, are you going to behave? Or must I arrange for you to go back to your apartment?"

"Should I ask Samantha if you're behaving?" Maisy asked archly, to the amusement of the audience. She stared innocently up at her towering son. The twinkle in her eye couldn't be missed.

The colonel interrupted. "How about we change the subject? When are you guys going to catch that killer? I heard about them finding that poor woman the other day."

That started the seniors all over again. Brandt threw up one hand in a classic stop gesture. "Silence!"

As Sam watched, Brandt's gaze slid over the seniors, his mother, and finally rested on Sam. He frowned. The room quieted, except Sam didn't think he'd intimidated anyone but her. Maisy's cronies were obviously used to him. They treated him like one of their own. Maisy looked like hell on wheels, for stirring things up.

"I don't know what case you're talking about. We're after several killers. You know I can't talk about any specifics. But the police are following up several leads. We're doing everything we can. So if you know anything that can help us – great. Otherwise, let us do our job." He sent a cutting look to his oblivious mother. "And don't set up a pool on it."

"Well, if we do, we'll bet on you. See? We know you'll solve these cases." His mother beamed up at him.

Brandt shook his head. "Is it safe to leave, Mom? Do you think you can behave for a while?"

"Of course she can." Several of the seniors glared at him.

Brandt rolled his eyes. "Sam, let's go."

Sam hopped up, but had to tug her hand free from Maisy's clasp. "I have to find Nancy and the cat."

"We'll stop at her office on the way out."

Maisy rose and wedged herself between the pair. "Sam, please come for lunch next week. Brandt, when can you bring her?"

"Oh no, I couldn't do that." Sam shook her head.

"Why not?"

Sam didn't know how to answer. She slid a sideways glance at Brandt. Their eyes met. She shrugged, not knowing how to answer the question.

"Mom, Sam and I will discuss it, and I'll get back to you." He tugged Sam further away from his mother. "Now, we're leaving."

"Not without a kiss. Official visit or not, I'm still your mother."

Brandt obediently bent to give his mother a quick peck on the cheek before snagging Sam's arm and pulling her down the hallway.

Sam felt the dozens of eyes following their progress out the door.

"What was that?" Sam glanced behind, sure she was being watched.

A line of curious faces watched every step they took. Maisy stood in the doorway, a satisfied smile on her face.

"The other side of my life," he muttered.

Sam easily read the adoration for his mother in his eyes. Her heart warmed. A guy who loved his mom had a lot going for him. "Uh, oh. Has she got the wrong impression?" Sam shook her head. "I don't know what just happened. I came to pick up an injured cat."

"What happened? My mother happened," he said wryly. "She's a force to be reckoned with."

Sam motioned behind her with her hand. "Is she always like that?"

"Yes. Unfortunately."

"She's lovely. You're very lucky." Sam couldn't help but wish she had someone so lively and bright in her world.

She felt, more than saw Brandt's eyes upon her. She refused to face him. Thankfully, they'd arrived at Nancy's office, so she didn't have to.

Just then, an overly large box appeared, hiding the skinny man carrying it.

"Thanks, Jeremy. Brandt, can you carry the cat out to the lady's car?"

"No problem. We're both leaving."

"Thank you, Nancy. The hospital will fix this guy right up."

Sam tried to peek under a corner flap of the box. An unholy howl erupted, warning against going any further. She grimaced.

"I'll definitely be leaving him in the box." She smiled at the other woman. "Thanks again."

Sam held the door as Brandt carried the box outside. Sam rushed to unlock the passenger side of her truck.

Brandt gently laid the box inside on the seat. It was a tight fit, which would help stop it from sliding around.

"There you go." He straightened and studied her. "Sorry about my mother."

What could she say? "I thought she was sweet. Thank you for carrying the cat." She unlocked the driver's door and got in, anxious to avoid awkward good-byes. "See you around." She cranked the engine and backed out of her spot. After turning the vehicle around she was ready to head onto the highway but Sam was forced to hit the brakes.

Brandt stood in front of the truck, stopping her from going anywhere.

CHAPTER ELEVEN

11:50 am

Puzzled, she lowered her window. "What's the matter?"

He grinned. "You ran away so fast that I didn't have chance to ask you about Stefan." He held out his hands, palms up. "If you have time, I thought we could go see him later today. What's your schedule like?"

Sam stared at him in shock, as excited jellybeans jumped in her stomach. "I can't right at the moment. I have to get the cat to the hospital for treatment."

"And I understand that. Stefan is only about fifteen minutes from here so we can go later. But if today doesn't work, we can plan it for another day."

"Really." This would be a godsend. She needed to talk to someone who would understand. "What about Stefan? Don't you need to check with him?"

"I spoke to him earlier. He suggested we come mid to late afternoon. I was going to call and ask you what would be convenient, then you showed up here."

She didn't want to lose this opportunity by putting it off. Who knew when this chance would arise again? "This afternoon would be great. Where do you want to meet? Here? Or at his house?"

"No, it would be easier if I come to Parksville. How about we meet around three at the vet's office, then we'll go in my truck."

"That would be great." Sam beamed. "I'll see you then."

"Bye."

Brandt waved as she drove past. Sam was grinning so hard, she almost didn't see it. She honked the horn once and drove off. The trip home went fast.

It was a good thing as her thoughts were in turmoil. She had a million questions to ask Stefan and didn't know where to start. Then there was the prospect of spending the afternoon in Brandt's company.

Thoughts and ideas popped and submerged, yet more mixed and brewed. She wasn't the same person she'd been a month ago or even a week ago. What had changed exactly, she couldn't say. Only that she didn't wear her skin the same. Looser, maybe – and not from losing weight. Maybe it was just a better cut, more suited for who she really was.

Strange ramblings from a troubled soul.

Sam sighed. Glimpses of who she was and what she was doing with her life flitted in and out like a hummingbird. Enough to see the color and glow. Not enough to grasp the meaning or details.

A black pickup pulled in behind her. Too close for comfort, but not quite tailgating.

Sam peered into her rear-view mirror, wondering if Brandt had followed her. The truck might be his. She couldn't quite see the driver's face through the tinted windshield. Did Brandt's truck have gradient tinting like that? She couldn't remember. Still, she'd have recognized him behind the wheel, and this wasn't him.

The truck moved closer.

Definitely, tailgating.

The big truck dwarfed her Nissan. She knew nothing about vehicles and this one gleamed in the late sunlight with enough chrome trim to blind anyone. The pair of ram horns on the front identified it as a Dodge. A wave of relief hit when she was able to identify that little bit.

Then the truck came so close she thought it would hit her. Sam's heart shot into her throat, and her stomach heaved. She tried to pull over and let him pass, but he slowed down behind her. When she was almost stopped, he drove forward and deliberately bumped her.

"Shit." Sam hit the gas hard, pulling onto the road. She searched her pocket for her cell phone. She punched in Bandt's number. Sam switched her gaze from the road to her rear-view mirror.

"Hello. What's up, Sam?"

"Some asshole is trying to run me off the road," she yelled as the truck zoomed closer. The driver grinned down at her. His features were little more than a white blur – vaguely familiar, only too far away to be placed.

"What? What are you talking about?"

"This truck pulled in behind me just after I left you. He started tailgating me so I slowed down to pull over, then he deliberately hit my truck. I couldn't help it. I panicked and hit the gas. Now he's on my ass and grinning like a madman."

"What kind of truck?"

"Like yours. Exactly like yours."

This time he was all business. "How far from Parksville are you?"

Sam searched for landmarks. "I think about 7 or 8 miles."

"Anyone else on the road?"

"There's been the odd vehicle. Right now the highway is deserted."

"I'm on my way. Keep driving. Don't pull over if you can avoid it. You don't know what this asshole wants."

Shivers worked down her spine. "Great. I feel so much better now."

"Hang in there."

"Then you'd better drive like hell because I'm doing thirty over the speed limit and this guy is still on my tail."

He snorted. "Don't you worry about that. I'm not that far behind you. You focus on staying alive. I'll be there in a couple of minutes."

Sam turned off the cell phone, keeping a wary eye on the truck staying on her tail.

The highway was flat and wide. It was also deserted. There'd be little danger of an accident if she did go off the road. Yet, the idea of having this guy stop while she was stranded out here alone, kept her foot on the gas. Her little truck rattled and shook at the high speed.

Alternately scanning the rear-view mirrors and staring out the windshield, Sam increased her speed again. A double lane opened up. She surged ahead into the slow lane hoping the truck would take off.

Nerves locked down as tight as her fingers on the steering wheel. As she watched the truck sped up. He pulled into the fast lane to drive neck in neck at her side. Sam felt the first stirring of anger. It helped to check the fear bubbling through her blood. The asshole was playing with her.

From her position, she could see the lower portion of the passenger side panel, and huge monster wheels flashing silver lights. Anger fuelled her next move.

It might not have been the smartest. Still, a compulsion unlike any other took hold.

Sam hit the brakes hard. The black truck raced past her. Sam whipped her small truck in behind the black one. It had no license plate. Crap. Fear shot skyward. Everyone honest and open had license plates.

She let the distance between her and the truck widen. She watched anxiously to see if he would slow down to torment her more or if he'd had enough. She wasn't looking for a confrontation.

The truck pulled ahead, gaining speed before racing around a corner ahead of her. Thank God. Sam settled into her seat a little more comfortably. And breathed. It had probably been a punk kid playing power games. The band around her temple loosened.

She called Brandt. "He just took off." Sam could see flashing lights up ahead.

"Did you manage to see the license plate?"

"There wasn't one. Another reason for my panic."

"Did he go straight ahead?"

Sam checked all her mirrors even though she knew the black truck was nowhere to be found. "Yeah. He's long gone by now."

"And where are you now?"

"Almost at the first intersection in town. I'm just a couple of minutes from the vet hospital."

"Okay, I should be in the parking lot by the time you're done in there."

Sam shut down the phone and proceeded at a sedate pace. The poor cat. She glanced over at the box, but it hadn't moved. There hadn't been a sound out of it either. She made a face. It had damn well better be in there. She didn't want to have to go back.

Sam kept a wary eye on her surroundings, but never saw the truck again. Once in the parking lot, she struggled to free the large box from the seat. The cat howled.

Moving slowly, she carried the cat into the first examining room and on to one of the small patient rooms. Valerie joined her almost immediately.

"I really appreciate you stopping to pick this guy up for me."

She glanced at her in surprise. "It was no problem. I was glad to help."

"Good, good. Now let's see what we've got here." She smiled at her. "Would you mind asking one of the girls to join me? I'm going to need another set of hands for this job."

Sam nodded. "Yes, you will. That cat is pissed."

The vet grinned at her. "And with good reason. Not to worry, we'll put him to rights, if we can."

Five minutes later, Sam stepped outside, not noticing the black truck until she was halfway across the lot. She stopped, her hand going to her throat.

"Sam?"

Oh thank God, it was Brandt. She blew out her pent up breath and walked toward him, relieved and comforted that he'd raced after her. "Hi."

"Hey. How are you now?"

Good question. Sam tried to take stock but found her mind shrinking away from what had almost happened. "I'm fine. Part of me thinks I might have overreacted. Yet, another part says I didn't react fast enough." She shrugged. "I don't know what that was all about."

"Could you see the driver?" Brandt stood, hands fisted on his hips, his gaze penetrating.

She frowned. "Not really, the truck was so much higher than mine. I only saw a vague blur." She hesitated, then figured what the hell. "I caught a glimpse of his face in his rear view mirror, and although I couldn't get a close enough look there was something...I don't know how to describe it. There was something familiar about him."

"Was he tall? Short? Could you see his shoulders above the dashboard? Was his head close to the top of the cab? Hair, bald?"

He fired the questions at her so fast, Sam stopped and blinked. "Tall, his shoulders were above the dash, and his head did come close to the top of the truck or it looked like that from where I was sitting. He had hair, some, I just don't know how much."

Brandt nodded. "Anything defining about the truck?"

"Yeah, no license plate." She bent down to check out the rusted back end and the bumper. "He hit me once and more than a little tap, but I don't see any paint."

Brant squatted down, inspecting the rear of the truck. "The height of the truck would determine where he hit you. His chrome bumper might show traces of paint from your truck, but not the reverse. The chrome won't leave any trace on yours. It might have left a dent – not that we'd be able to see it if it had."

Sam could see that for herself. Her truck body was a mess. There were dents and dings all over the place. Bits of colored paint plastered the truck in odd spots. Some paint showed through the truck's outer layer while some sat over top of it.

Brandt glanced sideways at her. "The techs might be able to lift something off it, but chances are good that the bump shook your paint loose, confusing the issue entirely."

"Great. So no proof again." Sam stood up. "That's the story of my life."

"It's tough. These assholes know that cops follow a set pattern of evidence and when that's not present..."

"Makes sense. I suppose that the killers of the world learn police techniques to stay one jump ahead. She pointed to the tailgate. This killer...not the asshole who bumped me, "but the *killer* – he's playing with you. He considers himself some kind of pro. A specialist that's evolved over time."

He stood up, his gaze sharpened to a laser point. "What makes you say that?"

Leaning against her truck, Sam crossed her arms over her chest and thought about what she'd said. That it felt right wasn't going to be good enough for him. Slowly, formulating her thoughts as she went, she said, "I think it's the impression I've received. I've connected to his energy once or twice when he's gotten excited."

"More killings."

"Maybe." Sam shifted, uncomfortably. She hadn't told him about last night's victim. "I don't know if it's the same or not. But I woke up inside a woman who was being seduced."

His eyebrows jumped straight up. "Is that normal – for you?"

She flushed, heat creeping up her neck. "No. I don't normally wake up in other people's sexual fantasies." She hesitated.

"What?"

"The thing is, this woman was drugged. Some kind of hallucinogenic. Everything looked bizarre and felt over the top."

"But it was consensual?"

Sam couldn't help the grimace. "That's the thing. I don't think it was. He hurt her. Oh not at the beginning. No, in the beginning he made her feel a lot, but there was some sort of resistance going on in her mind that was hard to sort out. I think it was the drugs. I don't think she'd invited him in. I still can't identify him because the drugs distorted her vision and therefore my senses and view." Sadness tinged her voice. "It's almost like he's trying out new things. Like a new drug."

"Then he might try this again?"

"No. Not the same anyway. He didn't like what it did to her. I couldn't stay until the end because she faded into some kind of drugged unconsciousness." Sam shifted uneasily at the reminder. "I don't quite know what happened. If she died at that point in time, she didn't know it. She just went comatose."

Brandt stiffened. "Can you describe her?"

Describe her. Hmmm. "Not really. Just as my vision saw really weird things, her thoughts were the same." A nagging memory touched her again. "There was something off about this. From her impression, I got the feeling she knew him."

"Which could help a lot – if we knew who *she* was?"

"I don't have many details. She could be considered a suicide. Or a drug overdose. It was just last night, so would she even have been found yet?"

Sam studied her memories. "It's possible she didn't die, but was taken to Emergency." She shifted slightly, dismay wrinkling her face. "Even worse, she could be slowly dying in her bedroom right now."

"Horrible thought. I'll follow up with the morgue and the hospitals." He eyed her carefully.

She frowned. "What?"

"I'm concerned about you." He shifted closer, peering into her face. "That was a traumatic drive home for you. I want to know that you're okay." He reached out to grasp her gently by the shoulders. "Are you sure?"

Sam gently rubbed her face, feeling the weight of the full day pull on her. "I'm fine. I still can't decide if I overreacted, or if he really was toying with me."

"It's a busy highway. To be empty for any length of time would have been abnormal. That meant the attack had been spur of the moment. Someone had taken advantage of the opportunity presented. But why?" Brandt studied her carefully. "Who would want you dead? Have you pissed anyone off recently? Not so recently? Or this could be just some crazy asshole and not a targeted hit, but on the off chance..."

Sam heard his words, but they stopped making any sense after his suggestion someone might be trying to kill her. She could feel the blood draining from her face. There was one person. Only one person who had reason to wish her dead. But why would he be after her now? She stared at Brandt, horror dawning. The police checked into her history. Could that have triggered this? What's the chance Brandt had spoken to him? Nightmarish possibilities swirled through her mind. Did she dare tell Brandt? Did she dare trust him?

Brandt frowned. "You need to tell me the truth here. We've already got a crazed killer running around. If there is a second asshole, then I need to know about him."

Sam sighed. "Do you have time? This could take awhile."

***

12:15 pm

"Hey Maisy, I hear your son came today on 'official' business." Bert, a retired plumber, yelled at her from the far side of the room. There might be something wrong with his hearing, but there was nothing wrong with his voice.

Raucous, good-hearted laughter broke throughout the large dining room. Maisy smiled at everyone. "He did indeed. And did you also hear – he brought his girlfriend?"

Ooohs and aaahs from the group of seniors filled the room.

"Maybe he'll finally settle down now, huh?"

Maisy made her way slowly over to her table and took her place. "I sure hope so. You should see her."

Rosie, a retired yoga instructor seated at the table behind her, asked, "Is she pretty?"

Maisy thought about that for a moment, then shook her head. "No, not in the sense that a little girl running through a bed of flowers is pretty. She's..." Lost for words, Maisy glanced over at the colonel for help.

He nodded. "She's unique."

"Aaaah," said the collective voice of everyone listening in.

Maisy nodded. "Fine boned, long hair past her waist and eyes that make you want to cry. She's got my boy tied up in knots. He wants to protect her and devour her at the same time."

Knowing grins broke out on the other faces.

"So, it's serious then?"

Maisy couldn't see who'd spoken. She thought it was Jim, a permanent resident. "You know, I think it might be."

Silence reigned as the first course of hot soup and fresh bread was eaten.

The colonel, with a twinkle in his eyes spoke up. "I can't believe I'm going to be the one to say this, but how come you haven't set up a betting pool for when he asks her to marry him?"

A gentle chuckle rose around the room.

Maisy, acting as if insulted, said, "Brandt was just here telling me I'm not allowed to do that anymore."

The chuckle grew louder.

"And since when do you listen to him?" The colonel beetled his heavy brow in a leer.

She grinned. "Never." She pulled her notebook from her pocket and opened it to a clean page. "Okay, who's placing the first bet?"

The room erupted with voices clamoring to get their dates of choice before they were taken by another person.

With a big grin, and a fat wink at the colonel, Maisy set up a pool on her son's love life.

CHAPTER TWELVE

2:30 pm

Sam and Brandt left their trucks behind the vet's office and stopped at the crosswalk. There was a cafe across the street with an outside patio. Traffic zoomed past until the lights changed.

It had already been a hell of a day. So, it was no surprise that the thought of answering the upcoming questions made Sam nervous. Questions always made her nervous.

They grabbed a table slightly away from the others.

A waitress walked over with menus. Sam shook her head. "Just coffee for me, please."

Brandt snorted. "Like hell." He motioned to the waitress. "I'll have coffee as well. Bring two chicken Caesar salads, please. Just make mine bigger with a side of garlic bread."

Sam stared at him. "And what if I'm not hungry?"

"Too bad. You need to keep your energy up to make the most of our visit with Stefan."

She didn't have an argument for that.

The waitress returned with two mugs of steaming coffee. Sam murmured her thanks, wrapping both hands around the cup. She stared out at the traffic whizzing by.

"Hey, are you there?"

Sam glanced up to see Brandt staring at her. "Sorry, my mind is just wandering."

"You do seem distracted. So talk to me."

She sat back and toyed with the cutlery. "It's not that easy."

"I presume this is about the car incident today?"

"I don't know if it is, or not. I guess so." She sighed. "Can I ask you a question first?"

"What do you want to know?" He took a long drink of his coffee, his eyes on hers.

Her lip curled. "That's the thing. I'm not too sure that I do want to know."

The table across from them had a family of five sitting around enjoying a cool drink. Sam watched their normal activity with a hint of jealousy. She'd never been able to have that type of experience. And she never would unless she could put this behind her.

She pursed her lips before lifting her own cup for a sip. "How much of my history have you dug up?"

"I had a surface history on my desk the first day you walked into the station. After taking your fingerprints and DNA, I learned a bit more." He toyed with the sugar packets. "I know you were in a bad car accident several years ago. I know you spent time in a mental hospital."

She closed her eyes, letting her head drop.

"I know you've helped the police in the past and at times, your help appeared to be more of a hindrance." He reached across the table, his hand covering hers. "I know you went to college where your best friend was murdered. You went to the police to offer your help and together, you managed to catch the killer."

"Lucy," she whispered. Memories flooded her mind. Lucy smiling with her wild and crazy coffee cups. She'd haunted curio shops for her next best mug. She'd been so open, so caring, and now she was so dead, just like the other victims. "You have it wrong. I went to the police to see if I could help. I thought I was getting somewhere and then Lucy was murdered. You see, she was murdered because of me. The killer, after finding out I was helping the police, came after me. He got her instead." Guilt tore at her. Her head bowed even more under the weight of the memories. She sniffled. "I couldn't save her. I couldn't save any of them."

"So you ran away. From your education, from your friends, and all of society."

The accusation stabbed into her. "That's not fair," she whispered. "I tried so hard to help those women. It broke my heart when I couldn't."

Brandt squeezed her hand gently, his thumb stroking the soft skin of her palm. Sam watched the slow movement, mesmerized by his gentleness. "Do you realize that's what I do, day in and day out? There are so many people I haven't been able to help. And some that I have. I can't quit just because I don't always succeed. It's important we just keep trying to save the ones we can."

She glanced up, caught by the strength of his gaze. "I didn't totally quit. I tried again, when several children went missing. I found I couldn't ignore the pleas for help. Not when I thought I could do something."

"Did you help?"

She beamed, a lightness inside, bursting forth. "Yes, I found a little girl that was missing. We saved her in time."

He grinned. "It feels great doesn't it?"

The light inside grew stronger. "Yes." Her smile dimmed and fell away. "Then, when the next child showed up dead, the suspicion fell on me again. It got pretty ugly."

Brandt nodded. He could just imagine. When a ship started to sink, all the rats either bailed or turned on each other.

She grimaced. "There was one cop, in particular. He disliked psychics. I think they all did to some degree or another, but he...he hated me." Picking up her cup of coffee, Sam bathed her face in the warmth drifting upward.

"Is that what you were afraid I'd find out about?"

The corner of her mouth tilted. "Yeah, sort of. If you'd talked to this guy, he'd have told you a whole lot of nothing good."

"To tell you the truth, I think I did talk to him."

Sam's stomach curdled. "Oh." She ran her fingers through the loose curls at her temple, the weight of her braid hot and heavy in the sun.

"Is that a problem?" He leaned forward watching her.

She grimaced. "If I show up dead, look to him first."

Brandt stopped and stared at her – his cup stalled mid-air. "Seriously?"

It was all she could do to meet his eyes. Eventually, taking a deep breath, she said, "We had a difficult last meeting." She ran her fingers across her neck. "As much as he hated me, he believed in my skills. It's just he wanted them solely for his use. I ended up taking off. Yes, running away and hiding from everyone. It was better than letting this asshole control my life. He threatened to kill me if I ever told anyone."

"But he was a cop."

"Deputy, actually. And a drug dealer on the side."

He glanced over the cup at her. "Are you sure?"

She nodded.

"Are you saying he could have been behind the wheel of the truck that tried to run you off the road?"

Her shoulders slumped. "I don't know," she half-wailed. "He hated my guts and..." She stopped talking, unable to tell him the whole story. Tears clogged her eyes, emotion clogged her throat. She couldn't believe that after all this time this deputy still had the power to destroy her. Surely, she'd moved past that. "I disappeared and hoped he'd forget about me."

"But once I called him, then he knew where to find you?"

She nodded again.

His gaze was intent on her face. Sam felt heat rise that had nothing to do with the sun.

He stirred his cup until Sam reached across and stilled his hand. "Go and get a second cup so you have something to stir." Even as she picked up her own cup, relief slowly spread through her limbs. Relief to have someone to share this burden with. Relief that she was no longer alone.

A smile twitched at the corner of his mouth. "Do you want another?"

"No, not if we're heading to Stefan's house soon."

Brandt glanced at his watch. "Let's head out then. We'll talk on the way."

"Great," she muttered.

"You'll be fine. We'll figure this out."

They crossed the street to his truck. He walked to her door and unlocked it before walking around to the driver's side. The small concession to old-fashioned courtesy made her feel good.

Getting into the truck was a different story. Her truck was lower to the ground. His had huge tires and no running boards. Fine for a six-foot male, but she barely crested five-foot-four and struggled to get up to the seats. Flustered, Sam finally managed to shut the door and get settled. A sidelong glance at Brandt's face didn't help. He was trying to hold back a grin.

Sam harrumphed and refused to look at him again.

As they passed the town's welcome sign, she ventured to break the silence. "How long have you known Stefan?"

Brandt glanced at her quickly. "Close to ten years now."

Sam raised her eyebrows at that. "That's quite awhile. Is he your age?"

That question brought a frown to his face. "I don't know how old he is. I'd say he's mid thirties. Then again, he doesn't look a day older now than when I met him."

Older would be better than younger, in this case. Sam could only hope he had decades of experience handling what the psychic life dished out. She needed to talk to someone who'd already figured this stuff out.

Brandt took a left turn off the highway and drove further into the country. Peace surrounded the area. Heavily treed on the left and rolling hills on the right. Stunningly beautiful and something she hadn't expected to see.

"He lives just a couple of miles further."

She nodded. "And he prefers to live away from people, just like I do."

"Yeah." Brandt snorted. "Stefan is different. There's really no other way to describe him."

Pursing her lips, she thought about that. In a way, the same description applied to her too. Better to wait and see just what that meant to Brandt. Maybe it would give her an idea of how he saw her.

***

3:00 pm

Brandt navigated the last turn onto Stefan's twisting driveway. The man had chosen a hell of a spot for a hideaway. Now that Brandt lived closer, he had a chance to visit and not just talk on the phone. Stefan didn't like phones. Then he bordered on antisocial at times.

Brandt regarded Sam's profile. Something was bugging her. In typical Sam style, she sat worrying on something instead of outright asking him.

The house winked at them from between the trees. Brandt drove around to the far side and parked. One side was glass that twinkled like diamond facets in the light. The rest was built of logs – huge logs. Evergreens surrounded the house on three sides. Stunning in colors, the air almost vibrated with an otherworldly appeal. Birds approved as they flitted and dipped between the foliage, chirping happily.

Sam appeared awestruck. Remembering how he'd felt the first time he'd arrived, with the sun bouncing off all the glass, he could fully understand her reaction.

"Ready?" He couldn't wait. Putting these two together in the same room should be interesting. Stefan wasn't the friendliest of males. But all women reacted to Stefan – one way or another. Over time, Brandt had come to understand the type of woman each was, by her reaction.

For that reason alone, he'd wanted to be on hand when Sam met Stefan for the first time. He needed to see Sam's reaction and see into the depths of who she was.

***

3:18 pm

Sam shut the truck door gently. Turning, she tried to take the scene in. She couldn't imagine being the man lucky enough to own such a place.

Brandt, several steps ahead, turned to her, one eyebrow raised. "Coming?

They walked toward the front door. "How long has he lived here?" Sam couldn't help it. Her head swiveled from side to side at the spectacular foliage, and unique wooden carvings peering out amongst the brighter-than-believable plants. The strong scents blended and fused into a fresh woodsy smell. "Everything appears like it's on drugs, for God's sake."

"Or you are." Brandt grinned at her. "He's got plants from all over the globe. Everything about Stefan is unique and indefinable."

"I'll say." Sam stopped at the front door. It was made from one solid block of wood with faces pushing out of the wood grain. Some laughing, some crying, yet all of them glowing with life. "Christ." She didn't know if she was praying or swearing, but there was no way not to react. Everything she'd seen so far came under the heading of stunning. Maybe not comfortable, yet undeniably thought provoking.

"Quite the place he's got, huh?"

"That's an understatement. I can't wait to meet our host."

Sam barely caught Brandt's sidelong glance. She wondered at it as he pounded on the door – stalling any chance of asking.

"Come in." The shout came from deep inside.

Brandt pushed open the door. "Hey Stefan. It's us."

"Yeah, I caught that. Let me just wash up. I'll be right there."

The voice came from the far left. Sam noted that in a distant part of her mind, as she stood in the front foyer, her mouth hanging open. The inside of the house shone with warm yellow sunlight bouncing off wood floors and ceilings. Streaming light struck and highlighted vivid paintings hung on every wall. The room had a surreal energy. The entire house was an artist's canvas.

"Hey Stefan. Good to see you." The two men slapped shoulders. Brandt's large shoulders blocked Sam's view.

Brandt stepped slightly to the side and motioned between the two people. His voice light and easy. "Stefan, meet Sam. Sam, Stefan."

Sam stared at Stefan. Her soul stirred. Overwhelming love and warmth flooded through her.

Stefan gazed into her eyes, his gentle lips curved into a welcoming smile. That same warm loving smile from her vision, that same man from Louise's car accident. Then he opened his arms. Without warning, she burst into tears and ran into them. They closed securely around her.

***

3:20 pm

Brandt's mouth fell open. He didn't know what to think or even how to jumpstart his brain. He was on shocked standby.

He'd never seen a woman react like Sam had. Ever.

Without trying to be too obvious, he tried to assess the clinch they were in. It didn't look lover-like. Neither did they resemble two strangers. He didn't know what the hell was going on. He'd sure like to though.

Interrupting them was out of the question. Whatever was going on was intensely personal. Even standing in the same room was uncomfortable. He walked over to stare out the huge window. The acreage around the house was as wild and impressive as the rest of the property. He heard soft voices behind him. He turned around to see the two smiling in a strangely intimate way.

He took several steps in their direction. "I gather you two know each other?"

They both stared at him in surprise.

Sam's answer stunned him. "What? No, we've never met."

***

3:25 pm

Brandt motioned toward Stefan and then at her. "Is that how you greet all strangers?"

Feeling heat rise on her cheek, Sam glanced over at Stefan, who stared at Brandt, an odd twist to his features. Christ. Stefan was as gorgeous in person as he was in her vision. A charming smile graced the model face. She turned to Brandt. "Oh that."

Brandt made a choked sound. "Yeah that?" He stared between Sam and Stefan. "So an explanation, please."

Sam glanced at Stefan to find him watching her.

"Go ahead."

Sam glanced down at the floor, knowing she was rocking slightly in place. Making a decision, she looked up to find Brandt's suspicious gaze firmly planted – on her. "Remember the car accident that I told you about. Louise Enderby? What I didn't tell you was that I saw a man in that vision. Not the killer, but a man who...at the time...I thought might have been someone close to Louise that had already died. Like her husband, a long-time lover, at least someone like that. He was trying to help me...her...get out of the car and cross over."

She glanced over at Stefan who had a benevolent smile on his face. "The guy left a very strong impression *because* there was so much love in his face. It radiated throughout his energy. He glowed like an angel."

Stefan snorted.

Sam smiled and continued. "I had no way of knowing who he was. Still, it isn't uncommon for a loved one to show up at the time of death to welcome the dying person. Except this guy had an incredible impact on me because he had such loving energy – and it was directed my way."

She gazed into Stefan's eyes. "That man in my vision was Stefan."

Brandt reeled backwards as if from a blow. "What?" He stared at Stefan, searching for confirmation. "Is that possible?"

Sam shrugged. "I don't know how, but it happened."

Stefan stared at them both. "It's a first for me too. I've never come across another psychic in my visions."

Brandt focused on Sam. "You're saying that you recognized Stefan here from your vision. And the emotions from that vision were so strong that when you saw him, you burst into tears and walked into a stranger's arms?" Hands on hips, head titled sideways, he stared at her in disbelief.

Sam knew how important her answer was. It was also important to her that he believe her story. She hated to admit it, but she'd come to enjoy his acceptance and now wanted his respect. "It is hard to understand. You have to consider the circumstances.

"I was caught in a horrible vision inside a burning car and a dying woman. Stefan appeared – yes, I'll say it again – almost angelic in appearance, and he saved me. The emotion that existed at the time was overwhelming. This man cared about Louise. I don't understand that part."

She glanced sidelong at Stefan who was listening casually. "But for me, it was as if he loved me, cared about me, and was trying to save *me*." She implored Brandt to understand. "It was pure instinct to cry when I saw him again. I thought he didn't exist...that he wasn't real. Then suddenly he's here, in front of me." She shrugged. "I just reacted."

Brandt shook his head, his fingers running raggedly through his hair. "Wow."

"Precisely." Sam found little satisfaction in his comment. She hadn't had time to adjust to this scenario either. Questions crowded her mind. She didn't know where to start and her energy levels had dropped alarmingly. "Stefan, can I go and sit down?"

Brandt made a funny sound. She glanced over at him, but he'd already reached her. His arm wrapped around her shoulders. "You look like you're ready to pass out. Come sit down."

Stefan moved ahead of them both. "You two get comfortable, and I'll put on coffee. It looks like we have a lot to talk about."

CHAPTER THIRTEEN

3:45 pm

Stefan walked into his kitchen, happy to escape the emotional energy of the other two. Coffee made for a great excuse.

Sam was an interesting development. As was Brandt's reaction to their meeting. Stefan wouldn't have said she was Brandt's type, but then she didn't fit his own type either – and he found her fascinating. That she'd managed to see and communicate on the etheric field was impressive all over again.

He stayed in the kitchen until the coffee dripped to a full pot. Pouring three cups, he carried them out to the sitting area. "Anyone need cream or sugar?"

"No, black is fine. Thank you." Sam reached for her cup and huddled over it as if needing the warmth.

Stefan considered her for a moment before sitting on a chair between them. He understood power positions and being between these two wouldn't be his normal choice, yet they obviously had issues.

"Sam, are you always cold?"

Both Brandt and Sam turned to stare at him. He allowed a small smile. "Not a trick question, just a simple inquiry."

Sam nodded. "Yes, I am. And that's getting worse with every vision."

"Is there any particular time when you are colder than others?"

Her head cocked to one side and Stefan studied the fleeting expressions washing over her face as she considered his questions. She had no guile, this girl. She was a newborn babe in the world of ageless freaks. He sighed inwardly. She needed a lot from him. Her survival potential, without it, didn't look good.

She was powerful but open. Her energy shone and flashed with no control. Worse, she didn't even seem to know there was such a thing. She bled energy like a hemophiliac bled blood.

She shook her head. "No, I don't think so. I'm cold all the time."

Settling deeper into his chair, Stefan ran a few basic tests. First, he checked her life force. Strong, this girl was a fighter. Next, he checked her aura. Right now, it spat in several directions while being conspicuously reticent about going in Brandt's direction. Interesting. She didn't want Brandt to see too much.

He smiled to himself. While everyone was busy not looking at each other, Stefan took advantage of the uneasy energy and opened his inner eye.

He turned to focus on Sam. And found Sam staring at him. He reared back in surprise. She frowned at him.

"What's the matter?"

Stefan quickly switched to his normal sight to find she still stared at him. Could it be? Could she flip between the two views or did she not know the difference? With a quick glance at Brandt, who hadn't appeared to notice anything, Stefan decided to ask.

"Do you recognize when you are using your inner eye?"

His question seemed to surprise her, only she answered readily enough. "Yes. I use both equally and switch between them easily."

That made sense, given what he'd just seen. It also elevated her skills another notch. This was a very interesting woman. Without any formal training, she'd found her own way. Without anyone to say right or wrong, she'd developed in ways that worked for her. Stefan could count on one hand the number of psychics the world over that could switch their inner vision as simply.

"Brandt has told me something about your visions." He stretched out his legs, crossing them, and with a quick glance at Brandt, he centered on Sam. "Maybe you could explain to me exactly what happens to you."

Sam winced. She stared at her coffee cup. It didn't take long to fill him in. Stefan didn't interrupt her. He waited until she ran down before asking questions.

"So you have no trigger that you know of? You have no awareness outside of the vision when you're in one, and you've been having these particular visions during the night?"

"Right. There have been a couple of other odd insights as well." Quickly, she filled him in on when she thought the killer had been hunting a new victim, and the car accident where she'd seen Stefan.

Stefan considered what he'd heard. "What would you like from me?"

Sam's face became a mix of contradictions. She looked hopeful, confused, and even full of trepidation.

Stefan leaned forward. What did she want?

"I was wondering if you could help me."

Stefan shifted, surprised. That's not what he'd been expecting her to say. "Help? In what way?"

Sam glanced toward Brandt.

Was she gaining strength from his presence, or expecting criticism? Stefan filed her action away to contemplate later. "The visions are extremely violent. My recovery takes quite awhile. I'm wondering..."

"Yes," he encouraged.

"Well." She stopped again, as if gathering her thoughts. Then the words rushed out. "The visions are hard on my system. My blood loss is huge. I was skinny before, now the pounds are falling off. I can hardly sleep." Her stream of chatter slowed down. "I'm scared these visions will kill me," she admitted softly.

Stefan didn't know what to say. She was right to be concerned. "Normally, the psychics with physical manifested visions, don't show the blood loss to a dangerous level – at least not for long."

She didn't seem to hear the last part, for she leaned forward, her eyes intent on his face. "There are others like me?"

"Absolutely. Some people will wake up with blood on their hands and not always know why. In this case, they've had an empathetic episode." He rubbed the side of his temple. "Some people walk in the gray area between life and death and will become comatose depending on how long they stay there. There are some who have died because they couldn't return to their bodies in time."

With a quick glance at Brandt – who sat quietly listening – he refocused on Sam. "I've often discussed with Brandt the number of misdiagnosed patients in mental hospitals who have psychic talents they never knew they had."

Sam did a double take. "Are you serious?"

Brandt nodded. "Unfortunately."

"Control." Sam jumped on that term. "That's what I need to do. I need to learn how to control my talents and to disconnect from the visions. The last time, I managed to keep one foot in both realities, only for the briefest of moments, then I lost it."

"Right. There are several techniques. But it's not going to happen overnight. It will take practice. I can help, but it will take effort on your part."

Sam smiled. "That's fine. The more control, the more I can use my talents to benefit others."

Brandt interjected for the first time. "What do you want to do with them?"

A becoming pink blush that started at her neck, washed upward. Stefan watched Brandt's mesmerized gaze follow the color trail. No doubt about it, he had it bad.

Sam licked her lips and Stefan almost laughed aloud. Brandt looked like he was choking on something.

"I want to be able to help people. Or maybe animals." She told them about the incident with the dog at the hospital. "I don't know yet the best way to help. Partly because I don't know my own abilities and therefore don't know what is possible *to* do. I just know that I don't want to hide, and I don't want to be helpless."

Interesting. "First let's set up time to work on your control. We'll sort out what your talents are, which are strongest, and which need developing. You can go from there."

Both Brandt and Sam nodded.

"That makes good sense." Brandt glanced at his watch. "We're going to need to go soon."

Stefan took note of the color surrounding the two. Their energy danced around each other, close enough to blend, yet staying separate – at least for now.

Long fingers of sunshine touched and warmed the atmosphere. Stefan watched the sunlight dance with their energies.

Sam spoke again, interrupting his musings. "Stefan, can I ask you about the vision where I saw you – what were you doing there with Louise?"

Stefan smiled. "I knew her, years ago before she married. By the time I arrived, it was too late for her. All I could do to help was escort her to the other side."

"Escort?" Brandt's curiosity jumped out. "You mentioned this before."

Sam stared at him. "Crossing to the other side. Death."

Brandt shifted in his seat, one eyebrow raised, listening.

Sam turned back to Stefan. "Was this an unusual occurrence for you?"

Stefan thought about it. "It doesn't happen weekly or even monthly, but if there is a connection on any level, then I usually know what's happening."

"Were you close?" Sam flushed. "I don't mean to be personal, but when I was inside Louise I felt...different."

Intriguing. "I loved her. But she couldn't handle my life."

Sam nodded as if understanding what he meant. Maybe she did.

"What was she thinking about?" He admitted to being curious. He'd never experienced a psychic vision like hers. He studied Sam's face, searching for the truth.

"It's hard to say. My visions are overwhelmed with the physical trauma, though a little of their thoughts mix with mine. I don't remember much of hers, though. We were both more concerned with the car that wouldn't respond, then the crash, the fire...you know." Sam held her hands out. "That's about it until I saw you. Then it was my thoughts. I wasn't sure whom you were talking to – Louise or me." She waited for his answer.

He frowned. "Louise mostly, trying to get her to leave her body. Until the end, when I was talking to you because at that point, you were holding her back."

Understanding dawned in Sam's eyes. "That makes sense now." She cocked her head sideways. "Do you know how she died?"

"She was in a car accident. Her vehicle drove off the highway at Emerson Point."

"You know that?" Brandt shook his head.

"Sure, I could see her memories. One of the last things to happen before death is a rewind of the movie of your life." He glanced at Sam. "Don't you see that part?

She shook her head. "No. Mine are always violent deaths, and they don't have much time." She sat up straight. "Could you see why her car went over the cliff?"

Stefan stared at Sam. She almost vibrated with energy. "No, I came in later. What about you?"

"Only that her brakes weren't working. She pumped them hard." She shrugged. "Then she went off the road."

"What connects you to your visions?"

Sam shifted uneasily. "Usually violence. Lately it's been murder."

Stefan studied her. "You think Louise was murdered?"

"I think so, yes."

He frowned. "Did you connect with the same killer, in her case?"

"I don't know. I think so. It's his energy on the car."

"At the time of her death?

"Just before." Sam rubbed her hands together to warm them up. "No. As we went over the cliff, I thought I saw his signature. Once we crashed and burned, I wasn't looking at anything, but the flames and then you."

"What does that mean to you?" Brandt interjected, sitting on the edge of his seat. "I don't understand this energy signature stuff."

Stefan explained. "When you touch something, it leaves a bit of energy behind."

"This energy can dissipate quickly or hang around, depending on the energy of the person touching it and depending on how long the contact lasted."

Brandt jerked his head, urging them to continue. "That still doesn't mean much to me. Are you saying this guy owned or drove the car? Or did he just work on it for a little bit?"

Both Sam and Stefan shook their heads.

Stefan. "It's not that easy."

"No. I'm not sure I can say very much about his energy in this case. I only saw it long enough to recognize it. For me that means he's responsible for Louise's death." She wrinkled her nose at Brandt. "The how and whys, well, I thought that was your job."

"Except, there's nothing left to investigate. The car burned to a crisp."

***

4:45 pm

Brandt and Sam drove to Parksville in almost total silence. Brandt's mind crowded with all he had to mull over, and he could only imagine what Sam was thinking. She'd set up the first session with Stefan in four days time. In the meantime, she had homework to do.

He, on the other hand, had regular work to do. He turned into the parking lot and pulled up beside her truck. Checking out the report on Louise Enderby was another priority. Stefan couldn't confirm that her brake line had been cut, yet he agreed that it was likely she'd been murdered.

"Are you okay?"

She nodded. "Yes, I'm good. Better than I have been in a long time." She collected her purse. "In fact, I should go home and review everything I've learned." She shifted to leave. "Thanks for taking me."

She opened the door and hopped out. "I'll talk to you later. Thanks again."

He walked around the truck to stand beside her. "Are you hungry? Do you want to go someplace to eat?"

Sam stopped and considered his offer. "You know, I think tonight I'd just like to be alone. My mind's a little overfull and I'd like some time to digest everything."

Brandt nodded. "Maybe another time?"

"Thanks, I'd like that."

Brandt didn't know if he should try to pin her down or not. He could understand her wanting to be alone tonight. He was the one that didn't want to be alone. Still, she'd been through enough for one day. Yet he couldn't leave it like this, he needed more. "I could pick up something and come down to your place tomorrow. If that works for you?"

Sam glanced back at him, startled. "That would be nice. Thank you."

"Good. I'll call you with a time when I see how the day is going." He walked to his truck. "Remember..." he said frowning, "be smart and stay alert. The killer is still trawling for victims."

"How could I forget?" She frowned at him. "I'm the one with the insider knowledge, remember?"

"Speaking of which, let me know if anything new pops up. Okay?"

"Alright."

Sam reversed her truck and pulled out of the parking lot in the direction of her home.

Brandt watched for a few minutes then headed back home. He could retrieve his messages from there just as well as from the office.

The house sounded hollow as he shut the front door behind him. Today was perfect for a cold beer and a medium rare steak – too bad he didn't have either in the house. By the time he'd showered, the coffee had finished dripping and he'd decided on a hefty ham and cheese omelet with hash browns. Easy, doable, and fast.

With a plate of hot steaming food, Brandt clicked on the television. His stomach growled with hunger pangs. He dug in while listening to the local news.

"The police have issued a press release requesting the public's help in identifying the owner of this ring."

The television screen flashed to a sketch of a ring with a four-leaf-clover pattern and missing one stone. Brandt bolted to his feet. "What the hell?"

He circled around the coffee table to get a closer look. There was no doubt about it. It was his sketch. His stomach warred with his nerves. How had the media gotten this picture? The announcer had said something about the police asking for help. The picture must have come from his department. From his office. Only not from him.

Trying to be fair, Brandt ran through those who knew about the ring. Basically everyone. He'd brought it out at the meeting after explaining it could be connected to the killer he was hunting. He'd been trying to identify the owner for Christ's sake.

"God damn it." He paced around the living room, his mind working furiously.

He couldn't believe someone had jumped him on this. Surely, that could only have been the captain – or someone on his team. But why? This wasn't even an official case. Sam's information was a tip, yet that's all it was. The others didn't even believe her. Damn it. This could blow up in the department's face. And put him into hot water. There were few people willing to own up to having a psychic help out. If the information wasn't any good, many people would be up for crucifying the idiots who brought the psychic in. And the psychic.

Jesus, what about Samantha? His heart stopped beating. No. Sanity swept in. No there was no way she could be identified by this. Relief sent his heart racing again. There could be serious repercussions. If Sam were right, and the killer saw this newscast, he'd be seriously wondering how the police knew about it. The killer could just laugh it off, or it might drive him into a killing fury.

There was just no way to know.

***

8:05 pm

The evening news rippled outward to another man enjoying an evening alone in his apartment.

"Life is good." Bill walked to his refrigerator and pulled out a cold beer. Raising the bottle to the sky, he took a long swallow. The television was blaring from the other room. He heard something about the police asking for help and walked to where he could see the broadcast.

"What the hell..." The tall slight man leaned forward, slamming the bottle down on the hewn wooden table beside the

World War II airport model he was building. He stared at the picture on the screen.

No way. No fucking way. How the hell did they know about his ring? He glared at the item still on his left hand. It had been his lucky ring for so long, he'd forgotten he was still wearing it. Pissed, he tore the offending thing off and threw it against the far wall.

Why would anyone be searching for his ring? He wiped his mouth with the back of his hand. What did they know? Could they have connected the ring to his women? No. He thought about it. There's no way anyone could connect the ring to his victims. The cops would be pounding on his door if they were that close. So who else? They couldn't have captured a picture from a camera as he always wore gloves.

Disturbed, he slouched into the couch. The newscaster's voice washed over him in a continuous drone. What had he missed? What could he possibly have forgotten?

God damn it. No, there's no way anyone could know. He'd didn't make mistakes.

In a dour mood, he drank his beer and went over every move he'd recently made. He shook his head, feeling better. He hadn't missed anything.

Unless the last woman had survived.

He shot to his feet, disturbed. Not possible. Surely not. She'd been cold when he'd left her. She had to be dead. Except her death hadn't been reported.

The problem was, anyone could have seen the ring. He'd worn it as long as he could remember. Someone was sure to have noticed it somewhere along the way. He pondered the implications. First, he needed to make sure that woman had indeed died, then he needed to find a similar ring and wear it to fool anyone who may have thought he'd had on the ring the police were asking about. That way when anyone doubled checked, it would seem like they'd made a mistake. And last – he needed to never, ever leave a victim until he was sure she was dead.

***

9:35am, June 19th

Sam finally slept through the night. No nightmares, no visions, just sleep. Stefan's homework had helped. Lying in bed, feeling rested for the first time in several days, she rolled over and curled deeper into her blankets. Relaxation rolled through her.

If it weren't for the animals waiting for her, she wouldn't bother getting out of bed. Then, room service was a little lacking when you lived alone.

Moving easily through her morning routine, Sam made it to the kitchen and fed her canine family before they had a chance to get upset at the wait. Soldier ate then stood at the front door. Sam opened it and stepped out on the deck. He moved stiffly under her watchful gaze as he managed the steps and the few feet to a clump of trees.

While she relaxed with her morning tea, the two dogs started a ruckus. Sam frowned. Soldier's bark was hoarse, almost a cross between a growl and a bark. Like one long unused.

She walked toward the door and heard the vehicle. Instantly, her nerves reacted. She rarely had visitors, but it was only recently that the sound of an approaching vehicle brought out a sense of dread. Her tension eased when she recognized Price Coulson's car.

The rent wasn't due for another couple of weeks and her landlord came about once a month to check up on her.

"Good morning. How are you today?" She opened the door wider to let him in. She did it every time he came and every time, he refused to step inside. A married man in a single woman's house wasn't proper according to his generational rules.

"The wife sent over a loaf of bread and some cookies for you." His face creased into well-worn wrinkles. "Also wanted to make sure you're doing okay."

"Of course, I'm fine." Sam leaned easily against the doorway. God, she was becoming a good liar. How sad was that?

The old man glanced at her, sharp intellect shining beneath the heavy folds of his eyelids. "It's very isolated here. Aren't you worried about intruders?"

Shaking her head, Sam hastened to reassure him. "No. I've always been comfortable living out in the country."

He shoved his gnarled fingers into his jean pockets. "Now that may be, only it's not the same world today as it was a few decades ago. There are some bad people out there."

"There always have been. The communication systems of today are better so we hear about more cases."

"Aye. True enough. Just last night the news said the police were searching for the owner of an odd-looking ring." He turned to look at the calm waters of the lake. "The wife, she said it looked like a devil's ring, what with the snake twisting through a garden."

"A ring?"

"Yeah. You don't have television down here so you wouldn't have heard about it."

Sam went cold inside. "They said the police wanted this guy?"

"Just that they were looking for the owner of the ring so they could talk to him."

Almost numb with the ice that had settled into her limbs, Sam shook her head. "Then it's probably nothing."

He pulled out one hand to run through the white fluff around his ears. "Aye. I told the wife that. But well, she worries."

That was the reason for his visit. The pair of them were concerned about her. Unaccustomed warmth melted through her. This was a new feeling. She savored the sensation. Someone actually cared enough to worry. And he didn't even know her.

She shook her head in bemusement. "Are you sure you won't come in for a cup of tea? You can tell me all about it inside."

Price shook his head. "No, no. I promised Mary that I wouldn't be longer than a few minutes." He twisted, pointing out Soldier. "I didn't know you had a guard dog. Mary will worry less knowing you have him down here."

Sam's lips twitched at the thought. "I don't know how much help he'll be. He's with me because he's recovering from surgery and needed a home to heal and be rehabilitated."

The old man's gaze sharpened. "Is he dangerous?" His wrinkles rearranged downward. "Don't really want something dangerous living here. He's too old to be rehabilitated." He stared at the dog. "A bullet might be kinder all around."

Sam refused to take offence, understanding his old-timer ways. After all, he hadn't said anything different than the vets themselves had expressed. "No, he was mistreated, and then hit by a car. Since he's been with me, he's spent his time healing. I don't think he's dangerous." She couldn't help crossing her fingers. "He'll be a great deterrent for anyone out to cause trouble. I think he's a trained watchdog. At least that's what one policeman told me."

The older man's shoulders relaxed slightly. "That's good then. If the police and vets are involved, then he's probably fine." He nodded as if satisfied. "Mary will be happy to hear this."

A little later, Sam, with cell phone in hand, watched his pickup head up the hill. Dear God. The ring had been on television. Surely, not the same ring? Why would Detective Sutherland do that? What else had the broadcast said? She didn't quite understand how she felt about this development.

"Hello."

"Hi Brandt. This is Sam. Did you release a picture of the ring to the media?"

A hefty pause stretched out over the line. "I didn't, no. One of the members of the department must have. The first I knew about it was when I saw it on television last night."

"The whole point of telling you about the ring was to help — I just hadn't expected to have it released to the media. I guess I'm more surprised than anything." She took a deep breath. "The thing is, I'd really like to keep my name out of this. I've taken care to build a new life here. I don't mind helping, but I'd just as soon do it privately"

"Understood. I'll make sure your name isn't connected. I don't know who contacted the media, but I will find out." His voice came across strong and determined, and that helped reassure her a little more.

Sam rang off and went to get ready for work. A quick brush of her hair and a check to make sure her face was clean, then Sam grabbed her keys and purse and headed for work.

She couldn't quite stop the flutter of nervousness inside. Why had it never crossed her mind that the police might go public with her information? Why had she never once considered the risk that her identity would be exposed?

And why had this realization come when it was too late to change her mind?

CHAPTER FOURTEEN

10:10 am

Brandt stood with his legs apart, shoulders straight and his hands locked behind his back. What the hell? He struggled to keep his mouth shut. He couldn't believe what he was hearing. Captain Johansen had called him into his office and Brandt was getting his ass kicked.

"Sir? If I could just interject for a moment." Brandt tried to interrupt the captain's rant, only the man was steaming. Brandt relaxed slightly, and stuffed his hands into his jean pockets. He eyed the chairs stacked high with papers. An empty chair sat off to the side – one Brandt hadn't been offered.

"Brandt? Brandt, are you listening to me?"

At the first call, Brandt studied the man opposite him. At the second call, he raised an eyebrow. "Are you ready to listen to me?"

"Damn it." Captain Johansen blew hard and rubbed his temple. Reaching for his coffee cup, he glared at Brandt. "Fine. Talk to me. What the hell were you thinking?" The captain's face flushed red as his voice started to rise again.

Brandt held out his hand to slow the man down. "I didn't do it." He enunciated slowly and clearly. "I did not give that picture to the media."

The captain stopped cold. He fixed his hard stare on Brandt. "What?" he growled. "If you didn't then who did?"

"I don't know," Brandt admitted. "I'd planned to ask you that question."

"Why?" demanded Captain Johansen. "I sure as hell don't know. Any ideas? And why wasn't it you?"

Brandt stared at his boss. "I'd prefer to have proof before I say anything."

"Not good enough." Johansen pounded a fist on his desk. "I want to know what you know – and now!"

What could he say? Brandt shrugged his shoulders. "I don't *know* anything, sir. I showed the picture at the debriefing meeting yesterday, so anyone who'd been there knew. As would anyone they might have shown the picture to."

"And yet, a couple of names on the force came to your mind." The captain glared at him, waiting.

Brandt avoided answering. "It's the why that bothers me. If someone wanted to help, you'd think they would have included me in the plan. Which means someone may be out to discredit me instead."

The captain glanced at his desk, a frown furrowing his brows.

Brandt added one other point. "Or the department." He paused for a moment, considering his next words carefully. "I'll tell you this. Kevin doesn't appreciate me having Sam onboard, except he appears to hold the department in high regard. And Dillon barely speaks to me except yesterday he came to talk to me about the ring. If he did this, he may have thought he was doing me a favor." He shrugged again. "In both cases, it could mean nothing."

"Did you give Dillon the picture?"

"He walked into my office with a copy," Brandt clarified. "All I know is I didn't give it to the media."

"Therefore someone else did." Captain Johansen played with his pen, thinking hard. "And because so many people had access to the sketch, anyone could have leaked it."

"I did fax it to two jewelry stores yesterday asking if they recognized the pattern. It's possible the media may have found out from them." The more he thought about it, the more possible that sounded. "Except they said the police were asking for help."

The captain picked up the phone. "Dillon, come into my office please."

Brandt straightened up. "Sir, I'd like to be able to call these jewelry stores before we accuse anyone."

"And so you should, but I want to know what his take is on this mess."

"Then I'd like to leave so he doesn't suspect me of pointing a finger."

Brandt turned and walked to the door. "In fact, it might not be a bad idea to question everyone," he suggested thoughtfully.

"I know how to do my job, thank you."

A knock sounded on the open door.

Brandt turned to see Dillon standing there, waiting. He smiled. "Hey Dillon. Your turn." He nodded at Captain Johansen and walked out. "I'll get to work, if there's nothing else, sir?" Without waiting for a response, Brandt walked out. Feeling like he'd just barely escaped, he headed to his desk.

Once there, Brandt sorted through the sizeable stack of files on his desk and pulled out two. He tried to focus on them, only his thoughts refused to organize. They kept returning to the news broadcast and the person responsible. Who could have done that?

Still, of bigger concern was the case itself. Picking up the phone, he continued to work down his list of jewelry stores.

***

10:30 am

That was close. How the hell had his name come up – and so fast? Self-consciously, he glanced around to see who might be watching. No one appeared to notice as he poured a cup of coffee and walked to his desk. Captain Johansen hadn't known much so maybe he was doing a check on everyone. Dillon grinned. Good thing he had such an honest face.

Besides, what was the big deal? So what if anyone saw the stupid sketch. After all, the whole point was to learn more about the ring. Who cared if the media asked the public for information? It was more or less a problem regarding chain of command. The captain was pissed because he hadn't known about it. Dillon smirked. Damn well time someone shook his goat. The old man was a control freak.

What had the department come to? What a joke. A psychic for God's sake. She was a joke. A pair of anorexic eyeballs. Talk about someone who should have been shown the door the minute she walked in.

He had to admit, there was an opportunity to cement his reputation here. He didn't know what form it would manifest, but he wanted to make the most of it.

Then there was Brandt. As far as anyone knew, he was here only temporarily. Dillon didn't think so. Brandt had plans he was keeping close to his chest. Dillon could respect that. He did the same thing. Yet, he wondered what was brewing. Brandt had managed several private meetings with Captain Johansen.

Plans could involve the psychic. Whatever she had going for her, Brandt seemed interested. And that was just as ludicrous. Unless mercy fucks were this month's good deed. Dillon chuckled. Yet, she had something to offer or Brandt wouldn't waste his time. Dillon quickly pulled a notebook from the left side drawer and wrote some notes on what he'd found out about her so far.

He didn't have much, just bits and pieces of gossip gleaned from hanging around Kevin's team. Adam was a great source, and of course the office grapevine. That had kicked in days ago. In a place like this, it could usually be counted on for accuracy. It was a start. He'd source out her history and all the rest soon. Very soon.

The bottom line? She needed watching.

***

10:35 am

Brandt spent the rest of his day following up leads. He'd put several phone calls out to hospitals and morgues, checking for anyone fitting the right age and sex of a victim that had been brought in with a drug overdose or as a suicide. He'd found one possible – in a coma at Portland General Hospital. Asking the doctors to let him know about any change on that woman at the hospital, he carried on with his phone calls.

The city morgue offered a second possible victim. This one had little to no paperwork at this point, as she'd just been brought in and would still need to be autopsied for cause of death. He asked to be notified as soon as they knew anything.

Brandt frowned. Thanks to Sam, he had a very good idea of a time frame. Sam. He had trouble explaining his interest. She pulled at his heart, his mind, his emotions. He felt a dull pain in areas he didn't know existed. She made him ache for better times, for happiness, for a life filled with joy.

Spending time with her was like a drug. He liked the effect while under, and hated the sensation when it wore off. After his head cleared, he wondered why the hell he kept going back. Except he knew. He'd been intrigued since the beginning. Sex had never been his goal. He'd long since outgrown his adolescent hormones. He certainly wasn't searching for a mate to have the little white house with a picket fence and the customary two-and-a-half kids like so many of his friends.

When attraction slapped him up the side of the head, normally he ran with it. This time, the way forward held a few roadblocks. Still, he didn't think they'd stop him.

Sitting at his computer, Brandt checked his watch. He had a few minutes before his five o'clock appointment at the university.

***

5: 25 pm

The sun dipped behind the mountain, casting golden beams rippling across the lake. Sam tilted her head sideways, wincing as the pounding inside her head increased. The sun's rays twinkled and disappeared under the water. Mother Nature had outdone herself. Exhausted, she lay in numbed limbo. She was still dressed in jeans and t-shirt because she hadn't had enough energy to go for a swim this afternoon.

For someone who preferred her own company, she'd been overwhelmed by people, recently. She had to watch out and keep centered.

Animals offered a respite for her senses. They exuded calm, peaceful energy waves.

People, on the other hand, lived on emotion. They constantly projected erratic bursts of painful energy. The larger bursts from strong emotions hurt her the most. Happier, lighter emotions were easier to tolerate. But when people were angry or upset, overwhelmed in grief or even sometimes when they were ecstatic, they exploded with energy. For Sam, these waves became almost solid walls pounding against her.

Everything impacted much more when she was tired. At those times, on top of lowering her defenses, her own talents increased because her ability to keep them shut down was weaker. Her energy both bled outward and sponged inward.

Working at the vet hospital had allowed her to make gains on her protective shields – in part, due to the animals and their energy. Stefan had given her hints on how to release the energy afterward. She should be euphoric at what she'd accomplished, instead she was too exhausted to feel anything except the headache clawing the inside of her head.

Today had been a tough day. It had taken everything she had to feed her dogs once she arrived home. She'd grabbed a chunk of cheese and an apple and walked to the dock. She'd actually slept in the warm sun after consuming that little bit of food.

A vehicle growl filtered down the hill. Moses raised his head, not growling, yet not totally at ease.

Sam tensed.

In the same half-aware state, she watched as Brandt's truck drove into view. Her heart leaped. She'd forgotten. He was supposed to pick up something and bring it down for dinner.

Sam rolled over to lean on her elbow. Blood pounded in her temple making her grimace. She closed her eyes halfway against the pain. Headaches were the bane of her health problems though she'd never seen a doctor about them. Her lips twitched, imagining trying to explain her issue to a local MD. She'd be referred to a shrink immediately.

Groaning as she stood up, Sam had to stop and breathe deeply as the hammer in her head was put down and a sledgehammer took over. "Oh God," she whispered to the empty air. "I so don't need this right now."

Walking very slowly, Sam made her way up to the cabin.

"Good evening." Brandt walked toward her with a large brown bag.

Sam nodded and immediately wished she hadn't as pain stabbed her right temple. Chinese food? Her stomach gurgled. The apple and cheese hadn't gone far and the food smelled delicious. Now if only the pain would go away.

"Are you alright?"

A wan smile slipped out. "Just a headache. I'll be fine." She eyed the bag he carried. "Is that Chinese food I'm smelling?"

Brandt eyes narrowed as he searched her face. "I found a new restaurant to try. Let's go inside where you can sit down. I'll find some plates and serve." As they walked into the house, he added, "I also have a few pictures to show you."

Interest flared briefly before being pounded down. Sam navigated the stairs and led the way inside. As much as she hated to, she took a painkiller for the headache before collapsing on the couch. She let Brandt deal with the food.

She closed her eyes. Paper rustled, china clanged, and the aroma made her stomach sing. She hoped he picked up her favorite dish – Chicken Chow Mein.

"Sam, sit up and eat. You'll feel better."

She opened her eyes to see Brandt holding out a plateful. She placed it on the table between the two couches. Brandt sat opposite her. He'd heaped her plate high with saucy noodles, chicken, and lovely crisp vegetables. She'd be lucky to eat half of it. The hot steam wafted toward her, both soothing and comforting. She took several bites and moaned with pleasure.

"I love Chinese food. Thank you for this."

He smiled and kept a steady eye on her. "You're welcome." After another quiet moment with only the sounds of food being enjoyed, he asked another question. "Are you sure you're okay? You look a little pale."

Sam nodded gently, her mouth too full to speak. "Yes, sometimes I get these bad headaches." He'd been right, she was feeling slightly better. The headache, although not gone, had receded slightly. To change the subject, she nodded to several pictures upside down on the table. "What are those?"

He flipped the pictures over and spread them out.

Four different pictures of snake and leaf designs lay in front of her. Interesting. She leaned forward to study them.

After a few minutes, Brandt shifted his position. "Well?"

"Hmmm."

"What does that mean?"

Sam looked up at him. "It means they're close, just not the same as the one I saw."

"How can you tell?" Brandt leaned forward pushing the papers closer. "They're all so similar."

She took another bite of noodles.

"Similar but not the same. In the left one, the snake wraps around the outside of a leaf, not a cloverleaf. In the right one, you can't tell if it's a snake or a rope or something similar."

Brandt, shaking his head, collected the pictures together.

At her nod, he stacked the pictures into a pile. "Have you had any more visions or seen anything else?"

"No, nothing yet."

They continued to eat in contemplative silence for a few more minutes. The corners of Sam's mouth slid downward and her eyes closed. God, she was tired. She put down her half-full plate.

"Are you sure you can't eat a little more?"

She shook her head without opening her eyes. "Sorry, it's my headache. Let me just close my eyes for a few minutes."

"No problem. Lie down and rest. I'll clean up."

Sam was past arguing. With a warm full tummy, fatigue drew her in, and she slept.

CHAPTER FIFTEEN

10:05 pm

With the dishes washed, Brandt sat on the couch opposite Sam. Now what? Should he leave her alone to sleep? Odd to be so unsure. Staring at her, he had to admit, the idea of staying and watching over her was winning. He glanced at the pile of blankets on the floor. Picking one up, he opened it and covered Sam.

There was something wild about her. Not necessarily in a good way. Maybe untamed was a better description. She appeared awkward in crowds, uneasy in close confines, and hated confrontations – she wouldn't walk away from a fight if she thought it mattered. She could hold her own.

She was trying to improve her life now, but what had brought her so low? Had it been the last incident with the deputy? He frowned. Had that car accident long ago wiped out her savings or had she been unable to work afterwards because of her injuries? He surveyed the small room. He doubted she'd had insurance. There was no sign of money here. In fact, poverty had moved right in. She dressed in oversized thrift store clothes that would fit any large man.

She needed a keeper. Someone to make sure she ate and rested. If there was no one else, then maybe, just maybe the job fell to him. That he'd even had that thought showed how far he'd come. A few weeks ago, he'd have run at the thought of caring for someone like her. This was stupid. He needed a decent night's sleep himself. He should be home in his own bed, not here keeping an eye on her. Still, it was early yet, and she'd looked wiped when he'd arrived. Staying awhile wouldn't be a hardship.

Moses slept on the floor in front of Sam and Soldier sat on guard at the end of the other couch – watching him.

Brandt peered into the blackness outside the window. Moments later he closed his eyes, too tired himself to muddle through the confusing array of reasons for staying there.

An odd muffled noise woke him.

Brandt turned his head, groaning as pain exploded through his neck. "God, what did I do?" Rolling his head from side to side, he leaned forward, trying to remember where he was. A muffled cry from the couch had him bolting upright, now wide-awake.

Sam jerked her legs out straight and arched her back. Her mouth opened, the muscles on her face and neck clenched into long cords, straining with effort. She screamed – silently.

The hairs on Brandt's neck stood straight up.

Sam jerked, her back bowed even tighter.

Brandt reached out to wake her from the nightmare, then hesitated, his hands inches from her shoulder. How many times had Stefan told him not to touch someone in a trance? But how did he know whether she was in a trance or a nightmare?

Sam collapsed, her legs sprawling at awkward angels. Her breathing stabilized, returning to a more even pace, slowly picking up a normal rhythm again.

Just when he thought she was fine, Sam's face twisted, her eyes opened wide with an opaque glassy look. Brandt bent over and stared directly into her eyes.

"Sam," he whispered. "Sam, wake up."

Sam arched again, then jerked spasmodically as if struck by invisible blows.

Jesus. Brandt backed up a step and stared at her. Ice raced through his body. What the hell was going on? He searched her face, watching every nuance, every tiny expression – it was easy to see she wasn't really here. She was seeing something, experiencing something that Brandt couldn't. Brandt had never seen any nightmare like this one. He wasn't sure he'd ever want to, either.

He glanced at his watch. 2:30 am. He must have fallen asleep. He could have sworn he'd been out for only a couple of minutes.

Sam made a gurgling sound, arched once, then twice before collapsing into a shuddering tremble. Then she fell silent. Brandt stared in horror. Cuts appeared in the blanket. He reached out, the raspy wool scratched his fingers. When he'd covered her up, the blanket had been tatty but whole. He couldn't see it completely from the awkward way it lay over her, but he could see several slices in the thick fabric.

His jaw dropped. More cuts appeared even as he watched. He leaned forward, shock making his hands tremble. This could not be happening. This was not possible. His rational mind knew that, yet his eyes wouldn't stop receiving the images. There, another cut over her abdomen appeared. No way. He leaned closer and sat again as bile rose up into his throat.

Blood seeped slowly from the last cut. Impossible. Brandt sat in horror as blood slowly oozed from the dozen cuts, soaking the blanket covering Sam. Was she hurt? She couldn't be – the cuts had just appeared. Only there was nothing there that had caused the injuries.

Soldier arrived at the couch, a high whine sounding from deep inside him.

"Easy boy. I don't know what's going on either."

Brandt studied his hands, not surprised to see them shaking, shudders even now moving up his arms. Christ, no one would believe this. Hell, he could hardly believe it himself – and it was happening right before his eyes.

His gaze dropped to a second blanket on the floor. Reaching down, he shook the folds loose and went to fling it across her form, when Stefan's warning drilled through her. *Never touch a medium when they are in a trance.*

The blanket dropped to the floor. He didn't know if a blanket counted as a touch and decided he didn't dare take the chance. A sudden thought jolted him. No one would believe him, just like no one believed Sam. Oh God. His stomach knotted and bile seared his throat, threatening to make him sick. Is this how she felt?

He watched in fascination as the blood dripped and ran to pool on top of the blankets beside her. Her face paled to a milky white, making his nerves jump again. Shit. He wanted to call for an ambulance. But what could he tell them? He knew logically there was no rational explanation. And he could be killing her by leaving her alone to bleed. Shit. Doubt paralyzed him.

Soldier stuck his nose closer to Sam, sniffing the blood. He whimpered.

Brandt grabbed his cell phone. Stefan, Goddamn it, please be home.

"Hello?" A thick sleep-filled voice growled at him.

"Oh thank God. Stefan, this is Brandt."

"Brandt." A thick throat-clearing cough bounced through the phone. "What's the matter?"

"It's Sam."

"Sam? What's wrong?" His voice turned businesslike.

"I'm in trouble."

"What else is new?"

"No, I'm here with her now and she appears to be caught in a vision."

"And?"

"Stefan. I've seen a lot of things in my life, but I've never come across anything like this. It's happening right now." Brandt took a deep breath and willed some stability into his voice. "There are cuts appearing in the blanket that's covering her and there's blood. Oh my God, there's so much blood. It's dripping on the floor." Brandt drew a shaky breath. "There's no weapon, or anyone, just the slashes without reason."

"But she's still in the vision?"

"That's what I'm saying. It's like she's experiencing someone else's attack. As I'm watching, she arches and reacts as if being stabbed, then slashes appear in the blankets around her. Within seconds, blood appears and drips to the floor. Christ, Stefan." Brandt bent, dipping his fingers in a pool of blood. He rubbed his fingers together. "The blood is real. It smells real, and it feels real."

There was silence for a moment.

"How can she survive something like this?" Brandt needed Stefan's reassurance. That it wasn't forthcoming, made him more nervous.

"Is she breathing?"

Brandt, his heart racing at the thought, bent over Sam. "Christ, she'd better be." He checked her chest for the telltale rise and fall movement. There. Ever so faint. He placed his hand to hover above her mouth. Yes. A faint waft of air. "Yes, she's alive. But not by much."

"That's okay. The deeper her trance, the more her body vitals slow down."

Brandt checked her over again. The blood had settled in, staining the gray material to rust. The smell flared his nostrils – the same metallic odour he knew all too well.

"Can you see any damage to her body, or are we just talking blankets and blood showing?"

"Is it safe to touch her? Hell, Stefan, how many times have you pounded it into me not to touch you when you're in a trance?"

"Lift the blankets and don't touch her body."

"Why is it I can't touch her again?" Brandt stared at Sam, trying to figure out a safe corner of the blanket to lift without touching her body.

"You'll snap her connection to whatever energy she's attached to. She could stay over there, snap back here, or get caught somewhere in between."

Brandt winced. "Right." Working carefully, he shifted a corner of the blanket away from her shoulder to peer at her slight body below. A slice deep into her abdomen made his gut clench. He groaned softly, sadly. She was dying, and he'd done nothing to help her.

"Christ, her abdomen is split open."

Stefan's voice remained calm and patient. "That's fine. Is she still experiencing new injuries?"

"That's fine! What the hell, Stefan? She's dying."

"No, she's not. In about twenty minutes, she should be almost as good as new. Check again. Are new injuries still appearing?"

Brandt stared at Sam, trying to check all of her at once. After a moment, he answered, "I don't think so. I think that part is over."

"Good, the blood should stop seeping too."

"It will?" Brandt studied the welling blood. Relief washed over him. "Actually, it appears to be slowing."

"Good. She should wake up soon."

"Should? I need her to wake up now!"

"Don't touch her." Stefan's voice was sharp, leaving no room for arguing. "When she wakes, she could be groggy, disoriented, and possibly scared. Give her both time and space. Try not to startle her, just watch as she recovers."

"Right. I guess that makes sense." Brandt moved over and sat across from Sam. "I'll call you in the morning. Or in a few minutes if she doesn't wake up."

"She'll wake up. Trust a little more." Stefan hung up.

Brandt tucked away his cell phone, Stefan's final words ringing in his ears – time to recover and heal. The heal part blew him away. If she experienced the same physical damage as these woman, then no wonder she looked like she could use a good square meal. Her body had to burn calories at a horrific rate doing something like this.

Sam stirred. Brandt rushed over to her side. She rolled her head from one side to the next before coming to a stop. A deep heavy sigh worked its way up from her chest. She opened her eyes, ones that widened in shock when they landed on him.

"It's okay Sam. It's just me. Take it easy. Take your time."

Understanding seeped into those beautiful eyes before she closed them again, drifting off into a light resting state. She licked her lips and whispered in a voice so low he had to bend to her lips to hear it. "I'll be fine in a couple of minutes."

Soldier whined and flumped down at her feet protectively.

Brandt ran a hand through his hair, relieved to hear her talking, but having trouble with the concept that she'd could be okay that fast. Was that possible? He wouldn't be – how could she? He watched her carefully. Could she recover from something like this on her own – without a doctor? How? Did Stefan go through this as well?

In amazement, Brandt watched as the blood thinned and actually appeared to be less. He leaned forward. The droplets on the floor remained. The slices in the blankets remained. What about her? Getting up, he gently lifted the corner of the blanket and checked her abdomen. Even as he watched, the wound shrunk down. It was only a couple of inches long now. He shook his head. He'd never have believed it. And he was open-minded about this stuff. He couldn't imagine Kevin's reaction.

"Brandt?"

"I'm here, Sam. Take it easy."

"I'm almost there. Just another minute and I'll be good."

"Right. Like I'm going to believe that." He snorted and sat on the coffee table across from her, accidentally nudging Soldier who lay protectively in front of Sam.

Soldier lifted his head, his lip curling at Brandt.

Brandt glared down at him. Soldier glared back.

"No, I'm almost there. Wait, let me check." She lifted her head to look at him. And cried out in agony, her body curling into itself.

Instantly Brandt was at her side. "Jesus, Sam. What the hell?"

Sam gasped for breath her face slowly gaining color with the effort. "It's okay. Honest."

Frustrated, he fisted his hands on his hips. "How? How can this be okay?"

He crouched down beside her, reaching out a hesitant hand. He desperately wanted to give comfort, yet was scared of hurting her further.

She opened her eyes to stare at him again.

"Oh God, Sam." Brandt breathed her name almost in prayer. The depth of her suffering and pain hurt his soul. Her eyes had gone black from her agony.

Helpless, he could only watch. "I'm so sorry, honey. What can I do to help?"

A tiny smile peeped out. "Wait."

He didn't think he could do it. "Sweetheart, there is blood everywhere."

The smile disappeared as she shuddered once, then twice. "Always is."

Brandt sank into a crouch beside the couch. "God, how can you do this – day in and day out?"

Her answer, so succinct and so honest blew him away. "Easy. I have no choice."

***

3:48 am, June 20th

Sam found the shift through transition harder this time. Having someone watch while she healed and returned to normal reality wasn't exactly fun. Self-conscious or not, she couldn't move before it was time. Shifting her glance to catch Brandt's expression, she winced and stared up at the ceiling. Barely concealed horror still rippled across his face.

She closed her eyes. She couldn't help him deal with this. It took everything she had to deal with it herself.

The research she'd done said that blood rarely manifested in visions. But in special cases, people woke up with their hands or bodies stained with the stuff. For her, the blood appeared wherever the injuries manifested, but less blood than if she'd truly been the one attacked. Apparently, the amount of physical manifestations should decrease as she learned to control her gifts. She could only hope.

Gently, Sam swung her legs over the side of her couch and sat up. Feeling dizzy, she took several shuddering breaths before fixing her gaze on Brandt.

Wild eyes stared back at her. She couldn't blame him. This stuff came straight out of a horror movie. She wanted to curl up and hide in shame. She'd hoped he'd never see her like this. Never see her so exposed, so...freakish. She could only imagine what he thought of her now.

A few last tremors worked up her spine. It was almost over. Her eyes still burned, swollen and dry. Even her bones ached.

She focused on Brandt instead of the pain. His rumpled hair looked adorable – at total odds to his eyes. She glanced at the clock, yawning at the same time. It was close to four in the morning. He must have stayed all night.

She slid her gaze over him again. He still appeared shell-shocked. It said much about his perception. He'd never be able to accept this part of her. The pain from her vision was nothing to the sudden pain in her heart.

Brandt sat down suddenly. She studied his features. In truth, it looked like his belief system, his very foundation of existence had been ripped out from under him.

Sam couldn't handle any more. Tears of shame burned. Freak.

"Christ." Brandt's whispered words were a soft prayer for understanding.

Sam knew how he felt. She also knew her prayers had never been answered. "What's the matter?"

He snorted, rose, and reached to poke a finger through one of the many slices in the blanket covering her. "This is what's the matter." He stuck his fingers through a bigger cut and waggled them.

Confused, Sam watched emotions whisper across his face.

He stared at her. "Does this mean...?"

Her bottom lip wobbled and she nodded. "It means another woman has been murdered."

Hearing her own words broke the dam holding back the anguish in Sam's soul. Brandt sat on the couch and tugged her into his arms. Sam went. Hurt, she curled into his chest and let her tears pour. Brandt rocked her gently, her broken sobs so soft they could hardly be heard. The pain behind them could hardly be ignored.

Brandt hugged her tight.

After the worst of the storm had passed, Sam thought she heard him speak.

She shifted slightly to peer up at him, wiping away the tears on her cheeks. "What?"

"I'm sorry to have to do this. I need to ask you some questions while this is all fresh." His gaze glanced off the blanket. He shook his head in a daze. "About the victim, not so much the process – which I admit to having some trouble with." As his hand continued to stroke her sore muscles, he became lost in thought. After a moment, he tugged her close for a quick hug before setting her back slightly.

Holding back a few stray sniffles, Sam shifted into a more comfortable position and let herself relax slightly.

"What happened was in real time." Tears welled again. Sam struggled for control, using her sleeve to wipe her eyes. "The slashes you saw appear on the blanket and on my body were the same injuries the victim received. The blood and cuts to the blankets correlate to the victim's injuries."

Brandt started.

"Are you saying that you are stabbed every time the victim is stabbed?"

The tears slid from the corners of her eyes. "Yes." Her voice was barely more than a whisper.

"No." Brandt shook his head. "No one could survive those injuries. They can't be happening to you, because..." Brandt shifted enough to remove the blanket. "Because you're fine. You'd be dead if that had happened to you. Like those women are dead."

Teary eyed, and tormented by the poor woman's fate, Sam nodded. "You still don't understand." She sniffled, rubbing her eyes with the sleeve of her sweater. Recovery might have taken a while longer tonight, it had also taken all of her energy. She was exhausted.

Sam locked her gaze onto his. "In a way, I am exactly like those other women." A quiver ran down her spine, shaking her entire body. Wrapping her arms around her chest, she took a deep breath.

"As each woman dies...so do I – I die every time."

***

10:10 am

"So what are you going to do about it?" The colonel shifted further out of the sun, the buckles on his ever-present suspenders glinting in the bright light. He hooked his cane onto the arm of the overstuffed easy chair as he sat down. He glanced over at Maisy again. "Well, you said it. Enough is enough." He grinned at her sour face. "So what are you prepared to do? The boy is full grown."

"Pshhh." Maisy snorted delicately. "Grown he might be, know his own mind, he doesn't."

The colonel grinned at her. "Oh, he knows his mind. It's just not the mind you want him to have. You don't like that he's choosing to live his life the way he wants to." He reached for his cup of tea. "Admit it. You want him to do it your way."

"Behave yourself, or you can go somewhere else for your tea." She harrumphed and busied herself straightening her sunflower yellow skirts.

The colonel chuckled and relaxed further into his chair.

"The boy should be married and have a family by now. That's all I'm saying." She tilted her face more into the sun. The heat from the sun's rays was wonderfully strong for this hour of the morning. It did her old bones good to soak up the healing rays. "Besides, I like this one."

"Which one?"

"You know perfectly well which one. The skinny one that's all eyes."

"I don't think they're really going out. That boy wouldn't recognize staying power even when it's there right under his nose. He's after other qualities." The colonel waggled his thick white eyebrows at her.

"He's a normal male." Maisy grinned at the colonel. "He probably doesn't even know what staying power is."

"Too bad. A girl like that – well she's a keeper."

"She looks like she's survived hell on earth."

The two sat in comfort, enjoying the simple things of life that had taken them decades to appreciate.

The colonel spoke up again. "Did you hear about that case the police are working on?"

Maisy glanced at him. "Which one?"

He waved his hand at the television. "The one they talked about last night. The police are trying to identify the owner of a ring with a four-leaf clover pattern and some sort of snake wrapped through the leaves. Apparently, one diamond is missing from the ring. They didn't specify why they were looking for the information, though."

Pursing her lips, Maisy thought about the many jewelry pieces she'd seen over the years. None had been in that pattern that she could remember. She loved jewelry, particularly unique pieces.

"Can't say that I've seen anything like that – at least not recently."

"When are they coming for lunch?"

Maisy recognized the sly twist to the colonel's face. "Meaning you don't give a damn about seeing him, you'd like to know more about the cases he's working on."

The colonel scrunched his shoulders like a young child who'd been caught with his hand in a cookie jar. "Call him. We need something new to talk about here." He stared at the blank television. "I'm pretty sure I saw that ring somewhere. I just can't remember where."

"Really? That's so exciting."

He harrumphed at her. "It's only exciting if I can remember where. My memory isn't that good."

Maisy smiled. "Isn't that the truth?" She surveyed the courtyard and the other seniors taking the time to enjoy the morning sun. Life was peaceful here – too peaceful. Stimulation was hard to come by and her son's career was the source of much of it. Still, it was a good excuse to get him over where she could work on him a little more. Besides, she shouldn't need an excuse. He was her son. She reached for the phone, ignoring the low chuckles from the colonel. "Brandt, good morning." She smiled at his sleepy voice. Poor guy, he didn't get enough sleep. "I wanted to catch you before you went to work this morning and got all caught up in your cases."

He mumbled something in response.

Maisy wasn't fazed. He was always like that. "The colonel and I have been talking. He saw that bit of news on the TV about a ring the other night. It triggered something for him."

"What does he remember?"

"That's the thing, he can't quite remember and he's getting really upset about it." She sniffled. Then she frowned. What was that?

Brandt cleared his throat. "We don't want him doing that. He'll remember better when he's calm anyway."

"Well, I know that. But try telling him that." Maisy caught a second sniffle halfway. She glared at the grinning colonel. "I'm really worried about him, Brandt."

"Tell him to relax about it, and if he remembers anything to give me a call. I won't be able to stop by today."

"I will." She hesitated. "Brandt, don't forget to bring Sam by for lunch one day soon."

"I know. It won't likely be this week though. Things are busy at work."

Voices sounded in the background. Maisy widened her eyes. "Brandt, where are you?"

Silence.

"Why?" He cleared his throat.

Another voice came through the phone, faintly recognizable. Maisy strained her hearing. Something about tea. Brandt and tea? She gasped. "Brandt, you're with Sam!" She squealed in joy.

Brandt groaned, "Ouch, my ears. And it's not what you think, Mom."

Maisy bounced on her chair. "I'm sure it isn't, honey." She grinned at the colonel, her thumb in the air. "When are you bringing her for lunch?"

"Not today."

The colonel poked Maisy. "Tell him I want some advice."

She glanced over, frowning at him. But the colonel kept nodding his head. She shrugged. "Brandt, I don't know if this changes anything, the colonel says he wants your advice on something. You know how he is. He'll worry himself into another heart attack until he gets the information he needs."

The colonel blustered at her side. She grinned unrepentantly.

"Okay, I'll try to stop by later today – alone. If I can't, I'll give him a call tonight or tomorrow morning. I can't promise any more than that."

"Oh, that's wonderful dear. We both appreciate you making the effort."

"I said 'try.' I may not make it."

She smirked at the colonel, her cohort in fun. "No, no honey...we understand. Your job has to come first over things like this. That's fine. It would be nice if you brought Sam though."

After saying good-bye, Maisy hung up the phone and turned to grin at her companion. "He said he'll try to get here later this afternoon, or he'll call you later today." She leaned forward slightly as she squeezed the phone to her chest. "He spent the night with Sam."

The colonel nodded. "Good. We should have a few hours to ourselves too."

She plumped her blue white hair and smiled teasingly. "What did you have in mind?"

CHAPTER SIXTEEN

8:25 am, June 21

Brandt found his mind wandering. After what he'd witnessed last night, it amazed him that he could function at all. Sam had been fully recovered this morning. He checked his email, hoping for leads of some kind. He needed progress. He already knew that the stone found in the bedroom of the one victim was a diamond. So, the news broadcaster had gotten it right. The police had nothing to go on – no semen or DNA was ever present. The cold cases he'd collected under his project were similar in that they also lacked forensic evidence. That alone made him wonder if Sam's killer could be the same man he was chasing.

It also reminded him that, according to Sam, another woman lay dead, waiting to be found. It could be days before this one was called in.

He tossed his pen on his desk and glared at the stack of papers waiting his attention. Maybe he should go and talk to the colonel instead. See if he could shake some details loose.

Shutting down the multiple open tabs on paranormal research on his desktop, he rubbed the bridge of his nose. He'd hardly slept. He'd stayed and tried to doze on Sam's couch until it was time to leave for the office. Now fatigue made it hard for him to focus.

His cell phone rang, pulling him out of his reverie.

"Hello." Brandt leaned forward, reaching for a notepad and the pen. At the familiar voice, he closed his eyes and sighed heavily. "Hey Stefan, glad to hear from you."

The thin voice on the other end sounded tired but well. "How is she?"

"She's fine. Better than I am." That was an understatement.

"Of course, she took a totally normal trip into the psychic world, and you've just blown your mind. Figures."

"I find I'm searching for an explanation today. What I saw last night, I'm doubting now in the morning."

"Also normal." Stefan sighed. "Your rational mind refuses to accept what your heart already knows."

"And what do I do about it?"

Stefan laughed. "You ignore it. You saw what you saw — now let it go." The irony in his voice was hard to miss. "If you stay with her, it won't be the last time you get to experience something on the wild side.

Brandt's mouth widened. "It's been a little nuts already, I have to admit."

"She's an interesting woman."

"Is that all you can say? Interesting?"

"Absolutely." A heavy, amused pause filled the air. "What would you call her?"

Brandt shifted uncomfortably on the computer chair. He didn't know what to call her at this point. Unfortunately, his friend had insider knowledge that gave him an advantage. Brandt winced, knowing what was coming.

Warm laughter filled the air. "You haven't figured it out, have you? Any woman that can twist you up like this, is...well, definitely interesting."

"Stefan," he started hesitantly. "I was way out of my element last night. She scared the hell out of me."

Stefan paused. "I have never met anyone with these abilities, so it's new for me, too. To have the cuts and the blood is an interesting twist."

Wrinkles appeared in Brandt's forehead with his confusion. "Why?"

"There is probably less than one person in ten million with her abilities. Maybe even one in a billion. Because of that, we don't know much about them. She has more than one gift, by the way. She's incredibly talented. As she learns control, these physical symptoms may change. Could disappear entirely."

Brandt shook his head. "Well, the whole thing left quite an impression."

"Does it change the way you view her?" Stefan's voice reeked with curiosity but not surprise.

Brandt shifted uncomfortably. "I'd like to say no, but I'm not sure that I can."

Heavy silence filled the phone line.

"Take some time and think about this. Particularly take some time to think about this from Sam's point of view."

"I know." Brandt rubbed a hand down her face. "God, her life must be hell."

"That's probably all she has known. Consider the amount of in-depth knowledge she's gleaned about the dark side of humanity. Take into account the amount of disbelief and mockery she's faced, and then consider how different she is from others. None of that is going to bring her hugs in this world. Kicks, however, are free."

Stefan was right. "She's spent some time in a psych ward. Just under four months."

Stefan's voice was tinged with weariness. "Haven't we all. It's society's answer for the unknown. If she is fully functioning at this stage of her life, she's learned to adapt, to cope, and to hide. All three are required to survive."

"And she's all alone."

"Easy to understand, isn't it? You're wondering why you haven't high-tailed it for the hills yourself."

Brandt couldn't argue that point. He didn't know what the hell he felt about Sam now. She required a little more acceptance and understanding than he had yet to be asked for in a relationship. He was sure he could give that – eventually, should he choose. That was the problem – he just hadn't worked it out in his head yet.

Stefan read his mind. "If you care at all, watch what you say and do right now. She's spent a lifetime under suspicion and receiving disapproval. If you want to be accepted by her, she needs to know that you can handle her gifts." Stefan coughed a couple of times. "If you decide that you can't handle them then don't let her know right away. The worst thing you can do today is to walk away. You'd be reinforcing what she's had a lifetime to learn – she's unacceptable in the eyes of the rest of the world."

"But that's not true," Brandt protested.

"Maybe not, but you'd have a hard time convincing her of that." Stefan tried again. "Look to her history. It's all there. Fear, distrust, hatred even. There's no acceptance handed out for people like her and me."

"You're different."

"No. No, I'm not. It took you time to trust me as it took me time to trust you. This is the same position you're in with Sam – learning to trust. Remember – it takes time."

Brandt was silent. "Can someone really live a life like hers?"

"She is." Bald and clear, there was no arguing with the logic.

"What if I can't?" There it was – the secret fear. The fear that had kept him awake all night as he lay on his couch as she lay opposite on hers. That sat stewing in his mind all morning, keeping him from focusing on his job. What if he couldn't accept Sam, couldn't accept the life she led?

Stefan's heavy sigh came through the phone. "If you can't, you can't. It would surprise me though. I've certainly pushed the envelope of your beliefs – so what's different this time?"

"This time I find I'm searching for an anchor, a point of reference. Something to help me place what I witnessed into my belief system, my reality."

"That is exactly how you felt the first time I spoke to you about a killer on one of your cases. I even told you something similar at the time."

Brandt vaguely remembered that time in his life. "Was I that bad?"

"Absolutely. You might also remember something you've said to me in the past. You told me that you'd never married because you couldn't see anyone accepting your life. Now you're thinking about rejecting her because you can't accept *her* life."

"I'm not rejecting her..." And he wasn't. He was rejecting her gift. God he was an ass. But Stefan continued to talk.

"Good. Think about this. See how you feel about it all tomorrow. Call me if you need to talk."

Stefan hung up after that, leaving Brandt alone with his thoughts. Brandt had seen a lot of things in his life. Police work often demanded finding a way through lies and deceit to arrive at the truth. In this case, the truth stared him in the face. He could no longer doubt what he'd seen. It had just taken some time to accept. That something impossible, something that broke all the laws of life as he knew them – had happened – whether he like it or not.

***

8:45 am

Not working a normal nine to five, Monday to Friday job made for a great week, but damn it, she hated to work on weekends.

Peering into the mirror, Sam curled her lip. It's a good thing Brandt had left early this morning. She resembled the homeless woman everyone thought she was. Her hair hung lank around her shoulders. If there were any highlights then they were hidden in the shadows. Pulling a brush through hair she didn't have time to wash, she ran.

She was ten minutes late.

Two other staff members worked at opening the front office while Sam started feeding the animals. It must have been a busy day yesterday. There were several new animals and Sam's heart bled for each and every one. It took hours to make them comfortable. The hospital was short-handed. Twice, she was called away to help the front staff, once with an unruly canine, and the second time with a tomcat that wasn't interested in having his wayward ways changed.

Working with the animals out front, helped Sam to see other aspects of the business. Working with the injured animals in the cages gave her a lopsided view. She loved seeing them before they ended up in her care.

"Good morning, Sam."

Lost in thought, she spun around, almost falling to the floor from her crouching position. "Good morning, Dr. Wascott."

"How is Soldier doing?"

A big grin split her face. The vet stopped, a stunned expression emblazoned on his normally peaceful face.

"Soldier is doing wonderfully. He's walking around more and slowly gaining strength. He had his last medicine this morning, and he should be fine now."

The doctor moved his head from side to side. "Honestly, Sam, I don't think I've ever seen you this happy. I'm glad the dog is bringing some life into your world."

Heat bloomed on her cheeks as she realized she'd been babbling. "Sorry," she muttered.

The older man sported a boyish grin. "No problem. It's quite a nice change, actually."

Still, she couldn't help a sheepish grin, feeling a little more of her normal reserve drop off. She felt more comfortable with him than she ever had before.

"There's a phone call for you, Dr. Wascott." One of the vet assistants walked into the room, smiling. "Good morning, Samantha. How are you today?"

Feeling unnaturally peaceful, Sam nodded to the other woman. "I'm fine, thank you."

"Good. There's fresh bread, a new grainy recipe from the corner bakery, in the lunchroom. Lucy also brought in some fresh creamed honey. Make sure you have some before your shift is over."

The idea of fresh baked bread made her mouth water. "Thanks, I'd like to try it."

"You're done now. There's a fresh pot of tea in there, too. Go enjoy." Dr. Wascott nudged Sam's arm before walking out of the room.

The treat sounded too irresistible to ignore.

Sam slipped into the lunchroom, slightly disappointed to find it empty. With a frown, she considered that. How long had it been since she'd relished company?

The bread smelled luscious. A fresh yeasty aroma wafted free as Sam cut of a thick slice. An open canning jar full of creamy honey sat on the counter. In the light, the honey had a deep opaque milkiness to it. Opening the lid, Sam sniffed the contents. Using the tip of her knife, she tasted a small bit and rolled her eyes as the flavor exploded on her tongue. Oh my God, that was so good. Quickly, Sam slathered the top of her bread with a thick layer before sitting at the small table with her tea.

"It's good, isn't it?

Sam started in surprise, so lost in the snack she hadn't heard anyone enter. With her mouth full, she could only nod.

Lucy grinned, cutting herself a slice.

Afterwards, Sam headed to the library for more research books. From there, it was a quick hop over to the grocery store for a couple of items.

She stood in line, waiting to pay for her purchase. She should have come here earlier and avoided the rush. Crowds gave her a headache. She reached up to rub her temple when she felt it.

A long finger of evil reached out and brushed her soul.

The grocery store disappeared, the line of people morphed into a small tidy room. The smell of medicine and aftershave assailed her nose. A gruff cough poured from her chest. Sam bent to rub her sore leg, surprised to see a cane in her right hand and plaid slippers on her feet.

Her hand went to her chest as she shuffled over to an easy chair, stiff movements jarring her spine with each step. Evil surrounded her – *him*. Only she didn't think he knew about it.

"Hey, old man?"

The male body she inhabited jerked in surprise, turning somewhat awkwardly. The other man had a huge old lady's hat with flowers…and Christ, something that resembled a bird on top. A silk paisley scarf wrapped around the lower portion of his face, obscuring all, but his dark voracious eyes. Sam's stomach dropped. She knew that gaze. She wanted to close her eyes but they weren't her own. She wanted to jump free, but she was tied to this soul.

"Who are you and what are you doing in my room?"

"Just taking care of details. The mark of a professional is in giving every detail the same level of attention – no matter how small." The voice was muffled and rasping. Sam knew she wouldn't be able to identify it in real time.

"What do you want?" the old man asked querulously. "Get out of my room." Sam wanted to run from the room, to force the old man to move toward the door. She had no control over his limbs or tongue. She could only watch, paralyzed with horror, knowing what was to come. She tried to catalogue the details for later.

"Oh, I'm leaving, colonel. But I'll be back – you on the other hand, won't be."

Pain exploded at the crown of Sam's head, colors danced, blinding her. She groaned. The carpet rushed up to meet her, as she collapsed to the floor.

Darkness swirled, coaxing her into the center of the morass before becoming an all-encompassing shroud then blinking out all together. Sam hung suspended between time and reality. Not moving one way or another. Caught. Lost.

At the last minute, Sam heard a faint voice weaving through the darkness, "Serves you right, you old bastard."

Then the darkness was complete.

"Excuse me." Sam was nudged gently and then again, not so gently. "Excuse me? Are you alright?"

Sam came to, woozy and still in a half-blind state. She could hardly focus. A woman's concerned face, blurry and of an odd size came into partial focus. "Yeess." Her tongue had a fuzzy, thick feeling and if that was her voice, something was wrong. Very wrong.

"You don't look it." The woman spoke bluntly, tugging Sam to a chair nearby. The grocery basket was removed from Sam's arms and she was gently pushed into the chair.

Sam's eyes went black with pain. This wasn't transition, it wasn't reality either. It seemed a step in between – still painful with any movement, yet no bleeding, or other physical manifestations as far as she could tell. It would be a couple of moments before she'd be able to check.

"Are you a diabetic? An epileptic?"

Sam managed to shake her head slowly. "No," she whispered. "I'm fine."

The woman didn't appear convinced. "Do you want to just sit here for a few minutes?" She rose, taking several steps away. "I can return in a moment or two and see how you are doing?" She stopped her escape. "Or I could call for an ambulance?"

Sam eyed the woman again. Her eyes were huge with worry. Sam closed her own for a moment then reopened them again. The process worked much better this time. She gave her a tiny gentle smile. "Thank you," she murmured. "I'll just sit here until I feel better."

"Okay." Relief washed over the woman's face. "As long as you are feeling better, then I'll leave. I'll check on you in a little bit."

Sam said thanks and couldn't hold back a sigh of relief when the woman left. She really didn't feel well. Yet, neither could she say that she felt really bad.

She couldn't explain in a way anyone would understand. Whatever had just happened had drained her energy. She needed rest, and soon. First, she needed to get out of the public's eye.

Surveying the area around her, she couldn't find her basket of groceries anywhere. They could be sitting close, waiting for her, not that she had the energy to look or to care. She'd shop later. For now, she'd be happy with getting to her truck.

Staying upright was a challenge. Using the wall for stability, Sam slipped through the double doors to the parking lot. Her truck was somewhere in the middle. She closed her eyes and leaned against the outside wall. The fresh air helped. Several deep breaths later, her eyesight had returned to normal. If she waited just one more minute, she might be able to walk there like a normal person.

Once at her truck, she struggled inside, shutting the door with more force than necessary. She took another deep breath and evaluated her state of health. Most functions had returned to normal. She didn't know about her speech. But the pain was gone. Achiness remained, yet that was liveable. Her motor functions had returned to normal.

She pulled her cell phone out and dialed Brandt.

"Hello."

"Brandt." She winced. No, her voice wasn't quite normal.

"What's wrong?" His voice had no problem – it damn near split her eardrum.

She held the phone away from her ear, groaning as her head pounded. "Don't yell, please."

He modulated his tone. "Then tell me what's wrong. You sound terrible."

"I'm just coming out of a vision." Sam coughed gently. "This one was weird. This time some old man was hit over the head."

"What?"

Sam could almost see his brow furrowed with concentration.

"Did you see the attacker?

"He was disguised as an old woman. The old man knew him. I think I've been at this place before. Not the same room maybe, but something similar."

"Sam. I have another call coming in. I'll call you right back. Where are you?"

"I'm sitting in the shopping center across from work. While waiting in line at the grocery store, the vision damn near crippled me."

"But you're okay now?"

"Yes. Call me soon." Sam rang off. She rested her head against the side window and closed her eyes.

CHAPTER SEVENTEEN

1:20 pm

Brandt answered the second call impatiently. He needed to call Sam. Damn it all to hell. His fingers rubbed the ridge of his nose.

"Hello." He couldn't help the shortness in his voice.

He listened for a moment, and with the cries from the other end of the phone ringing in his ears, Brandt grabbed his keys and ran out the door.

It was a short trip, barely fifteen minutes before Brandt drove into the parking lot of the senior care home to be greeted by the all too common sight of an ambulance. He strode forward into the empty hallway. Arriving at his mother's suite, he was surprised to find that empty, too. But maybe he shouldn't be. She could always be found at the center of any gathering – and medical emergencies definitely qualified.

He raced to the colonel's quarters. Turning the corner, his steps slowed. A crowd had gathered at the doorway to the colonel's apartment.

Brandt pushed his way through, his heart dropping at the sight. The colonel was on the stretcher, strapped down. An oxygen mask covered most of his face.

Pulling his badge out, he addressed the paramedics. "What happened?" He leaned over the prone man. The colonel's wrinkled grey face resembled clay that had been baked in the sun too long. Unconsciousness hadn't smoothed the deep wrinkles splitting his face. No injuries were apparent.

One of the paramedics walked over. "He was found on the floor. His pulse is strong and he appears to be suffering from a head injury."

"Head injury?" Brandt bent for a closer look, but only the corner of a blood-soaked bandage was visible.

"He might have fallen and hit his head," offered one of the many bystanders. "He wasn't as steady on his feet as he used to be."

Brandt nodded absentmindedly. The colonel used a walking stick most times. Sure enough, there it was leaning against the wall by his big recliner. The room was so full of people it was hard to move. He stepped out of the way of the stretcher as the two attending men pushed it out to the waiting ambulance. It was only as Brandt turned around to survey the rest of the room that he saw her.

His mom sat with her knees to her chin, her arms snugged tight around her legs like a young child. She swayed gently on the chair, tears in her eyes.

"Mom?" Brandt approached and sat close beside her. Wrapping one arm around her, he gently rubbed her arms. "Are you okay?"

She nodded. "I will be. Just a little upset."

"Were you with him when he collapsed?" Brandt hugged her gently, concerned at the frailty of this feisty valiant woman. She came across as such a powerhouse, then when knocked off balance, she folded.

Giving her time to collect herself, Brandt stared at the other curiosity seekers. Many had started to wander away in search of something more exciting. Still others were waiting, hoping to hear what Maisy would say. Brandt didn't intend to have anyone overhear them.

"Come on. Let's go to your place." He led her through the thinning crowd to her suite. Once inside, he set her in her favorite chair then closed the door on the concerned well-wishers mingling outside. "She'll be fine folks. She's just a little upset."

Turning back to his mother, he added, "I'll make some tea, and you can tell me all about it."

Without waiting for an answer, Brandt put on the teakettle and returned to her side. "Now I need you to tell me what happened. Why are you so upset?"

She lifted her head to peer at him. Torment and guilt gleamed through.

"Did you have something to do with his collapse?" asked Brandt, confused.

"I don't know." Maisy's eyes welled. "The dogs came today, so everyone was in the meeting rooms enjoying their visit. Everyone talked about everything, but the colonel was center stage because of the ring the police are trying to find and what the colonel was trying to remember."

Maisy chewed her bottom lip and didn't continue.

"Then..." prompted Brandt.

"We walked to his apartment where I left him while I went for lunch. After lunch, I came home to lie down."

She glanced up at her son, her bottom lip starting to curl downward. "When I woke up, I called him, except there was no answer. So, I knocked on his door." She shifted uneasily. "He didn't answer so I used my key and that...that's when I found him."

Brandt raised his brow at the mention of his mother having keys to the colonel's apartment – but that was the least of his worries now. "So you feel guilty for falling asleep and leaving him?" he deduced.

"If I'd stayed with him, he wouldn't have been left to lie there unconscious for so long."

Brandt frowned. "How long is so long?" He'd received the impression that the injury was recent.

"Probably half an hour."

"Half an hour is nothing to feel guilty about." Brandt reached over and brushed his fingers over her cheek. "He probably fell just before you arrived."

Her eyes begged him to be right. She suddenly blurted out, "The thing is, I locked the door when I left, and it wasn't locked when I returned."

Brandt shook his head. "Didn't you say you used your key to get in?"

"Yes I did, only I didn't need to because it wasn't locked."

"So why did you use your key?"

"I took it out, expecting to use it, only I didn't need to," she said, exasperation adding life to her eyes and fire to her voice. "Pay attention, dear."

Right. At least she was returning to normal. Speaking of not normal, he had to call Sam. Surreptitiously, he checked his watch. The call would have to wait.

Ignoring the key for the moment, he asked his mother, "Why are you concerned about whether the door was locked or not?"

"I don't think he fell."

Brandt sat up straighter. "What? What do you think happened?" He studied her face. She didn't appear to be in shock. "You think he was attacked?"

Maisy nodded.

"Why would anyone do that?"

"He said he'd remembered the significance of the ring and wanted to think on it a bit, try to figure the pieces out first. Then I fell asleep and now he's injured."

"Even if he did remember, it's unlikely someone would have attacked him over it."

Maisy leaned toward him. "They would if they were involved."

"True. I doubt anyone here is involved. They aren't strong enough for one thing," he said grinning.

She sniffed, such a haughty sound that Brandt had to laugh.

"Not everyone is ancient you know. We all have families that come to visit, and several members of the staff are certainly young enough to have committed murder."

Brandt had to concede her point. Still...it was unlikely. "But how would anyone know what the Colonel was trying to remember?"

Maisy's cheeks flushed pink then paled to pure white. She didn't say anything. Curious, Brandt pushed. "Mom, how would anyone know?"

She straightened her legs out in front and studied her bright red toenails. "I may have had something to do with that."

Brandt pinched the bridge of his nose with his fingers and closed his eyes. "You didn't set up a betting pool on it, did you?" He opened one eye to look at her carefully.

She reddened again. Guilt in pink. Damn.

"So in other words, everyone in the building knew and probably a dozen more besides. All because you wouldn't listen to me."

She opened her mouth as if to protest, then slowly closed it again. She nodded, her eyes full of remorse. "I didn't think it would be dangerous." She shrugged her shoulders in a dainty movement. "We just like to have fun here. You know that. So, we were all taking bets as to when the colonel would remember. There were some people who even bet that he'd never remember, given his age and all that." She sniffed in disgust at that suggestion. "He did remember though, and we were all cheering the winner of the pool. Then someone struck him down before he could tell us what he'd remembered. He said he was going to wait until he could talk to you first."

Brandt sat back. It was too stupid not to be true. Now he had to wait until the colonel awoke. Which, given his advanced years, could be the case *if* he woke up.

"Right." Brandt stood up. "Let's go to the hospital and see how he's doing."

It was a quiet trip with both of them deep in thought. Once there, Maisy insisted on waiting in a chair beside the colonel in the Emergency room. He'd been stabilized, but there was no prognosis yet. Two hours later, there was no change. Still the colonel hadn't woken.

A tall stooped man in green scrubs approached and offered his hand. "Detective Brandt."

"Hello, Doctor Sebastian. How are you?" Brandt watched the multiple frown lines smooth out into a real smile.

"I'm fine. Are you here officially?"

Brandt nodded toward his mother sitting, head bowed at the colonel's side. "We're here for a friend."

"Colonel Bates?"

"Yes, that's right. How is he?"

The doctor glanced at the apparently sleeping patient. "We're keeping him sedated at this time. He has a skull fracture. We'll keep a close watch on the bleeding and the swelling. If he makes it through the night, he should pull through. Given his age and health, well... It's hard to know how he's going to do. There's very little chance that he'll wake up before morning." The silent 'if at all' was very clear. The doctor nodded at him and left the room.

Brandt glanced over at Maisy who appeared to be lost in her own thoughts. "Did you hear that, Mom?"

She didn't answer.

Brandt walked over to crouch in front of her. "Mom, do you want to stay here for a while?

Maisy lifted her pain-filled gaze to stare directly at him. She couldn't speak.

Brandt's heart ached for her. "I'm sorry, Mom. But he's in good hands here. Why don't I leave you here for a bit and I'll come by in a couple of hours?"

She shifted her head in a miniscule imitation of a nod. "Find out who did this," she said, her voice thin and reedy.

Brandt frowned. She didn't sound very good. "Mom, I'll look into it, but that doesn't mean there is a 'who' to find."

Her gaze turned fierce. "This was no accident. Someone hit this dear old man over the head. Find him," she demanded. Then her shoulders sagged as she stared at her friend. "Find him, Brandt."

Brandt stilled. His thoughts turning to the phone call he'd cut short. Maisy's words a mirror of Sam's.

Maisy walked over to the colonel, taking hold of his hand. "Leave. I'll be fine."

Brandt couldn't help but feel dismissed.

***

2:15 pm

Sam opened her eyes, surprised to find herself sitting inside her truck, still parked outside the grocery store. Almost an hour had passed. She felt better physically. Mentally, there was a sense of uneasiness that wouldn't listen to reason.

She wanted to be home where she felt safe. She started the truck, remembering that Brandt hadn't called her again. He'd probably been called out on yet another emergency.

Or she'd missed him? There were no messages on her phone. Disappointed, she sat for a few moments to get her bearing. Brandt had somehow taken up residence in her life, in her heart even. She shook her head, surprised as the speed her feelings had developed. Her hormones had gone into overdrive too. From dormant to wanting to jump his bones. She laughed lightly. As if. Just because she might be willing to go a little further didn't mean he was that interested.

She frowned. Odd to think that she could only know someone for such a short time and already be at this point. She didn't do one night stands. So what was different this time?

Trust.

As she mulled it over, she realized she trusted Brandt. Probably for the first time, she could honestly say she trusted a man. Love, now that was a different thing altogether. That she was interested was obvious. That she might go out of her comfort zone and have an affair – was also a possibility. But the permanent ever after thing, she didn't think would ever happen. It would take a very special man to accept her gifts... Then there was the teensy weensy problem of living with them.

Not every man would want to wake up to find her in the middle of a vision.

A family walked beside her in the parking lot, laughing noisily, their laughter shaking her out of her reverie.

Time to go home. Not sure of her reaction time, she drove slowly and carefully down the highway. Her mind twirled around the various tidbits, trying to find a solution. Surely, the killer had better targets than an old man.

The traffic light turned yellow. She slowed before coming to a complete stop at the red light.

A black truck pulled up beside her.

Sam glanced at it, then away, before zipping back again. Her heart jumped. She glanced around at the truck. She couldn't see the driver as the truck was on the left of her and much higher up. Her gut clenched at the sight. It was identical to the truck from a couple of days ago...

The opposite traffic moved sluggishly through the intersection. Sam stole another glance up at the truck. A man stared at her.

"Shit." She glanced away and back again – just to make sure. And swore again. That face! Surely it couldn't be? Was it really *him*? That one person she'd hoped to never see again.

Her gut clenched. Her fingers flexed on the steering wheel. Trapped in traffic, panic clutched at her insides. Always, she felt so damned trapped. The cars ahead lurched forward. She punched the gas, made a quick right at the corner, whipping into a break in the traffic. She glanced in her rear-view mirror and couldn't see the truck. Oh God. Get a grip, Sam.

She checked to see if she were being followed. Theoretically, he shouldn't have been able to as the car behind her had moved up and taken her spot. Not wanting to take a chance, she turned several more corners and fed into the main road, where she could only hope she was miles behind the truck now.

Prying her right hand off the steering wheel, she wiped it on her jeans.

The trip couldn't end fast enough.

She hit a bad pothole, reminding her to pay attention. Still nervous, Sam found herself searching the surrounding countryside, afraid to find a boogeyman hiding in the trees. She still couldn't determine if it had been him. She'd thought so at the time, but now...?

Brandt hadn't called her back yet. She wanted to call again, yet hated to. He'd bolted so fast out of the house this morning, she wondered if he'd ever come back. It had been a lot for him to deal with last night.

But, she'd love the comfort of hearing his voice right now.

***

3:45 pm

Dillon straightened his charcoal tie to a perfect line. He liked to stay professional at all times, even mid-afternoon. One never knew when opportunity might knock.

He had plans, and he'd be damned if he'd let anyone get in the way. That included Brandt. Earlier, he'd seen Brandt bolt from the office. Very curious. Dillon wanted badly to know what was up, and whether it involved the little psychic chick.

After lunch, Dillon walked naturally into Brandt's office – Brandt's empty office. He grinned then wiped off the smile just in case anyone saw him and wondered. Better not to stir suspicions. Not that anyone would see him. Brandt's office was at the end of a long line of offices. Besides, the station was dead. Only a couple guys manned the phones and there would be the standard group hanging around the coffee machine, only Dillon wasn't planning on talking to them yet.

Even if someone saw him, he had a good excuse. He was looking for a specific file. It should be in Brandt's office. If he happened to find something at the same time, something that furthered Dillon's own career that would be good. If it helped him to put a finger on what made Brandt tick – even better. He didn't know if Brandt was going to be a problem or not, and he'd much rather be prepared just in case.

Quickly, he rounded the desk. The computer was still on. Perfect. He smirked and rubbed his hands in anticipation. Then he got to work.

***

4:15 pm

Brandt left Maisy visiting with the colonel. He quickly punched in Sam's number on his cell phone.

"Sam, let's go over that vision again."

It only took a couple of minutes, just enough for him to clear his head, connect the dots between the colonel's attack and Sam's vision. If he trusted Sam's abilities, then it followed that the colonel had been the old man she saw attacked. The only reasonable explanation for such an attack was if someone needed to silence the colonel – particularly when the attack was undertaken in complete daylight in a home full of people.

"Brandt?"

"Sorry honey, I'm here." Shaking his head, Brandt returned to the conversation and filled Sam in on why the room felt familiar. After giving her an update on the colonel's condition, Brandt headed to the station. Unfortunately, the incident was likely to be classed as an unfortunate accident until the colonel woke up. Without more information, Brandt had no reason to ask Kevin to open an investigation. A list of who had been at the center during that period was mandatory. Maisy was compiling hers and Nancy should have a partial list of visitors, repairmen, and staff.

Once back at the station, Brandt grabbed a mug, poured coffee and headed to the privacy of his office.

"Hey Brandt. Did you ever find out who gave that information to the station?" Adam called out from the common room.

Brandt didn't even turn around. "No, not yet."

He had one hand on his office doorknob before realizing it was already open. Frowning, he pushed the door open and stepped inside. The room looked the same. Brandt hated the suspicion coursing through him. He spun around to his desk. Where was his file on Samantha? It wasn't there. Right, he'd started locking it up in his desk. Pulling out his key ring, Brandt unlocked the drawer on the left.

There was the file as he'd left it. Opening it, he found the information on Sam lying on the top page and frowned. Had he left it there? Normally, he had those papers buried in the middle of the file. Uneasily, he replaced the material, taking care as to how he sequenced the information in the file.

Relocking the drawer, he searched around the office for anything out of place. It appeared to be the same. It didn't feel that way. His chair. He frowned. He'd rushed out of the office and couldn't remember how he'd left it. He didn't think he'd have pushed it in that far.

His monitor flashed for his login information. Brandt hesitated. His keyboard sat off center and further to the front than he normally had it. His hands didn't automatically rest on the keys properly.

Suspicion nudged the back of his mind. He had no way to know if someone had snooped through his office. His work wasn't exactly a secret. Logging on to his computer, Brandt quickly checked his files. Everything seemed normal. The knots in his spine eased, he rolled his shoulders, pushed his sleeves up, and started in on his emails. Communication was the mainstay of his network these days. However, he didn't share everything and made good use of security passwords to keep some information private.

He'd planned on putting in a couple of hours then heading to the hospital to pick up his mom. He opened a file where he typed in his notes from Samantha's call and the colonel incident. He saved the material with a different code. He admitted to a heightened sense of paranoia, but still...

CHAPTER EIGHTEEN

8:20 am, June 21st

"Hey Brandt, there's someone here to see you." Adam stood at the open door of his office the next day.

Brandt raised one eyebrow. He wasn't expecting anyone. "Who is it?"

Adam shrugged. "Deputy Brooker for Nikola County."

"What the hell?" Brandt's stomach twisted. He lurched partway out of his chair

Adam grinned. "You don't look so happy."

"Very odd," he murmured to himself. "No, I'm happy," he corrected Adam. "I'd like to talk with the little piss ass."

"Oh, there's nothing little about this guy."

Brandt, in the process of clearing off the top of his desk and locking up sensitive files, scowled. "Big? How big?"

Adam snorted. "This guy makes me look like an infant."

"Scary."

Adam nodded. "If I had to describe him, I'd say he was one hell of an arrogant SOB, far too used to getting his own way."

Shit. So, Sam was probably right about him. Well then, time to go see why he'd come and what he knew about Sam.

"Thanks, Adam. Anyone in the conference room?"

"I don't think so. Is that where you want to talk to him?"

"Yeah. I'm not sure yet, but this guy quite possibly needs to be behind bars himself. Don't want to extend too much courtesy, just in case."

"Sounds good. I'm heading down there now. Why don't I deliver him to conference room one for you?"

"Good. That saves me a trip and gives me a little more distinction. I could use that in this case."

"What kind of trouble is he?" Adam walked out of the office with Brandt.

"I think he's been a lot of trouble for a young girl."

"Then no special treatment for him. We don't need more of his kind."

"According to my information, he's also into corrupting law enforcement and running drugs."

He shared a look with Adam. They both knew other assholes just like this one.

"I need to make a quick call, then I'll be down."

Adam left and Brandt called his mom.

His call went to voicemail. Last night, Maisy had convinced the hospital staff to bring a cot into the colonel's room so she could stay with him. Brandt's protests had been shot down immediately. Chances were she was still there, but he'd feel better if he'd reached her. A second call to the hospital confirmed that his mom had spent the night and that the colonel hadn't woken up. As luck would have it, his mom was at the desk speaking with the nurse too. He spoke with her briefly, confirming that she'd gotten some sleep. She sounded more chipper this morning.

Brandt then headed to the conference room, quickly scratching down a few notes and questions he wanted to ask as he walked. Entering the room, he found a huge man with beefy shoulders – not a beer belly, rather a beer barrel that completely covered the belt holding up his pants. Dressed in uniform, the deputy's beady eyes held a voracious gleam that belied the smile on his face.

"Detective Sutherland?" At Brandt's nod, the older man stepped forward, his hand outstretched. "Thank you for taking the time to see me. I appreciate it."

Brandt shook the man's hand. Then motioned to a seat opposite his. He sat down, sliding his hand along his pants to wipe it clean before opening the conversation. "I'm surprised. Did you just happen to be in this region?"

"Nope. I came specific. This case, Samantha Blair, is way too important to leave to chance."

"Oh, you didn't mention that there was a case when we talked on the phone?"

Deputy Brooker shifted his bulk into the big boardroom chair. "I thought long and hard about it. But decided I needed to come and check this out. I'd just about given up finding her when I got your phone call."

"What do you want with her?"

"She caused me a bunch of trouble a few years ago. I believe she stole something from my family that I would really like returned."

Brandt frowned. Sam hadn't mentioned anything about that. "Stole something? Like what?"

"Files and folders. Our family history. We went to a spell of trouble to collect this material and we'd surely like it back."

The man was full of shit. Still, he was here. Therefore, whatever he wanted was important. Brandt didn't think any of it would be good for Sam.

"What was she like the last time you saw her?"

The beefy man hitched the front of his pants up over the lower portion of his belly. He shifted his weight; the chair creaked in protest. "She was a mouthy know-it-all. Just like she'd been every other time I'd seen her. The things that come out of that girl's mouth were something else. She's surely a liar, she is."

"A liar." Brandt barely restrained the desire to jump across the table and strangle the bloody fool. "A liar but not a fraud?"

"Nope, usually her visions were spot on. But that girl's a social misfit. She's not the same as you and me. She needed a keeper then and I'm sure things haven't changed."

"What is your intention when you meet her?"

"Just talk to her. See if she's had a change of heart in the meantime. Maybe she's ready to give the material back now. Or has she ditched it somewhere along the last few years?"

Brandt took a few notes, more to calm the fury inside than for later information. There was no way this asshole was getting close to Sam

"She had a bad car accident after she was in your neck of the woods. Did you know that?"

"I'd heard. And in truth, I thought maybe she hadn't survived. I'd called the hospital a time or two, but word was she was in bad shape and not expected to live. That's when I put it all away in my head. Until your phone call, then I hopped into my truck and came here."

Shit. Brandt *was* responsible for this mess. Truck? As in black truck? "Long trip. When did you pull into town?"

"Oh, I arrived a couple of days ago. Didn't want to come knocking right away. Figured you'd be mighty busy."

Brandt sighed, keeping his head down. The asshole was lying through his teeth. So he had been around when Sam called him screaming on her phone about some guy trying to run her off the road. Through the DMV, he could find out what this guy drove – putting him on the highway at the same time as Sam was a different story. How to prove that? "Yes, we're swamped. Portland is a big city and it's not like there's ever a down season."

The deputy laughed. "Crime never takes a holiday."

"Isn't that the truth?"

As much as Brandt would like to cuff this guy with the information he had from Sam, he knew in good conscience that he'd need to hear what Sam had to say about the deputy's truths.

Then he'd have another talk with the deputy...on his terms.

***

10:48 am

It had not been a good day. As a matter of fact, as days went, this one sucked. Bill had finally located the right hospital only to find out his drugged victim was still alive and in a coma. What the hell? If she died – great. If she stayed in a coma for the rest of her life – even better. He kind of liked that concept. But if she awoke, that was bad news. It couldn't be allowed to happen. He'd have to think this one over while monitoring the situation.

Then he'd gone on to the care center with his dogs. The dogs had been great, the staff had been great – the people however... What was with those old people? They all had a gambling problem for one thing. And for another, they were a bunch of busybodies. Like that one old geezer. Apparently, he knew something about the ring the media had flashed on the television. Those damn old folks were betting on when he was going to remember just what it was. Who could have predicted such a problem? Well, he'd had no choice, had he? The guy couldn't be allowed to remember anything about him – ever.

That little bit of violence had been just enough to whet his appetite, to rouse the beast inside, yet not enough to sate either. It had been too fast, not well planned...and that bothered him a bit. Yet, he'd had few options. Prudence said he should be home and out of sight right now. He'd actually been driving in that direction when he'd seen her.

She was perfect.

He pulled off the road to a small parking lot so he could watch her sashaying down the sidewalk.

The glare shining through the windshield irritated him. It limited his view. Rummaging in the glove box, he finally came up with a scratched pair of sunglasses. Better than nothing. Putting them on, he quickly searched the area in front of the drugstore that she'd walked into a few minutes earlier.

There. She was laughing at something someone had said, her head turned as she walked out the door. She strode with confidence in the sunshine. God, he loved that. Loved to see a woman sure of her sexuality, sure of who she was.

And she was so wrong.

That was the best part. Stripping away their innocence and teaching them about the real monsters of the world.

He leaned forward for a better view. She turned left and moved smoothly down the sidewalk. Look at her walk – liquid honey. He grinned.

Perfect.

He hopped out of the truck and followed behind at a steady pace. When she entered a small clothing boutique, he found a bench on the sidewalk and sat to enjoy the sunshine. He had nothing better to do, except follow her around. She loved her little boutiques and before the month was out, he'd know every one of them.

***

2:20 pm

The afternoon was gorgeous. Sam felt like shit.

Leaning against the front doorframe of her cabin, looking out to the rest of the world, Sam mentally ran through the various options. She still had a couple days before she started working with Stefan. In the meantime, she had some homework to do. If these visions would stop, she might actually have the energy to work on them.

Her phone rang. Butterflies took flight in delight at the number on her phone display. He'd slid into her consciousness like he'd always belonged there. When had he gone from a cop to a friend, and now to mean something so much more? "Hi Brandt. What's up?"

"I need to see you today. There's something I need to go over with you and it's better to do this in person. Are you going to be home this afternoon or evening?"

Sam's stomach dropped. In person would be great, except nothing about this sounded good. Now what? "I'm here all day and night. I'm going to work on Stefan's exercises this afternoon, then head to the lake for a swim." She hesitated for a moment. "What's this about?"

"Deputy Brooker came into the office today. His story is a little different than yours."

She snorted. "What? He's in town?" Sam gripped the cell phone in her hand, her knuckles turning white. "When did he get here and what is he driving? I think I saw that same black truck yesterday."

"What? Why didn't you say something?"

"I didn't know if it was the same vehicle or not. I was still in town, so took off around the corner. I never saw him again."

"He is driving a black Dodge truck, but that doesn't mean it was him. We're running a check on him now. You stay there and just be careful. If anyone shows up, but me, hide unless you know them. I'll get there in a couple of hours – earlier if I can."

She shook her head. Not good enough. Not even close, only what were her options at this point? None. "Then you damn well better show up soon, or I'll be coming in after you."

The phone closed with a snap. Sam let out a shaky breath. Okay. Another problem. She was good at those. She snorted. Like hell. In the past, she'd run. So what did she do now?

Stick around and fight.

CHAPTER NINETEEN

5:45 pm

The late afternoon sun danced on top of the glassy lake. Sam studied the inviting landscape. Yeah. That's exactly what she needed.

"Hello, Soldier." She smiled at the dog lying so peacefully in the sun. Healthier now, his coat was thick and although still grimy, it was no longer covered in blood. Most of it had dried and fallen off. She'd love to get him into the lake, except he still had stitches. The last thing she wanted was to have to manhandle the dog into the truck and back to the vet's office. Soldier accepted her presence as a necessity, but only as long as his independence and freedom never came into question.

Soldier surged to his feet and started growling.

Sam frowned. "Soldier?"

The dog turned to face the wooded area behind the house and growled again.

Sam peered into the trees, but couldn't see what bothered the dog. He growled again at the bushes behind her. The woods appeared calm, and should have been teeming with life. None of it showed.

The energy had a peacefulness to it. Then maybe it was the energy she was projecting. Stefan's exercises had a phenomenal effect. It was what she was imagined meditation could do for a person. A sense of ease, comfort, had slipped under her guard. It's not that she felt she could do anything, because she knew she couldn't, however she did have a better understanding of just what she was capable of doing. The exercises were basic. She had to start at the beginning, according to Stefan. Working on seeing energy, understanding the colors around people, animals, even plants. Then to understand what the markings and colors meant.

Sure she was tired, but a good tired. Her energy muscles, something she never knew existed, had been well and truly flexed.

It felt great.

So many things in her life felt great – especially Brandt. She had no idea where the relationship was going, or when. All she could think about was where it would end up – in bed. At least she hoped she was reading the signals right.

Delight wiggled in her belly. She hoped he felt the same way.

With Soldier on guard in the late afternoon sun, Sam headed for a swim. It was the perfect temperature for a cool, relaxing dip. Feeling physically stronger than she had in years, Sam stretched her abilities to the limit, swimming strong for thirty minutes before rolling over onto her back and floating. Calm and filled with peace, she waited for her breathing to return to a calm gentle rhythm. It took longer than she expected.

With a groan, she realized she may have overdone it.

In the aftermath of exertion, her body chilled quickly. Turning over, she fluttered her hands enough to propel herself gently in the right direction.

The silkiness of the water slipped over her skin, making her sensitized skin come alive. The chill quickly morphed into heat as she moved through the water under the setting sun. Now, if only Brandt were here with her. His hands sliding across her skin instead of the gentle waves. She stretched, reveling in the freedom of the night.

"Sam. Goddamn it, what the hell are you doing?" The yell stormed across the water.

What was that? She raised her head.

"Get over here."

Well, that was hard to miss. She rolled over in the water and searched around the house and the dock. Brandt strode toward the water. Even from that distance, she could see his grim face. Her pulse sped up at the sight of him. Even if he was mad at her.

"Sam, you're too far out."

Too far. Sam twisted around her and realized she'd unintentionally floated out even further. Still, she wasn't in trouble. At least, not yet.

Striking out strong, Sam headed in. Her energy petered out before she managed a dozen strokes. She shifted to breaststroke and continued shoreward. When she made it to roughly fifteen feet from the dock, Sam slowed and treaded water.

She watched Brandt's loose-limbed stride carry him to the end of the dock, heard him yell, "God damn it, woman. Get your sorry ass in here."

Tall and lean, he looked incredibly good with a gentle wind ruffling his hair. Moses whined beside him. Now, if only she hadn't spent the last hour imagining him in the water with her.

"Sorry buddy. It's not you I'm mad at – it's her."

Moses sat down.

Sourly, Sam watched their interplay. Moses may not have anything to worry about. Obviously Sam couldn't say the same thing. She felt like hissing. Damn it. She was swimming in the nude.

***

6:55 pm

Brandt couldn't believe it. The last time he'd seen her, she'd been caught in a heavy vision and experiencing huge blood loss. Now she was out there swimming in the middle of the damn lake. She'd have been better off relaxing and regaining her strength. He watched as she struggled the last few yards. She was worn out, but if he jumped in to help her, she'd be royally pissed. Go figure.

He scowled at the dog at his feet. Even Moses knew better than to swim right now.

Jesus. She needed a babysitter. She was as bad as his mother.

Watching Sam swim closer, he realized he'd probably overreacted here. Swimming would help rebuild Sam's strength and endurance. Exercise had many benefits and as long as she didn't overdo it, then swimming was a good way to go.

Somehow, that logic didn't matter because he was still pissed. Scary. He stopped suddenly, hands fisted on his hips. And all because he was worried – about her. He blew his breath out in a gust. Oh, God, this was getting bad.

The balmy evening breeze wrinkled the water before smoothing it flat again.

He frowned. The cabin was a long way from everything. Not only that, if she were to run into trouble, no one would know for days. Not until she didn't show at work. Damn it. His frown deepened.

The bushes rustled behind him. Instinctively, he dropped and spun around.

Deep yellow eyes glowed in the darkness.

That damn watchdog.

"Hello there, Soldier. How are you feeling? I see you're moving better." Keeping his voice even and calm, he kept a wary eye on the dog's reactions. He wasn't exactly growling. On the other hand, neither was he wagging his tail with joy.

The two males glowered at each other. Both silent and watchful. Both waiting for the other to move. Brandt knew better than to break his gaze first. The alpha male was the one who held the gaze the longest. If he were ever going to get close to Sam, then the watchdog had to accept his presence.

Splashes alerted him to Sam's approach. Keeping his eyes trained on the dog, he called out, "Are you okay, Sam?

She coughed gently, then again a bit stronger. "I'm fine." Her voice was reedy and thin. "I'm just getting out now."

Brandt stared at the dog, relieved. "You sound exhausted. You should never have gone for a swim. Or at least not for so long," he admonished.

"Like I'm going to listen to you," she scoffed. "You're arguing with a dog."

Brandt started. Indignantly, he said, "I am not."

Sam brushed past him, a towel wrapped around her body, droplets of water flying off with every step. She deliberately walked between the two males. Both sets of eyes immediately switched to the distraction.

Brandt swallowed. Her towel snuggled around her curves, shifting to accommodate the gentle movements as she walked. Water had soaked into the thin material, making it almost transparent. Brandt's imagination fired up. The towel hung loosely down the center of her spine. There were no straps on her shoulders.

He swallowed.

The towel cuddled her bottom, just barely covering the gentle curves. He couldn't see any sign of a bathing suit. The tantalizing thought both enraged and delighted him. Didn't she realize that anyone could have come down here?

This lady was just asking for trouble.

Yet, the thought of all that female flesh floating sensuously free in the cool water was a huge turn on. And gave him an intimate insight into her true character. Watching her walk ahead of him and not knowing whether or not she was nude, was an even bigger aphrodisiac.

The bushes rattled again. Soldier, now in front of Sam, turned. His lip curled, his spine humped up and the hair on the back of his neck stood straight up.

Samantha stopped.

Brandt instinctively freed his gun, staying close to her as he peered into the woods. "What is it?" he whispered.

Sam shrugged, her eyes searching the woods. "I can't tell." Her voice was low, balanced. "Soldier doesn't like it ...and neither do I. Something doesn't feel...right."

Brandt scanned the area for anything abnormal. He didn't know what she meant, but he couldn't help agreeing that all wasn't as it should be.

Sam hurried to the cabin, running up the porch steps. Brandt followed at a slower pace, a wary eye searching around him. Soldier growled and lunged into the woods.

"Soldier, no!" Sam watched and listened as the noises trailed off to the left. She turned to Brandt. "I'm going to get dressed then go after him."

Brandt couldn't stop his eyes from following that perfectly formed backside, highlighted by damp circles in the towel as she climbed the stairs.

With a shaky breath, he turned to search the twilight. The evening sun was setting, throwing long shadows across the yard. There was no sign of Soldier. Moses sat on the top stair staring off in the same direction. He wasn't growling, but his tail wasn't wagging either.

Sam came running down the stairs still tucking her shirt inside the waistband of her old blue jeans. Over her arm was the inevitable oversized sweater. Her skin sported a blue tinge. She held a leash in her hand.

"Damn it, you're cold. Stay inside and get warm. I'll go after him."

Sam shook her head. "I'm going. He doesn't know you, and he won't come if you call." Turning around, she spied Moses at the edge of the bushes. "Moses, come here." Moses trotted forward obediently. Sam snapped the lead on. "Only one dog missing at a time, please. Let's go find Soldier."

Brandt scoffed. "Moses won't find him, and Soldier won't come if you call either."

She shot him a dirty look before walking past him into early the night.

"Soldier," Sam called from the doorway, looking around. But the wooded darkness had swallowed him completely. They left the porch and headed across the lawn.

Howls and screams split the air, followed by a couple of quiet spits. Sam ran forward and stopped. A heavy crashing through the woods could be heard for a moment before dying off in the distance.

"Jesus," she whispered, her hand at her throat. Her heart smashed in her chest. "Brandt, were those human screams and gunshots?"

"Maybe. You stay here with Moses. I'm going to check it out." Brandt pulled out his gun and raced into the woods. The trees stood thick together. He headed in the direction of the shots. The silence blanketed everything, except his own passage. Leaves and twigs crushed beneath his feet. The wind started. Branches swished sending whispers through the night. Brandt moved quickly through the area. Nothing. He circled around to Sam.

"Any sign?" she called out to him.

"No. Whoever or whatever it was is gone." A few feet from the porch stairs, Brandt stopped and looked around again.

Ignoring Brandt's protests, Sam took a couple of steps into the darkness. "Soldier?"

Brandt came to stand beside her. "Can you see him?"

"No, but he has to be here?" She spun to the left. "Wait, what was that?"

A small whine sounded several hundred feet away.

"Soldier? Soldier! Come here, boy."

Twigs broke and the brush rustled with movement. Darkness had descended quickly. Sam backed up a couple of steps. "Soldier, come here, boy."

Peering through the darkness, she thought she saw something move. "Soldier," she whispered, "Is that you."

Soldier limped toward her.

Sam ran and put her arms around him in a quick hug. She coaxed him forward. "Come on boy. Time to go home."

"Is he hurt?" Brandt surveyed the large animal. The damn thing had to weigh at least a-hundred-twenty pounds. Uninjured and cooperative, he might be able to move him…injured and cranky – no way.

"I don't know." Sam gently ran her hands over the dog's limbs, ignoring the warning growls. "Come on Soldier, let's get you inside."

Once on the porch, they could see fresh blood on his side.

"Damn it, Soldier." Sam checked his wound, accidentally touching a sore spot. Soldier spun around, his lip curled, an ungodly howl erupting from his throat.

Brandt trained his gun on the injured animal. "Sam, get back." The evening stilled. "Don't touch him. He's dangerous like this."

Soldier turned slowly toward Brandt, then his spine arched, and the howl turned menacing.

Sam shuffled behind Brandt. Soldier had eyes only for Brandt.

She said in a quiet calm voice, "Brandt, I think it's the gun – put it away."

"Are you nuts? He could attack."

"It's the gun that's upsetting him. It's easy to check my theory. Just put the gun away."

Brandt snorted. "I've seen too many aggressive animals to do that." He kept his eyes on the dog, sparing a quick glance at Sam.

"Let's just try it – please."

He stared at the dog for a long moment, then slowly lowered the firearm and slipped it behind. Out of sight but not away.

The dog watched every movement. The growling lessened ever so slightly.

"I wonder." A sudden impulse rolled around inside. Using hand signals, he ordered the dog to sit. Soldier howled.

Brandt repeated the command.

Soldier howled louder.

Brandt made the command sharper, harder.

Silence.

Then in a shuffling movement, Soldier slowly lowered his haunches.

Brandt shook his head then gave the command to heel. Wanting the dog to walk at his side was safer than having Sam try to coax him up to the house.

This time, Soldier obeyed on the first go around, the movement slow and awkward, but he did it.

"Brandt?"

"He's been well-trained. I don't know to what extent though. There are some commands I can try. From the look of him, I'm almost ready to suggest he's been a police dog in his past."

"Really?" Sam stared from one to the other. "Do you really think so?"

"I think he's a trained guard dog and chances are good his training was more formal. It's possible he didn't work out and never finished the training."

Once at the cabin, the slow moving party made it inside. Brandt ordered the dog to lie down. Soldier, small growls from deep in his throat, grudgingly obeyed.

Sam quickly checked out Soldier's wounds again. Brandt and Soldier glared at each other.

"It's not too bad. Looks like he ripped a stitch or two and he's limping. That could just be his old injuries with the unexpected chase in the woods." Sam gave the dog a quick hug. "Poor boy."

Brandt snorted. "Why's that?"

"The vet thought he'd been abused. As far as Soldier's concerned, it's people who aren't to be trusted." Sam paused for a moment, sniffed the air, bent closer to Soldier's back then raised her head. "Did someone just shoot my dog?"

***

7:18 pm

Brandt sat on the porch steps, speaking with his mother.

Sam studied him for a long moment, waiting for his call to end, before walking out to join him. "I just poured you a cup of tea." Sam handed the cup to Brandt. "How are the colonel and your mother?"

He glanced at her in surprise. "No change."

"So can we talk then?" At his confused look, she added, "Deputy Brooker. Remember?"

"What? Oh, right. He's here. As I told you earlier, your Deputy Brooker came to see me today."

"Oh, God." Sam sat down – hard. She didn't need to look in a mirror to know that all the color had leached from her face.

"He's been in town for a couple of days already." Brandt sat opposite her. "I know it's easy to jump to conclusions, but we don't know any more than that yet."

It was too much. Sam had hoped to hide her history, hoped that past events wouldn't have to be dragged into her future. "Damn it."

"Keep in mind, he doesn't know where you live."

Hope unfurled deep inside then she remembered what had just happened. She searched his face. "You're dreaming," she scoffed. "He was probably the one doing the shooting out there tonight." She added, "I have no illusions. He'd kill me any time he had a chance."

Brandt studied her face.

She stared calmly back. If there was one thing he needed to believe, it was that Brooker was slime, dangerous slime.

"Alright, I can see you believe that. He said you stole something from his family. Information of some kind? Any idea what that's all about?" Brandt's supportive gaze gave her strength.

She laughed, a broken sound that made him wince. "I didn't steal anything. Don't you see? The information he thinks I have is what I picked up from him. My psychic abilities told me a lot. That's what he's afraid of. That I know too much." Pain knotted at the base of her spine, shooting up through her temple. She shivered. "And he's right. I do."

Brandt mulled this over.

She stared blindly out the dark window. "Remember my car accident?"

"The one where you were injured or the one where you saw Louise Enderby die?"

"No, the first one – where I almost died. That was him. He caused my accident – he tried to kill me."

CHAPTER TWENTY

8 pm

Sam bent her head.

Brandt stared at the delicate tendrils of hair curled around her neck. The rest hung in long locks down to her waist. Really? He mentally drew up the deputy's countenance and conceded that, yeah, just maybe it was possible. That guy had an agenda. One that had nothing to do with his supposed visit to Brandt's station.

Staring at her bent head, he needed to ask, at least once. "Are you sure?"

Lifting her head, Sam stared straight at him. Her eyes shone with tears. "I don't have any proof if that's what you mean. But I saw him."

"You saw him?" Brandt leaned forward, to search her face. "Are you sure?"

Sam got up and walked to where she could stare out the window, her hair dangling down her back. "After the crash, I couldn't move. The flames had just started to reach the windshield. The seatbelt buckle had locked, my leg was broken, and my collarbone had been dislocated."

She closed her eyes and leaned her head against the cool glass. Tremors started at the base of her spine and moved up. "He walked up while I was wrestling with the straps." She paused, her breath coming out in shaky gusts. "I pounded on the window and screamed for help. He laughed at me." Sam swallowed. "There I was in total panic, thinking that help had arrived and he..." she turned to face Brandt, "And he pulled out his gun and pointed it at me through the window.

Brandt swore. Then swore again. "Bastard."

"That he is." She stared at him, a tiny smile on her face. "Thanks for believing me. That helps a lot."

He snorted. "So what happened? Did he actually shoot you?"

Sam shook her head. "No, or I wouldn't be here. He just walked away. As he drove off, another man – a retired firefighter – arrived. He shattered the glass on the driver's door, unlocked it, cut my seatbelt strap, and dragged me free." She walked over to Brandt and sat down again. "So yeah, to answer your question – I am sure."

He watched her shorts ride higher on her thighs, wishing she'd sit closer. His senses were awash in 'what ifs.' With a shudder, he stared off in the distance. Clearing his throat, he asked, "Did you tell anyone?"

"No." She snorted. "Who would I tell? He *was* the police."

Right. Brandt groaned and leaned back. "God. What a mess." He ran his fingers through his hair. "The bottom line is that this asshole is here now, and he's searching for you."

"Right. Hence my question – did bullets score Soldier's shoulder?"

"Christ." He stared at her, seeing past the old fears and tough memories. She was a fighter, but against a stacked deck, she'd run – until now. There'd be no running now. She wasn't alone any more.

"Let me make some phone calls, see if we've got anything on him yet. One of my team is running his background."

Sam frowned.

"That means we can track him down and have another talk with him. Adam did confirm that Brooker drives a 2004 Dodge truck – a black one."

She shuddered. "So it could have been him on the highway." After a moment of contemplation, she shrugged. "Not that it matters, he's not going to admit to anything. Why would he? You'd need proof, like bullets or casing from tonight to match to his gun."

"True, but if you recognized his black truck..." he said, waiting and watching for her comprehension to kick in. Her eyes opened wide as understanding filtered in.

She frowned. "Yes, only how would he know what vehicle I'm driving?"

"The same way we can find out about his truck, run your name through DMV to find out what vehicle is registered under your name." He glanced at her truck outside the window. That thing should have been deep-sixed a long time ago. Surely, it wouldn't pass a safety inspection?

"But he couldn't have known that it was me on the road until he came right up to me."

Brandt considered that. "It's not out of the realm of possibility, that's exactly what did happen. And then he took advantage of an unexpected opportunity."

Sam wrinkled her face. "That's horrible." She grimaced. "At least, he doesn't know where I live." She chewed on her lower lip, her arms wrapped tightly around her chest. "Then again, it wouldn't be that hard with his connections, would it?"

Brandt tried not to watch as her breast plumped out against her skin. "As much as I hate to even suggest it, it's possible that he could have followed you, or even me."

Sam's eyes opened wide. "That's a horrible thought." She tilted her head, carefully considering him. "He couldn't have followed me, I haven't been anywhere today."

"No. Are you sure you lost the black truck yesterday?"

Her eyes widened in horror. "Oh, God."

He leaned forward gently patting her on the knee. "Don't panic. We're working on it. As soon as we have more information, I'll bring him in for a second and more informative talk." Excusing himself, Brandt headed outside to make the phone calls that would put things in motion. This needed to be dealt with now. As did something else. Just as he was about to walk out onto the porch, he called out, "Oh, yeah. I'll also be sleeping here tonight."

***

8:22 pm

"You want what?" God, the last thing Sam wanted to remember were other victims. She shook her head, hair flying widely about. No. No way.

"Please. It might help."

She stared at him. He didn't know what he asked. He couldn't. He'd gone outside to make his phone calls after dropping his first bomb. Then he'd come inside and had dropped a second one. The last remnants of her control fractured, splintering apart. He'd asked for details on other visions. She shook her head. This isn't how she'd imagined the evening.

"I suppose this could be difficult for you."

She half laughed, half cried. "You think?" she said, her voice rising. "You have no idea!" She spun away from him, her whole body shaking.

Brandt winced. "I'm sorry. If it's that hard then we won't discuss this. I didn't mean to upset you." He walked over, one arm outstretched to touch her gently, hesitantly before dropping it down to his side. "I thought it might help to give the victims a voice." This time, he placed an arm around her shoulders.

She stiffened, but didn't move away. In truth, she wanted to snuggle in deeper, only couldn't trust her emotions. "All victims or just those from this same killer?" She reached up gently to massage the nape of her neck. She hated her immediate defensiveness. There was no reason not to. After all, she'd wanted to be able to make a difference. Although, it might be a lot easier if she had a chance to talk to Stefan first. Maybe he knew how to help her through the process without the damage she knew would happen. She needed to ask him at the first opportunity.

Surprise lit up his voice. "I didn't know you could choose." He mulled over the concept. "If given a choice, and if there is the possibility of this killer having other victims, then that's where I'd like to start." He paused for a moment. "Although, if you have information on other cases, that would be a help too. We have an incredible load of unsolved cases."

"I don't know. I suppose I can try," she said. Her voice so soft and so sad, he thought his heart would break. "It might be easier on me if we do this after I work with Stefan a few times. Maybe he'll have a few techniques so I can protect myself." Sam watched the puzzlement wash over his face.

"Protect yourself? I don't understand."

He wasn't going to like her answer. "During recall, a lot of the same energy returns. I tend to slip between the visions and this reality."

"Whoa! Come again?"

A wry smile played around her lips. "Sometimes, the same method the person died from will manifest again — although to a much lesser degree," She rushed to add this last bit because she saw the horror starting to overtake his face.

"So you're liable to start bleeding again?" He shook his head. "Uh, uh. No way are we going there."

Sam couldn't help it. She laughed aloud. "The bleeding can be the easy symptoms."

He glanced at her in disbelief.

"Don't forget, one woman burned alive in a car accident."

"But we don't know that it wasn't an accident."

"No, you don't know. I do. Not only that, I know it was the same killer. I don't understand how or why, just that there was some connection."

Brandt shook his head as he pulled a small notebook out. "You're certain that these are all victims of the same killer?"

"Sure enough that you should do a search and link everyone they knew and every activity they participated in. The killer is there somewhere in the mess. Personally, I'd add Louise Enderby in there. She's the exception that could show you the rule."

Sam wondered as Brandt spent the next five minutes writing down something in a notebook. Then she realized she had something that might help, while not hurting her. "I'll be right back." She strode into her bedroom. They were here somewhere in one of the boxes. She rummaged through the first, and then the second stacked box before finding what she was searching for at the bottom. Sorting the books out, she grabbed up the one she wanted.

Brandt was on his cell phone when she returned. Not wanting to bother him, she refilled their cups with hot tea then sat down to wait.

"Right. Graph it out. I know it's far-fetched, but we haven't got anything else to go on so let's give this a try." He glanced over at her and smiled. "Let's pull all the data and cross reference with these other cases. If the information isn't there then let's get it." Brandt jotted down several notes in his notepad. "No. I'll come in early tomorrow. We can map out what we have then."

The conversation carried on a little longer and Sam blanked out. She flicked through the book in her hand, wincing at the notes. Very graphic and way too painful to read again, she wondered at her compulsion to write all this in the first place.

"What have you got there?"

Surprised, Sam looked up. "What?"

He folded and put away the phone. "So what's that you've got?"

"Here." She took a deep breath. Then as if making a decision, she handed the cheap, worn book over to him.

Brandt accepted it, glancing from her to the book and back again. "What is it?"

"My journal. It will have some dates and some details."

Brandt flicked through the lined pages, daunted by the sheer outpouring of her soul. "Is this about your visions?" He stopped, read a note, then turned the page. "How far back does this go?"

"It's close to being the first half of this year."

"This year?" Shock threaded through his voice.

"I have one I'm currently working on." She shrugged, unable to stop the self-conscious feeling. "I feel compelled to write down every detail I can remember after a vision. It's my way of letting the victims speak." She crossed her arms across her chest. "The thing is, I've never told anyone about these journals."

"Ever?

"No."

He bent forward, placing one hand on her knee. "Thank you."

A shaky sigh escaped. She nodded, a tiny smile on her lips. "You're welcome."

Brandt squeezed her knee gently, then sat up again. "So this is everything written here?" He slapped the book on this thigh, studying her face.

Soberly, Sam nodded. "Of those visions. I have more upstairs — at least twenty more."

***

9:05 pm

Brandt could feel the blood leach from his face. One of them? She had twenty more journals? Holy Shit. What kind of life had she had?

"A terrible one."

Brandt's head shot up in shock. His mind spun out of control. Did she just do that? Please, no.

237

"No I can't read minds. Your face on the other hand..." She grinned at his sour grimace.

He stared at the gold mine in his hand. He couldn't figure out what to focus on. She'd just handed him an incredible gift. Sure, he'd have to find proof, depending on her information, but she could give him a direction to start digging. Some of these cases might not even be in the files. Some could have been ruled accidental. Some could have been solved by now. Some killers could literally have gotten away with murder.

Sam's hesitant voice broke through his heavy thoughts. "I might be able to help in other ways."

He glanced at her in surprise. "You already have," he said lifting up the journal. "Can I take this?"

She cringed. "I don't really want the information shared with the rest of your team. Maybe read it over and see if there is anything useful. Take notes or photocopy the pages. I would like the original back."

"Absolutely. Photocopying is a good idea. And don't worry, I won't let Kevin or anyone else get their hands on this." Brandt knew the value of what he held. He wasn't planning on letting anyone else in on it until he could find the proof to match with the information. He flicked through the journal, stopping to read a page, wincing at the pain and the horror that dripped from the pages. Sam had come up behind to read over his shoulder, her long blond hair falling over his shoulder.

His nostrils flared as her fresh womanly scent sank in. He glanced up, still caught by her feelings so transparent, her torment so real, before just focusing on her now. How quickly she'd slipped under his guard. This gentle woman had experienced so much pain already. He wanted to make her feel better, to make the pain go away. Setting the book aside, he stood up and stepped up next to her.

She stilled, her eyes wide like a deer caught in headlights.

Brandt grinned and dropped a kiss on the tip of her nose. Sliding his arms around her, Brandt tugged her into a gentle hug.

When she relaxed against him, he rested his cheek on the top of her head and smiled.

He hesitated. Should he even broach the subject? Still, if this wasn't a good time, when would there ever be a better one? "You know you're never far from my mind, don't you?"

Sam tried to pull back slightly, when he wouldn't release her she contented herself with tilting her head up instead.

"Really?" Her voice came out as a gentle whisper, full of wonder and enchantment. Brandt immediately fell under her spell.

"Really." He stared down at her porcelain skin, the huge eyes that said so much, yet nothing at all, and those lips. He hadn't noticed them the first couple of times he'd seen her, now they were all he could think about — so red and full, so very inviting, so very ready to be loved.

He couldn't help himself. He bent and claimed them for his own.

***

9:15 pm

Overwhelmed by his words, Sam was blindsided by the touch of his lips. They coaxed, yet entranced. She'd never been kissed in such a way before. She wondered if she'd ever truly been kissed. She craved his touch. She wanted so much more. That there couldn't be a forever, didn't matter. She needed this, right now, right here...with him.

Letting herself slide under the spell he wove so magically, her hands slid up to either side of his face, and she kissed him back.

Her lips twitched at his startled pause. Excitement surged through her as he turned the tables on her and deepened the kiss.

A moan escaped. Oh, Lord. Her legs had turned to jelly — she'd never felt so weak. He tightened his arms, supporting her against him. He lifted his head.

"Sam?"

She opened her eyes. God, he was beautiful. Inside and out. She wanted what he offered. She wanted not to be alone — at least for one night. "Yes."

"Yes? Are you sure?"

Her smile turned to a full-blown laugh. "Yes, I'm sure."

Her answer darkened his eyes to an almost jet black. She smiled, reaching a hand to stroke the side of his face. "Yes, yes, and yes." She snagged his ear and tugged him toward her. "So what are you waiting for?"

"For you. For a very long time."

Sam's heart swelled. She knew exactly what he meant. She felt the same. She'd waited so long, she'd become so accustomed to the sensation, she'd forgotten what it actually meant. Now, she knew. She'd been waiting — for him. For this.

Still, she couldn't promise much. She frowned, not knowing how to let him know. He placed a finger against her lips.

"Don't. Don't think about tomorrow. Don't think about any of the many 'what ifs,' just think about us — tonight."

She closed her eyes, the tension draining from her shoulders, and relaxed against him. "You're right."

"I know. That wasn't so hard, was it?" He grinned at her even as he scooped her up in his arms and carried her to the bedroom.

"Always got to be right, don't you?" She couldn't resist teasing him. He set her on the bed, only she bounced to her knees and started opening the buttons on his shirt.

"Nope. Like right now. I think you're right." His grin blew her away. She couldn't help but respond to the lightness of his tone. She never knew lovemaking could be so much fun. She quickened her pace, pulling his shirttail out of his jeans and down his arms.

"Whoa, take it easy. We've got all night." He shrugged out of his shirt, dropping it to the floor.

Sam snorted. "Like hell." She reached for his belt buckle, when the tantalizing bulge just below sidetracked her. Her fingers wandered, caressing with exploratory strokes before finally wrapping around and gently squeezing.

"Jesus Christ," he yelped, trying to put some distance between them. "This will be over before we ever get started if you don't stop that."

Sam grinned, feeling a lightness to her soul she'd never experienced before. "I don't care."

"What?" he responded, outraged. "Oh you don't, huh? Well, two can play that game." In a smooth move she hadn't even seen coming, her sweater and t-shirt were pulled over her head and wrapped around her arms, holding them above her head. He applied gentle pressure and Sam found herself lying on her back. Using only one hand, Brandt easily held her there while undoing her jeans and tugging them down her hips, to send them flying across the bed.

He grinned, his smile sensuous and teasing. "Now, it's my turn."

Sam's eyes widened. Expecting to be ravished, his slow sensual assault slid under her defenses.

Ever so gently, his tongue stroked around her nipple. First on one breast, then the other. Tiny nibbles followed the moist path, close, but not quite touching her nipples. She sighed and moaned, twisting closer, then moving sensuously away.

When he did finally take her nipple into his mouth, she arched her back. "Oh God," she whispered almost in prayer.

"You don't need his help tonight. This is nothing you can't handle."

She groaned as he teased the other breast, his lips nibbling and nudging, but never quite taking. She struggled to free her arms, but he'd have none of it.

"Please, I want to touch you. I need to touch...you."

Her arms – instantly set free – wrapped around him, pulling him down on top of her. He groaned as his bare chest slid across her heated skin. Sam slid her hands down to his belt, only to find it and the jeans they'd held up were missing. Her hand stalled, then slid down to the smooth, muscled buttocks. His skin was so soft. She couldn't get enough of the silky expanse.

He willingly offered her every part of himself for her pleasure. Sam took full advantage. Pushing up on his shoulders, he rolled over onto his back, swinging her on top of him. Sam laughed joyously and accepted the invitation. Using her fingers, her lips, and her tongue, she traced, teased, and tormented Brandt until he could stand it no more.

Without warning, Sam found herself flipped over, tucked under him, her legs hooked over his hips. Brandt waited until Sam gazed into his eyes. Then dropping his forehead to hers, he plunged deep.

Sam cried out. Her back arched, sending him deeper. The sensations roiled through her. Her head dropped to the side, her eyes drooped slightly…she was overwhelmed by sensation.

Brandt moved once slowly, then a second time. Need twisted through her, sending her higher and higher. Fragile and yet edged in steel, Sam twisted against the tension whipping through her.

"Brandt," she cried out, almost afraid.

"I'm here sweetheart. Let's go together." He hooked her leg higher and seated himself at her very center.

Sam's senses exploded.

Dimly in the background, she heard Brandt cry out as he found his own release. A long moment later, he collapsed on top of her, rolled to one side, and tucked her firmly up against him.

Well-being and satisfaction permeated the air. Sam curled against him and closed her eyes.

***

2:10 am, June 22nd

The phone rang.

Brandt opened his eyes, struggling to orient himself to the unfamiliar lack of space. He raised his head to find Sam splayed out, fast asleep on his chest. Her bed wasn't intended for someone his size.

The phone rang again.

"Shit." Carefully, he extricated himself from her arms, reaching for his discarded pants and the cell phone in the pocket.

"Hello." Brandt's heart dropped at the voice on the other end. "Right, I'm about a half-hour out."

Standing up, he put the phone away and searched for his briefs. He didn't want to wake her. Neither did he want her to wake up alone. Putting on the briefs, he grabbed his jeans next. While closing the buckle, he glanced over at Sam. She stared at him.

He immediately went to her. "I'm sorry sweetheart." He bent down and kissed her. "I have to go. We have a new victim."

CHAPTER TWENTY-ONE

2:15 am

Ice slipped over Sam's soul at his words. At least they'd found her. She'd been waiting for someone to call this last victim in. She wrapped the blankets tighter around her. The cabin temperature had dropped with the news. Blue crept through her fingers, and her legs had already turned numb. She tucked her legs under and reached for yet another of the cheap blankets stacked on the floor beside her.

"It's her. The one we've been waiting for. The brunette. Her name..." Sam's voice caught in the back of her throat. "Her name is...was Caroline."

A shadow crossed Brandt's face. He nodded to her as he walked out.

"Brandt?" Sam raced to the front door.

Brandt turned to gaze at her, one eyebrow raised. "What?"

"Be careful."

He acknowledged her comment with a nod then he strode over to her, gave her a seriously dangerous kiss, and walked out into the night.

***

2:55 am

On any other day, Brandt would have made record time. But it was just after three on a Sunday morning, and the Saturday night partiers had the city in full swing. Getting to the city was no problem. Navigating to the crime scene was.

"Jesus, Brandt, you must have had a hot date tonight. You aren't usually this late showing up." The forensic team had already arrived. Brandt took their ribbing in good humor, without offering any clue to his whereabouts.

Walking into the suburban brick house, the sense of normalcy struck him. How often did a family-oriented neighborhood hide a heinous crime? Regular two-story homes on city-planned lots surrounded him. Somewhere close would be the elementary school with a high school a little further away, and within walking distance would be the standard corner store.

Bad things did happen to good people. Grimly, he walked into hell.

The odor hit him first – the flies second.

The crime scene had to be several days old. A body in the heat of summer decomposed quickly.

Photographers worked at detailing every little thing. One of the CSI crew stood over the victim, the flashes from his camera creating an irregular staccato pattern. A victim with brunette hair. Brandt stopped in his stride. Amongst the dried blood and body fluids, the pasty white skin shone with an eerie light. Brandt struggled for objectivity. He walked through slowly and calmly, giving each area close scrutiny. Not knowing what to search for, yet he knew he'd recognize it when he saw it.

At the victim's bedside, all attempts at a cool demeanor vanished. The scene was incredibly familiar. Too familiar. Not the hair, not the features...but the injuries. God, the injuries were all too familiar.

Her boyfriend had been out of town. Caroline was supposed to have picked him up at the airport. When she hadn't, he'd come looking for her.

"Hey Brandt. The killer took a trophy this time."

With a sinking feeling, Brandt turned to face Kevin and Adam. Kevin couldn't wait. "He cut off her ear."

Christ.

Brandt paused for a moment to honor the dead woman. Now, more determined than ever to catch this killer, he got down to work.

***

9:10 am

Sam checked the roster. There were two new surgical cases to deal with. One still under anesthesia, while the other was awake and definitely pissed. She couldn't blame the poor thing.

He was a lop-eared rabbit who'd lost part of an ear to a dog. A large bandage covered the right side of his head. Sam quickly cleaned his cage and moved on.

With the basics taken care of, Sam headed to the lunchroom to find a cup of tea. She'd held her thoughts locked up until she saw the lunchroom was empty. With a sigh of relief, she collapsed at the table and dropped her head to her arms. Her heart and mind were a mess. She couldn't help being worried about the colonel's fate. Maisy was such a warm loving character, Sam hated her to be suffering the pain of waiting and not knowing.

Brandt had been on her mind all morning, then that was to be expected after last night. Her heart smiled as memories flooded her. Only to be shut down as Deputy Brooker slammed into her thoughts. She looked around nervously. Could he have tracked her to her place of work?

The door opened, startling her.

"Good morning, Sam." A chorus of greetings startled her. She smiled at the group of noisy women collecting around her. Somehow, she'd managed to create friends, without even trying. She didn't know how or why, but found gratitude welling up inside. It helped not to be so alone.

246

Their chatter swelled and receded and swelled again. Sam rode the waves of utterly bewildering topics from the latest color trend in shoes to the murder victim reported on the morning news. She stayed quiet, not wanting to listen and found it hard not to. The last thing she wanted to do was relive the experience. The thoughts turmoiled around, keeping her off balance and struggling to focus. She worked on keeping her emotions under control. The very name of the victim hurt her deeply. That poor woman.

Eventually, the coffee break ended, sending everyone to their jobs.

The friendly atmosphere followed Sam as she returned to the animals. She realized this was close to the normal life of other people. Instead of an inherent wariness with a guard always in place, other people laughed and joked, at ease with each other. Sam was suddenly hungry for more.

Dr. Wascott came to check on the dog coming out of his drugged state. Sam waited a few minutes, watching the dedicated caring so evident in his actions.

When he was done, she brought up the one subject she'd been waiting to discuss. "Sir," she said diffidently, "Soldier has re-injured himself."

The vet frowned. "How bad? What did he do?"

When she described the wound, the vet nodded. He went over to one of the many floor-to-ceiling cabinets and took out a small tube.

"Here is an antibiotic cream. Use this on the open wound for a few days. If it doesn't get better then you'll have to bring him in."

"I don't think he'll like that."

The vet grimaced. "Truthfully, neither will I. Only we can't have him getting an infection from his ripped stitches."

"Okay, I'll see how he responds to this."

Her day almost done, Sam quickly finished up, grabbed the new cream, and headed out. Once free of work, her thoughts automatically returned to the one subject she'd refused to focus on. Caroline.

She grimaced. Caroline had become the ultimate victim and Sam had been acting like one all along as well. She'd let this asshole control her every waking moment and many of her sleeping ones too. In order to regain control, she had to stop being afraid. In order to control the fear she had to be progressive. And just how the hell was she supposed to make that happen? The fear wouldn't stop overnight. She'd possibly have it forever.

Running a hand over her tired face, Sam vowed to stop letting fear control her. It was going to take constant vigilance to stay on top of this. She'd been afraid most of her life and this wasn't going to stop simply because she'd decided differently this moment. Still, power welled deep within her. She couldn't just sit here any longer and wait for him to pull her strings like a puppeteer.

It was time she pulled a few of her own.

***

9:24 am

"Finally." He punched his heavy fist in the air. Jesus H. Christ, he could die himself before the fucking police actually got their heads on straight. He bet this was all over the Internet.

Bill rubbed his thick fingers over the top of his almost bald head. He'd need to shave again soon. But now he could relax. His victim had been found. Finally. He was tired but happy. There was no joy when his prize was decomposing without someone to watch and fuss over her. He grinned – that lopsided endearing movement as women described it. Before they got to know who and what he really was.

How long before the police actually received his surprise. He felt a moment of misgiving at his spontaneous action, then tossed it off. They'd never figure it out. He rubbed his thick hands together and gloated.

The gift should be nice and ripe by then.

***

10:03 am

Brandt yawned, feeling his face crack and splinter. God he was tired. He shouldn't have come in to work without catching a few hours of sleep, only he'd felt driven by the need to do something constructive. Besides, he might never sleep again. Not after that crime scene. That poor woman had been sliced and diced and Brandt could only feel grateful the killer hadn't been into cooking and eating too.

The forensic evidence wasn't in yet. The autopsy would be soon. All Brandt could do was wait.

He laid his head down on his crossed arms on the desk. He'd just rest his eyes for a minute. That's all he needed.

His phone rang a little later. Bleary-eyed he stared, uncomprehending at the noisy black machine. Sam? Rubbing his hand over his face, he reached for the receiver.

"Hello," he mumbled in a grainy voice. Reaching for his coffee cup, he took a drink to ease his throat. He choked and spluttered on the clammy cold drink, grimaced, and drank another sip. Caffeine was caffeine.

"Brandt, are you okay?"

Not Sam.

His mother. Damn, he'd forgotten. "Mom, I'm fine. How's the colonel?"

"He's still unconscious, but he does appear a little more peaceful now."

"But he hasn't woken up?" Brandt tried to smother a yawn and failed. He needed to talk to the colonel, if and when that was possible. He wanted to call Sam too, just to hear her voice. A warm light wrapped around his heart.

"No. Not yet."

Maisy sounded as tired as he felt. He hurt for her. It was hard to sit and wait when someone you cared about was hurting.

"Brandt, are you there?"

Brandt shook himself. "Yeah, Mom, I'm here." He checked at his watch. "Are you still at the hospital?"

"I'm here again now. I went home, had a shower, and came back in. I don't want him to wake up alone."

"It's almost lunchtime. Why don't I come by and pick you up? We'll go out for a bite to eat together." He could still check in with Sam, take his mom out for lunch and be back in time to tackle his heaped desk.

Maisy hesitated.

"Mom, come on. It would be good for both of us."

She capitulated. "Alright. But just for a bite."

Brandt checked his watch. "Good. I'll finish up here in another hour or so. Then I'll come by and pick you up."

Brandt rang off and stretched. He needed to check his emails and talk to his boss. Neither should take too long.

Bringing up his email, Brandt checked the couple of dozen messages waiting for him. One of them was from the librarian he'd met a couple of days ago. The librarian confirmed various ring patterns used over the decades for class rings and the similarity of the sketch to one used by a specific fraternity.

Brandt couldn't believe it. Finally, a breakthrough. His euphoria died as he read on. The ring design was in use for close to a decade with variations by year. Except it had been out of circulation for two decades. Over five hundred of them could have been purchased. The professor who'd informed the librarian, didn't have any figures or names available as the system hadn't been computerized back then. He did offer a few names of other people who might be able to help.

Brandt weeded through his messages, taking care of priorities. Before leaving for lunch, he walked over to the largest of the file cabinets and carefully hid, then locked Sam's journal inside. That would do for the moment.

"Hey, Brandt."

Brandt turned to find Kevin at the door. "Hey what's up?"

Kevin grinned. "The captain wants to see you. And for a change, I had nothing to do with this one. The grapevine apparently told him about Sam's vision and the latest murder."

"How the hell did the grapevine, or you, even find out?"

Kevin shrugged. "I don't know where I heard about it first, but it's true, isn't it?"

"Is what true?"

"She saw this victim as she died, didn't she?"

Brandt groaned and closed his eyes. "Shit, did I slip up and say something to Adam? God I must have been really tired to have done that."

Kevin snapped his fingers, almost laughing out loud. "Yeah, that might have been who told me."

Captain Johansen's door was ajar when Brandt arrived. He knocked and pushed it open.

"Come in, Brandt. Take a seat." The captain gestured toward the single chair not piled high with file folders.

Closing the door behind him, Brandt made his way to the lone chair and sat.

The captain glanced at him. "Brandt. What's this about your psychic and another murder?"

Brandt said, "It's true. Sorry, I haven't had a chance to catch you up on the latest since coming in from the crime scene."

"You know what will happen if this gets out?" Captain Johansen always had the department's image on his mind. "How close was she?"

"Spot on."

"Damn."

Brandt understood how he felt. "It's not as if we're the first department to have used psychics." Brandt swept his arm toward the wide expanse of glass. "Besides, this is department stuff and the media shouldn't ever know – unless someone tells them."

Captain Johansen glared. "What about her? How are you going to stop her from stepping into the limelight? She could make a huge promo out of this case."

"Sam's not the type."

Brandt watched in fascination as Captain Johansen's beetle brows crinkled, almost meeting in the center of his forehead.

"Everyone is the type. You just have to have the right circumstances to bring it out."

Brandt stared out the window, refusing to be drawn. Captain Johansen was a hard-ass who'd apparently run the department fairly for many decades. His beliefs were little enough to put up with.

"Well, I'm saying that Sam isn't like that – but believe what you want."

The captain shuffled the papers on his desk. "So what did she see and what did she miss?"

It took a few minutes to give him the rundown. He finished with the one thing Sam hadn't seen. "She didn't mention the trophy. And we don't know why her ear was cut off or where it is."

"That's how it works with psychics. They get some of the information right and they get a lot wrong." Captain Johansen doodled on a notepad in front of him, obviously deep in thought.

"True enough." Brandt leaned forward. "This isn't for discussion with anyone else, but I actually saw her go through a vision." He gave a brief version of what he'd seen at Sam's cabin that night. The memories of the cuts appearing on Sam's fragile body haunted him.

"You saw these cuts appear and disappear – and you weren't drunk?"

Brandt stared into Captain Johansen's eyes. "God's truth. I swear I watched the cuts appear and then disappear. There was blood everywhere. Jesus, I panicked."

"Why didn't you call 911?"

Brandt's lips twisted. "I almost did. I managed to get through to Stefan first."

The captain squinted up him. "That would have helped. Did Stefan have answers?"

Brandt nodded. "And thank God he did. I would have caused more damage if I'd touched her. Maybe permanently."

"I don't know what to think about this stuff, however, I know several good cops that swear by Stefan."

"Sam isn't as strong or as secure in her abilities as Stefan. The good news is he's going to help train her. Sam's fragile. She needs to learn to protect herself." Brandt geared for the blow. "And that includes being protected from this department."

The captain leaned forward, glaring at Brandt. "What does that mean?" Larger than life, the captain never backed down from a fight. He had no trouble calling a spade a spade, and he always stood by his men. At six-foot-six, he was built like the football player he used to be.

Brandt glared back. "I can't forget about the ring diagram incident. Someone could also take it into his head to release personal information about Sam." He paused.

"But why?" The captain pounded his fist. "It wouldn't be someone from here. They'd know the damage something like that could cause the department."

"More likely to discredit me."

He waited a beat. "There's another possible complication."

The captain leaned forward. "Let's hear it."

Brandt quickly related what he knew about Deputy Brooker and what had been done to Sam, years ago. And the couple of incidents in the last few days.

The captain very clearly, very succinctly, said one word, "Shit." He shifted his great bulk deeper into his chair. It took another few minutes before Captain Johansen spoke again. "Bring her in. I think it is time I met this person."

"And how am I going to do that?"

"I don't know. That's for you to figure out. Just do it."

Ten minutes later, Brandt reached Sam by phone. "When?" Her tone somehow managed to convey weary acceptance. Damn she sounded tired.

"Today. Now would be good." Now that she'd agreed, he didn't really care, just the faster the better.

"I'm at work. I have roughly another hour-and-a-half before I'm done. Say about 1:30 pm. Does that work for you?"

'That would be great."

He hung up the phone and then remembered. Crap. His mother. He glanced at his watch. He was going to be late. Ah hell. Grabbing his keys, he locked his office and ran.

CHAPTER TWENTY-TWO

1:07 pm

Sam sat stiffly in her chair in Brandt's office. As soon as she'd arrived, Brandt had excused himself. What the hell was up with that? He'd mentioned something about the captain wanting to speak with her.

Hearing a noise, she turned to watch as one of the clerks walked in, smiled, and dropped a stack of mail onto Brandt's desk. Of course, there was no Brandt.

Just when she'd determined to go searching for him, Brandt walked in, followed by a huge man who dominated the small office.

Sam shifted to the side, slightly intimidated at the outright bulk of the two males. She tucked her fingers under her thighs, hoping to still the nervous rapping on the chair.

"Sam, this is my boss, Captain Johansen."

Surprised, Sam could only smile and nod. She shifted to the one side of her chair again.

The captain gave her a gentle smile that was at odds with his size. "It's nice to meet you, miss." He sat down on the chair beside her.

Sam could feel her eyes grow wider. She struggled against the nervousness threatening to overwhelm her. The captain smiled again. It didn't make her feel any better.

"What can I do for you, Captain?"

"I've spoken to Detective Sutherland here." Captain Johansen glanced at Brandt. "And he's told me a lot about you."

255

Sam whipped around to stare at Brandt. "Did he now?" Her eyes bored a question into the hapless target. When he nodded slowly, she slumped into her chair and closed her eyes, just barely holding back a groan. "Great," she whispered barely above an audible tone.

"Now I'm not saying that I agree with all this stuff, but I'm willing to trust Brandt. He says you have some impressive data. The problem is, I don't really want the public to know that you've been helping us."

That made sense, sort of. "Good. Neither do I."

He pursed his lips, gave a decisive nod, and continued. "Then we agree on that." The captain fell silent, Brandt stayed quiet, and Sam didn't know what to say.

"Why are you're telling me this?" She felt suspiciously under attack again.

The captain gazed at Brandt, one eyebrow raised.

"Stop it. No silent conversations between you two. Talk to me," she snapped. She glared at the two men.

Brandt hid his smile.

Captain Johansen opened the discussion. "We'd like to be able to use any information that you have for us. Like the ring. You know about the ring sketch on the news, right?" At her nod, he continued, "That wasn't supposed to happen. Still, it is bringing in tips on our hotline. There is a slight possibility that other information was accessed at the same time, but only a very slim chance."

She didn't know what to say. "Am I in danger?"

Again, the two men exchanged glances.

"I don't think so. Your address is a PO box and not a house address, so that would slow down anyone searching for you," said the captain. He took one of her hands in his. "I just need you to be careful until we get to the bottom of this."

"That's a little hard when you don't know what the threat is or where it's coming from."

Captain Johansen spoke up. "The killer doesn't know about you – does he?"

That was a horrible thought. "No I don't think so. Unless someone told him, or he's psychic, too. The chances of that aren't great."

He nodded. "Right. So just be careful."

Paper rustled as Brandt casually sorted the stack of mail on his desk. There was a small padded envelope in the stack. Grabbing scissors, he cut the tape.

Sam watched him. "An early Christmas present?"

Brandt snorted. "Not likely. The paper came off and the top of the box followed.

"Ohh, God. What is that?" Sam cried out as a nasty odor permeated the room.

The captain dropped her hand and damn near pounced on the parcel. Bits of paper went flying. The lid was slapped down and both men donned gloves from a box sitting on the filing cabinet. As Brandt reached for the box again, the captain held his arm and nodded in Sam's direction.

Brandt, realization coming into his face, nodded and walked around the side of his desk. He put an arm around Sam's shoulders and urged her out the door. "Sam, come sit out in the hallway. I'll get you a coffee. There might even be a fresh pot, if you're lucky."

Before she had time to register the offer, she'd been seated outside, and he'd already returned with a hot cup of coffee and a stack of magazines. "I'll be right back. Sit tight."

Sam, her hands burning with the heat of the Styrofoam cup, sat in numb silence. For all their efforts, there was no way to hide the smell or the fast glimpse she'd seen. She couldn't be sure, but she thought the box contained an ear: a bloody ear, still wearing an earring.

Several men came in and out. She watched, blind to most of it. The office swelled with people. Someone dropped a stack of paper on the chair beside her, someone else came and picked it up. Sam saw a small piece of paper on the floor. Not bigger than a half inch and was mustard colored like the package. Surely, it was important, too. She couldn't let the idea go as people walked over it and beside it – yet always missed it. Taking advantage of a lull, Sam snatched up the tiny piece, before plunking down on her chair again.

Instantly, the station disappeared as an unexpected door opened. She couldn't think. She couldn't focus. She couldn't see. She was lost in a black haze. Her hand holding the hot coffee ceased to hurt. Her surroundings ceased to exist. She walked in a grey fog, pulled down a path she'd never walked before.

Evil called to her, laughed at her, and even caressed her arms as she travelled. She knew there was something she had to do. Some reason for being here. But what? She didn't want to be here. It was dark, scary, and so very cold. The smell, God, the smell resembled a garden planted full of decomposing bodies. She felt compelled to walk forward. The fear and uncertainty diminished. The need increased. By now, the blackness soothed even as it hypnotized. She walked forward, uncaring where she went.

Then she heard it.

Mocking laughter filled the air, her ears, and even her soul.

Sam screamed.

***

1:30 pm

Jesus. Sam.

Brandt bolted in her direction and still came in behind the group filling the hallway. Where was she? Her high-pitched scream shut off abruptly. Brandt wrestled through the crowd to her side.

The captain was already yelling at everyone. "Give her room. Come on everyone, move back."

The crowd grumbled, giving way under his orders – slightly. Brandt spun around and glared at them. "Come on. Give her some air for Christ's sake. Sam? Sam, are you alright?"

This time several of the spectators broke away and headed back to their own duties. Only a few of the braver souls remained.

One of them asked, "Do you want us to call for an ambulance?"

Brandt checked Sam over. Pallid whiteness defined her face. Blue veins pulsed steadily down the gentle line of her throat. She was breathing slowly, evenly. She was either right out from a vision, or she was comatose from an injury. As she hadn't been on her own long enough and there were no visible signs of injury, he presumed she was reacting on a psychic level. Her hands gripped a piece of brownish-gold paper clenched in one hand.

Not sure if he should be touching her at all, Brandt plucked the offending piece out of her hand and took a closer look. It appeared to be a piece from that grisly package. If so, it could explain her fugue now. Turning around, he found only the captain and Kevin remained.

"Is she okay?" Kevin stood to one side, doubt and confusion in his eyes.

"What's the matter with her?" whispered the captain, crouching down beside him.

Brandt opened his hand to show him the paper. "I think she touched this, unwittingly, and it's sent her in a psychic state."

"What does that mean?" The captain studied her. "She's awfully pale. Is she okay?"

"I think so. I don't really know."

Her position looked so uncomfortable. Her body slouched sideways. She'd fall any minute. His office wouldn't offer anything more comfortable. The captain was obviously thinking along the same lines.

"Can we get her into my office? We can lay her on the couch there."

"Only we're not supposed to touch her."

"But we can't leave her here. She's going to hit the ground in a minute."

Decision made, Brandt slipped his arms under her legs and back and carried her to the captain's office. Once there, he gently laid her down, her head on a pillow. She moaned with the jostling movements.

"Sam. It's okay. Take it easy."

Her eyes flickered. Brandt eased back in relief. She was waking up. He didn't know what had happened, though he could make an educated guess. She really had no control. When visions took her over, it was as if she stepped out. He couldn't protect her – not from her own abilities. Not an easy thing to admit. He admired her guts. But he was damn sure he could *not* live her life.

Sam's eyes had a glazed look as awareness slowly returned. She glanced around the room, a frown wrinkling her face. "Where am I?"

"This is the captain's office. We moved you in here so you could lie down. How are you feeling?"

"Huh? Did I have another vision?" Her frown turned pensive as she thought deeply. "There was such blackness. The world smelled dead." She turned to him, a wave of sadness making her eyes huge wells of pain. "It was her ear, wasn't it?"

At the reminder, Brandt winced. "I'd hoped you hadn't seen that."

"Just a glimpse." She rolled her head against the couch. "That was enough."

"I'm sorry. You should never have been exposed to that."

She grimaced. "Really, what do you think my nightmares are like?" Bitterness tinged her voice, melding with the sadness. Brandt managed not to wince again but just barely.

Staring around the room, he found the captain sitting at his desk, listening in. Kevin stood beside him, watching, a deep frown of concentration across his forehead.

"Did you..." Brandt hesitated, "Did you learn anything useful while you were in this place? Wherever it was." He studied her reaction.

"I don't know where I was either. I think..." she hesitated.

"Go ahead."

"I think I connected with the killer this time. But I can't be sure." She looked at each man, one at a time. "I think I was inside his mind. A black pit of darkness that lost its way a long time ago. He thinks you're all useless idiots and that you'll never catch him."

Kevin butted in. "That covers every criminal out there."

Brandt nodded, but kept watching Sam. "Anything else?"

"He's old energy. He's been doing this for decades. He won't ever quit. You'll have to kill him."

"My pleasure." And Brandt meant it. He'd bring him to justice if he could. However if not, well sometimes that was the best way all around. "Do you know anything about what he's planning next? Where he is? What he's doing?"

Sam's eyelids drooped and a faraway look came over her pale features. "He's waiting. He's rubbing his hands gleefully and imagining your face, your reaction when you open the gift."

"Why? That *gift* doesn't make any sense. We already have his victim. The ear makes no difference." The captain spoke up for the first time.

A large tear welled up in the corner of Sam's eye. Brandt reached over and gently wiped it away.

"It's not her earring. It's her ear, yet another woman's earring."

"Another woman?" Captain Johansen surged to his feet. "What, there's another victim?"

"He thinks you won't figure it out. It's an older victim. His trophy from the drugged one. He doesn't want to keep it. She's not a memory he wants to honor. She was a failure for him."

"Sam." Brandt gently tapped the side of her head. "Sam, wake up."

"Is she aware of what she's saying?" Captain Johansen came around his desk to bend over and see for himself.

Kevin jumped in. "Do you think she was telling the truth?"

"The truth as she knows it. Yes." Brandt stroked her cheek gently, willing her to come to awareness. It took another moment before she opened her eyes again.

"Please quit doing that, will you? It scares the hell out me." He was rewarded with a half-smile. "Are you back now?"

It was weak but it was a nod.

"Then sit up," he said and half tugged her upright to lean against the overstuffed couch cushions. "Maybe now you won't go under again."

Sam curled into a small ball, huddling with her knees to her chin. A blue color highlighted her cheekbones.

"Jesus, you're freezing." Brandt searched the room for something to cover her. Captain Johansen walked over to a coat stand in the corner and pulled down a large wool overcoat. Sam gratefully snuggled under the warm material.

Captain Johansen asked in a diffident voice, "I know you're not exactly recovered but...do you have any other information that would help us?"

Brandt jumped in. "If you connected to the killer, does he have his next victim picked out?"

Her answer came out on such a soft breath the three men bent to hear her.

"Yes."

Kevin looked to Brandt, shrugged sheepishly, then returned his gaze to Sam. "Can you give us any details? Anything helpful that we might help us to find her?"

Sam shook her head slightly. "Only that she's close to him geographically. He watches her, follows her everywhere. His hunger is building. He's enjoying this stage. Soon though, he'll have to appease his appetite. Not yet. He has time to play."

Brandt wondered. "Do you get a sense that he works or has a career? Does money ever enter his mind?"

Captain Johansen added, "What about his location? Can you see any landmarks? Anything that tells you where she might be?"

"Only stores, a drugstore, a coffee shop, sidewalks. I saw only some of the scenes from his mind." Sam rested for a moment. "She's Caucasian."

All three men stared at her, startled. "You can see her?"

"Only bits and pieces." Keeping her eyes closed, Sam, in a monotone voice, said, "She's tall. He's taller. She's young, mid-twenties with long brunette hair." She fell silent again.

The men exchanged glances, everyone anxious for the one or two details that could make the difference between finding her, or not.

Not wanting to disturb her if she were getting more information, only he didn't want her zoning out again either, Brandt murmured, "Sam, you there?"

She opened her eyes slowly, as if they were weighted down. "She has a vehicle."

Kevin snapped forward. "Can you see a license plate? Make? Model? Color? Sam – anything?"

Brandt shot him an approving nod. At least Kevin appeared to be taking a solid step toward accepting Sam's abilities.

"Red, small, two door. Can't see a license plate. He's watching her get in the car."

Brandt, on a sudden thought, asked, "Sam, is he sitting inside his car?"

After a long moment, Sam nodded. "I can't see much. The windshield is tinted blue green. The seats are dark green."

"Bench seats or individual?"

"Bench."

"Old or new?"

"Can't tell."

After that the questions came hard and fast from all sides. Some she answered and more she couldn't. After fifteen minutes, all three of them had run out. Brandt couldn't believe it. He was exhausted, so he could only imagine how Sam felt. In fact, he leaned over to find she'd fallen asleep. He reached to tug the coat higher up her shoulders.

Nodding to the others, Brandt followed the men outside and closed the door behind them. Once in the hallway, Brandt leaned against the closed door and looked at the other two. "So, what do you make of it?"

Captain Johansen grimaced. "I have no idea. I sure as hell hope she's giving us viable information. But we don't have much else to go on. Period."

Kevin spoke up. "We might find a different DNA on the earring versus DNA of the ear. That will give us some idea."

"That will help. Sam had mentioned this victim before. I came up with two possible women. One is in the morgue and one is in a coma at Portland General. We can check to see if one of the women was wearing the matching earring. If the victim is dead, then we're too late to help her. We'll need to check her for forensic information, but other than that, we should be trying to find his next victim."

Pursing his lips, Captain Johansen agreed. "I'll go to the lab now and talk to them. What do we do about her?"

"She needs to sleep this off. Her energy level drops quickly with these visions." That was a given. "I don't want to leave her for too long. She shouldn't wake up alone."

Kevin nodded. "Stay with her and I'll start with phone calls and running car data. I may just owe her an apology." Leaving, Brandt staring after him open-mouthed. He smiled and walked to his office. Brandt raised an eyebrow at Captain Johansen who shrugged. "Don't know, but I'm heading to the lab to make sure they don't screw this up."

Ten minutes later, after making a few phone calls of his own, Brandt opened the captain's office door to check on Sam. He must have woken her for she sat up, startled and nervous.

"Shh, Sam. It's okay. I'm sorry. I didn't mean to wake you." He walked in and sat at the edge of the couch beside her, close, without touching. She peered at him, still groggy.

"Wow. I guess I fell asleep?"

He smiled. "That you did. Not for long though, maybe fifteen or twenty minutes."

She stood up uncertainly. "What time is it? Can I leave now?" She searched around anxiously. "Where's my purse?"

"Take it easy. First, it's not that late. You've been here for just over an hour. Your purse is in my office, and yes, you can leave." He opened his arms, closing them around her as she walked into his embrace. "There, that wasn't so hard was it?"

She stared at him, fatigue pulling at her features.

Brandt hurt for her. She had to be exhausted. "I want you to stay and rest for a bit."

"I'm fine." She visibly straightened and produced a stronger smile. Brandt wasn't fooled in the least.

"Have you eaten?"

Confusion clouded her face. "I think so."

He nodded. " I may have found the drugged woman. She came in during the right time period – and with one earring missing. Her name is Annalea Watson. I'm on my way over to check it against the one that just arrived. The lab has taken swabs of it to match DNA, if need be. The woman is alive, but she's in a coma."

Sam's eyes widened. "But that's wonderful."

"So far so good. Come on, let's find your purse and get you some food."

***

1:50 pm

Kevin hurried to his desk. He couldn't believe what he'd seen. Or heard. His mind had been blown, and it still had a frazzled edge to it.

If he hadn't been there and seen it for himself... Well, he couldn't even go there yet. All his life, he'd thought he understood the ways of the world. He just didn't know anymore.

He did know one thing – she couldn't have been making this up. He'd watched her very carefully. Her eyes had been blind, the pupils dilated and unfocused. She'd been almost comatose at one point, then completely awake at another.

Her face had gone dead white, then flushed cherry red on her return. Her skin, God, her skin had been so thin and so blue. He shook her head.

No one could have faked that.

***

2:15 pm

Now wasn't that interesting? Dillon kept his face impassive as he watched the chaos going on around him. He'd been on the phone when the woman had screamed. Detective Sutherland had a hell of a reputation with the ladies – but not this kind.

Thinking she must be an informant of one kind or another, Dillon had initially ignored her. Until she'd screamed. Still he'd thought, hearing about the gruesome delivery, that it had to have been her reaction to the gift. But not after the preferential treatment she received in the captain's office. When that was followed by an intense session later, Dillon's interest was truly piqued.

So this was the psychic Brandt was working with. Unbelievable. He laughed.

By the time she walked out of the office, he had to admit, she did appear as if she'd been pushed through an old wringer washing machine. Brandt's careful handling confirmed one thing. Brandt must be sleeping with the weirdo witch. Brave man. And smart too. That was the best way to control a woman.

And while Brandt stayed focused on her, it gave Dillon a chance to move in and on up.

CHAPTER TWENTY-THREE

7:48 pm

The sun had lost its heat by the time Sam managed to get home. Seemed Moses couldn't contain his joy. She knew he hated it when she came in late. Soldier wagged his tail, his only concession to her arrival. It was a step in the right direction.

She should have gone home after the vision, except working around the animals helped recharge her psychic batteries faster than anything else. Though working didn't help her physical energy levels, they would recharge faster once her psychic energy levels were high again.

Sam survived by shoving everything to the back of her mind and staying on task. Only once, had she fallen off balance – when she'd noticed the blue dangly earrings in Lucy's ears. It had been all she could to hold back the memories...and the tears. After that, Sam had stayed away from the others.

Only when she tried to make it up her porch stairs and inside the cabin did Sam realize the hamburger Brandt had bought for her had been a long time ago.

The kitchen seemed empty and cold. Leftover dishes in the sink, and an almost empty fridge added to the forlorn atmosphere. It took a moment of rooting through the cupboards before she found a can of soup and half-a-package of crackers.

"Yeah, food." She turned on a burner and slowly warmed up the soup, munching on the crackers while waiting for the rest of the meal to catch up. Just before the soup had heated enough to eat, Sam fed her animals. Then it was her turn.

She turned off the kitchen light and sat in the fading sun's rays. At some point in the last few days, the atmosphere inside the cabin had changed. The normal sense of security had disappeared. The darkness, instead of giving her peace, threw long scary shadows. It didn't feel right anymore. The loss of its solace devastated her.

Feeling chilled, she cupped the cooling soup bowl, needing what warmth remained. She drank down the last of the broth then headed outside.

With Moses at her heels, she walked to the dock. Hearing something behind her, Sam spun around, surprised to see Soldier hobbling after her. Happy with his progress, she ran toward him only to stop at his warning growl.

"Damn it, Soldier. What do I have to do to gain some acceptance here?"

His growl deepened.

Crouched down close to him, Sam didn't know whether to continue outside or head in. The sound of an approaching vehicle decided it for her. She stepped further into the shadows, glad she'd left the house in darkness. She knew the sound of Brandt's truck by now only it appeared identical to the asshole's truck who tried to run her off the road. She wasn't taking any chances.

Silently, the dogs at her side, Sam kept to the darkness of the trees and watched as a vehicle approached. Powerful lights lit the way.

At the house, the vehicle parked and a man got out. Sam squinted through the darkness. He looked like Brandt, yet she couldn't be sure. She refused to be the first to make a sound.

The man approached the dark house warily.

Sam watched just as cautiously.

The man jumped up the stairs and knocked on the front door.

He knocked again. He pivoted, searching the encroaching darkness. There was no way anyone could miss her truck parked out front. "Sam, are you in there?"

It was Brandt. Joy lit the dark areas in her heart and filled them with a sense of security. Misplaced feelings or not, she was glad to see him.

"I'm over here."

Brandt turned in her direction. "Where?"

"Down toward the dock." Still, she didn't move, waiting instead for him to approach her.

"Why the hell are you wandering around outside in the dark?" He stormed in her direction. "And why the *hell* didn't you answer the phone?" As he approached, his face switched from worry, to exasperation, and finally to a building anger. "Do you know how many times I tried to call? Did you ever consider that someone might be worried about you – especially after the day you had?"

Sam stepped forward so he could see her. "Hi." She pulled her phone out of her pocket, saying, "It's a beautiful night. Why shouldn't I be out?" Flipping her phone open, she groaned. "Shit. My battery is dead. I'm sorry, I never even checked."

He shook his head. "Right. Of course, it is. There's no reason to be extra careful or accessible, huh?"

Sam defended her actions. "I said I'm sorry. Besides, I have the dogs with me."

"Not a lot of good they are going to be against a bullet or two, are they? Remember the last time?"

She didn't need this. "So did you have an official reason for this visit or did you just come to yell at me?"

"Sorry." He smiled slightly, reached out and snagged her into his arms where she cuddled right in. "I am sorry, but you scared the hell out of me when I couldn't reach you by phone. I've been trying for hours."

Leading the way, Sam walked to the cabin. "As you can see, I'm fine." She didn't wait to see if he caught up with her. As she passed his truck, he stopped and opened the passenger door. Curious, she turned in time to see him pull an overnight bag out before locking up the vehicle.

Sam glanced sidelong at the bag, but reality didn't hit until she'd opened the door. Excitement unfurled deep in her tummy. Her breath hitched even as a kernel of outrage sparked at his audacity. She didn't know how to react. How to feel. Excited and comforted, all mixed up with relief. She needed to know for sure. She turned around. "What's the bag for?"

"If you won't look after yourself, then someone has to do it for you." Brandt walked around her and stepped inside. "Therefore, you have a houseguest." He walked over to the worn out couch and dropped his bag with a heavy thunk. "Besides, I have a couple of questions I need answered."

Sam didn't want to give in so easily. He had a lot of nerve making this decision without her. And yet, she couldn't be happier. "Did you ever consider asking me?"

"Asking – oh yeah, that's one of the questions I'd planned on putting to you earlier. But... Oh right, you wouldn't pick up the phone. So now I don't need to ask, do I?" He kicked back on the couch, his arms behind his head. His grin split his face in two.

"Whatever." Sam pushed the door shut with a little more force than she'd planned. She reached for her answer to all life's ailments – tea.

"So why didn't you know about the souvenir?"

Sam stilled. Turning away from him, she pulled out two cups from the cupboard.

"I won't go away."

Sam sighed, poured two cupfulls before walking over to sit down opposite Brandt. "Are you sure?"

He grinned. "Positive."

Sam sat in silence, then sipped her tea, staring quietly at the irritating and highly amused man in front of her.

"Get it through your head. I'm here for the long haul."

Sam tilted her head to stare at him in confusion. Quickly, she glanced down again. Surely, he hadn't meant that, had he? But God, she hoped he had. She didn't know much about long hauling, but she'd like to.

He sat up and leaned toward her. "So tell me why."

She tried to focus on the conversation. As much as she didn't want to revisit the case, she knew he wouldn't lay off. "I didn't know because it was sliced off after the woman died. After I disconnected."

Brandt's face was a study of emotions as he considered her words. "Then I guess it's a blessing that you didn't know."

With a frown, Sam sat back. "I'm not always so lucky." Sam stopped, as emotion rose dangerously high. She swallowed heavily. "Once the victims die, I have a couple of minutes of adjustment. How they die and how long it takes them to disconnect, determines how long I am caught in limbo. Sometimes, I'm aware of what happens to their bodies after death if I'm still stuck there."

Staring down at the table, her fingers traced the old pattern showing through the melamine top. "And sometimes," she said, raising her gaze slowly. "And sometimes, people think the victims are dead, but..." Tears clogged her voice. "But they aren't a hundred percent gone yet." Sam wiped her eyes with the back of her sweater sleeve. "They, and I, can feel every little thing then."

Her vision blurred with tears and through it all she tried to see if Brandt understood. The look on his face broke her heart.

"I'm sorry. I shouldn't have told you."

"No. No. Don't feel that way." He reached across the table, his hand a protective cover over hers. He squeezed her hand. "It's just disturbing that you have to go through this all the time." His thumb stroked across the soft skin beside her thumb.

"Working in law enforcement, I'm exposed to every horrific human experience. I should be used to it... It still catches me sometimes."

Sam gently caught up his fingers in hers. "I know. It's the same for me. People can be vicious to each other."

His lips twisted in a wry grin. "That's often why relationships don't work for law enforcement officers. If we marry someone *not* in the same field, then the partner doesn't have the understanding of what we go through every day. And if we marry another officer, then there is no leaving the work behind. Living with this level of violence every day, slowly wears down the relationship until nothing can hold it together."

"How horrible."

Moses barked, startling her. An odd sound rustled outside the cabin. Frowning, she went to the front door and stared out the window to the one side. The blackness showed nothing untoward. She opened the door to let both dogs outside then followed them. Brandt was suddenly at her side.

"What did you hear?"

"I'm not sure. Something was moving out here."

"Wildlife?"

She shook her head. "No. The dogs wouldn't react like that."

In the distance, a faint rumbling sound could be heard. A vehicle.

"Can you hear the highway from here?"

"Occasionally. It depends on the weather." As her voice died away so too did the engine sound.

"It has to be on the highway."

"Unless someone drove part way and then walked the rest."

The two stared at each other, uneasiness hanging heavy on the evening air.

Sam stepped closer, linking her arm with his. "I forgot to say thank you for coming. I really don't want to be alone tonight."

Survival had meant being alone before. She didn't know what to do with Brandt. Having sex once was one thing – didn't other people easily toss sex off as a momentary passionate lapse? Twice well, didn't that constitute a relationship? She didn't do those. Or she hadn't done in a long time. And she was pretty sure, he didn't do them either. Better to clear the air and tell him, no matter how uncomfortable.

"I need to tell you that I don't do relationships." Oh wasn't that smooth, Sam. Good job, Sam? How to advertise your inexperience and total lack of social skills.

Brandt slowly turned around to stare at her. "Why not?"

Heat pooled in her tummy at the sensuous vibes emanating from him. Her cheeks warmed, but she stood her ground. "I'm no good at them," she said baldly.

"How would you know if you don't do them?" he asked in a reasonable tone of voice.

Sam stared at him, unsure of how to go on. "I tried."

"So that's it. You tried and failed so you're doomed to a life alone? Haven't we been around this block once before?"

"Yes. No. I don't know. Maybe." Sam shut up, too flustered to answer clearly.

"You don't know because you're too afraid to go on."

"So?" she challenged him.

"So live a little. Don't spend your life so afraid of trying and failing that you live alone. Take a chance and let someone in your world." He reached out and cupped her chin, raising her face to meet his gaze. "I want to be a part of your world. I thought I'd proved that already."

He was saying the words she'd yearned to hear all her life. Moisture collected at the corner of her eyes. It's all she could to not start bawling. In spite of herself, her bottom lip trembled.

His thumb smoothed even as it rubbed her lower lip, gently teasing it to a smile. Sam couldn't resist. She kissed his thumb as it made its next pass.

He stopped. "Dangerous."

Sam's lips twitched. His thumb moved again, this time much slower, more seductive in its sensual mission. The tantalizing movement slowed when it reached the middle swell, where it sat heavy and waiting. Sam raised her eyes to his.

His asked a question.

Sam hesitated. Did twice mean a commitment. Or given her lack of social skills and inexperience did twice mean still dating? Could she really walk away? Did she even want to? No. If at the end she was devastated, then so be it. At least she'd have enjoyed life...and him for a little while.

Closing her eyes, she let her body answer for her. Her lips parted slightly. Her tongue slipped out to caress his thumb. Sliding first to one side then to the other.

Brandt bent his head, his eyes absorbed with her every tiny movement.

From under half-closed lids, Sam watched his eyes deepen, darken. Sliding her tongue out further, she slowly curled it around the top of his thumb. Instinctively, she'd invited him inside. He didn't resist. His thumb gently caressed the inside of her lips. Sam closed her teeth on his skin, tugging his thumb ever so gently inside. She sucked it lightly, her eyes wide, watching him watch her.

His eyes became heavy-lidded, his breathing harsh and rasping. Sam half smiled. She sucked harder.

His mouth opened, his tongue gently licking across his own lips. His nostrils flared.

The wait became unbearable. Sam closed her eyes to enjoy the simple sense of arousal. Nerve endings she'd tamped down surged to life, making her body tingle in places she didn't even know could respond.

Then he pulled his thumb away.

Her eyes snapped open. Blinded by sensation, her whole being focused on his mouth as he lowered his head and replaced his thumb with his lips. Stunning, hot liquid engulfed her as Brandt kissed her slowly, leisurely, and very, very competently.

When he lifted his head long minutes later, Sam sagged against him.

Holding her close, his lips against her ears, he whispered, "Too much?"

She shook her head, and whispered, "Not enough."

He needed no encouragement: bending and lifting her in his arms, easily carrying her up the stairs to the single room upstairs. He lowered her feet to the floor. Lowering his head, he gave her a long, slow kiss. When he broke it off, she stretched on tiptoes to recapture his lips.

"Sam, I need to know – are you sure? I don't want just a moment. I want to see where this goes. To give it a try. To give us a try."

Sam didn't want to talk, but Brandt reached up to hold her face in his warm hands as he dropped soothing kisses on her forehead, her cheeks, her closed eyelids, and even the corners of her mouth – but never on her lips. "Are you sure?" he murmured insistently.

Sam moaned as his teasing lips moved to her ear and down the smooth line of her neck. Shivers ran down her spine. She melted deeper against him.

"Sam."

She smiled. Her tongue slid against his lips, darting inside to stroke his tongue. Brandt took her mouth in a deep drugging kiss. He finally broke off the kiss, breathing in deep sharp rasps. "Sam, answer me," he ordered.

Sam forced her heavy eyelids open to stare at him in confusion.

"Say yes."

With her gaze fixed on his, she whispered the promise they both needed to hear. "Yes."

***

11:00 pm

Brandt studied his surroundings. The bare bedroom fascinated him. What an insight into her personal life. All walls and the painted ceiling were bare, not even a poster to break up the bleakness. There were no dressers, closets, or storage of any kind. He could only imagine how her life had been up until now.

Her bed held cheap army surplus blankets with even more stacked on the floor. He glanced at the odd stack of blankets. His face grew grim as understanding crashed in on him. They were spares in case what happened to the one on the couch, happened again.

His cell phone rang. His heart sank. Gently, disengaging himself from Sam's arms, he hurried to find the phone before she woke up.

"Hello." His cell phone showed it was just past eleven. Moonlight cast a pale shadow on the bedroom floor.

"Brandt. We've got trouble."

Brandt listened, glaring into the night. "What the hell? Not again. Who. Did. This?"

"I don't know. I have called the station, but no one is talking. If it takes a court order, I will find out. The ring incident was minor compared to this. You need to warn Samantha."

"Oh I will. Don't worry about that. I get first dibs on the asshole that did this."

"Don't go jumping to conclusions," warned the captain.

"I'm not. Go ahead. Get all the proof you need – then he's mine." Brandt's mind fired on all cylinders. "They actually gave her name? How irresponsible is that?"

"They say it never occurred to them that she might be in danger. Many psychics need publicity to stay in business. I don't think they understand what they've done. But don't worry. You look after Sam, and I'll sort this out."

His voice brooked no argument.

"Fine. You get the first shot. Sort it out...or I will." Brandt hung up.

***

11:05 pm

"Oh Shit!"

Dillon leaned forward to stare at the television newscaster, his handful of chips frozen in midair. Sam's face filled the screen. Dillon chest constricted. He hadn't done this. He hadn't given the media a picture of her. Oh, crap. He dumped the chips into the bowl and rubbed his hands through his hair. It wouldn't matter if he'd done this or not. If anyone found out what he had done, he'd be blamed regardless. He was so fired.

He'd talked to the reporter, but had only mentioned a psychic being part of the investigation. How could they have put the rest together? He hadn't given them any details. He sure as hell wouldn't have given them her name.

They had to have a name to get a picture. Or the reverse. That's it! Someone could have seen and recognized her at the station. Then it would have been easy to have followed up on her.

Not that it mattered. Once the others knew he'd talked to the media a little bit, no one would believe he hadn't given them everything. Everyone would assume the worst. Given his behavior to date, he couldn't blame them.

The woman's face stayed on the screen so long Dillon wanted to throw something.

What was he going to do?

There was no doubt about one thing. If Brandt and Sam were right about a killer taking out women in the area, there was no doubt which woman would be his next victim.

He needed to save his neck. Shit. There was only one way.

He reached for the phone.

***

11:06 pm

"What the hell!" Beer spewed out of Bill's mouth. He leaned forward to hear the newscaster's voice clearer. "A fucking psychic."

The small apartment closed in on him for a long moment. The picture on the screen wavered before focusing in tightly again. Whoever she was, she looked like hell. The picture was grainy and old, the woman hardly identifiable.

He leaned back, unsure what to think. After a minute, he started to laugh. A slow rolling-barrel laugh pealed across the small room. "Oh God, that is too funny. Fucking incompetent cops. They can't solve anything. Their heads are stuck so far up their asses they had to bring in a goddamned psychic."

With his beer safely down on the long pine coffee table, he laughed and laughed. This was so perfect.

Abruptly the laughter died in his throat. He glared at the picture still on the screen, committing her features to memory.

She'd better not sense him. He'd fucking kill her.

CHAPTER TWENTY-FOUR

11:15 pm

Brandt gazed down at the sleeping angel beside him. God, help him, he was just as much to blame for this mess. There were so many things he could have done. He could have talked to the station himself about who supplied the picture of the ring. He could have put the fear of God into Dillon and Kevin – let them know he was suspicious of them. Most of all, he should have beat the shit out of that asshole deputy from her past. He closed his eyes and groaned. Guilt squeezed his heart. Stupid.

He'd never knowingly do anything to hurt her. Ever. But just as bad...he'd promised to keep her involvement private and he'd failed.

His arm tightened around the tiny woman that had broken into the locked places in his heart. Lowering his head, he dropped tiny caresses to the side of her face tucked into his shoulder. Unbelievable. He cared so much and just the thought of anything happening to her made his arms squeeze tightly.

With a muffled protest, Sam, still asleep, shifted slightly out of his grasp. "Sorry, sweetheart." Brandt shifted to give her more space.

His phone rang again. Casting a worried look at Sam, Brandt slid upward to sit against the wall, cell phone in hand.

"Hello."

Captain Johansen's next words had Brandt hopping out of bed to the far side of the room. He stopped in front of the window. "What?" he hissed.

Brandt shook his head at the next piece of information. "He what? What the hell was he thinking? Yet, he says he *didn't* give them her picture and name?" Brandt, remembering Sam was still asleep, took several deep breaths. "Do you believe him?"

Brandt, tucking the phone against his shoulder, quickly pulled on his briefs and pants. Trying not to wake Sam, he walked downstairs and into the kitchen.

The captain's heavy sigh was unmistakable. "Yes. I do. He's an idiot, mostly a harmless one. Do you have a picture of her in the file?"

"No, I don't."

"Right, and he wouldn't have gone to the trouble of digging one out. He's too damn lazy for that. Chances are someone else did it. I just don't know who yet. The station did admit this information came from a different source than the one who provided the ring – which confirms Dillon's story."

"Christ, what a mess." Knowing the captain agreed didn't help any.

"Brandt – you know what has to happen. I'll deal with Dillon. You have to get her to a safe house."

Brandt laughed a short angry bark. "That's not as easy as it sounds. She's not going to be happy."

"To hell with keeping her happy. At this point, I'm only concerned with keeping her alive. If she won't come willingly, you know what to do."

The captain rang off, leaving Brandt glaring at the phone in his hand.

Someone had deliberately put Samantha in danger. Whoever had done this might as well have pointed a gun at her head and pulled the trigger himself.

What if that was exactly what this asshole intended? Deputy Brooker came to mind. The more he thought on it, the more his suspicions grew. It shouldn't be too hard to pick him up. Adam had been working on tracking where he was staying earlier today. Brandt quickly made a couple of phone calls. Within minutes, an

APB was put out on the vehicle, and Adam was heading into the office to pull a photo off the database to circulate as well. Then he'd be taking the photo to the newsroom to confirm Brandt's suspicions.

Could anyone else have done this? Sam said only a few people knew about her skills. After today's mess at work, that select few had grown considerably. Several of those might have wondered about her skills before – not after today. God damn it. He highly doubted Kevin would have done something like this, particularly after seeing Sam in action today. Besides, he'd have never put the department at risk.

"What won't make me happy?"

Startled, Brandt turned around to find Sam, with a blanket wrapped around her shoulders, leaning against the doorway. Tousled and tiny, she appeared so lost Brandt couldn't help himself. He walked over, tugging her into his arms.

He didn't want to tell her. Brandt grimaced. There was no way around it. She had to know.

"That was the captain. One of our detectives has fessed up to telling the media that you were helping the police with this case. He swears that's all he said. But on the news tonight there was a little more to it than that."

"Exactly how much more was there?" Her voice was quiet, too quiet. So were her eyes.

His heart sank. She already knew.

"Your name and picture."

She froze. Brandt rubbed her back soothingly. "It's okay. I won't let anything happen to you."

Stiff and unyielding, Sam didn't answer. After a few moments, Brandt tilted her chin so he could gaze into her eyes. Searching deep, he tried to find out what she was thinking.

Her eyes were frozen blanks.

"Oh, God, Sam. I am so sorry." Brandt tugged her closer, rocking her gently in his arms. "Captain Johansen wants you to go to a safe house where we can keep an eye on you."

Sam shook her head vehemently. "I'm not going."

Brandt winced. "I'm afraid it's not a choice."

Sam reared up, glaring at him. Brandt, damn his hormones couldn't resist noticing the gentle sway of her breasts. Now that he knew what those God-awful sweaters covered up, he whole-heartedly approved of them. He didn't want every other male getting an eyeful. Christ, she was gorgeous when she was mad. Peach flushed her normally pale skin, giving her a lively bloom that was so often missing from her skin.

"Like hell. You can't force me," she declared defiantly.

He sighed and tried to tug her down against him, only she was having nothing to do with it.

"Actually, I can, but I don't want to have to." He shifted slightly, realizing his body's interest in her nude state wouldn't be received well at the moment, but knowing there was damn little he could do about it. "Sam, try to be reasonable. The killer now knows who you are and it won't take him long to find where you live."

"Do you realize what you've done? It's not just the killer. It's my job and my friends." Sam stopped, a stunned look on her face. She snorted. "Okay, so they may not be friends in the 'forever' sense, but they were friendly to me. Why is it, I'm only just understanding what that means, now that I'm about to lose them?"

"Not everyone will see the news."

Sam snorted. "This is a small town. Whoever doesn't see the news will be told by 9 am tomorrow."

She was probably right. "That doesn't mean they will treat you any differently." Besides, he couldn't let anything else matter. She had to stay safe. Nothing else was acceptable.

Fine tremors ran through her. "I don't think I can I live here if I'm an outcast again."

Brandt ran his fingers through his hair. He couldn't imagine what her life had been like up to now. She'd built herself a life here. He didn't want her to lose that.

"I can understand how you feel."

An angry laugh escaped. "Can you?"

Brandt could feel the slow burn he'd stomped on earlier, start to flare up. Her anger was nothing in comparison. He couldn't let it be. This was beyond serious. She had to leave and now. Staring out into the black of night, he realized they didn't have much time. The killer could already have found her location and be on his way. His voiced his thoughts. "You have to consider that he could be on his way right now."

Sam aged before him. His heart went out to her.

"I'm sorry, Sam. But this is the way it has to be."

Sam blurted out, "The animals. I can't take them to a safe house. Soldier needs this place as much as I do. To take him anywhere else will slow his rehabilitation, magnify his trust issues if you take him away from his new home."

She had a point — just a small one. He was concerned about her though, not the dog.

"Staying here is out of the question."

"Why?" she interrupted.

"There's too much cover for a predator. It would be hard to defend."

"Not true," she answered shaking her head. "Someone could stay in the house with me."

"We don't want to use you for bait. He's going to come looking for you and you know that. If we take you to a safe house, he won't be able to find you."

"Really? You mean until another detective leaks that information too. Thanks but no thanks. I didn't trust the police before, and the behavior out of your office hasn't changed my opinion one bit." Sam walked over to curl up on the couch with the blanket wrapped around her body.

Sadly, he watched as those beautiful curves disappeared from view.

"Besides, if he can't find me, he'll just kill other women. You..." her voice choked, "or someone else has already set me up as bait. So you might as well make good use of the opportunity." Bitterness edged her voice.

Shit. Brandt sat down beside her. "Sam, I'm wondering if this isn't part of Deputy Brooker's machinations. If the killer found you, it would be an easy solution to his problem."

Sam shot him a considering look. A sweater lying over the couch caught her eye. Dropping the blanket to her waist, she pulled the sweater over her head, tugging it down under the blanket. Oddly enough, it was that action that made him suddenly very nervous.

"God damn it Sam. *I* didn't set you up. You know what a media frenzy is like. Once they sniff out a story like this, there is no letting go."

"Thanks, but I don't need the reminder." Sam curled into a tiny ball and stared out into the night.

***

3:15 am

Now fully dressed, Sam curled up in a small ball in the corner of the couch where she could look out. Darkness still blanketed the valley, giving it an eerie glow. She wasn't going to leave her home. The police had created this situation, so they could damn well fix it. She wasn't being stubborn; she was being sensible. They wanted to protect her, fine. They could do it here.

Moses pushed his cold, wet nose against her arm. "Hey boy. That's right, isn't it? We couldn't possibly move you and Soldier. He's just starting to adapt to this place as it is."

She peered around at the simple room. This was her home and she wasn't leaving. She knew better than most what this killer was capable of doing.

Brandt walked down the stairs. Her heart twanged. She didn't want to see him. She didn't like this sense of betrayal. If Brooker had done this, then it wasn't Brandt's fault. Except he'd promised to keep her name out of this. Unfair or not, there it was.

She geared up for the fight to come. Still, the feelings of resentment were hard to maintain as he walked toward her. Her nostrils flared. Her heart and mind flooded with images of last night. It couldn't be. She refused to be swayed by sweet memories. Damn it.

Ruthlessly, she forced down tears.

Brandt gingerly stepped over the sprawled dog to sit on the couch with her.

"You may not be feeling very generous toward me at the moment, however, I need you to understand and believe in one thing – I didn't set you up. I wouldn't – couldn't – do that to you. And I will do everything in my power to keep you safe."

When she stared at him, but stayed quiet, his shoulders sagged.

"Please," he whispered, "Just believe in me, in us, that much. We'll work out everything else. I promise."

This time, she couldn't hold back the tears. They pooled at the corner of her eyes before slowly running down her cheeks. Burying her face in her arms, she tried hard to stifle the sniffles. When his arms wrapped around her, lifting her to his lap, the dam broke.

Brandt held her tight, murmuring nonsensical things in her hair.

Finally, her sobs ran down until she rested quietly in his arms. Where did she go from here? How to go on? She'd lived so isolated for so long, she didn't think she could handle being pointed and laughed at again. She shook her head slightly. Tough as that might be, losing Brandt would be the worst. For the first time, she was experiencing this connection, this sense of belonging with another person. He fit like her other half, making her whole.

"Honestly, I don't think many people will recognize you. Apparently, it's an old picture."

Sam stilled then tilted her head. "Did you read my mind?"

He smiled and dropped a tender kiss on her nose. "No. I figure that's your department."

She leaned against him, not sure how she felt anymore. She hadn't really thought he was to blame. That responsibility belonged with the asshole who'd released the information. Still, how much did she really know of Brandt? Sure, her mind mocked. You only know him well enough to have wild, uninhibited sex with him. Sam winced at the reminder.

"What's the matter now?"

Deciding to be honest, she answered, "I'm realizing that I've only known you for a few days."

His arms tightened. "You know all that matters."

She wondered about that.

***

6:10 am

Several sleepless hours later, Brandt walked into the kitchen expecting, even spoiling, for a fight. "I hope you've reconsidered."

She pulled the bread out of the toaster and buttered the two pieces and didn't answer.

"I hope you're prepared to be reasonable." Brandt knew he should shut up, yet found himself aggressively defensive. He needed her to understand, to care about staying safe.

She shot him a look. "Reasonable? Take another look at what has happened to my life, then tell me that."

"Damn it, I have. I wouldn't have wished this on you for anything. But it doesn't change the facts. You have to be protected, and we have to catch this asshole. This could be the same guy I'm hunting, or it may be an entirely different asshole. I don't care — we have to get him off the street. You have to stay safe." His voice rose at the end of his sentence. He visibly struggled to regain control, but it was tough. She was fighting him over something that was inarguable.

She finished buttering the toast on the plate and carried it over to the table. "I don't have a death wish, but I do want this to be over. I can't live in a cell, and I have to have some space for my..." Out of words, Sam wafted her hand in the air. "For my abilities or whatever you want to call them. I can't live the same as everyone else. Don't you understand? These things happen and I don't know when they will. I have to feel safe in my world." Glancing around at the cabin, she added, "It's not much, but it is home. I feel good here, rested. Being in the real world all the time hurts me." She paused briefly. "I don't want to leave this place."

Brandt leaned against the table, trying to give her a chance to express her needs. He didn't think she'd had much time or opportunity to have anyone care about what mattered to her.

She turned to face him, her hand out in a beseeching way that wrenched his heart.

Her voice continued the tug. "I trust you to keep me safe, regardless of the problems with your department. But if I go to a safe house, I won't have an easy time of it." Sam reached out, covering his hand with her own. "Brandt I just want this over. I don't want anyone else to get hurt — including me." At the furious look on his face, she backed off slightly. "I think you should use me as bait. Go ahead and involve Stefan. He has a great inner warning system, so use it."

Seeing his mouth open to protest, she held up her hand to forestall him. "But I will leave that up to you."

Brandt placed his hand flat on the table and slowly sat down, deep in thought. She had a valid argument in terms of her abilities. She wasn't the same as everyone else. Was it unreasonable to force her to go to a safe house? No. However, it would be intolerable for her. He had his orders, still... He straightened up and looked around the cabin, considering location and the problems of guarding her here. Using her as bait was out of the question. A policewoman now...that was possible. Stefan was also a hell of a good idea. He narrowed his eyes, considering her earnest face.

He knew what he had to do. Right or wrong.

"Alright. I'll talk to the captain. Maybe we can find another way."

She turned to look at him in surprise. "Really?"

At his nod, her smile burst free, warming and calming the fear inside him.

"Thank you."

He smiled grimly at her. "Don't thank me yet. The captain isn't going to be happy and may order you to be picked up regardless. Even if that means bringing you in for questioning where we can hold you for forty-eight hours."

She swallowed hard. "I understand and thank you... Thank you for considering my needs." She shrugged. "Maybe, he'll understand."

Brandt didn't think so, but he'd made his decision and he'd stand by it.

But he wasn't looking forward to telling the captain.

***

10:15 am

Sam kept to the rear of the vet clinic as much as possible. It helped that business was brisk and there were plenty of animals needing her attention.

It also helped her ignore the six-foot-four security guard that stood just inside the door watching her every move. He'd arrived at her house just before seven this morning. Open-mouthed, she hadn't had time to protest. As this guy had walked in, Brandt walked out. Not a good way to start the day.

She tried to stay focused and give the animals a little extra of her time. These poor things needed a warm, caring voice and a shot of love. She needed to stay away from the chaos in her mind. Somehow, she'd thought Brandt would be the one to stay by her side.

She stole a glance at the tall, silent ghost beside her. He'd introduced himself, shown her his ID and had stayed quiet ever since. Watchful, ever present, quiet – Sam, so used to silence, found his unnerving.

Lucy pushed open the door and walked toward Sam. She cast a nervous glance at the man standing silently to the side. "Sam, can you give us a hand? We need another person for a moment."

Sam nodded and followed her into the surgical ward. There was no animal on the table. She turned around in confusion. "What do you need help with?"

Three women converged on her.

"Sam, are you okay?"

"Why do you have a bodyguard?"

"Was that you they were talking about on the news last night?"

Their questions came hard and furious. She stared from one to the other, more than a little overwhelmed. It didn't take long to realize their questions came from a place of caring.

Dr. Wascott walked in. He headed straight for Sam, where he gave her a quick hug. "I can't stay and talk. But you take care of yourself. That psycho could be after you."

A wry smile lit Sam's face. "That's why the bodyguard."

"OMG!"

The girls' excitement and fear melded and blended until sentiments were impossible to tell apart. It took several minutes of explanations before they finally ran down. They gave her a big hug each and ran back to their duties. Sam stood there bemused, a warm glow inside and out.

So that's what having friends felt like. She could get used to this.

***

11:35am

Plans, plans, and more plans. He'd done what research he could. There was little enough to find. Bill hoped she was enjoying her celebratory status. Because soon he'd make her famous. He could see the headlines now: Psychic Who Couldn't See What Was Coming.

Serve her right. He preferred to study his victims, to learn everything he could about them. That was the best part. He loved finding out where the women worked, who their friends were, and especially about the lovers they slept with. Every tidbit helped him to know them just a little bit better. Once he'd collected all the little details then he could choose the perfect time and method for her death.

There was not time for all this now. He couldn't take the chance.

She also didn't fall into the same category as the other women. They were chosen. She was just an irritation to be taken care of.

He smiled. Cutting her brake line would be too easy. He already knew that she owned an old Nissan truck. He'd found that out within minutes of hearing her name. He used that method sometimes, just not with the chosen ones. Besides he couldn't guarantee the success like he needed to.

Many people deserved death. Not every one of them deserved his personal attention. Sometimes, men needed killing too. His old boss was one of them. The asshole had the audacity to fire him. Bill hadn't liked the damn job anyway. He frowned. That reminded him. That asshole had escaped. His damn girlfriend had borrowed his Mercedes, dying in his place. His stomach soured. Now, he'd be sure to take care of that bastard personally. But there were more pressing issues to take care of first.

Parksville was only a few miles away. The psychic wouldn't know what hit her.

The cops were particularly stupid. She'd be placed under police protection and the cops would be waiting for him. Bill was too smart for that. His mind spinning with ideas, he couldn't help but appreciate the extra challenge. It definitely added a little spice to brighten up his day.

CHAPTER TWENTY-FIVE

5 pm, June 24th

Sam slowly found a level of comfort with having a constant companion. Her daytime watchdog changed shifts regularly, and Brandt stayed for the nights. There'd been a suggestion of a policewoman moving into the house in Sam's place. She'd nixed that. What if the poor woman were killed? Sam didn't want that on her conscience.

Sam still looked over her shoulder at odd times. At unexpected moments, she felt eyes on her. No matter how fast she spun around, she could never find her stalker.

Still, as time passed, she adjusted.

The detectives were busy doing their thing. They'd found out where Brooker was staying. He'd denied anything to do with the media, and hadn't planned for Sam to identify that the picture shown on television had been taken during her time in Nikola County. He'd blustered for hours, but Captain Johansen, paired with Brandt and Sam's evidence, convinced the overweight bully into giving them a cowering confession. Kevin wanted him to confess for trying to run her off the road, but Brooker wasn't going for it – yet. A crew had gone to her cabin searching the area for evidence where Soldier had been shot, in an effort to pin that on him, too.

Sam didn't ask for the details. That asshole was a minor blip in her life now.

Brandt's mother was having an easier time of it, too, now that the colonel had woken up. He couldn't remember what happened, which wasn't unreasonable considering his injury and age, but he knew her. She'd stayed at his side these last few days, only leaving for showers and changing of clothes. Brandt would be heading over tomorrow to take both back to the care center.

As for Sam, she was surrounded by friends and her bodyguards were reserved, yet friendly. That suited her. Best of all, Brandt came home every night and slept on the couch he'd moved into her room.

She hadn't invited him into her bed again and he'd never mentioned it either. The unspoken word 'later' hung in the air. There would be time down the road to talk and sort through their convoluted relationship. Not that she didn't wake up in the night and reach for him, because she did, then hugged her pillows close when she found herself alone. The temptation to go to him often overwhelmed her. It was the knowledge that her advances wouldn't be welcomed that stopped her. He considered himself to be on duty.

She planned to present him with a ready dinner tonight. Return some normalcy into their lives. Not that they'd had a chance to experience such a commonplace thing yet. That was for other people, other relationships...

By the time she'd made pork chops with a creamy mustard sauce and stuffed tortellini on the side, with slices of cucumber and tomato in apple cider vinegar, she was feeling quite proud of herself.

Brandt arrived just in time, only stopping outside to speak with the guard briefly. Sam's heart lifted at the sight of him. Sam walked to the front door. "Hi, how are you doing?" There, that was just the right note, casual and friendly. She waved good-bye as the guard hopped into his car and drove off.

Brandt walked in, sniffing the air. "Whatever it is, it smells wonderful." He dropped his coat and laptop bag on the end of the couch and walked over to sweep her into his arms, where he twirled her around so he could check out the pots bubbling on the stove.

Laughing, she squeezed him before stepping back. "It's ready. Wash up."

"How was your day?" he asked, walking over to the kitchen sink.

Sam started serving the plates. "The same as usual. Yours?"

"Same old. How's Soldier?"

"Not impressed." Soldier had objected strenuously to the added male presences. One of the guards had made the mistake of walking too close. Soldier had barely missed snapping his hand off. Sam had been horrified, apologizing profusely and had gone to calm the dog down. The guard had been wary ever since and had passed the word on.

Soldier spent his days in peace and quiet, his mornings and nights on full alert. She appreciated the fact that he never ventured far away from her. The two of them had an unspoken truce. She helped him to heal and regain his strength while he kept her company and worked to keep her safe. That it kept the men away from her and him was a benefit to both of them.

By the time bedtime rolled around, Brandt and Sam had spent several comfortable hours talking. They discussed everything from global warming to hybrid cars and even favorite recipes. By bedtime, Sam had a warm glow of friendship around her. She'd really enjoyed tonight. Still smiling, she fell asleep immediately.

Sometime in the wee hours of the morning, Sam surfaced from her dreams to hear the unfamiliar sounds of voices in her living room. Listening from under her covers, she heard Brandt move around.

Something was wrong.

Concerned, Sam hopped out of bed, grabbed up her old terry cloth robe and slipped downstairs. Brandt stood at the bottom of the stairs, fully dressed.

"What's the matter?" she asked, frowning.

"The hospital' raised the alarm. Your suicide victim has been attacked."

Sam wrapped her arms around her chest. "Oh no," she whispered. "Is she okay?"

He shook his head. "I don't know the details. We put a guard on her too, once we matched the earring to her."

"You did?" Sam felt warmed at his concern for the unknown woman. He was a good man. "Why didn't you tell me?"

"Because you would just worry even more." He reached into his pocket and pulled out his keys. "The guard has been injured, as have two nurses."

"Oh, God." This asshole was a sick bastard. "What makes you think he's not on his way here?"

"The hospital security chased him outside and saw him take off in his car. The police have picked up his trail, heading north to Washington. He's probably planning to run across the border." He kissed her on the cheek. "Just in case, there's another cop on his way here. I'll wait until he shows up and then head out."

Sam wrapped her robe tighter around her. "I can't believe how many people he's hurting."

"He's a serial killer, and the noose is tightening. He's going to do everything he can to survive."

Lights shone through the trees into the living room.

"Here he is. I'll see you in a couple of hours." He walked to the door and opened it. "Get some sleep. Remember, the cops are on his ass and should have him in handcuffs within hours."

Sam frowned. "He's pretty smart for that."

"Not this time."

David, an older man,, walked in, smiling at her. "Good news, huh?"

"Yeah. But I'll feel better when he's behind bars." With one last glance at Sam, he said, "I won't be long, but it's important to get to the hospital as soon as possible. We need every bit of evidence we can to nail this bastard. I shouldn't be more than a couple of hours."

Sam nodded, giving him the reassurance he needed to leave. She couldn't quite believe that this was almost over. This worry had been with her for so long. It didn't seem possible that the end was near.

She smiled at David. "Thanks for coming. I'm heading to bed. Maybe I'll be able to sleep for the first time in weeks."

David tipped his cap. "Go rest easy. We'll get this guy."

Sam nodded, as expected, and walked to her room. She didn't have the same level of confidence. She knew this asshole had evaded cops for decades. A car chase was small change for him. He'd taken out a guard and injured two nurses tonight alone.

Who knew what other damage he could inflict this night?

***

2 am

Brandt drove fast, carefully. The long, twisting dirt road didn't offer much opportunity for speeding. He hated to leave Sam. Reaching for his cell phone, he called Captain Johansen for the latest.

"I don't have an update. I'll get one and call you back. Where are you?"

"Almost twenty minutes out from the hospital." Brandt hung up, turned on his sirens, and slammed his foot down on the pedal. His stomach churned with nerves. Leaving Sam was the last thing he wanted to do. They'd better have this bastard locked up by the time this night was over.

His cell phone rang.

"Hello." Brandt glanced in his rear view mirror. Other than a semi that he'd passed a few miles ago, the highway was deserted.

"Brandt, turn around," yelled the captain. "The cops pulled the car over. A stupid assed kid had been paid a hundred bucks to drive the car north as far and as fast as he could. The cops tracked the car. It was stolen yesterday."

"Shit!" Brandt hit the brakes. His tires squealed loudly as the vehicle spun sideways before coming to a violent, rocking stop across the highway. He turned the wheel and hit the gas. "Call David and warn him. I'm on my way."

If Brandt thought he drove fast on the way into town, he burned rubber heading to Sam.

A diversion. A fucking diversion to leave Sam open – and defenseless.

Christ.

He tried calling Sam's cell phone. No answer. Shit! She hadn't turned the damn thing on. He called David. No answer.

Oh, God, please let him be in time.

***

2:24 am

Sam curled up in bed. She couldn't help feeling terrible about the guard and nurses. She didn't even know how the victim had fared in that confrontation. Hopefully, everyone would survive. Sam really wanted a happy ending to all of this. With the blankets pulled up to her chin, she found herself listening for the phone downstairs announcing the good news. Uneasy, without explanation, Sam found herself giving extra thanks for her bodyguard downstairs. Brandt...well, he'd be home whenever he was done.

Home. That had such a nice cozy ring to it. Maybe when this mess was over... After twenty minutes of not being able to stop her mind from circling uselessly, she compromised and took a, herbal sleep aid. It wouldn't knock her out the same as a sleeping pill.

Brandt. A warm contentedness filled her mind. An irritating pinch on her arm made her frown, but then his hands slid over the smooth surface of her hips. Mmmm. Heat flushed through her veins, awaking nerve endings she'd forcibly capped for the last few days.

Moving sensuously under his soothing caresses, Sam moaned in joy. She reached for him, but let him turn her hands aside as his caresses explored the soft valley of her abdomen. He was purely delicious. He was also too good at what he did. Lost in the sensations of building lust and the unique experience of enjoying her lover's attention, Sam slid deeper under his spell. Placing her hand over his, sliding her fingers gently through and over his, Sam explored his strong muscled hands before sliding slowly up his wrists. They felt different.

He still had clothes on.

With a slight moue, she tugged at the sleeve that interfered with her exploration. Gently, he grabbed her hands and raised them over her head, holding her in place. She murmured in delight and tried to tug. It didn't work.

He bent his head and nuzzled the plump side of her breast through her pajama top.

Sam moaned and twisted under him. Her stomach roiled, at odds with the rest of the sensations happily flickering though her body. She frowned in confusion.

His mouth fondled the pouting nipple under the cotton material.

"Please," she pleaded.

Silence.

A tiny bit of doubt crept under Sam's guard. It seemed so real. But so were her visions. A weird fog rolled through her mind. Shit. Realization was slow to come. Brandt was gone. This was another vision. No. Surely not. Sleepiness mixed with the images overlapping in her mind – all in bright Technicolor.

Heat flashed over her skin at the memories of her previous lovemaking with Brandt. Overlapping were sensations on her skin even now. Hands moved to cup her breasts and squeeze gently. She sighed. But her mind wouldn't relax. Caught in limbo between worlds, she struggled to stay real in another woman's dream. Wanting it to be Brandt, yet knowing the killer had taken another victim.

His mouth tugged and teased, tantalizing her nipple, bringing her back to a sensual high, all the while her mind operating in the background, struggling to remember Stefan's lessons.

Teeth clamped lightly on the end of the sensitive nipple.

Then bit down hard.

The woman screamed. Sam screamed.

Her spine arched and she tried to curve away from the pain. Her hands were held above her head, keeping her captive. Her eyes opened. Then closed again in despair.

Oh God. It *was* him. She was caught in another vision.

Sam struggled to separate the vision from the reality.

Oh, God. Oh, God. The poor woman. Sam knew she could do nothing, but endure. Locked inside her mental labyrinth, Sam felt the victim's pain and horror, as she finally understood.

She twisted and struggled, hearing the words. "Please don't hurt me." Were they from the victim or her? Sam didn't know. It didn't matter. Both of them wanted this to be over. They wanted to be saved. And they both knew it wasn't going to happen.

Low masculine laughter filled the room.

"Please," pleaded the same voice. "Let me go."

Her arms were wrenched above her head and held in a punishing grip. The attacker pressed down hard on the wrist bones. Pain squeezed through injured nerve endings, ripping scorch lines throughout her body.

Sam, desperate to separate herself from the woman's pain, tried to seek the blackness of the etheric world. This torture was just beginning. Sam didn't want to be here and most definitely not this early on. She normally came in at the end, those precious few minutes to help the victims cross the line to death.

She was part of this experience to help the victims and if she could, to help the police find justice for the victims. She wasn't here to suffer. Her mind waffled then raced in different directions from what had to be drugs, sliding insidiously through the victim's veins. She wanted out. Stefan had given her some tips to try, what were they? Right. Grounding herself by following the line of her skeleton down to her feet and imagining them coming from the center of the earth. Except, she hadn't expected to do this under these circumstances. Concentrating was almost impossible. The woman's terror, her pain dominated. Sam struggled to free herself of the dark sucking energy.

"Samantha."

Sam's mind froze. Then her heart slammed into her chest.

Who called her?

Her eyelids flickered and she was suddenly more afraid than she'd ever been in her life. Never had a vision called her name. She wrinkled her nose. A fetid odor filled her head. Something awful wafted through the air. A metallic bloody smell. God, she didn't want to open her eyes and see what she knew would be there.

"Look at me, Samantha."

She forced her eyes wide.

And found herself in her own bedroom, staring up at the same whitewashed ceiling. She was home. Oh God. She was not alone.

This time, she was the victim.

***

2:29 am

Stefan slammed into awareness. Shoving his bedding back, he came to a standing position before he'd even realized what had happened. He couldn't see where he was, his bedroom was seeped in darkness. His curtains were open – still no light shone in.

Looking around, his hand went to his throat. Jesus. Sam. She was in danger. He reached for his phone. No answer. Shit. He called Brandt. It was busy. Fuck.

Pushing into a sitting position, he crossed his legs and sent himself deep into a trance. He had to find Sam. Soon. She needed help. Evil was wrapping her up in the dangerous torrent. He had to make her aware...and fast.

He tried to block out the unwanted thought, then realized it was stopping his gifts. Better to acknowledge the possibility so he wouldn't be crippled by the fear. He knew that before this night was over she'd be fighting for her life

Or...even worse, he'd be helping her cross over to the other side – to her death.

***

2:39 am

No!

She tried to struggle. Panic dimmed her sight as she realized there'd be no waking up this time. There'd be no last minute rescue for her. It was her turn to die.

It wasn't supposed to happen this way. Where the hell was Brandt? Even as she panicked, vestiges of old resentment rose to the surface. Why was there no one there to rescue her? Wait. David. Her security guard. Oh no, the poor man.

I'm here.

Stefan.

Call Brandt!

He knows. He's on his way. Keep fighting.

I'm trying.

Fight harder.

Stefan's voice started to fade. *No. Wait. Remember your lessons. Disconnect.*

Her mind cried out for him. There was no answer.

She glared at the asshole that had hurt so many people. She'd never even seen him before. This time he had no mask. Why? As she tried to focus in on the details of his face, his features zoomed out, leaving her with a faint impression of dark wide-set eyes with heavy brows and thick cheekbones and prominent nose – his eyes black empty holes. His face look oddly colored, out of proportion.

Drugs. Of course, he'd given her drugs. Different ones this time. Her mind tried to puzzle through the convoluted maze of thoughts, then quickly frazzled out. It didn't matter anymore.

"What kind of useless psychic are you? You couldn't even see this coming." His mouth twisted into a malevolent mockery of a smile.

"What did you do to my bodyguard?" She spat the words at him. She twisted in vain.

He reared backwards. "Must have been a cop. Just as useless as the rest of them." He shifted slightly for a better look at her face. With a big smirk, he added, "You were supposed to be a bigger challenge, being a psychic and all." Coarse laughter filled the room, grating on her ears and sending terror running through her soul. "I was looking forward to this." He stared around in disgust. "Nothing to it. Or you. God, what a loser. Look at this place. It's a dump."

Evil glistened from his eyes, sourced deep in his soul. It would be a bad day for those who'd crossed him. Like her.

She, remembering Stefan's lessons, searched for lightness inside her center of being. His blackness was overwhelming. The light sustained her. If she let the blackness gain control, it would be over. If it were her time to die like all the others, then she'd rather go kicking and screaming – and taking a piece of him with her.

She reached out in her mind's eye. She could barely sense the bodyguard. He was still alive. The dogs' energy was outside her bedroom door. She could almost hear them whining. The bastard had shut it, locking them out. No sign of Brandt or Stefan.

"Damn you to hell." She glared at him, furious at herself, and the situation.

He laughed. "Not like you planned, huh?"

She twisted her head to check the window. It was wide open.

If she screamed, the dogs still would not be able to get through the door. There was no lock, still she had yet to teach any animal to open the door latch. Soldier was an incredibly determined animal. He was strong enough to break the door down if he wanted to. Or if he were mad enough. If she could find the right trigger. What had she called him in the vet's office so long ago?

At the top of her lungs, she screamed, "Major, git!"

"Whoever you're calling — let him come. I'll kill him too."

His knife slid upward without warning, cutting her throat under her chin.

Sam screamed. The drugs gave him enormous size. Nothing was needed to emphasize his natural cruelty. He was too big for her to move. Furious and in pain, she struggled for freedom. He laughed again, placing a knee on her chest. In a startling motion, he stabbed the knife into the mattress beside her ear, cutting locks of hair and grasping her throat in both hands.

"I want to squeeze the life from your body myself, you stupid bitch."

Black dots appeared before her eyes. Static filled her ears. She automatically grabbed his hands, trying to free her throat from his grasp. She gurgled for air, bucking to get rid of him. To no avail. With her strength gone and almost no air, she collapsed back down. This was the end then.

Her mind went cloudy. The killer's face blurred. The rage and joy in eyes blended into something pure evil. Her arms fell to her sides.

The last of her air bubbled from her lungs. Suddenly, the weight was lifted off – she was free. Sam gasped frantically for air, her hands circling her own throat, protectively. She rolled over into a tightly curled up ball, coughing as she gulped for air. "Oh, God," she whispered, her voice barely recognizable.

Noises penetrated the fog in her mind. Growling, and yelling, thuds and blows surrounded her. She shuffled on the bed to huddle at the headboard, trying to avoid bodies that crashed down beside her. Teeth bared, fur flying, Soldier had locked onto the killer's shoulder. Moses had locked on the man's leg. The killer grunted and punched, kicking any area he could as the three rolled in mortal combat.

The bedroom door swung in the cold night air.

Sam winced at the heavy thud of boot on bone. Soldier howled.

God, Soldier was already injured. She had to help him. Her body refused to respond to her orders. The shine of the blade, still embedded in the mattress, caught her eye. She focused on the shine.

Her hand grabbed the hilt just as the killer grabbed her arm pulling her back. Sam punched with her free hand and tried to kick. There was too much dog in the way and too many drugs in her system. She stumbled.

Finding an opportunity, she collected the last of her cohesive energy and lunged, digging her right hand, fingers stiff like claws, into the soft spots of his throat. Her left hand stabbed upward with the knife. He raised his arm defensively. The blade caught his arm and sliced upward, deflecting off bone. He screamed. "Bitch."

His much longer reach latched around her throat. Sam screamed at Soldier again, "Major. Kill."

From the corner of her eye, she hardly recognized the dog. His fangs dripped saliva and blood, and the howl coming from the back of his throat was...otherworldly.

Soldier was on a mission, and she was in the way.

His lip curled, his shoulders hunched up. Sam pushed herself away in a clumsy movement that tumbled her backwards onto the mattress. She needn't have worried. Soldier's jaw replaced her hands, ripping into her attacker's shoulder. The knife was jerked out of her hand.

Soldier's howls, dragged from deep down and forced through his clenched jaw, scared her shitless.

She turned slightly. The killer had the knife raised to bring down on Soldier's spine. "No!" She grabbed his knife arm with both hands and tried to stop him. "You bastard, leave him alone." Her arms trembled. Still, she fought. He grinned at her. She couldn't beat him. He was too strong, and knew it. Soldier continued to howl, splitting the air with his tone. The noise drove through her brain. She groaned, her knees collapsing under her weakening body.

"God, Brandt, where are you?" She needed him. She screamed silently into the dark of night. *Now*.

***

2:44 am

"Jesus." Brandt swore he could hear Sam yelling in his head. It was bad enough hearing Stefan screaming though the phone at him a few minutes ago and knowing no one else could get to her before him.

The sounds coming from inside the house sent terror stabbing through his heart. 'Hang on Sam! I'm coming," he yelled. Brandt raced through the living room, barely noticing the body collapsed in a pool of blood on the porch. The screams and howls from upstairs pierced the night. He took the stairs two at a time. The scene that greeted him made his stomach churn.

Blood splattered everywhere. Soldier and Sam were locked in a death fight with a large male, Moses reduced to a crumpled heap of fur on the floor.

Brandt jumped into the fray, knocking the knife from the killer's hand and pulling Sam loose. She stumbled a few feet then collapsed to the floor. The killer ignored him. Bent on destroying the fury chomping through his shoulder, he immediately locked his hands around Soldier's throat, squeezing tight.

Bloody bubbles foamed out of Soldier's mouth. Blood coated his fur. The sound coming out from his mouth, an unholy alliance with hell.

His gun trained on the two still caught in a life and death grip. "Sam, talk to me. Are you okay?"

"Yes," she mumbled, managing a small nod to reinforce her statement. "I think so." She reached up to her throat, barely able to touch the raw skin. "Save Soldier."

He spared her a quick glance, slightly reassured that Sam had crawled to Moses and was talking – not very coherently, still she could communicate. "Stay back. I have to get Soldier off first. I don't want to have to shoot him."

Brandt turned his attention to the still-howling dog locked on to the killer's shoulder. "Let the dog go. I'll get him off you."

"Like hell.," the killer gasped. "This asshole should have died a long time ago. Worthless piece of shit."

Brandt didn't know what he was talking about, and it didn't matter right now. Somehow he had to save the dog. For Sam's sake. The killer be damned. "Let go of the dog, or I'll shoot."

"Fuck you." The killer grinned at him through bared teeth as he removed one hand from Soldier's throat and with a quick twist of his wrist slid a dagger free from his belt and threw it.

"Brandt!"

The dagger stabbed into the wall behind Brandt, missing him completely. Brandt didn't miss the killer. The bullet hit him low in the left shoulder. The grin fell off his face as he stumbled to the floor.

Soldier, now with the upper hand and caught in a blood lust of his own, lunged again. He reclamped his jaws into a tighter grip.

"Soldier!" Brandt ordered. "Soldier! Stand down." He repeated it twice before the dog stopped trembling and unlocked his jaw. Brandt stepped closer, the gun trained on the killer.

Soldier curled his lip at him.

"It's okay, boy. You've done good. Move, Soldier."

The dog dripped blood from open tissue shinning wetly in the dark.

"Soldier. Down."

In the distance, the sound of sirens grew stronger.

Brandt didn't think the dog was going to listen. Finally in a crippled shuffling movement, the dog slid to the floor. He was hurt, and badly. Brandt kicked the knife away. The killer glared at him, blood pouring from both shoulders.

Sirens filled the air, colored flashing lights filled the room.

"It's okay Sam. The ambulance and police are here."

"Sam?"

Silence filled the room.

Brandt spun around to look, his gun still trained on the killer. "Sam?" Fear spiked his voice to a scream. Crumpled in a bloody pile on the floor, Sam lay between the two dogs. All three looked dead.

CHAPTER TWENTY-SIX

Sam walked slowly down to the dock, Brandt at her side. Soldier hobbled behind them. Moses, moving much slower, brought up the rear. Sam wouldn't want it any other way.

She tried not to dwell on the events of that night. She didn't remember much and that's the way she wanted to keep it. She'd been rushed to the hospital where the doctors had frantically tried to stop the spread of the poison from the cocktail of drugs guaranteed to kill her. If it hadn't been for Brandt she would have died. Chills ran down her spine at the reminder.

It had been late the next day before she'd surfaced – screaming. Brandt had been at her side, a place he'd stayed during the first week of her recovery. Once out of hospital, they'd enjoyed the time alone at the lake. A healing time. But then he'd had to go back to work.

Sam had returned to the clinic soon after.

At the clinic, she'd refused to talk about the events, hoping the chatter would die down and with time – it had. Still, David, a good family man and an off-duty cop pulling extra time, lost his life when he'd stepped outside for a cigarette. He'd wandered out to the deck and never had a chance to draw his first smoke-filled breath.

The dogs had been rushed to the clinic where they'd both undergone surgery. Thank God, the vets had done it for free. Sam didn't have that kind of money, and although Brandt had joked that his department should pay the dogs' medical costs, she hadn't wanted to ask for it.

She didn't know what the future held, although more people than she'd ever thought possible stopped her on the street to ask what she saw in their futures. Her fame as a psychic had spread after the details of the attack had leaked to the press.

Speaking of leaks, Dillon had been reprimanded and transferred to another station.

As for Deputy Brooker, Brandt had matched shells picked up from the woods around her place to his gun, finally. He'd followed Brandt to her place when Soldier had caught his scent in the woods. His truck was the same as the one who'd tried to run her off the road. He wasn't admitting anything more at this point. She didn't know what he was going to be charged with at the end of the ongoing investigation, yet she could count on Brandt to make sure he'd be out of commission for a long time. Sam had agreed to testify and help their case in any way. She wasn't looking forward to seeing Brooker face to face, only knew she could do it and survive. She was stronger now – in many ways.

Captain Johansen had apologized profusely. Every time he saw her, in fact. He'd even thanked her. Who knew how long William Durant would have continued killing women if not for her visions. She could grin at the captain now. It had taken awhile, but she was slowly getting used to being around people.

Brandt had helped with that. So, too had Maisy, Brandt's mother. The colonel had recovered. He'd recognized the ring as being on the hand of the dog handler that brought the animals in to visit the patients at the center. A very subdued Maisy confessed that the dog handler had been there when she'd established the pool on when the colonel would remember what he'd forgotten about the ring. She'd actually asked him if he wanted in on the bets. That had sealed the colonel's fate...or nearly.

Even Soldier's story might have been connected. Although, chances are they'd never know for sure. The dog had certainly known what to do when the time had come. William Durant hadn't survived surgery. Sam found it hard to care. The world was better off without him and this way she didn't have to go through two trials.

Brandt was backtracking the guy's life, searching for links to other murders in his files. He was hoping for evidence to close dozens of cases – not to mention bring closure to dozens of families.

It would take some time. As a dog trainer, Bill had exposure to people, care homes, and even the hospital where he took animals in to visit with the patients. This allowed him to travel to various locations without raising suspicion. Teaching obedience training gave him access to hundreds of women. An opportunity he'd taken full advantage of.

Louise Enderby's long-time partner had come forward after seeing the news. He'd been on the board for the city's animal shelters – he'd fired William from a part time job at the pound where he was to rehabilitate last-ditch cases. He'd been caught abusing the animals instead. An organization that relied heavily on donations, the pound hadn't wanted any negative publicity and agreed not to press charges if Bill disappeared – for good.

They could only speculate, yet it appeared that Louise had become an innocent victim of a war she hadn't even known about.

The best that Sam could understand, Bill picked his victims out of numerous loving couples where the man had been supposedly considered to be 'the best' man – theoretically underlining that, Bill himself, wasn't good enough.

Sam didn't understand the psychology of it all. Who could understand a twisted mind like his? Who would want to?

Stefan had even shown up at her cabin during the first week of convalescence, threatening to do her serious harm if she ever got herself into that situation again. Said it had cost him ten years off his life. He'd also pulled her training forward to avoid a repeat of this mess.

Sam smiled. Stefan was a special man and she loved knowing he was in her life. They had a closeness that she had never known was possible. She could only imagine it was similar to the relationship between twins.

As for her and Brandt, well they were slowly adjusting to life as a couple. They both had things to learn and Sam wasn't sure she was ready to live together, although the topic was under discussion. At the same time, she didn't sleep nearly as well alone. Not that she had the chance to.

It was Brandt who refused to sleep alone. According to him, he was planning on always waking up with her beside him. She hoped he meant it. She wanted to believe in a 'happily ever after.'

Her visions weren't ever going to stop, but she'd become accustomed to them. It wasn't about accepting them any longer, it was about understanding and utilizing them. Progress.

Her visions didn't make her an easy partner, then Brandt's job wouldn't be easy on her. They'd work it out. For the first time ever, she could see a future. It was bright and rosy. She'd like to have had a vision that told her Brandt was her future and she'd be spending the next forty years happily at his side, but as she'd found out, visions didn't work that way.

***

Brandt glanced at Sam, standing at his side, staring out over the water. He couldn't help but feel protective of this woman, so slight, so strong, and so damaged. She'd been a tormented soul who walked with one foot on the dark side of the universe. Now there was a lightness to her.

She was everything to him. He stepped closer, wrapping his arms protectively around her shoulders. He'd do anything to keep her safe. In this world and the next. They were a matched set. Their future wouldn't be the standard two-storey house and white picket fence life. No. But it would have its own rewards.

And he was going to make sure they received each and every one of them.

<u>Hide'n Go Seek – Book 2 of the Psychic Vision Series</u>

A twisted game of Hide'n Go Seek forces an unlikely alliance between a no-nonsense FBI agent and a search-and-rescue worker.

Celebrated search-and-rescue worker Kali Jordon has hidden her psychic abilities by crediting her canine partner Shiloh with the recoveries. But Kali knows the grim truth. The Sight that she inherited from her grandmother allows her to trace violent energy unerringly to victims of murder. No one knows her secret until a twisted killer challenges her to a deadly game of Hide'n Go Seek that threatens those closest to her.

Now she must rely on FBI Special Agent Grant Summers, a man who has sworn to protect her, even as he suspects there's more to Kali and Shiloh than meets the eye. As the killer draws a tighter and tighter circle around Kali, she and Grant find there's no place to hide from themselves.

Are her visions the key to finding the latest victim alive or will this twisted game of Hide'n Go Seek cost her...everything?

<u>Touched by Death – adult RS/thriller standalone</u>

Death had touched anthropologist Jade Hansen in Haiti once before, costing her an unborn child and perhaps her very sanity.

A year later, determined to face her own issues, she returns to Haiti with a mortuary team to recover the bodies of an American family from a mass grave. Visiting his brother after the quake, independent contractor Dane Carter puts his life on hold to help the sleepy town of Jacmel rebuild. But he finds it hard to like his brother's pregnant wife or her family. He wants to go home, until he meets Jade - and realizes what's missing in his own life.

When the mortuary team begins work, it's as if malevolence has been released from the earth. Instead of laying her ghosts to rest, Jade finds herself confronting death and terror again.

And the man who unexpectedly awakens her heart - is right in the middle of it all.

<u>About the author:</u>

Dale Mayer is a prolific multi-published writer. She's best known for her Psychic Visions series. Besides her romantic suspense/thrillers, Dale also writes paranormal romance and crossover young adult books in several different genres. To go with her fiction, she also writes nonfiction in many different fields with books available on resume writing, companion gardening and the US mortgage system. She has recently published her Career Essentials Series. All her books are available in digital and print formats.

Books by Dale Mayer

Psychic Vision Series
Tuesday's Child
Hide'n Go Seek
Maddy's Floor
Garden of Sorrow
Knock, knock...
Book 6 (Jan. 2014)

Death Series – romantic thriller
Touched by Death
Haunted by Death - (Fall 2013)

Novellas/short stories
It's a Dog's Life- romantic comedy
Sian's Solution – part of Family Blood Ties
Riana's Revenge – Fantasy short story

Second Chances...at Love
Second Chances - out now
Book 2 - Winter 2013/2014

Young Adult Books
In Cassie's Corner
Gem Stone (A Gemma Stone Mystery)

Design Series
Dangerous Designs
Deadly Designs
Deceptive Designs – fall 2013

Family Blood Ties Series
Vampire in Denial
Vampire in Distress
Vampire in Design - out now!
Vampire InDecision – coming soon!

Non-Fiction Books
Career Essentials: The Resume
Career Essentials: The Cover Letter
Career Essentials: The Interview
Career Essentials: 3 in 1

Connect with Dale Mayer Online:
Dale's Website – www.dalemayer.com
Twitter – http://twitter.com/#!/DaleMayer
Facebook – http://www.facebook.com/DaleMayer.author

Made in the USA
Middletown, DE
10 November 2018